PRAISE FOR T
COLBY M.

"Colby Marshall has written a book that deserves to be called *thriller.*"

—R. L. Stine, *New York Times* bestselling author
of the Goosebumps series

"An intricate puzzle that will keep you guessing until the very end!"
—C. J. Lyons, *New York Times* bestselling author of *Chasing Shadows*

"Colby Marshall's sterling debut may transpire over more than six or seven days, but like me you'll probably finish it in a single night, racing the dawn to flip the last page. A classic concept updated to fit our politics-wary world."

—Jon Land, bestselling author of *Strong Rain Falling*

COLOR BLIND

COLBY MARSHALL

BERKLEY BOOKS, NEW YORK

THE BERKLEY PUBLISHING GROUP
Published by the Penguin Group
Penguin Group (USA) LLC
375 Hudson Street, New York, New York 10014

USA • Canada • UK • Ireland • Australia • New Zealand • India • South Africa • China

penguin.com

A Penguin Random House Company

This book is an original publication of The Berkley Publishing Group.

Copyright © 2014 by Colby Marshall.

Library of Congress Cataloging-in-Publication Data

Marshall, Colby.
Color blind / Colby Marshall. — Berkley trade paperback edition.
pages cm. — (A Dr. Jenna Ramey novel)
ISBN 978-0-425-27651-8 (paperback)
1. Synesthesia—Fiction. 2. Serial murderers—Fiction. 3. Suspense fiction.
4. Psychological fiction. I. Title.
PS3613.A7726C65 2014
813'.6—dc23
2014025979

PUBLISHING HISTORY
Berkley trade paperback edition / November 2014

PRINTED IN THE UNITED STATES OF AMERICA

10 9 8 7 6 5 4 3 2 1

Cover design by Jason Gill.

For David,
a deep, rich navy blue

ACKNOWLEDGMENTS

As an author, I have the special opportunity to let the world know about the people whose help I simply couldn't do without. With the honor of thanking those who have given me so much comes the very real, terrifying possibility that I might leave out someone important. So if by my mistake this happens to you, I ask you to forgive my scatterbrained, last-minute writing of these acknowledgments and accept my heartfelt thanks for your role in this book's "birth."

To the wonderful people at Penguin/Berkley: First and foremost, a huge thank-you to my fantastic editor, Faith Black, for believing in Dr. Jenna Ramey and *Color Blind* enough to take on this new series. I am grateful not only for the confidence you've shown in me as a writer, but for the way you've infused the publication process with such enthusiasm. Thank you for your steady, fervent leadership and for the natural sapphire blue hue you bring to the table for me. To Jason Gill and the cover design team for bringing *Color Blind* to life visually. A million thanks to my publicist, Loren Jaggers, for your guidance and gusto in launching this book into the world. To all of the many wonderful hands at Penguin/Berkley that have touched and shaped this book in the production process, I appreciate everything you've done to take *Color Blind* from a story in my head to a tangible work for many to see. And of course, to my publisher and editor in chief of Berkley, Leslie Gelbman, for making this book possible, I am forever thankful.

To my agent, Rachel Ekstrom: nothing I can say can adequately thank you for your guidance, patience, wisdom, and passion for my work. More than anything, I'm thankful for the way you've renewed my faith that synergetic author/agent partnerships can exist and flourish (which no doubt plays into why I see you as the bright yellow color of daffodils). In addition to Rachel, a huge thank-you to everyone at the Irene Goodman Literary Agency for the hard work you put in every day to make sure books like mine make it into the world. I also owe an enormous debt of gratitude to Danny Baror and Heather Baror-Shapiro of Baror International. I'm humbled and thankful that because of your hard work and tenacity, *Color Blind* will be read in several languages throughout the world.

Research will perpetually be a favorite part of the book-writing process for me, but without the colorful array of willing victims— erm, *sources*—in my life, my interviews would be a lot more boring and my work, much less accurate. In all of my writing, I owe many of my baddest of the bad and craziest of the crazy characters to Dr. Richard Elliot. But for this series in particular, for your expertise and insight into the job of a forensic psychiatrist, I thank you, Richard. To Ashley and Jared Carson, thank you for your theme park wisdom as well as for allowing me to make my "niece cat" into a character. With any luck, your actual little princess will remain nothing like this character for which I've borrowed her name. Massive thanks to my +2 Friends of Nerd-dom—Ashley Carson (again), Herbie Hatlee, Amy Etheridge, and Chris Etheridge—without whom I would have embarrassed myself profoundly with my lack of knowledge regarding online role playing games. You guys are speced for awesomeness. Thank you to Laura Voss for your classic film knowledge and how it helped bring to life a vital piece of this book's puzzle. Dad, thank you for your "expertise" in that—*cough*—one "little" thing. And to The Possum, the mysterious benefactor responsible for helping me with weapon information that I may have later bastardized in the name of fiction and with the hope of suspension of disbelief, I thank you.

To Matt Stine and 27Sound Entertainment, I continue to be thankful for your web design brilliance and for making my crazy ideas like SWAT into a reality. And to Ken and Stacey, I will forever be grateful to you for your support of my writing career. You will always be my first "family."

Many people both cheered on this manuscript as well as tore it a new one in order to make it worth a look. A huge thank-you to George Berger, Rick Campbell, and Lisa Brackmann for taking the time to read it, give suggestions, and encourage me to press on. And to Pat Shaw, who I'm now lucky enough to consider my friend, for nurturing me as a writer. Thank you for everything you've taught me—not only about writing and editing, but about perseverance and staying true to my voice. For the record, you do—and always will—appear as a vivid hot pink.

I'm lucky to have friends and family to whom I can vent frustrations, brainstorm with, and turn to for gentle words of encouragement—or occasionally, for a kick in the pants when the gentler coaxing doesn't work. To my Purgies and Pitizens, I can't thank you enough for your support throughout the years, even when I disappear for months on end. To my Ynots, what can I say? The good, the bad, the vandalism, and the CDs . . . you all deserve keys to a beach house for weeks for how many times you've been there for me as a writer and as a person. Many thanks to my theatre and dance families at Theatre Macon, Macon Little Theatre, and Hayiya Dance Theatre, as well as to my friends at the Central Georgia Alzheimer's

Association for cheering me on, inspiring me, and helping to spread the word about my books.

To Will, Danielle, and Nikki: thank you for your selfless contributions to both my writing and my life. I'm so grateful to know I can count on each of you at any moment—for *anything*—without question, no matter how inconvenient or strange. To Courtney: not only do I appreciate your expertise in all things nursing, but it means so much to me that you love my books and spread the word to others. Compliments from you are truly some of the highest praise I feel, and the spirit of your words boosts my confidence.

And to Meg: I love knowing you're always there to pick up right where we left off. I couldn't handle any meltdown without the knowledge that you would keep up a sense of humor even when I lost mine. Thank you for your covert recon operations and for just plain being you. You're so loved.

To Ashlee: I could write a whole book of acknowledgments about all the ways you build me up and keep me together (and put up with my rambling when I need to talk about writing to re-ignite my excitement about a manuscript). Thank you for being the nine to my three, and for always reading along with everything I write. We always say we're twins, but the truth is, real twins don't get to choose each other. I'd pick you for my twin every day of every week.

To Mom and Dad: if there are more wonderful parents that exist in the world, I certainly don't know where they are or how they could do anything better than you. You've believed in me through trials and cheered on my achievements. You've never let me give up or give in. If I can be even half the parent you both are to me and teach my own children to follow their hearts and dreams the way you did me, then I will be sure I've done my job as a parent in a way I can be proud of.

For the littlest members of my family, you'll never know how much you inspire me, keep me going, and bring light and love to my life every day. One day when you're old enough to read this book, I want you to know that I loved you when I penned these acknowledgments, and my love for you has done nothing but grow since the night I wrote these words.

And to David: I have no idea what I did to deserve someone like you to champion my every effort, to push me to be my best, and to comfort me when I'm at my worst. You're my pillar of strength and my perfect companion. You make me bold and brave, but most of all, you bring out the best in me. Thank you for the long nights, the pep talks, the midnight runs for goldfish crackers, and for duct taping the sheets. But most of all, thank you for everything you are . . . and for everything you are to me.

Finally, to the readers of this book as well as those who've been with me since *Chain of Command* and *The Trade*: In today's busy world, finding the time to read a book can be hard to come by, so I thank you for putting your faith into this story and in me. Whether it was the back cover copy that drew your interest, that you enjoyed a previous tale of mine, that I have blackmail information on you, or just that one character happens to be a dachshund, I'm thrilled you've chosen to spend time with the characters in my head. I wish you happy reading, many surprises, and a heart-pounding ride. And as always, I hope this story keeps you reading late into the night.

COLOR
BLIND

Prologue

saac Keaton shifted the scope of his M16 from the five-year-old tripping on his own shoelaces to a forty-year-old guy ten paces to the side of the boy outside the Futureland Chow Station. Kid might grow up to be stupid and pathetic like the man Isaac was about to gun down, but hell, he might've spared the next great. Kid might grow up to be just like Isaac, hoping and praying someone would take out his parents with two quick shots. Isaac laughed.

Idiots, all of them. Treat kids like they need to be protected from these kinds of valuable experiences. Teach 'em tolerance, make sure they know it's okay to cry. Media screamed for a national campaign to stop school bullying after those two kids lit up that high school in Colorado. Parents freaked out about what kind of music their teens listened to, whether or not a trench coat hung in someone's closet. Morons didn't realize that if those two kids hadn't shot up the school and then themselves, they'd have had a lot worse on their hands a couple decades later.

They'd have had someone like *him*.

The guy in Isaac's crosshairs licked at his ice cream cone, which dripped over his grubby fingers. Maybe coincidence. Could be fate. Either way, this dude happened to be sitting right in Isaac's line of vision under the cable that carried the little fairy from the top castle turret over the park of wide-eyed, middle-class imbeciles every night. He glanced at his stopwatch. Thirty seconds. Twenty. Ten.

Time to fly.

He squeezed off round one, and a hundred faces pinched and looked in his direction. He watched the ice cream guy slam away from him into the bench he was sitting on.

No time to think. Anyone obviously over thirty equals goner. The grayer the head, the easier the mark. He took down three more: a tall, slim black woman in faded jeans, dude with a lip ring, fat Indian chick. The crowd ran in different directions, some into each other, others ducking. Then they all scattered, screamed. Isaac's head was quiet. His scope slipped over two kids, up to the dad holding one's hand, urging the kid to run. *Bang.*

The dad dropped. Isaac coursed over the crowd. Old Asian man, brunette with a fanny pack. A ginger-haired theme park worker yelling into his walkie-talkie. One by fucking one.

When he had fewer fresh targets than people he'd already hit, he finally heard them coming. He laid the M16 on the ground, turned around to face them, hands in the air. They wouldn't understand, of course. Give them time.

"Freeze!" the lead cop yelled, gun trained on Isaac's chest. Guy had probably never shot a man in his life.

Isaac ducked his head. "Don't shoot!"

His hands were twisted behind his back, his face pressed into the floor. He had the right to remain silent . . .

But he didn't want to remain silent. These half-wits had no idea. The fun was just beginning.

"Dad! Have you seen my keys?"

Jenna Ramey turned over couch cushions, squatted to look under the baby's playpen. "Dad!"

Her father appeared in the hallway, holding Ayana on his hip. Jenna's towheaded daughter held her pacifier in one hand and Jenna's ring of keys in the other. In her thirty years of life before her daughter, Jenna had never once lost her keys. Now they found their way out of her purse daily.

"Whoever thought to make giant key rings into toys, I'd like to see," Vern said.

Jenna smiled and pecked her father's cheek. "Ayana, can Mommy have those?"

Her little girl plugged her paci in her mouth but stretched the keys toward Jenna.

"Thank you, miss," Jenna said, and she kissed Ayana's forehead. Then, to her father, "I'll be back in a few hours, I hope. Don't know the damage yet."

"Must be bad if they're calling in a bigwig like you."

Jenna pressed her middle finger against her thumb and flicked her dad in the arm. "I was an FBI profiler, Dad. I can detect sarcasm."

"Go get 'em, El Tigre."

The sun shined in Jenna's eyes the whole drive to the Orlando Police Department. Her duct tape job held the visor on but didn't allow her to fold the thing down. So helpful.

While en route, she'd talked to Supervisory Special Agent Hank Ellis, the man she'd reported to and worked with every day back when she was with the FBI's Behavioral Analysis Unit.

"Let me get this straight, Hank. You guys *caught* a serial killer operating in mid-Florida this morning, and *now* you're inviting me in? No offense, but what for?"

"Oh, boy," Hank replied, his frustration seeping through. "Thought they'd told you more when they called you from the OPD. Shit."

"Hank, I'd love to rant with you about the incompetent lackey who called me, but I'd rather know what I'm walking into."

"Right. You're right. I apologize. Yes, we caught a serial, but not one only operating in Florida. They've been up and down the East Coast. You already know about them."

"Them?" Jenna couldn't hold in her surprise. "You can't mean what I think you mean."

She pulled into the OPD parking lot.

"Yep," Hank said. "The Gemini. But we only caught one of the pair, and he says he'll *only* talk to you."

Officer Mel Nelson met Jenna at the door and led her through the halls toward the interrogation room. "So cool to meet you in person, Dr. Ramey. Heard all about you, of course."

If only her reputation wouldn't precede her quite so fast. "Thanks. Catch me up, will you? I know next to nothing."

Hank had told her enough, but getting it from different sides helped. Someone might throw in a crucial detail.

Nelson straightened, seemed to shake off the starstruck. His short steps quickened, stocky frame moving faster to impress. "Right. Suspect apprehended at the top of the castle. Had already put down his weapon, hands up. The gun was an M16, standard. Twenty dead, seven more wounded. Suspect is Isaac Keaton of Norton, Virginia. Still trying to run backgrounds, but not much on the guy. Asked for you almost right off, didn't say why. They said you were coming with the BAU. I thought you weren't with the BAU anymore. Thought you were in a private practice now."

Typical. Someone reads about you in a textbook, they think you're as good as best friends, or at least next-door neighbors.

"I'm not," Jenna said. "And I am."

They'd come to a closed door, which Nelson put his hand to. "You gonna do that color thing on him?"

Grapheme-color synesthesia—Jenna's ticket to the spotlight for better or for worse. Since she could remember, she'd associated everything—letters, days, numbers, people—with colors.

"It doesn't work like that," she said and nodded toward the door.

Nelson twisted the handle. Inside, the man standing in front of the one-way window turned to them.

"Detective Arnold Richards, this is Dr. Jenna Ramey," Nelson said.

The hulking bald figure stretched out his palm. "Dr. Ramey. Good of you to come. BAU team is in the air. They'll be here within the hour, but we thought it best to bring you in right away. I'm the head of the task force for the park shootings."

Chin lifted, smile that didn't extend to his cheeks. That extra note of authority in his voice telling her she was only there because it was *his* idea.

The man gave Jenna a curt nod, and Jenna nodded back.

Richards turned to Officer Nelson. "Thank you, Moose."

Nelson backed out and closed the door. Richards's eyes followed him, then cut to Jenna. "He's Canadian."

He focused on the two-way mirror, and Jenna did the same. Aside from his hunched shoulders and the bags under his eyes, the man sitting in interrogation on the other side of the glass might've walked straight out of an Abercrombie & Fitch catalog. His fawn hair was cut in a trendy style that was shaggy but still neat, maybe even highlighted. Clean-shaven, strong jaw. Fit.

"Do you mind if I ask what color you see him as?" Richards asked.

"No, I don't mind," Jenna replied, "but I can't answer that. I haven't met him yet."

"Your interviews said it didn't have anything to do with what you felt about a person."

Isaac Keaton rocked back and forth in his metal chair, his palms flat against his dark trousers. Interesting. Jenna closed her eyes, then reopened them to look again, specifically attempting to gauge color. Nothing.

"It doesn't. Anything on the other shooter?"

Detective Richards's hands went to his pockets, jingled his keys. "Ballistics not back yet, but looks like a Magnum .308. Six dead."

Jenna blinked a few times as she tried to compute. "Wait a second. Officer Nelson said twenty dead, seven wounded. That by him"—she nodded toward Keaton—"or is that total?"

"Total," Richards replied. "Fourteen dead and three wounded near the castle, six more on the other side of the park, DOA. Four wounded there. Near the ferry."

Jenna filed away the information about the second shooter and returned her attention to Keaton. "And what of the interaction with the suspect?"

Richards's brows creased. "Arresting officer said he'd already ceased fire, dropped his gun. He went easy."

"Too easy," Jenna mumbled. This guy either *really* didn't want to die, or he *really* wanted to be caught. Or both. "And they recovered Keaton's weapon?"

"Mm-hm. M16, standard issue. Stolen, probably. We're on it. Recovered one slug at the ferry site, hopefully others from the victims. For twins, their gun choices pack a different punch."

Thirty rounds, and Keaton squeezed off a good many of them. Still, it'd take some time for police to hear the shooting, react, and find where it was coming from. In theory, firing an automatic rifle—even in single fire mode—he should've managed to fire many more.

Jenna was speaking before she realized the words were coming out. "The newspapers might've nicknamed them the Gemini, but don't be fooled. Chances are they'll be two entirely different beasts."

"Meaning?" Richards asked.

Jenna stared one last time at Isaac Keaton from behind the glass, where she could view him as a completely objective party. Then she stepped toward the door to the interrogation room. She might not still be with the branch of the FBI that was called in to analyze the behavioral patterns of mass murderers, kidnappers, and serial rapists, but once you'd studied these monsters, you didn't forget how they worked. To get into their heads and discover their motivations took some part of your humanity, not because you became them, but because you had to understand why they would possibly do what they did. "In serial pairs, one will always be dominant. The other is the follower, submissive. In other words, one is the soldier, the other the general. Before we do anything else, we have to figure out which one we have."

3

Jenna entered the inner room. Isaac Keaton's head was down, eyes hooded. Fearful? Defensiveness intentional? Only one way to know.

"Isaac. I'm Dr. Jenna Ramey. I understand you wanted to speak with me?"

He glanced over her, a slow perusal from head to toe, reading. This guy had just shot more than a dozen people at a theme park for children, and here she was introducing herself as though they were business associates. The job was never boring.

"So you're the famous Jenna Ramey," he said, his voice weary.

Colors flashed in. She pulled up a rolling chair across the table from Keaton. "Why did you want to speak with me specifically, Isaac?"

He leaned forward, squinted. Worry lines creased his forehead. "You were the only person I could think of who'd understand. You know. How someone can be a whole person, even if they do a very bad thing."

Jenna pursed her lips. She knew exactly what he was referring to, but she wasn't ready to give him that much yet. Granted, many people knew about her mother, but the fact that he referred to her so specifically spoke volumes. The years had taught her not to assume. "That I do. Are you saying you've done a very bad thing?"

He nodded emphatically, rocked again. "Uh-huh. I did. I killed those people."

Different colors struck her, but Jenna didn't try to reel them in. Her deeper brain would settle on one when it was ready.

She tossed the facts, quick and furious. He'd picked a vantage point that boxed him in, no escape, but then hadn't tried to shoot his way out. Hadn't committed suicide, either. Yet now he appeared tortured, remorseful. Wanted to be caught, not killed. Definitely wanted to get caught.

To end it or to play?

"Why did you put down your gun?" she asked evenly.

"I didn't . . . I expected it to stop the pain. Then they were dead. Blood everywhere, people hurt. My fault. I knew I should talk to you."

Interesting, but I didn't ask why you shot them. The vacillating colors coalesced, and a shade flashed in her mind. It lasted only seconds, but it was enough for Jenna to file it away, to use the ever-growing database of her color associations to define what the color said about Isaac.

"Would you like a drink of water, Isaac? I think you should have one. Keep your strength up. It's been a long, hard day," Jenna said, standing.

She stepped out of the box, where Detective Richards waited.

"Keep your strength up?" Richards repeated.

Jenna stared at Keaton, who was still rocking himself. He knew he was being watched.

She turned back to Richards to answer his earlier question.

"I see him as red."

"Huh?"

This part was never easy to explain. "Red. He could be either of the team, the mastermind or the submissive. He either picked a spot where he was sure to get caught, or someone chose it for him. He wasn't *afraid* of being caught. Backed into a corner, but didn't take everyone down with him. Could mean he wanted to stop, but not necessarily. He also knew to ask for me. Again, could've been told to by his superior. But when I asked about the gun, his speech pattern was strange. I asked him a question, and he answered something totally different. He's pushing his own agenda. He comes in as red."

Most people associated red with anger. To Jenna, it was less definitive. Her color associations proved more random and yet not random all at the same time. She never knew them until she felt them, saw them. The color would flash in, but after the flash, even when the color wasn't readily present, if Jenna closed her eyes and thought about a person or an event, she could draw up the color she tended to associate with them or it. A color association for Jenna was just like any other detail she would note about a person that might affect her perception of them, no different than the way she might read into someone's body language or note a person's tone of voice. The initial flash was fast, but it left its brand on something forever. In the bizarre color dictionary in her brain, red could mean wrath or love or a host of other things. Red often showed up for people she saw as strong, type A. Isaac Keaton headed the Gemini. He was the general.

"In this case, red tells me he's a power player. He's the dominant of the two, and for some reason, he wanted to get caught."

"I thought you said the color thing had nothing to do with emotions," Richards said.

"It doesn't."

Richards put his hands up. "Whatever. Where do we go from here?"

Jenna walked to the water cooler, filled two cones from the dispenser. "That's what I'm trying to decide. If he wants us to believe his act and we call him out, he might button up. If that's the case, better we play along."

4

Jenna reentered the box and handed Isaac Keaton, who was wiping his palms on his pants, the little cone of water.

She watched as Isaac lifted the cup, sipped. His hand didn't shake. The cone tilted smoothly, the water slid down easy.

Done.

Things were about to get either good or bad. "Good show, Isaac."

His chin tilted upward, and his hazel eyes met her own. In an instant those eyes transitioned from wild and scared to focused, calculating. Intense.

The side of his mouth turned up first, then he chuckled. "Whaddaya know? You're *not* a complete fraud."

Jenna's stomach knotted. Just because she'd suspected this outcome didn't make her less uneasy about it.

"I'd hate to think all that training was for nothing," she countered.

Isaac laughed again, hard and loud. "Oh, come on, Dr. Ramey! We both know your gift didn't come from one of those 'I have a high school diploma and can carry a gun' training courses!"

Gift. Kind of like the "gift" of foresight. "Tell me about your partner."

Isaac's thin brows lifted. "Partner is an interesting word choice. Implies equality."

"And he's not your equal," Jenna supplied. It wasn't a question. "Most people aren't, are they?"

Isaac threw his head back. "Oh, Dr. Ramey! You're shrinking me, aren't you? That's cute. Can I try? You like saving people. You saved your dad and brother, but you can't come to terms with the fact that you couldn't save your mom. You rescue other people to make up for the guilt."

Bile rose in Jenna's throat. "I'm not shrinking you, Isaac. Not any more than you want me to. I'm trying to wrap my head around why you did what you did. That I'll admit."

"Of course you are! That's your job."

Certain brands of sociopaths were like that: oppositional kinder-gartners wanting to be both first *and* not first for show-and-tell. When they showed the propensity, refocusing on something else tended to do the trick. "Tell me about the other half of the team."

"Third."

"Okay," she conceded. "The other one-third."

"Did you always see your mother as black?"

Flashes of the steak knife jutted in. *Bloody palm prints dotting the kitchen countertops, a sick trail to the door. Freedom.* "We're not here to talk about me, Isaac."

"Hmph," he smirked. "*I* am."

Jenna's heart clenched. Panic built in her chest. Something ugly pressurized it, readying it for explosion.

Chill out.

This psycho shot a bunch of people and hung around to be caught. Couldn't be *only* because he wanted to talk to the "famous" Dr. Jenna Ramey, no matter how bored he got. No. He was stalling. Waiting for something.

His smirk made purple flash in. Grapheme-color synesthesia worked for Jenna like inverted colorblindness. Where for most people, traits blended in, the colors that flashed in her mind at certain statements or mannerisms could make a quality stand out like a brunette in a sea of bald heads. In this case, the purple that crossed her mind brought up thoughts of narcissism. Flattery would get her everywhere.

"I don't believe for a second that you *let* yourself get caught so you could shoot the breeze with me, Isaac."

"You tell me, Dr. Ramey. Why would I *let* myself get caught?"

Notoriety. *You're playing a game, proving you're smarter than we are.* "You didn't enjoy your knitting class?"

"I wouldn't *want* to be caught, would I?"

Normal people didn't want to be caught. Isaac did. "You already told me the other guy is only one-third of what you are, and *he's* out there. By your own reasoning, either you're underestimating him, or you're lying to me. Which is it?"

"Did you know *she* was lying, Jenna? Your mother? How could you tell? The news stories said you had a hunch about her based on the color you associated. They said you couldn't explain it. They said your colors had nothing to do with your emotional feelings for someone, Jenna, but they did, didn't they? You didn't want them to, but they did."

She swallowed the surge of angst that crept in. Isaac was quite a fan.

But Jenna would rather donate a kidney to this guy than talk to him about her past. Best to keep him on task. "Speaking of your partner, if this guy is only one-third of what you are, why team up with him? Seems like a liability."

Isaac puffed out his cheeks, then let the air out by pushing on his cheeks with a handcuffed hand on either side of his face. "You know the answer to that, don't you?"

"If I knew, I wouldn't ask."

5

Sebastian Waters blinked into the fluorescents overhead. Damn, he was groggy. He couldn't feel his left side. *What the—*

Then he remembered. Pops. Bullets. People falling. He'd yelled that someone was shooting from above them, from the castle.

He jumped when he saw the nurse in the corner of his eye. "Who's there?"

The young brunette nurse with the sleek ponytail smiled. "I didn't mean to scare you, Mr. Waters. I'm your shift nurse. You're at the hospital. Do you remember what happened?"

Boy, did he.

"Yeah," he said, his voice solemn. So much blood.

"A bullet got you in the shoulder. It passed straight through, thank goodness. No major damage, didn't hit any arteries. You do have a good gash on your stomach where you fell. The doctor put in five stitches. You were one of the lucky ones."

Lucky? Try preordained.

"Did they . . ." Sebastian winced. The stitches in his side burned when he talked. "Did they get him?"

"The police will want to talk to you as soon as the doctor gives them the okay, but yes. The police caught the castle shooter. Unfortunately, he wasn't the only shooter. Another one shot people by the ferry. He's still out there somewhere."

"Unbelievable," Sebastian whispered. The magnitude of the whole thing shocked him, amazed him. It seemed so impossible. It reminded him of an arcade tournament he'd played in once years ago, how the adrenaline coursed during what seemed like a never-ending event. But all of a sudden, this huge moment was over, and you could only look back in shock that you'd won or lost.

"I know. Unreal, isn't it? But they'll find him. It's only a matter of time," the nurse replied.

"How many"—Sebastian's breath caught again—"dead?"

The nurse frowned. "Are you sure you want to talk about all this so soon, Mr. Waters?"

"Yes. I have to know."

The nurse took a deep breath, exhaled. "Twenty. Seven more wounded, you included. Some are still critical. Others'll be all right. Physically, that is. You're probably in the best shape of all of them, to tell you the truth."

Sebastian thought back on his morning. He'd gone in dressed as a cast member for customer convenience, in charge of making sure tourists found the attractions and rides. At one point he'd disappeared into one of the crew tunnels, headed away from the castle. He'd finished business, gotten back to the castle right when the shooting from above started.

Just like Isaac had told him to.

Jenna leaned in and propped her elbows on the gray metal table in the conference room. Time to switch tactics. "All right, Isaac. You want to talk about me so bad. You asked for me because you know about my mother. You said you read an article, huh?"

For a second, Isaac's eyes narrowed. He hadn't expected her to concede so easily. Then he smiled, smug. "Yeah. Read a few of your interviews and things."

She hummed what might have sounded like agreement in the back of her throat. "And you want to know if I always saw my mother as black?"

Isaac's gaze bore into her, excitement radiating off him. Mind-fucking at its finest.

"Yes, Dr. Ramey, I'd very much like to know that," he said, practically salivating.

She leaned back, folded her arms. "You know what I think, Isaac? I think you're a liar."

"That's pretty textbook for you, isn't it, Doc?"

Jenna smiled, though none of this was funny. Remaining genial was key to keeping him talking. She'd met his breed before. To stay engaged, this type wanted something from her. Her best guess was that he craved a worthy adversary. If she didn't fulfill this requirement, he'd either zip up or start spouting off complete bull that wouldn't tell them anything.

"I mean you're lying about the article research. You didn't read my interviews, or you'd know I never saw my mother as black. You assumed. Popular misconception, of course. Nope. I didn't give that information in any interview."

Isaac Keaton tossed his honey-colored bangs out of his face, blinked. Grunted. "Touché. What color *did* you see her as?"

Finally. The upper hand.

"That's for me to know, and you to bargain for."

Isaac winked. "Now you're the one assuming, Dr. Ramey. Assuming I'll play along."

"You will if you want me to play, too," Jenna argued. "Are you going to tell me about the other killer?"

Isaac glanced around the blank pea green walls of the room. "Don't I get a phone call or something?"

Not your everyday I'm-playing-a-game psychopath request. The ones caught for the allure of infamy weren't often looking for someone to bail them out. "A few more questions."

As usual, he changed the subject. "Most people like you want revenge, Dr. Ramey. You know. *Victims*. What do you do when you can't get revenge? Or do you even want it, if the person who hurt your family *is* your family?"

"Is that what this was, Isaac? Revenge?"

He snorted. "Of course not. I asked because lots of people *do* want it."

Where was he going with this? This was coming from somewhere. Had to be. "Who wants revenge? The other killer?"

Anger flashed across his face as his jaw tightened, then in an instant, complete calm replaced it. "Do yourself a favor and forget the other killer for a second."

So he wants this to be about him. Or wants it not to be about the other killer.

"Okay. Like who, then?"

Isaac folded his hands on the table, twiddled his thumbs. "I've spent years talking to people, Dr. Ramey. In fact, we're something alike, I think. You listen to people, I listen to people. Difference is when they talk to you, they're paying a professional to help them. When they tell me their problems, they don't pay. They're confiding their deepest, darkest secrets to a friend."

"Okay, and what do they have to do with anything, these people? Did they make you angry somehow?"

Isaac chuckled again. "I answered your questions. How 'bout that phone call now?"

6

"No way in hell you're getting a phone call if you want it that bad, buddy," Officer Nelson said.

Richards dismissed Moose with a flick of his hand after taking a bite of pizza. "It's not that simple," he said, but he looked to Jenna to explain.

The Isaac Keaton in the box now was very different from the one she'd left last time she'd come out. The rocking, confused mess from before now sat straight up, completely still, a slight smile playing on his lips. He was actually enjoying himself, wasn't he?

"He wants us to assume he'll call the other killer," Jenna said. "Which most likely means he'll call anyone but. You can bet he has a plan for this call. Otherwise he wouldn't keep asking for it."

"What kind of plan?" Moose asked.

"Who knows? But I'm gonna try to find out. How far out is the BAU team?"

"Just landed, so they should be this way in a half an hour or so," Richards responded.

"Good. Keaton can cool his heels in there a few. Wonder what I'm up to. In the meantime, is there somewhere quiet I can make a couple phone calls?"

J enna stared at the photos strewn across the desk as the phone rang on the other end. Twice. Three times.

Finally, someone picked up. "What's shakin'?"

"Where's Dad?"

On the other end of the line, Jenna's younger brother clanged a pot onto the counter, yelled, "Hey, hey, hey! No, ma'am, Ayana! Crayons are for coloring *only!*" The phone crackled, and he picked back up. "Dad is currently washing the chicken-potpie-disgusting off his arms. Turns out the terrible twos isn't a misnomer after all."

"Charley, I told you not to turn your back on her with the crayons! They go straight to her mouth—"

"Unlike the chicken potpie."

"They were the fat crayons, right? She could choke—"

"Heya, Rain Man. You're acting like I'm a virgin in the middle of a prison riot here. Why so keyed up?"

Jenna yanked her eyes from the photo of Korbin Dale, victim number four. "I know, I know. Sorry. It's this new case. I'm stir-crazy waiting on BAU to get here. I just wanted to let you guys know I'll be a few more hours. Can you hold things together until then?"

"Depends. How much duct tape we got in the house?" Charley asked.

Charley used his middle name, Padgett, as his last name now, but he still spoke like a true Ramey. If duct tape couldn't hold it together, they didn't need it.

"I'll pick up a couple extra rolls on my way home just in case. Give Ayana a kiss for me," Jenna said, and she hung up before Charley could say anything else. Right now his face stuck in her mind, but not the current picture of him with a bandanna tied around his head, his chin scruffy with a meager beard. It was a younger image she saw, the waxy, pale one from when he was six.

Jenna looked back down at the pictures she'd spread on the desk, pictures from another case entirely. Four dead men she knew too well to have never met them in person. *Can you do this, Jenna?*

The other half of Isaac Keaton's team was still out there, and somehow she had to wheedle information out of Isaac. Over the past few months, the Gemini had terrorized the East Coast, killing more than a dozen people across different states. But those attacks were smaller. Isolated. The killers had doubled that in one day today. With one shooter in custody, the media would crucify the OPD, launch a witch-hunt if they didn't make another arrest soon. Sure, she could work with BAU to form a basic profile of the UNSUB, the Unknown Subject of the Investigation, but the profile would be *better*, more *useful*, if she knew more. Even if Keaton *was* stalling, her best chance was to let down the drawbridge and let in the Trojan horse.

Isaac was right. She *did* save people. She tried to anyway. Damn it. Isaac Keaton had already gotten into her head.

He'd messed with the UNSUB, too. Sociopaths had a knack for finding that one button, then peeling down to the raw nerve until it was exposed and vulnerable.

It might be a dangerous tactic, but at least once the enemy was inside, she'd have a chance to take a swing at discovering and pushing *his* buttons.

"Back so soon, Doctor?" Isaac asked as Jenna came in. "After the first five minutes I assumed you were waiting for backup."

Astute. "Is that why you paired up, Isaac? Backup? You don't strike me as the type to need backup."

"Aha, Dr. Ramey. *Need* and *want* are two very different things."

Jenna settled in the chair across from the killer, crossed her legs, and leaned toward him. "Fair enough. So did you *need* backup or *want* backup?"

Isaac rose from the wooden chair an inch and slammed back down at the same time he hit his hand on the table. "Now, that's why I like you, Dr. Ramey. You didn't assume that because I corrected your statement, it meant I wanted rather than needed backup."

His wild eyes settled, calm confidence replacing the excitement.

Still no answer to the question. *Let's try this a different way.* "You don't like assuming, and yet you assumed I was holding out for backup. We have different sets of rules?"

Of course, she already knew that answer. Isaac was a sociopath, and all sociopaths, be they Ted Bundy, Jeffrey Dahmer, or Jenna's own mother, shared certain traits. One of those traits: they always played by their own rules, rules that set double standards—one standard for only them, and another standard for everyone else.

Isaac seemed to know where she was going. He nodded emphatically, mocking and humming his agreement. "Grandiose sense of self, feels the rules don't apply. I've heard this a time or two." He winked. "Yes. Agreed. I assume things about people. I'm typically smarter than they are."

Jenna didn't doubt it. Still, she'd heard it from plenty of monsters, and many times. Overestimating their intelligence was where they went wrong. *Play to it.* "What are my rules, if you don't mind my asking?"

Isaac cocked his head, studied her for a moment. Finally he said, "Both. Wanted and needed."

A reward for asking the right question. His pupils were dilated. He liked her.

"Am I right to *assume* my next question won't get an answer?"

"Phone call yet?"

Jenna glanced at her watch. They couldn't hold him forever without that call, but the hell if she had to give it to him without having some clue why he wanted it. Hank and his team had to be here by now. "Who's your phone-a-friend, Isaac?"

"Who's the first person you ever saw as one? A color, I mean," Isaac countered.

Jenna pushed away from the table, stood. Always the damned colors. "Let me see if I can find a timetable on that call for you."

7

Thadius Grogan's knees creaked as he rose from the recliner. He snapped the dusty hardcover shut and tossed it on the pile of other books and magazines decorating the sofa. Concentration was about as likely right now as America electing Pee-wee Herman to the presidency by write-in vote. Reading about the life of that poor girl kidnapped at ten and kept for six years as a sex slave couldn't hold his attention, even if it *was* in the interest of reminding him how very much worse Emily's situation could've been. Howie Dumas would be letting him know the latest on the case any minute now.

Not like he'd been able to read since "it" happened anyway. Leastways, not anything for enjoyment. For the past five years he'd stuck tight to pieces about unsolved murders, burning the suspect images into his mind in case maybe, just maybe, he'd see one on the street and could help someone like himself. Worst-case scenario, he picked up a book like this one and pored over the crimes, thanking God at least Emily's killer let her die the same day and not after years of torture.

Small consolation. Em was in vet school at the Florida Calhan University, her sights set on a job with the Birmingham Zoo a state over. She was supposed to marry that scrawny little dude with the 'fro haircut. Hell, maybe they'd have a kid or two by now, and he and Narelle would sit for them on Friday nights so they could catch a movie at the dollar theater. Em loved the dollar theater.

Thadius paced, flipped his phone over in his pocket.

Instead, that bastard took them both away from him. Well, technically just Emily, but Narelle went, too. Thadius would never forgive the bastard.

For that matter, he'd never forgive himself.

"Y ou yelled for help just before you were shot. You don't remember seeing anything, anyone after that, Mr. Waters?"

Sebastian's eyelashes felt glued together, but he forced himself to stay awake. Pain had flared in his left side as the morphine wore off, and before he could stop her, the nurse had given him another shot to take the edge off. Because of that, the interview with the police was technically off the record. The questions thus far had been cursory, since they figured they already knew any information he might provide. If only they realized what he might reveal in his drugged state. One foggy slip and they would have the interview of their lives.

"Nothing else I can remember," Sebastian muttered. *Isaac always said less was better—unless it wasn't.*

The detective pocketed his moleskin notebook. "That's all we need for now, but please call if you think of anything. We can't officially tell you how to handle the media, but I suggest keeping a low profile." He coughed. "As low a profile you *can* keep. You're headlining the news now. The—er—incident is headlining, I mean. They'll follow you, hang out in your front yard. Point is you don't want to draw attention to yourself for obvious reasons."

The detective walked toward the door, and Sebastian's head lolled over on the pillow. God, he needed to sleep. "You mean the other shooter, huh?"

Luckily, the slurred quality of his voice made the note of bitterness sound like fear. Not much on the news about *him* at all.

The detective turned back, looked him in the eye. "Yes. Unfortunately."

"Gotcha. No media," Sebastian said. He already knew about the damned media. All part of the process.

"Feel better soon, Mr. Waters," the detective replied.

Sebastian finally let his eyes flutter closed as the man left him in peace.

O h, boy. They were on the run now.

Isaac sat in the box, daydreaming of popping off the rounds in the theme park. That high was nothing compared to his discussions thus far with Dr. Ramey. He hadn't expected things to be so enjoyable before the main event began. Woman had it.

Like mother, like daughter.

By now, Sebastian would've been questioned, cleared. This time tomorrow he'd be on his way home. Of course, Isaac could ask how Sebastian Waters was doing, but showing interest in his victims wouldn't help his cause, would it? Right now, they didn't suspect. Best to keep it that way.

Behavioral Analysis Unit hadn't arrived yet, though. The real test was about to begin.

8

Jenna rubbed her temples with both hands. She followed the path toward the main police station intake. Moose could've led the BAU team to the box, but when Hank texted her that he was five minutes out, Jenna volunteered instead. She needed the air.

They'd have to give Isaac a call. Not really a way around it.

Hank swung the door open as Jenna entered the lobby. For a short second their eyes met, and Jenna caught the splay of hazel around his pupil that matched Ayana's. She'd gotten the eyes from him, all right.

In the next moment Jenna shook it off. This wasn't the time.

"Jenna," he said, curt, though his eyes said something different before they, too, broke free. He indicated the boxy brown woman about Jenna's age who was trailing him. "Agent Saleda Ovarez, this is Dr. Jenna Ramey."

Jenna introduced them to Officer "Moose" Nelson, then motioned them to come with her.

"What's happened so far?" Hank asked, matching stride with Jenna.

She couldn't stop the dry laugh that came out. "He either wants my deepest thoughts about my family life or a phone call."

"Winner," Saleda said from behind them.

Hank shot a look at Jenna, questioning, but she shook her head. "He's not going to call the UNSUB. He's too smart for that. I can tell by the way he asks for the call. He's thought this through."

Saleda spoke up, her Boston accent surprising. "Does he assume he has a constitutional right to a phone call?"

Jenna turned to face Saleda and backpedaled through the hall. "I'm not sure, come to think of it. Why do you ask?"

"Common misconception," Saleda answered. "We don't *have* to give him a call. It's not a right, even though it's usual practice."

Such a small detail, Jenna had never questioned it. But now that Saleda mentioned it, the concept brought up more than one interesting point. The first would be they had the option not to offer Isaac a call. The second and more interesting implication: Isaac Keaton might've overlooked a detail. What did that misconception say about his profile?

"Crazy people miss things, I guess," Moose said from behind all of them.

"He's not crazy," Hank muttered.

"That's the problem, actually. He's very sane, and he's a planner," Jenna added.

Moose grunted. "Seems like a big thing to miss for someone who masterminded something crazy. Even if he isn't crazy."

"Most likely means he knew he could get around it in some way, shape, or form. Lawyer?" Hank continued.

"Public," Jenna answered as she reached the door. Richards had filled her in on the lawyer situation when she first arrived. "But Keaton thinks his lawyer's an idiot. He's probably right."

They entered the box, and Jenna introduced the BAU team to Richards. Nods and handshakes went around the room, and everyone lined up at the window to view Isaac as though they were at a zoo exhibit.

"The M16 he dropped at the scene doesn't match any of the ballistics from the other Gemini killings," Hank said.

"Bastard has a lot of guns," Jenna said. She'd read in the case file. Every shooting seemed to utilize a different firearm.

"And he left it," Saleda ventured. "So, not his most prized possession."

Jenna nodded. At Richards's questioning look, she said, "In other words, not his .50 caliber with the specs tweaked just for him."

"What about the ferry shooter's .308?" Richards asked.

"Same deal. Different guns every Gemini shooting, and this .308 matches none of 'em. Only thing we have at the ferry site that's different are a lot of strays," Hank replied.

Jenna tossed that around a moment. "The M16 discharged . . ."

"Seventeen shots, seventeen hits."

"Too weird," Jenna said under her breath. The ferry shooter was either a really bad shot, or his heart wasn't in it. Steel blue flashed in her mind, the same color she'd seen at age five when she was considering jumping off her dresser to land on the bed, doubting whether or not she could leap the distance. The steel blue was unmistakable. Very different from the berry hue she associated with incompetence. The ferry shooter lacked guts.

"In theory the .308 should be the more precise of the two," Saleda said. "The guy with the M16 goes in firing at anyone and everyone, takes out whoever happens to be in its path. The .308 is less of a standard issue. Seventeen out of seventeen with an M16? Homeboy Isaac is way out of the UNSUB's league," Saleda echoed Jenna's thoughts.

"Or the UNSUB is out of *Isaac*'s league," Jenna replied.

Richards folded his lips, but Jenna could tell he wanted to ask more questions. *Get over your hang-ups, Detective. Serials don't happen every day in every precinct, thank God.* "Could be a variety of reasons for the strays—"

Saleda picked up for her. "Clumsy. Lack of conviction. Nerves. Less training—"

In the box, Isaac's tongue lined his teeth beneath his lips. Jenna's mother's face filled her brain. Claudia had worn such a sick, smug smile at the defense table while Jenna testified at her competency hearing after Claudia was arrested for the murder of four husbands, then charged with one murder and the attempted murder of Jenna's father and brother.

Before Jenna could stop herself, she threw in, "Less enthusiasm."

Hank shifted his weight just enough so his elbow brushed hers. "I say we give him the call. We don't know where he's going with this, but we need more to go on."

Jenna's skin prickled from Hank's touch as she shook her head. "He's not gonna lead us to the shooter, Hank."

Don't do something stupid because you're trying to protect me.

Hank shrugged. "Maybe not. But it'll lead us somewhere."

9

Jenna entered the box behind Isaac, but she knew he'd heard the door open. She stopped moving, waited.

"So, dear Doc," he finally said over his shoulder, "what's the verdict?"

Jenna plopped the cordless onto the table, slid into her seat. "Time for your call, Isaac. I assume you know the drill. Collect call, so whoever answers will have to accept the charges. Phone call recorded, all that good stuff."

"Oh, goodie." There was no inflection there. He stared at her with cold eyes, then picked up the phone.

She watched him dial, tried to read his expressionless face. Hank was right. They had no leads on the ferry shooter, and Isaac's call might give them something to go on. Still, she couldn't ignore the pit in her stomach that said this phone call would end up being a curveball in the dirt. They'd chase it, just like he planned.

"Isaac Keaton," the killer said, apparently reaching the prompt for his name.

Jenna filed the information away. Whoever he was calling knew him by this name.

The phone couldn't have rung more than once, because Isaac spoke almost right away. He snapped off only three sentences. "I can't talk long. I'm all right. B, please."

He was quiet for a moment, the phone still pressed to his ear. Then he added, "Love you, too. I'll be in touch."

The color of cement flashed in. Anytime Jenna thought about her family, saw other family members embrace, rose. Friends arm in arm showed marigold. Couples sharing intimate moments tended to register deep burgundy. But this comment, this was cement. Flat.

Isaac ended the call and placed the phone back on the table between them.

"Close-knit family, huh?"

Isaac slid the phone back across the table to her. "You should know."

Jenna snatched up the phone a bit quicker than she'd meant to. *Relax your fingers.*

He noticed. "How's *your* family, Dr. Ramey? Why'd you move them back here, after all this time? You could've gone anywhere after the big, bad BAU. Why back to the Sunshine State?"

A lump formed in Jenna's throat as the images of the house on Oak Hollow Road flashed in her mind like a picture reel: she and Charley playing tag in the front yard while her dad pushed the old, stinky lawnmower just past the wooden fence. Her dad hoisting her to the peak of the Christmas tree to plop the star on top. Running through the house, passing bloody streaks on the walls. Standing in the kitchen doorway when the police took Claudia away. Watching from her SUV as the wrecking ball dealt the old house its first blow.

She bit back her reaction, swallowed hard. No more Oak Hollow Road house with its perfect picket fence and perfect driveway. Now she had wrought iron gates and the generic, impersonal parking lot of a high-rise apartment building. Better.

"You from around here, Isaac? You sure do know a lot about me for someone who's not," she snapped back.

"Vern doing well?" he countered.

"Daddy issues, Isaac?"

A smirk crossed the killer's face. "How about Charley? Ayana?"

Motherfucker.

"Back in a while, rock star," Jenna countered. It was a weak response, but it was the best she could do at the moment. She'd lost this round, but she wasn't down for good.

Isaac winked. "You stay out of my family, I'll stay out of yours."

Even though he was waiting for the call, the vibration of the phone made Thadius jump. He fumbled the cell as he pulled it out of his pocket. Second ring. Third.

"Please be there. Please don't hang up," he mumbled. He finally reached the button to answer. "Yes?"

"Mr. Grogan?" A woman's voice, Australian accent.

Thadius gripped the phone harder. "This is he."

"Mr. Grogan, this is Sheila, Howie Dumas's secretary. Mr. Dumas is tied up this afternoon, but he asked me to pass along the information he's collected for you."

He concentrated on easing up on the phone. Wouldn't help if it broke before he heard. "Yes, ma'am. I'm ready."

"The gun was purchased at Pembry Pawn on Forty-fifth. Purchased the day before, no waiting period."

Thadius's pulse quickened. The police had released almost no details about Em's death, not even to him. He'd believed them, depended on them. Trust the system, he'd thought. They'd find him, the sick freak.

Over the years he'd come to realize they weren't withholding because they knew something crucial. They weren't telling him anything because they had no freaking clue what they were doing. It was the exact reason he'd hired someone to find out *for* him. Someone *competent*.

"No bullets purchased, but we expected that, since the gun wasn't loaded or fired," the secretary continued.

Thadius beat his head into the main beam of the living room doorway, eyes shut tight. If only the coward *had* shot her. At least it would've been over fast. As it was, one of the few things Thadius *had* been able to discern from the snippets the cops had told him was that the bastard used the gun to scare her into letting him inside. It'd been found in the smoldering ruins that were her house.

"I'll e-mail the full report. Will that work?" the secretary asked.

Thadius nodded, then remembered she couldn't see him. "Yes. Fine."

He clicked his phone off, pounded his head against the door frame one more time. Then he sniffed hard, blinked away the moisture in his eyes. Coat, keys, wallet.

Thadius didn't bother to lock the door on his way out.

He wasn't planning on returning home.

L yra Mintelle dumped the contents of the bathroom drawer into a garbage bag. No. A garbage bag was a dumb idea. The fireplace was better.

She grunted as she lugged logs inside, threw them into the little cove. Flames danced in front of her eyes after she lit the pile, and for a minute she couldn't turn away. Seductive. Appropriate.

Next, she knelt beside the white plastic bag of the drawer contents, pulled out the first piece of paper. Sure, Isaac hadn't told her to do this, but she had to protect him. Even someone as brilliant as him couldn't possibly think of everything, right?

Then again, Isaac would be furious if he knew what she was up to. Lyra'd seen evidence of that temper more times than she'd like to admit. She clenched her teeth as she threw the first envelope into the fire, where it crinkled into itself, a slug dying in the hot sun. Soon it collapsed into a pile of black soot. Only ashes remained, just like her memories.

"You told her we went to Seattle together?" Isaac yelled, standing from the dinner table.

"I . . . I didn't know I wasn't supposed to," she stammered. Why did he care that she told someone she was taking a trip?

Isaac's face reddened, his height seeming to double with the angry breaths expanding his chest. "Lyra, you don't understand how people are! They talk to each other!"

She threw up her hands. "So you took a few days off work for us to spend some time together. Big whoop! People do it every day!"

He snatched up his plate of lasagna. "I'll eat upstairs. Things to do."

"But, Isaac! I haven't seen you all day! You'll be gone to the Dallas conference all week. This isn't fair!" Calling him that had taken time, but now it was second nature.

He wheeled back around, nostrils flaring. "Fair? Don't lecture me about fair, Ly-RUH! Unfair is you going around telling people our private business!"

Her own name sounded foreign in her ears, the way he said it—emphasis on the opposite syllable than he used in affectionate times. "I'm . . . I'm sorry," she stuttered.

He laughed, loud and cold. "Sorry, huh? You're sorry. That does me a lot of good."

Lyra's eyes filled with tears, which she hastily tried to blink back before her brother caught them. One dripped off her chin and plopped onto the pinewood table. "I didn't mean to . . ."

At this, Isaac sighed heavily, and before she knew it, he wrapped her in his arms, kissed the top of her head. "Don't do it again, Lye, okay?"

"Promise, promise," she parroted, just like she had when they were kids.

Now Isaac was in trouble, but he'd trusted her to keep herself together. He'd trusted her to follow through, to handle it. Yet here she sat, burning items he hadn't told her to and without his consent.

Lyra tossed paper after paper into the bizarre bonfire and muttered, "Stupid, Lyra. You're such an idiot."

She sniffled. Such a disappointment, as always. She'd called Thadius Grogan just like Isaac had told her to. She'd followed the plan, done her part. Isaac always came through, and she had to believe in him, not divert. But because she was such a whiny moron, she had to do this one thing, this thing her gut wouldn't ignore.

She extracted the final envelope from the bag and stared at it a long moment. To her lips she brought it, kissed it like a dying lover. Then she tossed it into the flames. *He trusts me.*

Lyra hugged herself, rocked, and repeated the thought over and over in her mind. The mantra calmed her, a sedative.

He trusts me. Only me.

When Jenna exited the box, Saleda was on the phone with the BAU's technical analyst.

"Trace on the number went to a landline. A dummy company set up under the name of Howie Dumas," Saleda repeated what the technical analyst was telling her.

Hank's eyebrows lifted. He had to be thinking exactly what Jenna was.

"Big mistake to make, leaving that number traceable," she said.

"Not a mistake," Hank replied.

Saleda pressed a hand to her ear to block out noise, nodded to the person on the other end. She lifted her chin from the phone to talk to them again. "Call went from that number to a Thadius Grogan two minutes after hang-up. Waiting for more on Grogan now."

"Anything to go on with the dummy office?" Hank asked.

"Not yet, but the tech's working on it after he finishes tracking Grogan. Better him since we have a name," Saleda replied.

"Good call," Hank said. He rolled his head around, then spoke more quietly to Jenna. "I'll send Saleda to interview the Gemini victims at the hospital. You up for a road trip to find Thadius Grogan or the mythical Dumas, whichever comes first?"

Ayana's face flashed in, followed by the ash gray of guilt. Dad or

Charley could read her *Green Eggs and Ham* tonight maybe. But *only* tonight. "You sure know how to woo a girl, Ellis."

Hank's unamused grunt said more than anything. "You know what they say. You don't make the big bucks without being a ladies' man."

"Is *that* what they say?" Jenna asked. Then she added, "Sure. I'm game, but you're paying for gas."

Three hours later, Jenna rode shotgun in the black SUV the FBI field office had sent for the BAU team members. They traveled the expressway nearing Jacksonville after an hour of trying to find a judge to sign a search warrant based on a phone call. It'd been a long drive with Detective Richards's constant, one-note hum from the backseat presumably every time he picked up his pencil to add to the notes he was reviewing, but the city was too close for them to have taken a plane.

Hank chatted with his technical analyst on his cell. Jenna had worked with Irv at the BAU. She could still picture the chunky Goth kid turned pro hacker plugging away at his desk, his long hair pulled back into a ponytail to keep it from getting in the way of his quick fingers.

"Really? Wait a minute, let me put you on speaker." Hank jammed the phone's side and tossed it in the cup holder between them. "Hit me with that again, Irv."

"Hey, yeah, boss. Thadius Grogan, Jacksonville native, fifty-five. Owns a local pizza place turned chain called The Big Cheese."

From the backseat, Richards called, "Love that place. Best bread-sticks anywhere."

"Shh!" Jenna hissed.

Irv was undeterred. "Independently wealthy, self-built the em-pire. Franchised the place last year. So far, seven Big Cheeses have been built around Florida. Seems like Papa Bear has the life, but he isn't so lucky. His daughter, Emily Grogan, was murdered five years ago while she was in school at Florida Calhan University. Police never caught the UNSUB. No leads, no closure."

"Other family?" Hank asked.

Irv groaned. "Second pothole. Married Narelle Phillips in 1977, mother of their only child, Emily. After Emily was killed, Narelle spiraled into depression. Took her own life about a year after Emily's murder with a fistful of painkillers and nothing but a note to say she was sorry."

"Christ," Hank mumbled.

"Still working on Thadius, but Papa Bear seems to check out. No trouble with the law, no history of violence that we know of. After Emily's death, he got heavily involved with a local victim support group, big into rights of victims' families, donates to a lot of victim support funds. He's there every time the doors open, advocates every waking minute. Seems to be work, work, and more work for this guy."

"Or action, action, and more action," Jenna replied. "Anything on the police investigation into the daughter's death?"

Jenna heard keys click on Irv's end.

"Ha. The police investigation was kept tighter than a Baptist's butthole, so not much was released to the public. Not much released to the *family*, either. They spoke out in the media several times about their frustration, looks like. There are a couple articles here that'd make good toilet reading when you have the chance, but the gist is the cops never gave an official cause of death, nothing. Said they needed to keep it closed for investigational purposes. They didn't even sign a death certificate 'til three years later, and then with the cause of death in the report listed only as injuries related to homicide."

So the manner of death was specific and gruesome. Check. But what the hell did this have to do with Isaac Keaton? Could he have killed this girl? Killed her and was torturing her family by calling them now? It didn't make much sense.

Yet.

"Okay, that's the official version. But even Baptists are at the mercy of a good proctologist," Jenna coaxed.

"One rectal, coming right up," Irv laughed. More key clicks. "Oy."

"What?" Hank said as he made a right-hand turn into The Pines subdivision, the entrance to Thadius Grogan's neighborhood.

"Emily Grogan was beaten, stabbed, sexually assaulted, and strangled. Still not entirely sure what got her first—blood loss from stab wounds or asphyxiation . . ." Irv's voice trailed over the last word.

Jenna closed her eyes as the deep crimson flashed in. At crimes she'd investigated in the past, her mind seemed to reserve the carmine color for only the most brutal of violent crimes. She blinked it away. "Asphyxiation with what, Irv?"

The technical analyst took a long pause. "Her . . . um . . . her own intestine."

Jenna swallowed hard as Hank put the SUV into park in Thadius Grogan's driveway. "Irv, find out everything you can about Grogan. Medical history, military past, phone records . . . anything you can get your hands on. I have a feeling we're going to need it."

"Left in a hurry?" Richards ventured as the three of them stepped into the foyer of Thadius Grogan's mansion.

"Something like that."

The front door had been unlocked, not even completely closed. Even if Jenna hadn't read so many Nancy Drew novels growing up, she'd still think it was a bad sign. This wasn't the type of house you left unlocked on a *perfect* day, but the timing of the phone call to Grogan from Howie Dumas's "office" bumped absentmindedness to about number ten on the growing list of reasons in Jenna's head why the man would rush out the door and leave it unlocked.

She knelt in front of a framed photo on the hallway table. The young woman grinning goofily up at the camera from where she was stretched out on a patch of grass had to be Emily Grogan.

Hank squatted beside her as Richards paced the hall. "Where to first?"

Jenna shrugged, tearing her gaze away from Emily's photo, noting the lack of any other knickknacks or pictures. "Best place I know to get acquainted with somebody is the bathroom."

"Remind me not to invite you to any parties," Hank answered, falling in step behind her.

Instinct led Jenna toward the stairs and into the master bedroom. The spacious bathroom was papered in pink, and his and her sinks adorned either side. Newspapers, books, and magazines covered the counters along with bottles of various soaps and household cleansers, used paper towels, Band-Aid wrappers, and crumb-covered paper plates. She noted the color of the earth her mind showed her. Since she was a kid, messiness showed up in three ways: natural, based on the personality of the person; eggshell when she visited someone's home who simply didn't have time to pick up; or the color of wet dirt when someone stopped cleaning because they no longer cared.

The last was the same color she'd noticed in her dad for months after her mother went away.

The whirlpool tub was grungy but not entirely neglected. Not for years anyway. More like days.

"He still cleans or has someone do his basic cleaning," Jenna said out loud, more for herself than anyone else.

Richards wrinkled his nose at the stacks of water-stained books surrounding the bathtub, the papers littering the floor. "If you ask me, if he *does* have a maid, she isn't a very good one."

Jenna moved on to the cabinets, picked up a prescription bottle half-full of Xanax. "I said *basic* cleaning, not full-on scouring. From the water stains on the books, he seems habited, set in his ways. These books stay where they are, splashed or not. If it's a housekeeper, he'd have her scrub the tub but never touch his stuff. Have Irv find out about the doctor on this bottle, but I'm guessing family physician, not psychiatrist." Jenna passed Hank the prescription bottle. She glanced over the stacks of papers on a stool by the tub, the open book on the back of the toilet.

Hank whipped out his phone and snapped off a text. "I'll get Irv on a possible cleaning person, too."

In the corner sat a hamper, empty except for a pair of boxers and a white shirt at the bottom. "Laundry's done, but there's no toilet paper," Jenna said, nodding to the empty roll on the wall holder. "He has the energy to do the laundry but not change the toilet paper roll? Doubt it. Still, if he has a cleaning lady, he hasn't slipped so far into depression he doesn't care about certain things."

She picked up the book from the back of the toilet. *Too Young: The Story of Bailey Frumpton.* "It's a memoir by a girl kidnapped at twelve."

Hank turned over the book at the top of the stack by the tub. "Yep. This one's true crime, too. The whole pile is."

"So maybe a little more obsessive with a purpose than depressed," Jenna said, turning back to the counter and opening the cabinet below the sink.

"How do you know it isn't him getting himself through?" Richards asked. "You know, reading from people who know. Commiseration?"

Jenna shuffled through the contents of the cabinet, but saw nothing interesting. "Do you see any self-help books lying around?"

Richards didn't answer, but she hadn't expected him to. He wouldn't find any. Whoever Thadius Grogan was, he didn't want to be pulled from the world of death and evil monsters. It looked like he'd collected every true crime book sold in the city over the past five years. Then when he got his hands on all of those, he went to the next town and the next. Nope. This guy was staying in this world, even if it was because he was stuck here.

"Did you see a computer?" Jenna asked Hank.

"We'll have to check," Hank replied.

"Let's take a look for that, but I want to tour the bedroom on the way out."

"After you," Hank said.

Jenna reentered the bedroom. She'd glanced over it when she'd walked through on her way to the bathroom, but she had purposefully not given it much thought or time to register. Now she allowed herself to take it in like a new city, the sights hitting her senses, giving first impressions, and colors danced in her eyes. The stacks of folders, papers, and books continued into the bedroom right onto the double bed, where it culminated in a mountain that took what would've been his wife's place. The bed was halfway unmade on the side next to the stack of open reading material and a smattering of pens and highlighters. "Cleaning woman doesn't come daily."

She moved to the bed and perched on the end of the unmade side. At the top of the pile of books lay an open volume on forensic techniques, and next to it, a legal pad scribbled with notes on the material. "Looks like he was researching on his own in addition to the true crime. See if Irv can get anything on who worked his daughter's case, Hank. We might need to touch base there next."

A warm, half-empty bottle of water on the nightstand. Advil. Nothing ridiculous. The guy wasn't an alcoholic. Didn't seem to be a druggie, either. The Xanax had been in the bathroom, of course, but the thing was pretty full. No other signs.

His pillows sat propped against the headboard like he'd been sitting up and reading. The position didn't scream "sleep." *Did* he sleep?

"Let's look at the other bedrooms."

Richards led the parade down the hall toward the other doors: three open, two closed. One open door was another bathroom. Across the hall, another open door led into what looked like a never-slept-in guest room. The third room contained a collection of every piece of exercise equipment ever sold on an infomercial. They moved on to the first closed-off room, which turned out to be filled with plain brown boxes sealed with packing tape.

Hank stepped into the room and read the labels scrawled in

Sharpie marker on the box tops. "NARELLE'S COOKBOOKS. NARELLE'S PAJAMAS AND GOWNS. MISCELLANEOUS NARELLE—CRAFTS. It's his wife's stuff."

"May be worth coming back to," Jenna said, but she was already three paces toward the last door, pretty sure of what she'd find.

Sure enough, she knew instantly the room had once been occupied by Emily Grogan. White wrought iron daybed with a blue paisley comforter. A tan, shaggy rug on the floor next to a rolling desk chair with a seat made of bungee cords. A vintage record player sat on the dresser a few feet away from various tubes of lipstick. The room had the normal wear of a teen's after she'd left for college: a rubber bin of Christmas wrappings out of place on the floor by the door, a small, broken television shoved inside to be out of sight until someone had time to fix it.

Richards eyed the wrapping box and TV. "Kids' rooms always turn into storage when they go off, huh?"

Jenna scanned the pictures taped to the vanity mirror. Emily with friends at a birthday party. Emily with friends dressed up like *Star Wars* characters on Halloween. "Standard. It's actually how *untouched* it is that bugs me."

A picture of Emily with Thadius himself. His grin shone under his mustache and graying beard as he looked straight into the camera. Had Narelle taken the photo? Emily stood next to him pointing at the T-shirt that bore the words NUMBER ONE DAD stretched across his round belly, her lips rounded in an exaggerated "oh."

Richards wrinkled his bushy brows. He turned to Hank and back to Jenna again. "Lots of parents of kids who die suddenly leave their rooms intact, right?"

Jenna popped open the oak jewelry box on the dresser. Silver bangles. A string of pink pearls. "Yes. That's not the odd part. The weird part is all the daughter's stuff is left as it was the moment she died, but the wife's is all neatly packed up and shoved out of sight."

Hank opened the bedside table's drawers one at a time, shaking his head. "Not *that* weird. His wife committed suicide. She *chose* to leave him. His daughter was taken. Polar opposites."

"Maybe," Jenna said, but she was only half paying attention. Yet another open book had caught her eye on the daybed across the room, but this was different. This time, it was the only book in the room.

Jenna's heart picked up before she lifted the book. Then when she did, it surged an extra few beats for good measure. Her hunch had been right—a journal.

She sat on the daybed with Thadius Grogan's writing, probably where he wrote his most private thoughts in his slain daughter's space. Jenna flipped the pages wildly, her brain struggling to connect dots she couldn't see. It didn't matter, though. Even if the dots might not be apparent yet, she already knew the picture they'd form when she connected them. Thadius formed more in her mind, a color latching itself to him from the journals. Bright red. And yet it wasn't red for power like Isaac Keaton. This red was action.

And rage.

The journal wasn't just entries about Thadius's nightmares, social anxiety, and trouble sleeping, though God knew there were plenty of those. No. Every other page had a picture of a person or place with scribbled notes about their possible role in Emily's death, how they might be tied to her killer. Some of them made a bit of sense. Others were outlandish, the stretch of an imagination desperate for closure. One picture featured a pizza boy who'd apparently delivered to Emily's rental house on two occasions. The note beneath it said: *Possible stalker. Check into.*

"Thadius has done the thing right. I'll give him that," Jenna said as she read.

"How so?" Hank asked from where he was now studying the pictures on the vanity.

"He's researched to a fault. Almost overresearched. That's going to be a problem."

Jenna flipped another page and another. With every page, she felt sicker. That sickness was Isaac Keaton. The guy was a psychopath all right. He knew exactly what he was doing, and unfortunately he was brilliant at it. Somehow he'd contacted a guy with just the right amount of anger, grief, and frustration. Easy to push off the ledge of depression. Maybe suffering from PTSD. She might not know everything, but she knew Thadius had a serious vendetta and that Isaac Keaton was in his head.

When her grandmother passed years before, she'd seen before her the gentle pearl of acceptance. Since then, she could see the same shade in victims and bereft families when they had the quiet calm of peace with a passing. This was different. This was the lava she saw when a loved one wasn't past that one stage of grief when it hurt less only because you could wield it instead of feeling it. Anger.

Unable to tear her eyes from the pages of Thadius's obsession, Jenna muttered, "Hank, we need to find out where Thadius Grogan went after mythical Howie Dumas's office called him. If we don't act fast, we might have a revenge killer on our hands."

T he bell on the door dinged when Thadius Grogan entered Pembry Pawn. The owner, a clean-cut man about Thadius's age, looked up but said nothing. The guy turned his focus back to the glass cabinet he was polishing. Thadius bolted the latch on the door, flipped the sign to CLOSED.

Thadius approached, afraid to speak. He needed answers first. There'd be time for the rest later.

When the guy realized Thadius was heading toward the counter, he spoke up. "Help ya, sir?"

"You Marley?" Thadius asked, even though he already knew the answer.

"That's me," the pawn shop owner replied. "What can I do ya for?"

Thadius had the SIG out faster than Marley could react. He let the pistol linger in the air a second longer than he had to before laying it flat on the counter. "You sell a lot of guns like this?"

Marley squinted, tipped his glasses down to look over them. "Yeah, fair amount. Looking to sell?"

This guy had no idea. "Not exactly. How many of these you sell, would you say?"

Marley's eyes trailed up from the gun to Thadius's face. "Eh, decent few, I guess. Maybe one every couple months, depending on what comes in. What's this all about?"

The air trapped in Thadius's chest wrenched his breaths, making them fast and heavy. He cocked his head toward the gun. "What kind of waiting period you got on something like that?"

Marley flinched, but his face recovered in the next instant. "Standard, of course. Three days minimum."

Moron thought he was a cop.

Thadius lifted his other hand, peeled open the manila envelope, and removed a DVD. He laid it on the counter next to the SIG Sauer. "Guy bought one of these guns here a few years ago. You sold it to him. I need to know who he is."

"Sorry, man," Marley replied. "Can't help you. Client confidentiality and all."

Marley's face wasn't on Thadius, but rather, on the counter where Thadius's hand now gripped the SIG. Marley shifted, and Thadius jolted the SIG level with his forehead.

"Uh-uh, cowboy. No alarm buttons or funny business. All I need is anything you can remember about the guy on this video footage, and we'll be square."

Marley lifted his hands, which shook like an alcoholic's days off a binge. "Man, I don't know what you want from me! I can't read DVDs with my palms, ya know! And I don't got a way to watch it here!"

Thadius brought up the envelope and dumped the contents on the counter. He'd stopped by Kinko's on his way here to print out images. "Lucky for you, I brought pictures. Talk fast. And put your damned hands down, for crying out loud."

Marley blinked rapidly. He slowly lowered his hands, tilted his glasses again. Thadius watched Marley pick up the stack of the photo stills taken from the video, flip through them. Toward the end was a zoomed-in shot of the guy in the AC/DC T-shirt.

The guy who'd killed his Emily.

"I don't . . . God, that was a long time ago," Marley stammered, eyeing the date stamp in the picture's right corner. "I don't remember him, really. Do you realize how many people come in here?"

"Yes, and I also realize very few of them scare my daughter into letting them into her apartment waving around a gun *you* sold them before *killing* her. A gun you sold him without a waiting period. It's only *one* guy, come to think." Thadius jabbed his pointer finger hard onto the picture on the table. "*This* guy. Now, Marley, you've gotta remember something. Can't be every day a college kid comes into your store wanting to buy a military-grade handgun with no bullets but can't seem to wait three days. Give me *something*."

Thadius leaned forward. The barrel of his own fully loaded SIG touched Marley's forehead, and the shop owner slammed his hands on the counter at an awkward angle, trembling.

"All right, all right. I don't remember much, though. He was average height, average build, just like in the video. Didn't say *that* much. Said he needed the gun ASAP as a prop for a film he was shooting. One of the local art students. That's why he didn't need bullets. Made sense to me, so I tried to throw the kid a bone."

And instead, you helped out a murderer and got my daughter killed. "Okay, what else? Name? Records of a name? You have to have records . . ."

Marley started shaking again. "Dude, I wish I did. We had . . ." Marley stuttered, shook harder than a pine twig in a twister.

Thadius pressed the butt of the pistol into his head. "Keep talking!"

"Okay, okay, okay! We had a . . . a . . . a fire, and it wiped out a lot of our records. Lot of trouble with the authorities after that. Managed to pull out all right, but only by the skin of our teeth. But no records—"

Marley stuttered more, faster as Thadius pushed against his head with the gun. "But but but I do remember him asking me if I knew where around here he could buy some fireworks. Said he was having a New Year's party, wanted to shoot some off. He must not've been from around here, come to think, or he'd have known they sell fireworks everywhere from stands on the side of the road to Walmart. I pointed him to a friend of mine up the road a piece who sells. Pretty sure he was planning to visit the guy."

Thadius's throat went bone dry. This ignorant scum on the bottom of his shoe wouldn't know, of course, that Emily's house was in shambles when the police finally got to her. The coward who killed her had used a black powder explosive to demolish the house and cover most of the evidence.

The same black gunpowder used in many fireworks.

"Guy's name?"

Marley sweat fat droplets now, which ran down his cheeks, soaked his neck. "Woody. Name's Woody."

Thadius shoved Marley's head onto the counter with the SIG. "You're shitting me, Marley."

"I'm not!" Marley screamed at a high pitch, eyes shut tight. "That's his name! Now please, just leave me alone!"

At this, Thadius wrenched the gun away from Marley's head, knocking Marley backward into the wall behind the counter. He leveled the SIG with the pawn shop owner's face. "He didn't have *any* waiting period, and you saw the news stories about a young college girl murdered the next day, didn't you? You *had* to have. Why didn't you call the police, Marley? Say *anything* to *anyone*? Didn't want to get in trouble? Didn't want anyone to know you weren't following rules?"

"I don't know what you're talking about!"

But Thadius wasn't listening anymore. The anger and pain building inside him were taking over, the disease that had festered in his heart for years. "You wouldn't have to worry about shit like that if you hadn't done something wrong, Marley. If you hadn't *sold* it to him!"

"I . . . I . . . I made a mistake! People make mistakes! I didn't mean to—" Marley cringed, hands over his face, pulling at his own hair.

"Yeah, well, mistakes slide sometimes. Other times they get corrected."

He pulled the trigger twice, but the first time was enough.

Thadius's head pounded, blood pressure up. He rounded the counter and stepped over Marley's body. He didn't look at the guy's face, just bent to his side and took the key ring from his pocket, stepped back over him toward the side office.

Nothing could make this better, he knew. None of this would do anything to bring back Em or Narelle.

He pressed eject on the old-fashioned VCR recording the shop events, stuck the tape in his pocket. He could only live a pseudo-life for so long, pretend victim support was helping. Imagine he could ever move on.

At least this way, if there was a life after death, he'd see Em, see his wife if *she* wanted to see *him*. And when he saw his family, they wouldn't have to ask why the people who did this to them got to live when they had to die. Nope. This way, he could look Em in the eye and tell her he took every single one of them down with him.

13

"So are you thinking this Grogan guy could be the second shooter?" Richards asked as they climbed back into the SUV.

"No," Jenna replied. She knew what his next question would be. "Why?"

First of all, Isaac Keaton had called *him*. Not directly, but he had to have known they'd follow that call straight to Grogan. He wouldn't give away the other shooter that easily. Not to mention, Grogan didn't fit her limited vision of the other shooter. Not even close. Keaton was type A, and Grogan, however different, seemed to be, too. Their motives might be different, but they had a similarity, as well. Red and red—regardless of the differences between the connotations the colors pulled up—wasn't a likely combination. She was keeping an open mind, but in a pair like this, the combination of red and blue was far more likely. Thadius came nowhere near that submissive, cool blue.

"Too alike." That'd suffice.

"But if Grogan isn't the other shooter, why do we care what he is?" Richards asked.

Million-dollar question. "Keaton wanted us to find him. While I don't think letting Isaac run the game is a good thing, it's the only lead we have right now. Not to mention, we have a possibly volatile man being provoked by a psychopath. If we *don't* intervene, we'll probably have a lot more to answer for later."

Hank hung up the call he was on. "Detective on the Emily Grogan case was Jerry Hardeman. He'll meet with us in the morning. Irv's looking into the cleaning woman and whoever placed the phone call from Howie Dumas's pretend office. Cops in the vicinity checked the office building. Cleared out completely. Neighbors said no signs or people were ever there. Dead end. Getting phone records, Thadius's web history, all that good stuff. APB out on Thadius Grogan's vehicle. In the meantime, you ought to go home and rest. This'll be a long week."

"I want to talk to the shooting victims," Jenna replied.

"They need sleep, too, Jenna. Saleda didn't turn up anything of note, and she's good. Besides, you know as well as we do that they're out of it. They need some simmer time."

"I can take another crack at Keaton." She couldn't put this down. Not right now, when she knew he was toying with them.

"*Or* you can go home and see your little girl."

Jenna bit back her retort. As if she were the only one ever to put the job—the lives they were trying to save—ahead of Ayana. She bowed her head, closed her eyes, and took a deep breath, remembering how as she was laboring to deliver that precious little baby girl that was somehow made of equal parts of her *and* Hank, she'd asked the nurse to call Hank just *one* more time. The phone had rung and rung, but no answer.

Hours later, he would show up, hold the pink bundle in his arms. He would coo at her, make funny faces, and tell Jenna she was the most gorgeous baby he'd ever seen. But at the end of the day, she hadn't been his priority. Never would be.

Richards hummed uncomfortably in the backseat.

I can go home and see your little girl. "Fine."

A few hours later, Jenna turned her key in the apartment door, facts still rustling around in her head. Grogan, Keaton. Keaton, Grogan. What would *her* father do if he were Thadius Grogan? What was her mother's effect on his mind-set?

Jenna swung the door open. "Hey, Da—"

Charley's face met hers. He grimaced, finger to his lips. His eyes held hers. His finger drifted from his mouth, and he jabbed it toward Ayana's bedroom.

"Really?" Jenna whispered in disbelief. "At ten p.m.?"

Most toddlers fell asleep by eight, but Ayana's body clock worked in reverse from every kid Jenna had ever met. She was usually just getting started at ten, and every night was a battle royale.

Charley nodded once. He gestured to the hallway, and they filed out. Her brother could read her so well.

"Need to talk?" he asked as he pulled the door to.

Jenna leaned against the wall, crossed her feet. "Ay never goes to sleep this early. What gives?"

Charley mirrored her on the other side of the hallway. "The usual. I was writing a new song, she's an eternal critic. Fell asleep before I hit the first chorus."

"And Dad?"

"Boredom is contagious? He went to bed, too," Charley said, shrugging. "Must be some case if you're heading it off talking about the nocturnal habits of the Ramey family."

Jenna folded her arms. "Gemini killers."

Charley's eyes widened. "No shit?"

"Yep. Theme park killings? It was them. One in custody, the

other, who knows. We have a random lead concocted by the devil himself, and a bunch more bodies on the way, I'm guessing."

Charley nodded. "Sounds all in a day's work. What am I missing?"

Before she had a chance to answer, a ring cut the air. Both she and Charley leapt for the door, but Charley's hand reached it first. He dashed across the living room toward the cordless, but already, Ayana was crying.

Her brother swore under his breath as he punched the on button of the phone. "Earplug Factory, how can we help you?"

He listened, then stretched the phone toward her. "It's for you. Shock and awe."

Jenna took it. "Yeah."

"Sorry to call you so late."

Hank.

If she thought Hank called because he assumed Ay wouldn't be asleep, this wouldn't be half as annoying. But seeing as how he had no clue she didn't normally sleep like an average toddler, the call made her want to pummel his face with the phone until he begged for mercy. "No big deal. News on Grogan?"

Silence.

Finally, Hank answered. "Not exactly. Isaac Keaton made another move. I'm not sure how to tell you this."

Jenna gripped the phone, frustrated. She could eat the entire contents of her refrigerator right now, and trashy TV hadn't seemed so enticing since she was on pain meds post wisdom teeth removal. Her entire family was under the same roof right now, so whatever Keaton had up his sleeve couldn't be *that* bad. "Just spit it."

"All right. Keaton sent a letter. To Claudia."

"What?" Isaac hadn't been indicted, wasn't even an official inmate yet. How could he send letters? And what in God's name could he have to write to Jenna's mother about?

"When was it mailed?"

"I'm looking into it," Hank replied. "I debated on whether or not to call, but I knew if you got in there and he told you first, he'd have a serious advantage."

"You haven't told me what it said," Jenna shot back.

"Jenna, you don't need to do this. He's messing with you, trying to distract us—"

"What did it *say*, Ellis?"

The phone crackled with the heavy breath Hank blew out. "It said, 'In regards to our previous discussion, I have one further question. If you could do one thing over, where would you say you failed?'"

14

Jenna blew past Hank at the police department and headed toward the box. "Don't even try to talk me out of this, Hank. Bad idea."

She'd left Charley with a screaming Ayana, no time to catch him up with what her ex had told her on the phone. No need to anyway. Her brother worked too hard *not* to think about Claudia to have to hear that in one fell swoop, this evil son of a bitch had drawn her right back into Jenna's life. She wanted to know what the hell Isaac knew about her mother, and how he'd managed to talk to her.

"Jenna, you know better than I do that this is what he *wants*. You go in there ready to strangle him, he takes one look at your face and knows he got a reaction. He feeds off this bullshit, and—"

Jenna whirled around. "Say one more thing to me, Hank, and you won't have to worry about all that pent-up anger he'll see, because I'll take it all out on *you!*"

He stared at her, stern, but said nothing. He didn't have to. His eyes scolded her enough. Accused her.

Knew her.

Back when she'd worked at the BAU under him, she'd felt those same eyes. The ones that had once viewed her as the most fascinating woman he'd ever met. Where, later, the spark of respect would dim, replaced by a cloud of shame.

She'd gulped in deep breaths of oxygen as the Butcher of Anaheim fell to the ground at the mercy of her bullet. Then she herself had fallen to her knees into the cold, wet dirt. The threat past, she dropped her gun beside her and keeled forward, catching herself with her palms. On all fours, heaving precious air, she thought of Ayana, and how moments before, Jenna had charged into the darkness of the forest, unwilling to wait for the rest of the team. She knew he was there. The color in her mind had pointed the way, and if she waited for even another minute, another girl could've died. A girl that now would be going home to her mother, a woman Jenna had watched cry and beg in the same way Jenna would for Ayana. As she hunted this hunter, with every step, she hadn't known if her little girl would ever remember her.

A yell from behind her had told her the others had heard the commotion. She wasn't alone.

A hand grasped her forearm, yanked her upward. But no embrace came. No relief.

The firm hand released her, and she spun to face Hank.

"What the hell were you doing, Jenna? You know the protocol!"

"He was here, Hank. She's here. Back there." Jenna pointed to the place in the forest where they'd find the Butcher's last attempted victim tied topless to a tree. "She's okay. Needs fluids, food. But she's alive!"

Hank didn't make a move for the trees, nor did he smile or even breathe a sigh of relief. Instead, he squared his shoulders to her as the other team members came racing into the backyard from various points in the home they'd been searching. As her team leader, he had the authority to manage her, but while technically superior, the team leaders in the BAU usually tried to stand as on par with the team as possible. A cohesive unit flourished in this environment where everyone had their place and everyone held each other's respect.

"*Jenna, you knew the plans, and you know the rules. You don't go into an unknown situation without backup,*" he'd barked.

Her face flushed, adrenaline still rushing through her veins. She wanted to draw herself up to full height, to stare him down, scream in his face that because of her, a girl would live. That she'd made the right decision.

But in her peripheral vision, her teammates' forms loomed. She couldn't do it to him even if he could do it to her. Maybe that was what made him a good leader. Who knew.

But in that moment, standing in the dark, spurned by the eyes that used to have such confidence in everything she was, Jenna had known that even if that quality made him a great Special Agent in Charge, it made him a really, really shitty boyfriend.

Now she looked down, exhaled the fiery breath she'd been using to berate him, and felt her shoulders droop. After one more calming lungful, she clenched her fists and looked up at Hank again. "Listen, I know the same things you know. Trust me to be smarter than him."

Hank frowned. "I *do* trust you, Jenna. I don't trust the situation. This is your family."

Jenna raised an eyebrow at him as she stepped toward the interrogation room. "Claudia is *not* my family."

She pushed through the door to confront the monster.

*S*he's *b-a-a-ack.*

Isaac sat still as he watched Dr. Jenna Ramey bolt through the door to come and pick his brain again. Only the red-splotched patch of skin where the neck of her T-shirt dipped into a soft V told him news of his little surprise was what brought her back to the precinct so late this evening. "Dr. Ramey. Always a pleasure."

She slipped a picture out of a file folder she carried, but she laid it on the table facedown, the folder on top of it. "Who's Thadius Grogan, Isaac?"

Despite himself, Isaac smiled. She didn't want to give an inch, did she? "Are you really here to talk to me about Grogan, Dr. Ramey?"

"You pointed us toward him for a reason, Isaac. I'm playing the hand you dealt."

"Do you actually think I'll answer that question *for* you? I knew you guys had it easy, but you've at least gotta *try* for it, Jenna."

Her eye twitched. "We're on a first-name basis now?"

His mouth twisted into a crooked smile. "You've been on one with me for hours now."

She didn't answer, but he could smell the perspiration under her arms through the cheap deodorant she'd no doubt swiped on haphazardly this morning. He pictured her in her bathroom, freshly out of the shower, standing in her sensible bra and panties in front of the mirror and checking out her towel-dried hair. She'd scrub her teeth with the kind of abhorrent-tasting toothpaste made by a company that manufactured baking soda and cat litter.

Jenna plucked the picture from under the folder, flipped it over, and slid it across the table toward him. "Know her?"

A striking picture of a girl met his vision. Even as gray as the morgue table beneath her, she was prettier than half the girls Isaac had taken to bed. He leaned in toward the photo, then away, squinting. "I don't have my glasses, of course, but I'd venture to say no."

"You don't wear glasses."

"And you already know I know who she is."

Jenna leaned back and folded her arms. "If you know her, why'd you lie about it?"

I didn't. "You're the psychiatrist. You tell me."

The good doctor didn't know what to say to that, so her response was to push back from the table and pace. "How do you know Emily Grogan?"

Isaac leaned back, tapped his toes. Question-and-answer sessions entertained more when you answered with more questions. "Don't you already know enough from showing me the picture, *Doctor*? You *were* showing me the picture to see if I'd salivate over her dead body, right? Get excited, pupils dilate? Maybe start humping the table? Well, no, Dr. Ramey. I hate to break it to you, but I'm not excited by Emily Grogan's death pictures, because they don't help me relive a thing. I had nothing to do with her murder."

Her lips pursed a second in annoyance before she controlled them. So fun and easy to make people wiggle, wonder.

"Does the other shooter have anything to do with Emily Grogan, Isaac? With Thadius?"

"Now, *that's* a good question, Jenna! Gold star."

Jenna plopped back into the chair, slid the picture of Emily Grogan back toward her. "Any chance you'd like to tell me how?"

Not on your life. "We haven't even talked about why you really came here tonight, Jenna. It was a good question, yes, but if I told you everything now, it'd ruin all the fun."

"Right! Of course! What was I thinking?" Jenna said loudly, her voice just the right cocktail of gusto and sarcasm.

Come on, Dr. Ramey. Take a bite.

"Maybe you'll tell me how you know Emily Grogan if we talk about why I really came. You seem to be into that sort of thing."

Isaac licked his lips. Tricky. "Don't put *too* many words in my mouth, Doctor. But sure, let's talk some about why you came to visit. You'll have to ask me, though, because I must say, I'm not entirely sure what you're talking about. Everything isn't always as it seems, so I want to make sure I clarify . . ."

Jenna leaned forward. "You contacted my mother. You said you'd talked to her. How?"

"By letter, Doctor. You know that."

Jenna sighed. "I mean before that. How had you talked to her before that? When?"

Isaac rubbed his chin with his thumb and pointer finger. "You know, it was a while ago. I may not quite remember the details. Perhaps you should ask your mother. She might pass on a thing or two."

"Got a mother, Isaac?" Jenna asked, elbows on the table, head propped in her open right palm.

Isaac cocked his head, searched her eyes. Green, intense. "What? You suppose reptiles like me are hatched?"

"Mommy issues, too, huh?" she retorted.

A distant memory flashed in, and he promptly cataloged it, neatly folded it, and placed it back in the compartment reserved for such things. "Yeah, I think you should ask your mother. That visit might be more educational for you than this one. And who knows? Maybe you'll get something out of it. You never answered me about revenge against your own family, after all. I realize you're on the right side of the law and all that, but you know how it is, don't you, Jenna? When it's dark—when *you're* dark—sometimes nobody'll see."

"Thoughts?" Hank asked as Jenna exited the box.

"I hate this job? I don't know. He's definitely trying to steer my attention away from something. The old 'look over here so you don't look at the real action' sort of trick. Question is how much of a truth line there is in his game."

Hank shrugged. "Most sociopaths have a truth line in there somewhere. Still doubt he actually talked to your mother. Wouldn't hurt to check records just in case, but odds are, he's bluffing."

"Yeah," Jenna said. "Odds."

She yanked back out the medical examiner's photos of Emily Grogan, the ones Emily's family and the media had such trouble getting hold of. Amazing what could happen when a murder case kept so quiet suddenly became tied to the most prolific serial killers the country had seen in years.

Richards stepped in, crowded Jenna's personal space. Up until this moment, he'd been sitting quietly in a chair in the corner, but now his movements were jerky, agitated. "Aren't we paying this Grogan guy way too much attention if he isn't the second shooter? I may not be the expert here, but shouldn't we spend more time pro-filing *that guy?*" He jabbed at the window toward Isaac.

"We are," Hank muttered.

Jenna shook her head. Richards wouldn't accept Hank's answer, however true it might be. "We don't have anything on Isaac yet. According to public records, Isaac Keaton doesn't *exist*. Thadius Grogan *is* Isaac's profile right now. He's one of the only connections we have."

Richards threw his hands up. "You said yourself he's trying to distract you!"

There, she couldn't argue. But it was more complicated than that. Isaac Keaton had his own agenda, for sure. The question was: better to chase the person Isaac took them straight *to*, or dig a needle out of a proverbial haystack and find one eyewitness from the theme park?

A third option existed, but right now that option was on Jenna's list right after stabbing her own eyes out with a rusty spoon.

She glanced at Hank, hoping for help.

"Your call," he said.

Funny. He'd said the exact same thing when she'd found out she was pregnant with Ayana. Something she had never been able to forget. Or maybe forgive.

Now her mind cinched around the answer on the spot: which-ever one wasn't Hank's. "Richards is right. We need to talk to the people who were at the park, starting with the coherent ones in the hospital. I want to interview the victims myself."

The stubby night shift charge nurse at Simons Medical Center didn't act happy when Jenna, Hank, and Richards showed up on her floor at 1 a.m. wanting to talk to the park shooting victims. "These people need their *rest*, Detectives!"

"Ma'am, we hate to interrupt the sleep of anyone who's been

through such a traumatic experience, but it's crucial we speak to them as soon as possible. Our job is to bring the people who hurt them to justice," said Hank.

Jenna was thankful he hadn't bothered to correct her inaccurate moniker "Detectives." It was only a matter of time before the media swooped in and realized the two shooters at the park were the Gemini, but for now, the fewer who realized the FBI—and *former* FBI—were involved, the better.

"And it's *my* job to see my patients get their rest," she said, her pudgy cheeks reddening to match the color of her frizzy hair. She turned and continued to file folders in the cove behind her. "What happened? I thought they said they'd arrested the nut who did this."

This chick clearly didn't watch much TV. "The evidence points to multiple shooters."

The nurse clicked her tongue. "People are crazy these days. Imagine! Shooting people at a *theme park!*"

"We'd love to make small talk, ma'am, but we need to get these interviews rolling. Which room should we start with?" Richards asked, voice seeping with annoyance.

"Listen, you—"

"Twyla," Jenna cut in after a glance at her name tag, "we definitely don't mean to disrupt the order of your wing."

Hank took over. "Maybe you could check to see if any of the patients are awake?"

Nurse Twyla shot a glare at Detective Richards, then turned back to Hank. "Well, I suppose I could check. I'm not makin' any promises, though."

She waddled out the back of the nurses' station and down the hall. As they watched her go, Richards grunted. "We could burst through that door and interview anyone we wanted, this case what it is."

Jenna smiled. Working as a doctor in a psych ward for several years would teach anyone not to mess with an overworked, underpaid member of the nursing staff. "We could. But what we *could* do isn't always the best route. Trust me. Keeping friendly with the gate-keepers is a good thing."

Nurse Twyla ambled back toward them. "Only have one awake. He says he'll speak with you, but I'll be watching. You upset the balance in here, and you leave lickety-split. This way."

She buzzed them in, and they followed her down the hall. "Yancy Vogul—"

"Twenty-four-year-old male, superficial gunshot wound to the left arm, hospitalized for observation only," Hank said.

"Why's he in the ICU, then?" Richards asked.

"People like you," Twyla replied. She stopped at the next door they came to. "Keep it brief."

Jenna took the lead and passed through the already open door. Yancy Vogul lay on top of the covers, fully clothed.

"You guys *did* bring pizza, right? I only agreed to this because she said you brought pizza," Yancy said quickly, maybe a little nervous.

Jenna took in his full appearance as best as she could but kept her focus on his eyes. "Mr. Vogul, we appreciate you speaking to us so late. I'm Dr. Jenna Ramey. This is S.A. Hank Ellis and Detective Richards of the OPD."

"Call me Yancy," he said.

He didn't meet *her* eyes, though. Jenna followed his to Detective Richards, whose gaze was at the foot of the bed.

"Oh, yeah, don't worry too much about that," Yancy said, tapping the side of his curved metal prosthetic foot with his hand. "Repels bullets."

Wisecracker. Fast talker. From the darting pupils, his tucked-in body language, both were covers for nerves, shyness. Maybe a touch of Asberger's? Maybe just cool.

"How are you feeling?" Hank asked, no doubt to draw attention away from the awkward focus on the young man's disability.

Yancy dry-laughed. "Better than a bunch of people, I guess."

PTSD was definitely on the table, especially if Yancy's foot was MIA from an encounter with guns or explosives. Violence.

"Yancy, this is a difficult question, but we'd appreciate it if you can tell us anything you might remember about what happened at the theme park, no matter how insignificant it seems. Anything strange you noticed, anything you saw right before—or during—the shots."

Yancy's head stayed down toward his chest, but his eyes rose to study Jenna, a frown on his face. "I noticed lots of stuff, but none of it'll be important for what you need, I'm sure. I was walking near the ferry on my way to one of the shows at the castle. That's why I was there—a friend of mine plays Cinderella. She kept bugging me to come watch her. I finally did. Picked the wrong day, I guess."

"What happened next, Yancy?" Hank prompted.

"I heard someone yell. Heard pops. Screaming. People running everywhere. About ten feet away, maybe, blood spattered on the concrete. Next thing I knew, my arm was on fire, my balance went wonky. I hit the ground. By then, I knew what was happening. From where my face planted, I could see a few bodies. They weren't moving. I didn't try to move. Played dead."

Most people would panic, but this kid had instincts. Or training. A soft yellow color started to form in Jenna's mind. "You said you heard someone yell *before* the shots?"

Yancy nodded. "Yeah. Don't know what he said, though. I couldn't make out the words."

"Definitely he?" Hank asked.

"Oh, yeah."

"And definitely *words*?" Jenna reiterated. That tidbit could be important.

"Yes."

"Okay. So you played dead. What happened next?" Hank asked.

Yancy shook his head like he was trying to dislodge the memory.

"People kept shrieking, running. Nobody helped me, really. Some people ran over me. A guy stepped on my back at one point. I didn't react, but I doubt it would've mattered if I had. Eventually, the pops stopped. Screams died down. I saw medics around the other bodies and lifted my head. Someone came over to me."

"Do you have any idea how long it was before the pops stopped?" Hank asked.

Other people at the park told Saleda it was anywhere from three to twenty minutes. Still, Yancy's take would be interesting.

"Sorry, but I left my stopwatch at home."

"How many pops did you hear?" Jenna asked. Long shot, but if Yancy's face was planted and he had any military or police training, he might've counted, if only to block out other things. "Or was there *anything* you might have counted?"

"After I was on the ground, maybe three more pops? They weren't fast. There was time in between them. Seemed to last forever, but it was probably only a couple of minutes."

The ferry shooter, according to the slugs recovered, had only fired nine times. Yancy's account was pretty close—much closer than the fifty shots many witnesses claimed.

"Let's back up," Hank said. "What about before, during your morning in the park? Did you notice anyone around you acting odd, doing anything suspicious?"

Yancy's head fell back against the pillows. "Dude. I've watched the news. I know you guys think you're doing yourselves some big favor by keeping the guy you arrested a big secret, but it'd be a lot easier to tell you something if we knew what we were trying to remember."

That was the problem. "You're right, Yancy. We haven't released a picture yet, but it's because we want to—"

"Maintain the integrity of the eyewitness testimonies. Yeah, yeah. I know. I'm just saying it's something you might want to consider. I can tell you all day about what the shrieks sounded like, or how it felt to have no idea if I'd be gunned down if I tried to see if the girl ten feet away from me was still breathing. But I can't tell you anything that might be hiding in my brain unless you jog it a little."

Jenna pulled the door of Yancy Vogul's room closed and started down the hall. "Let's get some more information on Yancy Vogul. He's got some kind of serious background."

"Already have Irv on it," Hank said.

"Yancy might be right, you know."

Richards caught her stride. "You think we should release Keaton's photo? What about people thinking they saw him even if they didn't? I keep thinking it would give us a chance to find people who know who he *really* is if we just pasted his picture a few choice places, but you guys said it wasn't a good idea."

"*Yet.* I said we didn't need to do it *yet.* We can use it as a tool later, but we want to play our cards close to the chest. Keaton wants the attention. He'll have thought about us releasing it. Right now the damage it could cause might be worse. If I'm right about the ferry shooter, he's nervous. He's not a cucumber like Keaton. He spooks. He might get more violent," Jenna answered. Then, to Hank, "But think about it. We could show it selectively. Maybe someone saw Keaton with the other shooter in the lead-up."

"Eyewitnesses under pressure are close to useless, Jenna. You know that. Besides, Yancy Vogul's already tainted. He admitted he's watched the news."

"He had plenty of exposure time once he was on the ground. He didn't have a gun *in* his face to distract him—"

"Yes, I'm sure the people trampling him were only a minor diversion. Oh, and the bullet wound."

"Eyewitnesses with a police background and trained observers are more accurate than average," Jenna insisted.

"We don't know he *has* a background," Hank reminded. "What do you make of the yelling?"

Jenna considered for a moment. In a less premeditated attack, she'd have thought the yells were a rage response to some outside stimuli. In this case, it seemed more like a battle cry. "Yelling words is interesting. Not something he'd do spur of the moment, not something he'd do without picking out something exact. Combine that with the hesitation between the shots—"

"You're sure it was hesitation?" Hank cut in.

"You're not?" she replied.

Hank shrugged. "Guess it couldn't have been very targeted, given the place. So the hesitation between shots makes you think he needed to prepare for the shooting? Jack himself up?"

Jenna nodded. "Maybe. It's also an attention-seeking behavior right before killing people. A risk. He was convinced it was the right thing to do. He felt validated."

"Probably because Keaton knew the ferry shooter couldn't work up to it on his own."

"Exactly."

Hank's phone dinged with a text, and he whipped it out of his pocket. "What do you know? You're right. Yancy Vogul used to be an intern at the Florida Department of Law Enforcement."

As soon as he said it, his phone started vibrating in his hand. He held up a finger. "Yeah?"

"You don't know the kid, then?" Jenna asked Richards. He was a detective. For all she knew, he could've worked with the state's version of the FBI.

He shook his head. "Nope. Only been with the PD, and haven't run into him, for sure. I'd remember the foot, I think."

Maybe. But he might've had two feet back then.

Behind them, Hank talked feverishly with someone on the cell. "That's after the intersection of Corkery and Wilcox? Christ. All right. We're on our way."

Hank pocketed his phone and moved for the door. "Gotta wake up Saleda. They found Thadius Grogan's truck in a pawn shop parking lot. Grogan's gone, but he left a body behind."

J enna hopped out of the SUV at Pembry Pawn Shop after the chopper lifted them a few towns over. She flipped her badge to the guards at the crime scene line, then ducked under it behind Hank and Saleda and walked into the shop. The bell tinkled to announce the big guns were here.

The cops there stood around, waiting for them as they'd been instructed. This crime scene was officially FBI territory now. One of the men stepped forward, offered his hand to Hank. "Lieutenant Glease, Gainesville PD. You must be—"

"Hank Ellis, Special Agent in Charge. This is my team. Special Agent Saleda Ovarez, Dr. Jenna Ramey. This is Detective Richards of the OPD. What do we have?"

"Shop owner. Marley Ostin, forty-six-year-old male, shot twice in the head at close range. The place is covered in prints. Perp made no effort to clean up other than that it seems he took keys off of Marley. Bloody footprints led to the office, which probably explains the missing security tape. Not sure why he took it since we have so many prints and a vehicle. We're running the prints, but I understand you probably have a good idea who they belong to."

"Why would he take the security footage and leave prints and the truck, you suppose?" Hank asked.

"My guess is he's shaved or dyed his hair," Saleda answered. "Oops. Irv calling. Be outside."

"She's right," Jenna said. "Or he's otherwise disguised. He's got more work to do."

Hank stepped toward the counter behind which Marley Ostin's body lay splayed. "I'm pretty sure he didn't hesitate."

Jenna's eyes roamed the wall, the glass behind the counter, which provided the sickening canvas for where Marley's brain matter had exploded out the back of his head. She looked down at the cheap countertop, which shone with massive palm prints. The palms were set at a strange angle. Thadius had questioned the guy. Interrogated him. Held him here, gun to his head. What had Thadius asked?

She looked back at the gunshot victim. "Double tap. Thadius wanted him extra dead. Maybe one shot for the kill, the second for good measure—and appeasing anger."

Hank looked up at her from where he squatted next to the body. "And what did this joker have to do with Emily Grogan's death, do you suppose?"

Jenna shrank to the floor next to Marley and gave him the once-over. His pupils were fixed straight ahead. "I don't know. Maybe we're asking the wrong questions. We'll know more after we talk to Detective Hardeman about Emily Grogan's case. Let's get some people on the details of what the pawn shop sold in the past several years, possible relationship between Grogan and Marley Ostin. In the meantime, I think we need to find more people who *knew* Thadius Grogan. Who he hung around with, where he ate dinner, that kind of thing. Isaac Keaton *met* Thadius Grogan somehow. Had to have. Find out more about Thadius's activities, maybe we can find someone who knew Isaac Keaton."

Hank stood and turned his back. "Or what Isaac Keaton saw in Grogan to make him think he could set him off. Better yet, why did he want to?"

"Now *there's* a good question. Is Keaton doing this for fun or for a reason?" Jenna followed Hank out of the pawn shop.

"I'd say both."

Saleda was on the phone outside. When she saw Hank and Jenna, she signed off with Irv, telling him to let her know as soon as he had any more information on Marley Ostin.

"No records of a housekeeping service, no checks cleared that look like they might be to one. And the mythical Howie Dumas has a phone number, but that's about all he has. No records of anything else anywhere, including birth or death certificate," Saleda said.

Hank nodded. "I'll line up a press conference about Grogan. The public needs to be on the lookout. I want you and Richards door-to-door in Grogan's neighborhood. See if anyone's seen a housekeeper coming or going. Also, float the name 'Dumas' by the neighbors. See if it rings a bell. Maybe a van in the neighborhood with those letters, anything like that, though I doubt Keaton would leave that kind of a trail. Keaton called the person who phoned from the Dumas fake office. They have to be in cahoots somehow. Jenna and I are going to talk to the detective in charge of Emily Grogan's murder case, see if that'll open up any new holes. Richards, can you put together a lineup containing Isaac Keaton's photo to show to Yancy Vogul?"

"Sure thing."

So Hank thought her idea was a worthy one, after all. Yancy Vogul's chances of having seen something at the theme park were good, even if Yancy didn't realize he had. Stranger things had happened.

"I know this is a long shot, but do we have any video from the park?" Jenna asked.

Hank shook his head. "Park video had a technical malfunction the night before, and it wasn't up and running again, as luck would have it."

"Luck," Jenna repeated. "Big coincidence, don't you think?"

"May be. Worth checking on. We better get a move on. We'll be late for our date with Detective Hardeman," Hank said.

As Jenna climbed into the front seat of the SUV the local FBI branch had waiting for them on the scene, she couldn't help but picture Isaac Keaton sitting in his holding cell, thinking about what other surprises he had planned for them. He'd written her mother a letter. What next?

"Hank, do me a favor," she said, hesitating.

"Yeah?"

"Get the visitation logs for the Sumpter Building. I know it's doubtful, but I want to see exactly who's visited Claudia in the past few years."

S ebastian Waters sidled into Conference Room B on the first
floor of the hospital, hovered near the wall, and poured himself a cup of coffee. The nurse insisted on bringing him down
in a wheelchair, but as soon as she disappeared, he'd ditched the
chair. Made him feel too conspicuous.

Others chattered in groups of two and three. Everyone seemed
to know each other, just like Isaac told him they would.

"Hi! Are you new here?"

Sebastian turned toward the voice behind him. A wraithlike girl
with drapes of hair the color of a raven stood in front of him. Before
he could stop himself, he winced at the battlefield that was her face,
the right side scarred and melted.

She shrugged. "It's okay. Not everyone's used to it. I've had a few
years. I heard you were in the big park shooting? What was that like?"

He blinked at her, not sure how to answer. As instructed, Sebastian had told the staff psychiatrist about how nightmares plagued
him every time he closed his eyes. Had to look pained, the consum-
mate victim. "They won't look at you twice," Isaac had said.

Them, too, huh?

The psych had told him all about the support groups for traumas like this, how in fact, one met in this very hospital. The doc got him a meeting schedule, told him to have the nurse bring him down to the next one if he was up to it.

In the meantime, he'd spent a lot of time imagining how to interact with these people, to seem like one of them, like his life had been disrupted on one random day instead of every day of his life he could remember. Now here was this girl, acting like he'd just filmed a movie with Denzel Washington instead of being shot.

"Um, well, it's been a blur," Sebastian replied. Strange, how the honesty came out easily when someone actually asked his opinion.

"I know what you mean," she said. Her lip caught her gums when she spoke. "Mine was a chemical bomb."

"Those happen?" he blurted out.

She laughed, and a slight sucking sound emanated from her throat, like the weird straw the dentist used. "Hard to believe, huh? Yep. Some kids set off homemade bombs at my high school. Not really sure why. The whole day is foggy to me."

"All right, folks, come on down," a heavyset black guy in his forties called to them from the front of the room.

The group meandered away from their little cliques and queued up in the metal folding chairs.

"I'm Les Quaney," the guy at the front said. "I run things around here, but please, don't think that means I have any control over the quality of the coffee. It's all donated."

Most everyone laughed.

"If you're new to the group, welcome. We're pretty informal in here, but we're also into keeping things real and calling people on their crap. So whatever you do, don't feel *too* sorry for yourself. We allow everyone their own quota of personal pity parties, but we also want you to self-soothe. We're all dealing with our own recoveries, so we can hold hands, but we can't mop you off the floor, if you get my drift. Those needs are better addressed with your pdoc upstairs. Now then, who wants to go first?"

"I will," the girl Sebastian had been talking to said.

"Go for it, Zane," Les Quaney said, and he lowered his hefty frame into a chair.

The raven-haired girl stood. "Hi, everyone. I'm Zane, and I'm a survivor of a violent crime."

"Hi, Zane!" the group echoed.

She gave a sunny little wave. "Since our last meeting, I've had a few bad dreams, but nothing I can't handle. I haven't journaled any, but I've been busy with planning the event next week. By the way, I hope you'll also consider coming out to the City Walk this weekend. There'll be lots of music and acts. We have some live bands, dance troupes. And no worries, because they'll have plenty of nonalcoholic drinks and snacks for everyone. Big celebration of healing."

Sebastian started to zone—maybe the atmosphere, maybe the morphine—but he kept snapping back to attention. Zane's voice grated on him, but it also lulled him like a stiff drink.

He shook his head hard. Isaac would kick him clear *into* the weekend if he knew he wasn't paying attention.

But Isaac wasn't here now. He was sitting in jail. Zane giggled again at something she'd said, the suction of her laugh catching in her throat. For someone who'd been marred for life by a random bomber, she sure was in a good mood. In fact, all of these people seemed to be.

You can do this. You have to.

Sebastian ripped his gaze from Zane's mottled cheek, the way her lip curled with words that started with a vowel.

You deserve to do this. Just like Isaac said.

18

"Detective Hardeman, thank you for seeing us," Hank said to the slight man who greeted them with a nod in his garage shop.

Hardeman hadn't exactly made any concessions for their visit, of course. His wife had answered the door, brought them here. "Tolerating" would've been a more accurate term than "seeing."

"Mm," the middle-aged man grunted, his focus returning to a bottle on the table in front of the old exercise bench where he sat. He picked up something that looked like one of those plastic back scratchers from the dollar store and hooked a flat Lego to it. He inserted it into the skinny mouth of the bottle, deposited the Lego into the wider chasm within.

Words flew through Jenna's head. Patient. Calm. Pensive. Unhappy.

"Don't keep me in suspense," Hardeman growled. "What do you want to know about the Emily Grogan case?"

Haunted.

He continued plugging away at the Legos in the bottle, but spoke softly out of the corner of his lined mouth. "Saw your press release on the six o'clock early news. Thadius Grogan finally snapped, I guess. Question is, why does the big bad FBI finally care?"

"Thadius Grogan might be involved with another case we're looking into," Hank answered.

"Hmph. Figures," Hardeman grunted again.

"Detective Hardeman, you said 'finally.' I take it Thadius has been unstable for a long time?" Jenna asked.

Hardeman placed the next Lego gently atop the bottom one inside the bottle. "Unstable. Angry. Grieving. Perfect storm."

Grieving was an interesting word choice. "*Did* Thadius Grogan grieve his daughter's death, Detective Hardeman?"

For the first time, Hardeman's hand stilled, and he glanced up and drank in Jenna's appearance. "Of course the man grieved. Someone murdered his daughter, Detective."

"Doctor," Jenna corrected. "Don't misunderstand. I know he was aggrieved by his daughter's death, but he may not have attended to the process of grieving. Everyone handles grief in their own way, but he might not have accepted the loss. If he turns that energy to creating a space where he doesn't *have* to accept it, we have a different ballgame than if he was grieving and had, say, a psychotic break where he's hearing voices."

Hardeman squinted at her, and the waxy skin on his face constricted. "If you wanted to know which grief *stages* he went through, you can stop at anger and denial. He displayed shock, guilt. But he never passed those initial ones. Probably my fault in the end, of course."

"How do you mean?" Hank prodded.

The detective let the hooked stick rest on the table, smoothed his hands through his sandy hair. "Ah. I thought I was doing the right thing by his girl. Kept everything close, tight. That way, when we found the bastard who did it, we'd know it for sure, no question. Thought I was doing right by *Thadius* that way, too. Narelle. Thought their lives would be better if I could make an arrest they'd never doubt. That way, they'd know Emily's killer didn't go free. Turned out it kept 'em from a death certificate. Lots of awful stuff happened. Phone calls to the house from phone companies, wanting to sell Emily a new long-distance plan. Mail to 'em from the Gap about a sale on blue jeans."

"Detective Hardeman, did Thadius Grogan's behavior change when that mail came, the phone calls?" Sure, it was torturous, but if he'd developed a habit of fixating himself on finding the killer, those were unlikely triggers.

Hardeman shook his head, glanced at his bottle. "Not his behavior. Narelle's. It's probably what spurred her forward to ending it."

Now *that* made sense. "Did you notice his interest in the case escalate after Narelle's death? A renewed interest in forwarding you leads on the case, sending articles about new police procedures, anything like that?"

"Eh, probably the opposite, now you mention it. Before, he was calling every other day, telling me some new idea he had or tidbit he thought might be of consequence. After, he stopped calling as much. Thought at first the support group he was involved in was influencing him for the better. He had people to talk to and all that. Then someone pointed me to a website he'd started about Emily. It had lots of stuff. Antipolice rants, ways families who'd gone through this sort of business could help themselves. Had a timeline of events leading up to her death, even a letter to her killer."

In other words, everything Isaac Keaton would've needed to key him into Thadius's exact frame of mind. Still, the timeline could be quite useful. "He was reaching out to the killer?"

"More like warning him," Hardeman replied.

So already, Thadius had ventured into a personal manhunt. People who launched vigilante operations did several specific things with a few variations. "When was the last time you spoke to Thadius Grogan?"

The detective stood and paced. His clothes hung around him as though they belonged to someone with a bigger budget for meals.

"I guess a few years ago, not too long after Narelle died. We still hadn't released all the information we had about Emily's murder—still haven't, to this day, in fact, though I daresay at this point it's more about the chief not wanting to eat crow than anything else. But yeah, Thadius had gotten really interested in paying for the details of the case file."

The detective stopped short, biting back further comments.

"What was that conversation like?" Hank asked.

"I—" Hardeman cut off, hung his head. "I hate it. I really do. I could've played it all so differently."

"You did the best you could, Detective," Jenna replied. No one knew what to do in these situations, and gut was all a good investigator had.

Hardeman folded his lips in a pained smile. "That's what I try to tell *myself*, too."

"What did Thadius say that last time you spoke?" Hank asked again, putting an end to the awkward tension left hanging by his last statement.

"Tried to pay me for the information," he said after a long pause.

"You mean he tried to bribe you?" Hank confirmed.

Hardeman folded his lips again. He was protective of Thadius. Hardeman's name solidified in Jenna's mind in a light blue. Did he have children? Maybe he saw himself in Thadius.

"I wouldn't tell him anything. Didn't. I knew by then it'd come to no good," Hardeman said.

Time to change directions. "In the time you knew Thadius Grogan, did he have any good friends? Did any new acquaintances become prominent in his life after his wife died?"

The detective sat back down at his ship in a bottle, resumed the tedious task of inserting the Legos into their delicate places. "Nah. Not really. That victim support group was really the only place he ever mentioned going that I can think of."

Victim support. A breeding ground for anguish and eggshells.

"Thank you, Detective. We may have some follow-up questions later," Hank said, acknowledging Hardeman's return to his ship as his signal that his patience with the interview was over.

"Hmph," Hardeman grunted as Jenna and Hank walked out the way they'd come.

"Victim support," Hank echoed her thoughts as soon as they were out of earshot.

"Only place better to suck in someone who wants to believe would be a church," Jenna mused. "I want to see that website, too. Once Thadius decided to find things for himself, he'd have looked for someone more sympathetic than the police. Or someone who *seemed* sympathetic. Biggest issue now is which came first for Isaac, the support group or Thadius?"

"Has to be Thadius, right? Surely you can't wander into an AA meeting hoping to stumble upon the perfect target," Hank said.

She glared at him. "Are all victims and survivors alcoholics now?"

"Emphasis on the anonymous, Jenna."

Jenna stopped walking. "But they *aren't* anonymous."

"What?"

She'd never found the beauty in getting together with a bunch of people who "shared" her journey in being part of the lives and deaths of a psychopath. Maybe it was because she knew she'd never be understood. The other people in those meetings didn't help *catch* their mothers.

Still, just because Jenna didn't want to sit with a group of strangers and sing "Kumbayah" didn't mean others didn't. Her own brother was one, in fact.

"Anonymous is a misnomer. These groups aren't anonymous. It's one reason Charley started going by Padgett, so his music career wouldn't suffer for his name being Ramey, but also to divert media attention. He didn't want there to be a record of him at meetings."

"They don't take attendance, right? Participation would take a serious dive . . ."

"No, they don't take attendance, but the odds of people who meet there *staying* strangers are slim to none. They get to know one another, become friends. Overlap of names is inevitable. So-and-So knows Billy Bob Smith from survivors' assistance. So-and-So goes out into the community to—I don't know—a play, where So-and-So meets Whatsername. They sit together, and pretty soon, they're looking at their programs. Billy Bob Smith's name appears in black and white. So-and-So says, 'Oh! Billy Bob Smith! I know him! He comes to survivors' assistance meetings with me!' Bam! Anonymity blown."

"Why did Billy Bob's parents not own a baby name book?"

"*Point is,* we turn up some names of the people in that group with Grogan, we narrow our list of potential Isaacs to something manageable."

Hank smirked. "You think these not-so-anonymous people who've had enough crime in their worlds to last them a few lifetimes and then some will walk willingly into a police investigation? I think you of all people should know better than that."

Jenna put her hands on her hips. "You underestimate the value of being one of them."

Red flashed in. Empowerment. If Hank wasn't the one she was talking to, she might've never felt challenged. Yet here she was, volunteering to open up to people she didn't know at all. By her own account, it was the exact thing Thadius Grogan had done that got him into trouble.

Hank couldn't hide his slight smile. "You said it, not me."

19

Thadius Grogan stepped off the bus at the Greentree Shopping Center, thoughts of the teal stripes in his head. Em had always been artistic, eccentric. She liked lots of makeup around her eyes, bright colors. One day, she'd come home with teal stripes in her dark hair.

A dilapidated storefront toward the left end of the shopping center bore a sign in the shape of an Acme rocket bearing the words SPARK YOUR INTEREST. This was the place.

The sun shone on his face as he crossed the parking lot, envelope clutched tight in his hand. If only he hadn't told her he thought the stripes were silly. It might've been different then, right?

The sign on the door said, BACK IN THIRTY MINUTES. Thadius cupped his hands to the glass and could see the man inside, sitting at the checkout counter eating a sandwich. He rapped on the glass with his knuckles.

Guy must not have many people ignore the little plastic clock on the door, because he stood almost immediately. He dug a key out of his pocket, twisted it in the bolt. "Can I help you, sir?"

Thadius glanced behind him. No one in the bare lot, the bus gone. He shoved the man backward into his store. The man hit a tower of Roman candles behind him, sending the cardboard display crumbling to the floor, the contents scattering.

Thadius closed the glass, rekeyed the lock. "Help me? I doubt it."

"What's wrong with you?"

I didn't tell my daughter her hair was gorgeous. Thadius pulled out the gun and leveled it with the man's head. "You better hope you're Woody, or this interview will be very short."

The man blinked and straightened his glasses where they were skewed on his face, his mouth slack. "Mister, the cash is in the drawer! Take whatever you want!"

Thadius took a step toward him. "I don't want your money. I'll ask again. Are. You. Woody?"

The man nodded like a bobble head. "Yes. Yes, I am. How can I . . . be of assistance?"

"Perfect," Thadius replied, and he gestured with the SIG toward the back. "Let's talk in there."

The man, reluctant to turn around, backed toward the rear, nearly tripping several times over fallen Roman candles. They reached the small back room. No windows, only white walls and a desk. Thadius indicated the chair. "Sit."

Woody did as he was told, and Thadius dumped the same video surveillance photos he'd shown the pawn shop owner onto the desk next to the computer, the coffee mug full of pens and pencils. "What do you remember about the guy in the picture?"

The shop owner blinked rapidly as his brain clearly tried to process what was happening. He touched the very edge of the grainy surveillance photo, leaned over it.

"Where was this taken?"

"Marley Ostin's pawn shop. Ostin said he sent him here. This was a few years ago. I need to know everything you know about him. Go!" Thadius barked.

"Sir, I can't possibly remember something that long ago. This picture's dated five years ago."

Thadius closed his eyes. Five years and two days ago, he'd told Emily no respectable businesswoman had hair that looked like it came out of a gumball machine. Five years and two days ago, he'd canceled their date to go eat Indian food and told her they'd reschedule when she washed the mess out.

"I'm aware," Thadius whispered.

Woody blinked more, tweaked his glasses again. He touched his face a lot, the picture. The desk. His face.

"Talk," Thadius growled.

"I think he might've been in," Woody said, but he sounded more like he was trying to appease than anything.

Thadius thrust the SIG into Woody's neck. "Gonna need more than that, buddy."

Now Woody blinked double time, shook his head. "I can't think with that thing in my neck! It's all I can focus on. Please! I'll do anything I can, just give me some room."

Thadius took one step back, eased the gun away from Woody's skin. The man released his held breath, which transformed into a fast pant. His eyes homed in on the zoomed photo. "Okay, okay. I think he came in. Yes. He definitely came in. I remember him because he had a backpack he put the fireworks in. Maybe was a student. Looked young in the face."

The camera angle didn't show the kid's face well, but Thadius bought the youthful description. "Tell me more about his face, clothes. The backpack. Anything."

"I could tell you about his face, but I probably wouldn't be right," Woody said. "It was so long ago. The clothes . . . shady. The backpack.

It . . . had a weird button on it. The MM Society. I remember thinking the words 'secret society,' but I don't remember anything else. Didn't ask about it or anything."

Thadius cocked his head. Woody was calmer, more helpful than Marley Ostin. Smart. "A logo?"

Woody nodded, blinked more.

"Draw it," Thadius commanded.

Woody looked straight on, never eyeing Thadius. He plucked a piece of paper from his printer, grabbed a pencil. He sketched feverishly, two letter M's with the word "Society" down the middle of them.

"I think it was red with black letters, but I'm . . . I can't be sure."

Thadius grabbed the paper, folded it, and pocketed it. "One more thing. Did you sell him fireworks?"

This time, Woody faced him, looked in his eyes. "I . . . yes. I'm sure I did. This is a fireworks shop, and he came in to buy. What is this about?" The man blinked some more, then said, "How can I help?"

Thadius's imagination had gone wild in the aftermath of Emily's murder, and he had a clear picture of what her body might've looked like. It flashed in, charred beyond recognition, all except her face. Her striped hair.

"You can't . . . Jesus. Did he say what he planned to do with them?"

Now sweat stuck Thadius's shirt to his chest. It had seemed so obvious. All of it. But right now Woody wanted to help him, even with a gun to his face.

Woody smoothed his palm over his mouth as he thought. "No. I don't think he did. If he did, I don't remember it at all. Sir, is there someone I can call for you?"

Thadius kept the gun on Woody and backed away from him. "Don't move."

This couldn't be happening. It wasn't right. *Emily.*

"I'm sorry for this," Thadius whispered.

20

Jenna sat at the kitchen table typing on her laptop, Hank beside her. Try as she might to ignore her father's disapproving eye from where he sat on the floor with Ayana and her farm puzzle, Jenna kept getting distracted.

"Shouldn't she be off that thing by now?" Hank asked.

Jenna swiveled her chair so she couldn't see Vern anymore, who was muttering something angry under his breath. "She's still a baby, Hank."

"Pacifiers can cause tooth problems, can't they? I tend to think the longer you wait to take it away, the more attached she'll become."

"And I tend to think she'll stop using it when she's ready," Jenna replied. Jenna modified the search criteria, hit the return key on the keyboard. "Bingo."

Hank leaned in to look at her screen, which now bore Thadius Grogan's self-made website about his daughter's murder. "Look no further for how Isaac Keaton knew what he did about Grogan."

"It certainly tells a thing or two about Thadius's mental state anyway."

Jenna's cursor naturally fell onto the tab marked "To Emily's Killer."

Unlike the rest of the site's soft pastels, this page's stark white background contrasted with plain black lettering. The note described all of Emily's activities, friends, charitable causes. It went on to tell the murderer he would be punished, labeled him everything from impotent to unintelligent.

"Assumes a lot," Hank said. "Takes for granted the killer didn't have anyone who loved him, berates him for not knowing what it is to have family. Presumes he's pathetic even."

Jenna shook away the orchid color that flashed in at Hank's words. The shade corresponded in her color vocabulary to elitism and a mind-set of superiority, but she couldn't let Hank's ideas influence her. The color had popped up at his words and didn't relate to her own gut feelings. It was something she'd learned to distinguish the hard way over the years.

"Says much more about Thadius's own healing process than anything else," Jenna agreed. *Or lack thereof.*

Stop profiling Grogan so much. It's what Keaton wants you to do.

Jenna clicked away from the letter—the obvious draw—and hit a tab of friends' and family's tributes to Emily Grogan. "Emily was bubbly" and "Emily was loved" graced the page, but nothing that might help figure out where Isaac Keaton originally found Thadius Grogan.

She out-clicked on the "Articles" tab. "If I were scouting for a volatile male with buttons to push, where would I go?"

"Would you like me to Google that for you?" Hank answered.

Jenna skimmed a piece about Thadius and Narelle visiting Emily's grave on the anniversary of her death not too long before Narelle killed herself. The website lined up a virtual tour of *where* to meet

Grogan, but someone would've had to have his name—or Emily's—to search him out on the Web.

"I guess you *can* Google 'vigilante justice,'" she said.

Her fingers pecked the words into her search bar. Lots of definitions popped up, several articles about various episodes of vigilantism over the years. A parent killing a perp who molested his child, a woman opening fire on her rapist. The article about the rapist's death had a few quotes from other crime victims.

"Have Irv get me every article he can find where Grogan's name is mentioned *not* in conjunction with the details of *Emily's* murder case," Jenna said. "Not specifically anyway. Anything commenting on other victims' rights issues, stuff like that."

"Got it." Hank opened his texts. "He says he just sent you a listing of all of the violent crime support groups Grogan has known involvement with. The main one is the Florida Families of Victims of Violent Crimes."

Jenna logged in to her e-mail. Some of the victims would sympathize with Thadius's mission, maybe even have struck out on their own to find the person who hurt their loved one.

Like a brick to the face, it hit her: any one of them might've helped Thadius get revenge.

She'd been around Charley, whose support group was all about forgiving the perpetrators who'd hurt their families. For a time, it hadn't occurred to Jenna that not all survivors tried to heal. Now she knew she'd been too close to be objective. Just because Charley didn't believe in the death penalty didn't mean everyone who went to a group like his felt that way.

"Hank, let's say you're Grogan. You try to bribe Detective Hardeman for information and fail, so you're seeking out someone who understands your plight. Someone in your support group maybe. What do they tell you?"

Hank shrugged. "Where to buy a gun?"

"Or what PI to hire." Jenna laughed out loud even though it wasn't funny at all. It was the sort of thing her mother would do.

"Howie Dumas." Jenna and Hank spoke the words simultaneously.

"How did Grogan not pick up on dumb ass?" Hank asked.

"Eh, people miss a lot of things when they lose someone. It's not exactly the clearest your head's ever been," Jenna answered. "Thadius wasn't looking for Keaton. He was looking for whoever killed Emily. Keaton snuck in, playing with him." *Playing with us.*

Jenna clapped the laptop shut. "Did you ever get that list of visitors from the Sumpter Building?"

She hadn't realized she was clutching the computer so tight until Hank's hand entered her vision, where it folded over hers. His thumb stroked the hook-shaped birthmark on her wrist. The same place his hand had fallen the first time they'd kissed.

Behind the inferno that had been, ironically, a firehouse years and years ago, Jenna sat wincing in the back of the ambulance while the paramedic stitched her chin.

"Could be worse," Hank said as he approached from a few feet away, still wearing his FBI-issued Kevlar vest over his white dress shirt. The raid on the hideout of the dangerous serial arsonist they'd been tracking had almost gone to plan. Except, of course, for that little moment when that bastard Toby Van Shore, who'd been hiding under the basement steps, had clotheslined Jenna on her way down to secure the room. She'd hit the concrete hard, heard her chin crack against the cold floor. Rookie mistake.

Luckily, Hank had been her backup, and he'd put a bullet straight into Toby's skull. And just like that, her first case with the BAU had ended. Her first encounter with a madman who wasn't a relation, done.

And she'd lived to tell the tale.

Hank had glanced around, checking that none of the others were nearby. Then his hand had folded across hers, his thumb caressing her birth-mark.

"Don't be too hard on yourself," he'd said. "Happens to the best of us."

She shook her head. "No, it doesn't. That's why the best of you are still breathing."

He'd squeezed her hand as the medic finished up, told them he'd want to watch her another five minutes to make sure she didn't have a reaction to the pain medication he'd given her. Hank promised to notify him of any change, and the medic had seen what every other profiler in their unit hadn't—either by chance or by choice—and left them alone together.

"You think they know?" Jenna asked softly as Hank boosted himself into the back of the ambulance to sit beside her.

"If they don't, they're not the team I thought they were," he said.

But it was a moot point. No one else had followed Hank to check on Jenna. They all knew.

"I think they're exactly the team you thought they were. After all, the number one rule on this team is not to profile another team member," she said, staring down at their hands clasped together, the light and the dark perfectly contrasting.

She looked up, expecting to see him looking at their hands, too, but instead, she'd met his eyes. Dark brown with a ring of hazel splayed around each pupil. If a teammate had been shrinking her right now, they'd probably note her shallower breaths, the way her own pupils dilated as she took his in.

"I didn't say anything about kissing a team member, right?" he asked.

Before she could say anything, his mouth had met hers, and she'd leaned into his kiss. First case over, something else insane begun. Check.

Now Hank waved his hand in front of her face. "Earth to Jenna? Come in Jenna."

She shook away the memory. "Sorry. Must just be tired. What were we saying?"

"I was telling you nobody out of the ordinary was on the visitors' list at the Sumpter Building, Jenna. Lawyer, consulting state psychiatrist. That's it."

Figured.

"All right. Let's pay the Florida Families of Victims of Violent Crimes an office visit, take Richards's lineup with us. We'd cut out a lot of guesswork if we just ask if they've seen this guy."

Jenna crossed into the living room, kissed Ayana atop her head.

"Off again so soon?" Vern sulked.

"Duty calls."

"Bye-bye, Ay!" Hank said, waving goofily to his daughter from the door.

Jenna's chest clenched painfully as an image emerged from somewhere deep in her memory of that same goofy face hovering above Ayana's crib when they'd all lived in the apartment together, before they'd decided to admit it was time for both of them to walk away while they still could, mostly unscathed. The first time she'd ever heard her own daughter's laugh had been as that same face peek-a-booed from behind a soft, knit afghan Hank had held.

Some things never change.

Now Ayana giggled and grinned from behind her pacifier. She pointed a chubby finger at Hank.

"Geen!" the baby squeaked.

Hank shot a look at Jenna. "Gein? Like Ed?"

Jenna rolled her eyes. He *really* wasn't around her enough, was he? "You work with too many serial killers. Green, Hank. She's pointing at your tie."

He glanced down. "Oh. Right."

Jenna walked out the door and closed it behind her, started toward the stairwell. "You should know I'm not teaching Ayana about Gein until she's at *least* four."

"Five and a half," Hank countered. "And incidentally, *you* might be *reading* too many serial killers. The real Gein doesn't meet the traditional definition of a serial. Less than three murders attributed to him. Hannibal the Cannibal, he ain't."

"*Proven*. Less than three *proven*. Claudia didn't fit the traditional definition of black widow. She was only *charged* with one murder and two attempted. That doesn't make her less of a serial. What do you make of that, by the way?"

"Make of what?"

"No visitors to the Sumpter Building other than the lawyer and the state psych."

Jenna felt more than heard Hank's steps slow behind her. *Here we go again.*

"He's bluffing, Jenna. That's what I make of it."

She descended the stairs at a steady clip. This wasn't the time.

"Don't underestimate her, Hank."

Hank sped up again behind her. "Don't you mean *him*, Jenna? Don't underestimate *him?*"

Her feet whirled on their own, her body controlling her. "What is that supposed to mean, Ellis?"

"Jenna, this is about Isaac Keaton, not Claudia. Even if it was about Claudia, she's *still* considered legally insane. Black widows are psychopaths. Claudia is manipulative, but she's very likely schizophrenic. They've said it over and ov—"

"And *I've* said over and over that Claudia has everyone snowed."

"The best psychiatrists the state—the *FBI*—can conjure up? She's spinning every single assessment at her competency hearings?"

Jenna glared at him but didn't answer. He wouldn't hear her if she did, because Claudia didn't fit the textbook. She didn't kill for financial gain or have a history of sexual abuse, never made a violent move toward an animal. After all this time, Hank still didn't understand how Jenna could know everything she did about psychopathy and still reject the repetitive findings of the court systems. Jenna ignoring the conventions baffled him.

But Claudia *was* a psychopath, all the more dangerous because she shirked the parameters.

Jenna turned and kept moving.

Outside, as Hank hopped in the driver's seat, Jenna clicked off a text to Irv: Need reports on everyone who's worked in the Sumpter Building over the past thirteen years. Keep on the d.l.

Some things, logic couldn't explain.

Lyra squirted the syringe of blood into a purple top tube. "All done. What a champ!"

The seven-year-old smiled, revealing his top two teeth missing as she smoothed a Spiderman Band-Aid on his arm. He'd screamed like a steamboat when she told him she was going to use a syringe to draw blood rather than stick his finger, but it ended up being less painful for him than he'd thought.

"Thank you," the mother said, and she gave the kid a quick hug.

"No problem. The doctor will be back with these results in a jiffy."

She left the room and took the tube to the lab. "Heading to lunch, May."

In the break room, Lyra took her ham and Swiss out of the mini fridge and settled in at the card table facing the twelve-inch black-and-white TV that stayed on all day, every day. It was tuned in to one of the few channels the TV got, the one that usually showed soap operas by twelve thirty when she had her break. Today, however, she'd taken lunch early, so the midday news was just beginning. The leading story revolved around the theme park shootings and the breaking news that the two murderers were actually the serial Gemini killers.

They had it all wrong, of course. Isaac had nothing to do with the Gemini killings. *She* knew why he'd turned himself in. The question was, how long would he go on with the charade?

He'd be furious if she tried to intervene. She couldn't. And yet the more time he was in jail, the more worried she got. They were railroading him. He needed some kind of defense, didn't he?

"The Gemini killers gunned down their first two victims at a gas station outside of New Haven, Connecticut, three months ago. The team of killers next hit two people at a company picnic in Delaware before the next massacre last month in Charleston, South Carolina. The most recent strike took down a couple in Georgia dining at a local Red Lobster," the newscaster said.

Ridiculous. Isaac had never even been to Connecticut.

And yet . . .

Three months ago when those shootings happened, Isaac was at a work convention in Los Angeles. He couldn't have been anywhere else.

But then again . . .

"Why didn't you get a picture of the Hollywood sign while you were there? You know it's the one thing I wanted to see," Lyra said when she picked him up from the airport.

"Lye, you know I don't have time to sightsee on business trips."

"Oh, come on. Surely you've had time to snap a few photos on some of these trips. You never take pictures anymore. Why not?"

That was when Isaac's voice shifted from relaxed and drowsy to cold and firm.

"Drop it, okay? I didn't take any fucking pictures! I didn't need to! My memory is fine!"

Lyra set her ham sandwich back on her plate. Queasiness washed over her.

She shook her head hard and whispered to herself. "Trust issues. He has trust issues, and he doesn't like people to know where he is because of that. That's why he doesn't take pictures."

"Who doesn't take pictures?" May asked from behind her. The other nurse grabbed her brown paper sack lunch from the mini fridge beside the TV table. She sat down next to Lyra.

"Oh," Lyra said, releasing a fake laugh. "My brother. I always ask him to use the camera I bought him for Christmas, but he never remembers."

Three months ago in Los Angeles. What were those dates again?

The Florida Families of Victims of Violent Crimes office didn't seem to Jenna like the sort of place you'd find lives touched by evil. The door bore a wreath of bright flowers, and inside, bulletin boards covered the walls like in an elementary school hallway. The tables, chock-full of brochures of different sorts, were the only signs that the organization assisted victims. Pamphlets on depression, dealing with holidays, insomnia, ways to reach out to others—all so personal, a stark contrast to the side of crime Jenna dealt with and its bare, cement walls.

"Help you?" the receptionist asked from behind a sturdy glass window. Apparently, the group was friendly, but also smart enough to keep up a barrier until they vetted newcomers.

"I'm Special Agent Hank Ellis with the FBI. This is Doctor Ramey, our consulting forensic psychiatrist. We have a few questions." Hank flashed his badge, then laid it on the counter so the receptionist could examine it. These people would have read enough—been *through* enough—to expect a bit more proof of identity than a badge flipped at them for a fraction of a second. Anything could be faked.

The woman opened the window a crack and slid Hank's identification through. "What's this about?"

"One of your regulars. Thadius Grogan. An acquaintance of his may or may not be connected to a crime we're investigating. Would someone in the office know Thadius Grogan or talk to him frequently?"

A smile crossed the woman's lips. "Oh, everyone knows Mr. Grogan! He's one of our biggest donors. He's had a hard time of it—"

"Who here does Thadius work with the most?" Hank cut in, but not before the marigold tone of friendship flooded Jenna's vision.

The receptionist nodded, eager to please. "You'll be wanting to talk to Bronx. I'll let him know you're here."

The lady retreated from her desk into a hallway behind her, and Hank turned to Jenna. "Grogan's well liked. Must not be that much of a hermit if everyone knows him. She practically beamed at the mention of his name."

"Yep. I don't think he's a major depressive. Not outwardly anyway. He probably inspires a lot of people with his activity actually."

The door on their right opened.

"Come on back," the receptionist said.

They followed her through the carpeted hall to a conference room.

"Agent Ellis and Dr. Ramey, Bronx," she said.

"Bronx" turned out to be an aging Japanese guy who looked a head shorter than Jenna and about thirty pounds lighter. However, as soon as he opened his mouth, the nickname made sense.

"Nice to meet you guys," he said, the word "guys" in two syllables that included a "w." "I'm the executive director of Double-F Double-V C. How can I help?"

Jenna perched on the end of one of the overstuffed chairs at the table, spread the police lineup in front of Bronx, and let her mind settle on the vermillion hue it brought forward for him. He was clearly a good leader. Just the right mix of friendly and assertive. The colors lined up with her initial reaction to him the same way they did with everyone else. "We understand you've had some contact with Thadius Grogan?"

Bronx's gaze lingered on the paper, probably searching it for Thadius's face. "Um, yeah. He's been in here a lot over the years. I assume you know about his daughter . . ."

"Yes, sir. We do. To be frank, Thadius Grogan is a suspect in an ongoing investigation, and we need some more information about him."

Bronx's forehead creased. "What sorta investigation?"

Jenna felt Hank glance at her. "A murder."

"Oy." Bronx frowned. "Can I ask what happened?"

The news conference would've run again on the midday news, but unless the staff here caught that broadcast, they wouldn't have seen anything about Grogan unless it had reached CNN. So far, they'd managed to keep Grogan's name separate from the Gemini killings. No telling how long that'd last.

"Thadius Grogan's truck was discovered in the parking lot where a shooting occurred," Hank answered simply.

"Right," Bronx answered. Poor guy was dumbfounded. Couldn't blame him.

"Does anyone in this lineup resemble someone you might've seen with Thadius at any point, anyone you might recognize from Double-F Double-V C?"

Bronx cocked his head at her use of his lingo, then returned his focus to the page. He scanned the photos but wagged his head side to side. "Not anyone I recognize."

"Could you look one more time? Just to be sure," Hank prompted.

Jenna watched Bronx's eyes rove the page. They stuck to no photograph, and he didn't display any nervous ticks at all. He was telling the truth.

"No one," he said again.

"Is there anyone in the age range of the men on that lineup he *did* hang around within the group? A sponsor or buddy of any sort?" Jenna asked.

Bronx scooted the lineup back toward her. Now he shifted in his seat. "I'm sure you understand I don't want to jeopardize anyone's privacy. The only reason most people come to us to get help is because they know we won't put it on a billboard. If we don't have trust, we don't have much to offer."

"Believe me, I know better than a lot of people about wanting privacy for this sort of thing," Jenna answered slowly.

Bronx's head jerked back as though Jenna had appeared in front of him for the first time out of thin air. "Ramey. Dr. Ramey, the forensic psychiatrist. You're Claudia Ramey's—"

"Daughter. Yes."

"Christ. I'm sorry," he said.

You and me both.

"I don't really know who Thadius talked to outside this office. He'd come in any time I wanted a word with him, needed a donor to sponsor a fund-raising event. That sort of thing. I can't promise they'll be receptive, but the best people I can think to talk to would be Amy and Shawn Snow. Their daughter was killed when she was in high school, and I think the two families stayed in touch. I can give you some contact info, but again, I stress that they've been through a lot. Might not be as willing to talk to you as others."

"Right," Jenna replied, noting the coal color that came to mind. She should know; it was the same guarded shade that flashed in anytime someone mentioned Claudia.

Jenna and Hank trailed behind Bronx back to the front. He flipped through a box of index cards to Amy and Shawn Snow. Even though Jenna could obtain the same information from Irv in less than sixty seconds, she and Hank waited while Bronx copied the phone number and address for them on a sticky note. Bad policy to remind people the FBI could dig into their lives any old time they wanted.

As Bronx wrote, Hank cleared his throat. "You don't happen to recognize the name 'Howie Dumas' at all, do you?"

Bronx glanced up from the Post-it. "Howie Dumas? Doesn't ring any bells."

"What about a name of any private investigator popular with the people who come to your support group?" Jenna asked. "Do you ever have members who aren't satisfied with police investigations who try to look into things themselves?"

Bronx frowned, then turned his gaze back to the address to finish writing. "Comes up every now and then, but we don't provide resources for anything like that. Usually that sort of thing isn't healthy for victims or their families. We encourage 'em to move on, not stay put."

"So Mr. Grogan never mentioned anything of the sort?" Hank pressed.

Bronx pulled the note from the top of the stack, stretched it toward Hank. "Not to me."

"Thanks," Hank said as he accepted the piece of paper.

He made for the door, but Jenna lagged. It was risky, but at this point, better to ask than not know. The connection would get out as soon as they revealed Keaton's name, but protecting that name wasn't nearly as important as what they'd gain if Bronx recognized it. Keaton had to have been here, met Grogan in association with this place. It was the most logical explanation.

Isaac Keaton didn't exist. The name had no trail. But . . .

He was narcissistic. Organized, but not without his shortcomings. One of those shortcomings was that he liked that name. He'd given it to them so easily. Readily, even. He'd have used it other places before, and those places would be anywhere it wasn't used in fixed, traceable form.

"One more thing," Jenna said, her heart pumping faster. "Have you ever heard the name Isaac around here? Or Keaton?"

Bronx's eyes turned upward as he racked his brain, but again, he shook his head.

"No, and I tend to remember names. No Isaac or Keaton."

22

Dread suffocated Jenna as she walked up the path to Amy and Shawn Snow's split-level home in the Willow Woods subdivision. Yard was kept meticulously, every blade and leaf trimmed tight. Garage open, cars inside. Both clean. The garage *itself* was spotless, no oil stains or outside debris.

If Jenna was them, she wouldn't want to talk to her, either.

The door behind the screen opened, and a brunette of about fifty stared back at them through empty eyes. She cocked her head, but didn't speak.

"Hun, who's at the door?" a male voice asked from behind her.

The man Jenna assumed was Shawn Snow appeared, tall and looming.

"Mr. and Mrs. Snow, I'm Special Agent Hank Ellis, and this is Dr. Jenna Ramey—"

"Oh, God, you've found him! You got him! After all these years! Why hasn't Detective Plieban called? Where is he?" Amy Snow squeaked, high-pitched, giddy.

Behind her, Shawn licked his lips, put his hand on Amy's shoulder. "Is it true?"

Uh-oh.

"I'm sorry, but we're not here about your daughter's death," Jenna said in little more than a whisper. They hadn't even thought to look up details of the Snows' daughter's death yet. Hadn't bothered to think about what the couple might make of this visit. Rookie mistake, not doing any homework.

Hank cut in. "We're here to talk with you about a man you know. Thadius Grogan. Would you mind if we came in?"

Hank offered his badge, Jenna her own identification.

Shawn Snow opened the screen door, but he stepped onto the porch. "What's this about?"

"I'm not sure if you've seen our press conferences on the news today—"

"Oh, we don't watch the news anymore," Amy countered. "Too much to be sad about out there. I have enough to worry about without worrying over everyone else's problems."

Such a statement would normally seem upbeat and bring visions of vivid colors to mind, but instead, Jenna's mind settled on a strange orangey-brown hue surrounding Amy Snow. Denial? No. It wasn't quite the color she usually saw as denial. Close . . .

"Right," Hank replied. "Thadius Grogan has been connected to a recent shooting. In Thadius's perception, the victim may've had something to do with his daughter's murder. We believe he may be intent on harming others. We need to know—"

"We think someone encouraged him to perpetuate these acts. It was most likely someone who seemed sympathetic to him. Someone he might've known through FFVVC." On instinct, Jenna picked up where Hank left off. No way to explain it except the truth.

Shawn's face reddened. "You're not suggesting that we—"

"Of course not, Mr. Snow," Jenna cut in before Shawn could finish. "We thought you might be able to tell us some about Mr. Grogan's lifestyle, people he talked to regularly, seeing as how you were acquainted with him."

Shawn cackled, wild and angry. "If Thadius hurt someone involved in Emily's murder, I can't say I blame him. You want me to help you *stop* him?"

"No."

Jenna's response came out so quickly, she wasn't even sure *she'd* said it at first. Shawn's statement had drawn forth a strange, tempered cerulean. The blue didn't match at all the red anger in his voice. He was furious, but his personality screamed the cool blues of defeat.

"We want you to help us find out who *targeted* Thadius. The person who encouraged this behavior is not his friend," Hank said.

"And you people *are?*"

"Mr. Snow, the person who set Thadius on this path may be the same type of person who harmed his daughter. Your daughter. This person will most likely be a male between the ages of twenty-five and thirty-five. White. He'll most likely have never been married, but he'll be charming, possibly even handsome. The person who did this to Mr. Grogan is a sociopath, and a vicious one. We need to know if you have any idea who this might be."

Shawn Snow looked at his wife, who had wandered to the corner of the porch and was staring across the street at nothing. Everything.

"Thadius Grogan didn't have any friends that match that description. Not that I know of," he said. His eyes didn't leave Amy as he spoke. Maybe the cerulean Jenna's psyche had assigned Shawn was his defeat mingled with *devotion*.

Hank's phone bleated from his pocket. Jenna nodded to him to take the call.

"Excuse me," Hank said, and he walked across the yard.

"Is there anyone else you can think of who he might've trusted?" Jenna asked.

Shawn Snow's face turned maroon again. "Thadius didn't trust anyone. I know that much."

Even you?

"Do you know if Thadius had a housekeeper?"

"What?" Shawn Snow asked, surprised.

"A housekeeper. Or someone who came in and did laundry. Anyone like that?"

Shawn shook his head. "I don't think so. It wasn't the sort of thing we talked about."

"What about you, Mrs. Snow?"

Amy continued gazing in the distance but twisted her head left and right. A tear dripped down her cheek, streaking her caked-on makeup.

"No," she whispered.

"Do either of you know the name 'Howie Dumas'?"

Amy Snow continued to stare blankly across the street. Shawn glanced at her, turned back to Jenna, and shook his head. "Never heard of him."

Shawn crossed to Amy, squeezed her shoulders. "We'd better get inside. This isn't the best time of year for Ames to be out."

Jenna fished in her pocket, extended her card. "Call if you think of anything, will you?"

Shawn said nothing, just accepted the tiny slip of cardboard and tugged his wife's hand, directing her into the house. The door closed in Jenna's face.

Jenna turned to locate Hank, who was talking on his phone at the curb. She trotted toward him but stopped for her own phone's steady ring.

"This is Jenna."

"The list of Cuckoo Nest workers is in your in-box when you have some time, but I'm guessing it might be a while," Irv said.

"This about the phone call Hank just took?"

"Oh, so you haven't heard yet. Our friendly neighborhood Punisher strikes again."

"Grogan?"

"Yep. All for the greater good, I'm sure. He stopped by a store in a nearby shopping plaza. Greentree. Talked to the owner. But there's good news this time. The dude's still alive."

23

Jenna and Hank ducked under the crime scene tape at the fire-works shop in Greentree Shopping Center, which wasn't too far from the Pawn Shop where Marley was shot. Woody Fine sat calmly behind his desk, polishing his glasses with his shirt tail.

After introducing himself, Hank started off by asking what Woody and Thadius talked about, how Thadius seemed.

"Calm and deranged at the same time, if that's possible. Angry and sad. He asked me if I sold fireworks to this guy he had pictures of. Surveillance camera footage from years ago. I do actually re-member him a bit. I told him the guy was a customer. Wasn't about to lie to him."

"Did he mention Marley Ostin to you?"

Woody nodded. "Yeah. Told me Marley'd given him my name. Guess he got these from him?"

Not exactly. "Mr. Fine—"

"Woody, please."

"Woody, did this man mention his visit to Marley Ostin to you at all?" Jenna asked.

The shop owner propped his glasses back on his nose. "Naw. I assumed."

Regardless of whether or not Thadius's conscience weighed on him, he'd shot Marley Ostin after he questioned him. What had Marley done that Woody hadn't? Or what had *Woody* done where Marley had fallen short?

"Did you fear for your life at any point, Woody?" Hank asked.

"He *was* pointing a gun at my head."

"I think what S.A. Ellis means is did you *believe* this man was going to shoot you?" Jenna clarified. *Such an important distinction.*

Woody was quiet while he thought, maybe even reviewed the earlier incident in his mind. "No. I don't think I did. Believe it, I mean."

So one of a few things went on here. Either Grogan went into both places with his mind made up *not* to kill Marley Ostin and Woody Fine, and something happened between Thadius and Marley to provoke Thadius to kill the pawn shop owner. Or Thadius went into both places planning to kill both people, and something *stopped* him from killing Woody. How to figure which?

"What were you able to tell him about the surveillance photos?" Jenna asked.

"Not much, that's for sure. Couldn't remember the kid's face or stature. I told him about the young man's backpack, or rather, a button I saw there. Random thing, but the logo struck me as strange at the time, even back then. He had me draw the button for him. Then he asked me if I'd sold the kid fireworks. Told him I'm sure I did if the kid tried to buy them. I'd have had no reason not to sell 'em. The guy asked me if I'd known what the kid planned to do with them. I asked the guy several times if I could call someone for him. He seemed so distraught, not stable."

"Back up a minute. What did you tell him when he asked if you knew what the kid planned to do with the fireworks?" Jenna asked.

"Told him the truth—that I had no idea. I don't ask usually.

People buy 'em all the time to set off on beaches or on holidays. It's legal around here. What else *would* he be doing with fireworks, other than setting them off?"

A muted celadon permeated Jenna's psyche. The color she'd associated with the law and anything related since she could remember.

Legal.

"Hank, have Irv check Marley Ostin and the pawn shop's records to see if his dealings, particularly firearms sales, were done by the letter."

"On it."

"Woody, can you draw the same sketch for us as you did for the man who held you up?"

"Of course."

One of the cops in the shop ripped a sheet of paper out of his notebook for Jenna, and she passed it and a pencil he handed her to Woody. "Take your time."

As Woody's pencil scratched the paper, she pulled Hank away. "Thoughts?"

"Thadius is still somewhat rational. He's deciding who lives or dies, probably based on how culpable he perceives the individual."

"Do you think it has anything to do with Woody's offer to help him?"

Hank shrugged, but Jenna could tell he was doubtful.

"I think it's more likely that he's determining how much he blames them," Hank said.

"Judging them," Jenna filled in.

"Exactly."

"Who's next on Grogan's list is the hundred-thousand-dollar question. And how did Thadius get a lead on Marley in the first place?" Jenna asked.

"Grogan built his business into a franchise—he had connections. Someone might've hooked him up with a private investigator."

"The surveillance camera photo stills," she remembered out loud. "Those had to have come from a private investigator, right? Has to be Dumas's cover."

"That's what I keep thinking, too, though surely Grogan would've met with the PI before he hired him. He couldn't have known the PI *and* Isaac Keaton if the PI *was* Isaac Keaton," Hank replied.

There, he had her. "So maybe the second UNSUB is the PI."

Even as Jenna said it, she didn't believe it. The Gemini may have been partners, but Isaac himself admitted they weren't equals. Anyone who had to perform and convince someone as competent as Grogan had to be a terrific actor. Something told her the subservient ferry shooter wasn't that good. Had to be Isaac.

"Finished," Woody called to them, and they turned back to him.

He pushed the paper across to them. He'd drawn a circle with a small emblem on it.

"What colors were the letters? The background?" Jenna asked.

"The M's were black. I think all of the lettering was. Red background."

Hank already had his phone out and was snapping pictures of the drawing. As if Irv didn't already have his hands full.

"Thank you, Woody. We appreciate this. I may have a few more questions, but that's it for now," Hank replied.

Hank read another text as they headed for the store's exit. "Detective Richards wants to know if we're ready to put the lineup in front of Yancy Vogul. Chase the MM Society or head back to Yancy?"

Good question. As tempting as the button emblem might be, Grogan was the goose chase, not the golden egg. Keaton had orchestrated this whole thing. Even if they tried, they couldn't beat Thadius Grogan to his next target, even if they knew more about the emblem.

That would require knowing everything about his thought process, and unfortunately, even Jenna couldn't read minds. They needed to visit Yancy and show him the lineup. If he recognized Keaton, this would be a new ballgame.

"Let's put Saleda on the MM Society. I want to see Yancy Vogul's reactions."

24

" point out the lack of pizza to you guys, and you *still* don't bring the pizza," Yancy said when S.A. Ellis, Dr. Jenna Ramey, and Detective Richards showed up at the door of his one-bedroom apartment. Cops. *Can't live with 'em, can't get away from 'em.*

"How're you feeling?" the pretty brunette Dr. Ramey asked.

On second thought, she wasn't a Fed or a cop anymore. She was a shrink. Perfect.

"Get back, Oboe!"

Yancy nudged the dachshund away from the doorway with his prosthetic. He noticed all their eyes were drawn to it. Typical. "Some people call it a challenge. I like to think of it as genetically enhanced."

"Do you mind if I ask how—"

Yancy cut off Special Agent Hank Ellis. "Aw, no. But the genetically enhanced thing was a joke. I wasn't born with it. Crushed it in an elevator shaft, believe it or not. Training exercise while I was with the Department of Law Enforcement. The trainees were conducting a firearm training simulation that was supposed to be a routine sweep of an abandoned building, taking down the people playing the bad guys as we went. Part of the exercise involved rescuing someone playing a victim from an elevator shaft. Unfortunately, that building had been *really* abandoned, and its structure unchecked for too long for it to be used for games like these apparently. I went in to assist in the rescue, came out without a leg. Now I run websites. Good excuse for playing on a computer all day. Funny how freak accidents can make you a freak."

Both Ellis and Detective Richards kind of jerked, uncomfortable. Jenna Ramey smiled.

"You're dark. I like that," she said, smooth.

She would, of course. Some things you can't afford *not* to joke about. Not if you wanted to survive.

He'd read all about her during his internship. Most people had at some point or another. She'd published several great articles about profiling, but mostly, people in the field knew her because she'd been the first person to suspect her mother of being a sociopath. At only thirteen years old, she'd begun to profile her mother, keep detailed records of her thoughts and findings. That journal led to Claudia Ramey's arrest—and maybe to Jenna's dad and brother's own attempted murders. Apparently, if her mother was going down, she wasn't planning to leave any witnesses. Too bad for her that her daughter turned out to be really good at wielding a shower rod.

"Feeling better, by the way. 'Twas merely a flesh wound," he said in a mock British accent.

"*And* a Monty Python fan."

He laughed and plopped down in the leather recliner. "Got the whole collection on DVD. So what brings you folks out here without time to stop for a large supreme?"

Richards opened his briefcase, removed a few sheets of paper. A lineup.

"Yancy, we'd like you to look at a few photos and tell us if you saw any of these men at the park."

The detective offered the laminated papers to him, and Yancy focused on the pictures. The lineup was like a Who's Who of All-American Football Players.

"Nobody told me this killer was a former Mr. America. How long did it take you guys to find enough prisoners pretty enough for this lineup?"

Nobody answered. *Stop trying to be funny, cool guy.*

The first page, nothing. Second, nothing. On the third, his gaze fixed on the last photo. He pointed to it. "He looks familiar."

"From the park?" Ellis asked.

"Familiar. Maybe the park. I don't know. I guess I could've seen him anywhere in the city, but I can't place where. Just familiar."

The guy's face floated in Yancy's mind. He'd been walking. No—running. Where?

"Yancy, can you remember any details? Was it indoors? Outdoors?" Jenna Ramey asked.

"I'm almost sure it was out. He was moving somehow. I can picture it vaguely. I want to say I passed him."

Yancy shut his eyes tight, held the face. *Motion. Jogging. Bumped. "Sorry," the guy said, but he wasn't. Guy was in a hurry.*

"I'm sorry," Yancy said. "I'm just not sure."

His one chance to really help somebody, to do what he'd been trained for, and he couldn't. *Are you a good enough investigator to detect failure, cool guy?*

"So asking for a name would be—"

"Setting me up for the privilege of saying, 'I have no idea'?" Yancy cut off S.A. Ellis's question.

Ellis opened his mouth to say something but glanced down instead. "What the—"

"Oboe! Stop!" Yancy leapt out of his chair and scooped the dachshund from where he was happily humping the Special Agent's left shin. "Excuse me. Excuse *him*. I'm so sorry. He probably needs to go outside. Always tries to get attention when he does. Be right back."

Yancy pulled a leash from the coat rack, clipped it onto Oboe's collar, and pulled the wiener dog out onto the back porch.

"Seriously, dude," Yancy mumbled, "I don't know why you do this to me. I'm not kidding. I don't want to snip your manhood, but you're leaving me no choice."

"Oh, I wouldn't be too hard on Oboe." Jenna Ramey joined him on the back porch. "Hank deserved it. He's humped a leg or two in his day." She closed the door behind her. "Thought I'd come out here and—"

"Profile me a little? Talk to me about my abandonment issues?" *Shut up, smart ass!*

Jenna Ramey laughed. "Well, it wasn't what I had in mind, but if you want."

"Not in the traditional sense maybe. I can't figure out why no one *will* abandon me."

She leaned against the porch rail and crossed her arms. "I'm familiar. Believe me. No, I actually just needed the fresh air myself. I've been around those two all day. Breathers are good."

"I take it you aren't notifying everyone like this, or the lineup would be all over the news. What makes you think I can help you, Dr. Ramey?"

"Call me Jenna if I'm supposed to call you Yancy," she said. "I guess I could give you some BS about how your color clued me in to your photographic memory, but it wouldn't be true. It's what most people hope for, though."

She was *real*. Rare. "That's good, because I don't have a photographic memory. What's the boring truth?"

"We dug up your file and found out you had a history in investigation, thought you were a more reliable witness than most."

His shoulders sagged of their own accord. "Sorry to disappoint."

She waved him off. "Memory's a weird thing. It still might come to you. In the meantime, we'll check other angles."

"So this isn't any kind of victim profiling?" he asked. *Nosy bastard.*

"I wish. Having a victim profile makes things easier, but the Gemini don't work like that. The victims seem random. No discernible connection other than they were all killed in public. All from different states, races, socioeconomic backgrounds. Of course, we're running victim profiles like in any case, but we'd be wasting our time to focus on it."

God, he wanted in on this investigation. He'd tried so hard to stay out of drama since his accident, to stay away from people. And yet somehow it *found* him, magnetized to him. Had to be the metal foot.

"The Gemini *aren't* after one-footed wonders, then?" he cracked.

She smirked. "Doubtful. Probably more like thrill-seekers, people who want to lord the power of life and death over others. That sort of thing . . ."

"Only one would be that, though, right? You've written about team killer mentalities in journals before and said that." He jerked his head toward the apartment. "The one in the lineup is the ringleader, huh?"

Jenna squinted, lifted her chin. "What makes you say that?"

"Uh, he's handsome. Groomed. Probably charming, but I'm basing that on looks, so I could be wrong to the point of detriment. I remember his voice actually. He said, 'Sorry,' when I bumped into him. It was cold, but not meek. I think the ringleader idea is just a gut feeling."

"Hm," she said.

"It's part of his game, right? That's the ringleader, and he'd pull in the other guy purely because it would amuse him . . . being able to manipulate someone weaker into doing something that evil. Am I right?" *Press your luck, smarty-pants.*

"*Jenna!*"

The yell came from the front of the apartment. Oboe pulled to the end of his leash, barking insistently. "Stop it, Oboe! Shut up!"

S.A. Ellis grabbed the drain pipe at the side of the building to rein in his turn as he charged into the backyard. His dark face was as pale as it probably ever got, panic across it like a mask.

"Jenna, we have to go. We need to go now. Ayana—"

Jenna went pallid. "What's wrong? Jesus, Hank! Tell me what's going on!"

S.A. Ellis stopped, hands on his knees, trying to catch his breath. "Your father got a package at the house. It was addressed to Ayana. Jenna, it's from *him*."

25

J enna crashed through the door, saw Charley sitting on the couch, head in his hands. "Where is she? Where's my baby?"

Vern appeared in the doorway holding Ayana, her daughter's skinny bird legs wrapping his waist. "We just read *Goldilocks and the Three Bears*, didn't we, Ay?"

Jenna blinked rapidly, shook her head. How could he be this cavalier when he knew a psycho knew about Ayana—was *contacting* Ayana? Knew her *mother*.

Ayana clapped her hands and rocked in her grandfather's grasp. "Locks!"

The pressure of Hank's hand on Jenna's shoulder corked the spew of panic about to erupt. Deep breaths. He was right. No need to get Ayana worked up.

"I want to see the note," she said to Vern sweetly as she kissed Ayana's cheek.

Charley took his cue to take Ayana. "Come on, Ay. I'll show you how to put the puzzle together so you never have to fix it again . . ."

"Charley, if you duct tape that farm puzzle, I swear—"

Her brother cut Vern off. "Duct tape? You can *see* duct tape." He lifted Ayana onto his hip and pressed his nose to hers, Eskimo kissing her. "We're using superglue!"

Ayana giggled, and her pacifier dropped to the ground.

Jenna picked up the pacifier. "We probably need to superglue this, too."

She followed her father into the kitchen. She rinsed the binky under the faucet before turning to look at the box she'd seen her dad pick up. Hank was already examining the contents with latex gloves, though her father and brother had probably already compromised some evidence by handling it bare-handed, not to mention the mail carrier and whoever else had touched it in between. Still, prints and fibers should be somewhat intact, so no need to disregard procedure entirely.

Hank pulled out a stuffed purple and blue dragon, sniffed it, gave it the twice-over. He plunked it into a plastic evidence bag.

Hank used a pair of tweezers to lift the note out of the box at its fold, and it fell open.

"'Dear Ayana, do you have a fishhook birthmark, or is that just your grandmother's? Let me know. Love, Uncle Isaac,'" Hank read.

Heat washed over Jenna's face, and her eyes darted to her own birthmark on her wrist, then to Hank, purposefully avoiding her father. No way she could handle that right now.

"Handwriting?"

"We'll send it to an expert, but it's block lettered, so even if he didn't pen it himself, it won't tell us anything," Hank replied.

"Postmark?" Jenna countered.

"Denver, Colorado, but it apparently was mailed there from elsewhere, and before that, from somewhere else. He had a string of people sending this one so it couldn't be traced."

"I want to know every human being who touched that package," Jenna said.

"We're on this, Jenna."

Did he not realize a serial killer had sent their *daughter* a stuffed animal? "We need surveillance at post offices where it was handled. Talk to whoever delivered it, the mail workers, everyone in the radius of where it was mailed—"

"Jenna. This isn't my first rodeo," Hank said slowly.

"It isn't mine, either. I'm going to the Sumpter Building," Jenna blurted out.

Now it was Vern who spoke up. "You can't be serious, Jenna!"

They were *not* talking her out of it this time. She didn't want to go any more than they wanted her to, but it was the only way.

"He's met Claudia. There's no way he could know about the birthmarks if he hadn't," she argued.

"The sick fuck could've seen *yours*, Jenna."

But Hank shook his head. "He'd have no way to mail the thing since he's been in lockup. He's under tight surveillance."

"Oh, surveillance, shmerveillance, Hank! You know how those places work!" Vern said, his face the shade of a radish.

"Dad, he's right. Anything can happen in jail, but Keaton's been in the box and in a holding cell. There's nowhere and no one he could've slipped anything to yet. He had to have mailed that before he called me in there. Before he was caught. It's postmarked Denver, for crying out loud." Then, to Hank, "When was it postmarked?"

Jenna's stomach flopped like a fish in a shallow bucket. She didn't really need to see when it was mailed. The planning that had to have gone into the whole thing, the attention to detail. The targeting. She'd known from the moment he'd called her in that he'd researched her, known about her. Yet somehow she'd thought he was some sort of twisted fan. It wasn't like she hadn't had them before.

This was different, though. This whole thing had been orchestrated not just with her as a piece of Isaac Keaton's weird puzzle. She was woven much deeper in his plan than she'd realized.

"Two days ago. Jenna, are you sure you want to do this? You know what these guys are like. He's messing with you. He *wants* this. I can send someone else over there to question Claudia," Hank said, his voice a plea.

"You think someone else can figure her out?"

"The chances of you getting anything from her but gibberish and nonsense are slimmer than—"

"Look, Ellis, I know you think Claudia is more cuckoo than a Swiss clock, which is exactly why *I* have to be the one to talk to her. I know what to look for. I did before, and I will again."

Vern sat in a kitchen chair, biting his lip. Jenna knew he'd always believed her about Claudia. Always had. Still, he'd given up trying to convince other people long ago. Too bad. Right now it would be nice to have the backup.

"You don't hear voices if you're sane, Jenna," Hank pressed.

Memories flashed in, the ones she beat away at night when she tried to sleep: *August 15,* she wrote. *Mama got home from the airport about four. She cooked macaroni and cheese for Charley. I ate SpaghettiOs. We ate about 5:15. He started feeling sick sometime before bath at 7. Ran to the bathroom three or four times. Diarrhea, I think. First time he's had it in a week.*

More flashbacks jutted in. Her mother's steps padding the carpet outside, her frantic movements to shove the journal into the backside of her bear, where she kept it. Pushing the bear into the back of the pile of stuffed animals in the net suction-cupped into the corner of her room. Claudia walking in, eyes trailing from where Jenna sat on the floor with her homework and lingering on the net above, which was still wobbling from the movement from the moment before.

Now Jenna leveled her gaze at Hank. He had no idea what Claudia was capable of, and that meant he had no idea what Isaac was, either.

"You don't know to *lie* about hearing voices unless you're really good at what you do, Hank. I'm going. Are you?"

26

The cold metal doors slid back, and Jenna followed the orderly into Hall D of the Sumpter. Hall D held the dangerously criminally insane.

Jenna's spine tingled as the doors slammed behind her, locking her in on the same side as the vile woman who shared her blood.

As she followed Gema, the orderly, her mind wandered back over what had led to this day. In a perfect world, Claudia would be in a maximum-security prison on death row, even if Charley would disagree. However, Claudia had put on the razzle-dazzle at the competency hearing, and she was sentenced to six months in Sumpter, where the judge ordered state mental health professionals to "restore her" to competency to stand trial.

Seventeen years later, thanks to Claudia's brilliant plan and her sleazebag lawyer, she was still here at the Sumpter, unmedicated and living the luxe life, while her lawyer continued to file petitions to keep her here. His argument was simple and probably true: the state could not medicate her to stand trial without endangering both her health and her case.

"You know the rules, right?" Gema said as they came closer to the glassed-in "fishbowl" in which Claudia lived.

Of course she did. Jenna walked this hall every now and then for different reasons, most of the time her own consults or patients.

"Don't pass her anything that hasn't been approved, especially no writing utensils or sharp edges," Jenna recited. "No cross-visiting with other inmates, no contraband or electronic devices that aren't approved. Stay back from the glass. Objectionable behavior will end my visiting privileges. Anything I'm forgetting?"

"Gold star," Gema replied. "Luck to ya."

When Jenna's eyes found Claudia Ramey, bugs crawled on her arms. The woman had become thinner, waxier than the last time. The years hadn't been good to her. Frown lines sprawled in unsteady paths from her eyes and lips, and her previously bleached-blond hair had faded into a ratty brown color turning gray at the roots.

Claudia paid no attention whatsoever to Jenna, and instead, tapped on the glass at Gema. "Biscuit time?"

Jenna repressed the shudder at the guttural, scratchy voice that had at one time called after her as it chased her down a blood-spattered hallway.

"Not 'til morning, Claudia. It's late for that right now. Brought you a visitor."

Claudia's yellow fingernail tapped again in front of Gema as though she hadn't even heard the orderly. *Oscar-worthy, Mama. Really.*

"Biscuit time? Jelly?" Claudia asked, a concerned expression blanketing her face.

"A few hours," Gema repeated. "Be back to check on you kids shortly."

Claudia's eyes followed Gema as she left the hall, her finger still tip-tapping at the glass until Jenna heard the doors of the hallway close and latch shut.

The woman's face turned toward Jenna, the mask dissolving like sugar in water. "Well, well, well."

This time, Jenna couldn't hide her surprise. Her eyes widened, and she took a step back. Un-fucking-believable.

Claudia inclined her head toward the corner surveillance camera. "Surprised I'd speak to you with that there, right?"

Jenna didn't answer. Couldn't. Her blood was too busy thundering in her ears. Someone had to be watching this. Finally!

"They don't like to pay for nonstop surveillance, I guess. Blinking light, on. Solid light, off," Claudia explained through a smirk.

Leave it to Claudia to figure out from a fishbowl how to transform herself based on whether or not she was being recorded. Leave it to her to somehow team up with a monster from behind bars.

"Brilliant," Jenna spat.

"*Tsk, tsk*, Jenna. You should know sarcasm doesn't inspire confidence in patients."

"You're not my patient."

Claudia half laughed. "Thank God. You'd have me on a lifetime supply of Thorazine by now."

"No, I'd have you declared legally competent to fry by now."

Her mother leaned against the wall closest to her, her face close to the glass. The side of her mouth turned up like a scythe. "Charming. You didn't stop by to catch up then?"

"What do you know about Isaac Keaton?"

The slits of Claudia's eyes contracted. "Isaac . . . Keaton, did you say?"

Oh, she knew all right.

"Don't play with me, Claudia. If you know something, tell me," Jenna breathed.

"And here I thought you called me Mumsy!" Claudia said, throwing her head back with a wicked laugh. "Must be causing *some* problem, you come here to ask me."

"Who is he, Claudia?"

Claudia drummed her fingers from thumb to pinky on the glass one by one. "I don't have a clue. Why do you ask?"

Snarky smile, sure. But Claudia's eye position was level, no tension. Of course, a good sociopath could bald-faced lie without any tells, but even the best gave something away if you knew what to look for. Could it be she *didn't* know?

"You may not know *him*, but he knows you," Jenna said.

Claudia's eyes flashed. "Is that so?"

"Definitely."

Claudia twisted her head and lowered her voice conspiratorially. "He tell you that, huh?"

"You know better than to think I'd be here if he'd come out and told me."

"Aha. So you *are* talking to him. Caught one, have you? Or just corresponding with one? He's *one*, right? That's why you're here."

Jenna collapsed back against the concrete wall and folded her arms. Then she unfolded them. Too guarded. "I guess it won't hurt to tell you that much."

"Big case?"

God. It was like a weird after-school moment, a parent asking her child how her day at school went. Only, they were in a psych ward, and her mother happened to be a murderer. Hell, all families had their little problems.

"Which one is it?" Claudia asked.

Jenna stared at her.

"Oh, don't look so surprised. You've got serial written all over your face. Missing body you need him to fess up to? A live one hidden somewhere? Come on. You don't know all his secrets, you're looking too hard. You need help. You came to me for a reason," Claudia said, almost panting. "Why don't you show me his picture? If I've met him—"

"You're about as likely to tell me as you are to inform the courts at the next hearing of your lucidity," Jenna replied.

"Maybe. But you're *here*. You think I'll tell you *something*. I don't know Isaac . . . Keaton, did you say? Nope. Nothing. But then . . ." Her voice trailed deliberately. She grinned.

"What?" Jenna said. Damn. She sounded like a petulant teenager.

"I guess I'm wondering why you *haven't* released his picture. Surely if it was a matter of utmost urgency, you'd be willing even for *me* to take a look. But he's under your hat. Why?"

"You said you don't know him, so it shouldn't make any difference," Jenna said.

Claudia looked down, tapped each of her toes in turn. She leveled her eyes with Jenna's and tilted her chin up. "And you believe me?"

"No," Jenna said. "That's the point. I don't."

"Your brother singing these days?" Claudia asked, tongue between her teeth like a snake.

Jenna bolted up from the wall. It was time to leave.

"Oh, come now, Jenna. Surely we're *past* all that, right? You came in to seek my *counsel*. We're practically pals!"

She couldn't help it. It was what Claudia wanted, and yet it seethed to the top and boiled through before she had a chance to stop it. "How dare you . . ."

"What was it, Jenna? You never did say. How did you know when no one else saw?" Claudia asked, eyes scanning straight through her, x-raying.

Funny. Isaac Keaton asked the same thing in the letter he sent.

"Wouldn't you love to know. You can figure out surveillance cameras and conning orderlies, but you have to live with that one mistake. One mistake, and believe me when I say this: you will never know it."

Jenna turned and stormed away. Stupid, coming here. Claudia knew nothing about compassion and help. Dangling a need in front of Claudia and expecting her help was something akin to scraping your knee on the ocean floor and not only expecting the shark swimming nearby to resist the urge to attack, but to offer you a Band-Aid.

"Of course I know who he is," Claudia said, monotone. "Not Keaton, mind. But I know you've caught a Gemini. Right?"

Jenna stopped cold. She turned around. "How do you figure?"

Claudia smirked again, then leaned straight into the glass with her forehead, no hands. "The walls have ears."

Pros, cons. Cons, pros. "Okay. Yes. We have."

"And he says he's met me, so I'll venture a guess he's the smarter of the two. Why no picture released yet? Come, come and tell your mother, Jenna," Claudia said. Forehead still against the glass, she winked. "After all, I'm on your side."

If Claudia knew him and had any way to communicate with him, telling her was a horrible idea. *Not* telling her, on the other hand, might *spur* her to communicate with him. Delicate balance. Still, one thought echoed harder in her head than any. *She thinks like he does.*

"The other is still at large. We need to find him and not spark him to go to ground if he thinks we're on to him."

Claudia pushed back from the glass with her palms, and for a minute, Jenna could see her oily fingerprints lingering there like they had on the knife that night so long ago. "You want my opinion?"

"Probably not. Shoot anyway," Jenna answered.

"From what I hear about those two, the second one wouldn't run if you 'spooked' him, so to speak," she said matter-of-factly.

Claudia wasn't a shrink. She had no basis on which to believe this, and probably knew little to nothing about the case. Still, Jenna couldn't help but be intrigued.

"What makes you say that?"

"Why do you suppose he does anything he's done, Jenna?"

"I don't know, Hannibal. You tell me."

Claudia crinkled her nose. "You flatter me. But surely you've been through a lot of, er, *schooling* to not know this one? Elementary."

Jenna shrugged. "I don't know. Rage. Revenge. Boredom."

"Try all of them, only *simpler*."

Jenna stared at the woman who'd killed husband after husband, and not for revenge or money. This woman had made her own child sick, and for one reason only. The chrome color of fame popped into her head.

"Attention," Jenna whispered

"Oh, very good, Jenna! A-plus!" Claudia said, clapping her hands, patronizing. "And what do we take from this little lesson?"

Claudia might have more ulterior motives here than a politician buying a puppy, especially if she *was* lying about knowing Isaac. He puts her up to setting off the ferry shooter just like he set off Thadius Grogan, and then bodies sizzle from here to Timbuktu. And yet no denying Claudia had a point.

"You think he'd be pissed he wasn't getting the credit?"

"Wouldn't you be? Go to all that work just to have What's-His-Name take your glory and your spotlight like every other time in your lowly, unnoticed life?"

"How do you know he was unnoticed?" Jenna prodded.

Claudia raised her eyebrows. "How do you know he wasn't?"

The scream Yancy described before the ferry shooter started firing, the subservient nature, hesitancy to shoot. All of it said he didn't get cold-blooded pleasure from the killing, but had his own reasons. The profile did suggest he wanted attention. Damn.

"Do it, Jenna. Make *him* come to *you*."

It seemed too easy, too wrapped in a bow. All kinds of things could go wrong, too.

"Why would you tell me this?" Jenna asked, even though she knew she wouldn't get a straight answer.

Claudia looked at her pinky nail, started to wiggle it at the joint. "If this Isaac Keaton does know me, he'd expect me not to tell you what I really think."

Then her mother lifted her eyes and looked straight into Jenna's. "And I *do* hate to do the expected."

On campus at Florida Calhan University, it wasn't hard to blend in. Cap on, jacket—he could be just any other professor who'd eaten too many donuts, heading to the dining hall for lunch. Why the cops didn't have men watching the campus for him, Thadius would never know. Then again, they didn't have any way to know he'd be here. Not yet anyway.

The kid who'd killed his Emily was a student, or had been at least. Thadius was sure of it from what Woody had described. Now, to find the MM Society.

He looked up at the building in front of him. No better place to ask someone to show a stranger around than the Christian Life Center. Those people had to be nice to you, right?

Thadius pushed through the creaky wooden doors. "Excuse me, miss. I'm looking for a kid I met at the coffee shop who said he'd give me a good deal on setting up my wireless network. He gave me his number, but I can't find it anywhere. He's in some club on campus, though. Hoping I can find him."

It was a crappy story at best, but he was under a lot of pressure. Waving a gun in this girl's face wasn't on his to-do list.

The redhead turned from where she was spraying Windex on a curio cabinet filled with faceless angel figurines. "Do you know his name?"

Lie. "Pete Something. Sommerton, I think."

She shook her head. "Don't know him, sorry."

Thadius fished in his pocket, pulled out the sketch Woody had drawn. "He had this on his shirt. Does that mean anything to you?"

The girl looked into Thadius's face, skeptical. Did she know? Had she seen him on the news?

Then she looked at the drawing, and the doubtful look faded.

"Oh, yeah. That's the Movie Making Society emblem. They're over in Baynor Hall. If you go down this road and turn right on Paine, it's the little brick building next to Shillings. That's where they have the meetings anyway. Not sure of the meeting schedule, but it's probably posted in the Student Center."

"Right. And which way is that?"

She gestured behind her. "Back up towards McDavid. White columns."

"Got it. Thanks," Thadius replied.

He turned and left the Christian Life Center. Hell if he was wasting his time with the Student Center. Somewhere around here had to have Wi-Fi.

Thirty minutes later, Thadius strolled into Grover, one of the coed dormitories on campus. After a while at the computer in the library across from the Christian Life Center, he'd found the meeting schedule for the Movie Making Society. It didn't meet again until next Monday. Luckily, he'd also found the name of the president of the club. A quick search of Hallie Majors's name on the campus web-site showed she was also a resident assistant in Grover, so the chances of her hanging around there were pretty good.

He smiled at the girl manning the front desk. Some old guy look-ing for a girl in her twenties was bound to look crazy, so his best hope was to appear like a worried father so she didn't call security before he got to ask question one.

"I'm trying to find Hallie Majors," he said, his expression wor-ried and confused.

The heavyset blonde quirked her head. "You've found her."

"Oh! Hi!" he stammered.

"Can I . . . help you?" she asked, suddenly wary.

"Yeah, yeah. I'm sorry. Didn't mean to . . . here," he said, laying the piece of paper out. "I'm looking for a guy who used to be part of your film society. Back in oh-seven, I guess it would've been."

Now he'd come to it, the part that wasn't explainable. Holding the girl hostage in the middle of a dorm wasn't an option, both because she had nothing to do with this *and* it was impractical. Should've thought this through better.

"This is kind of embarrassing to admit, but my daughter used to go here, and she dated this kid. He, uh. Well, my daughter is, um. She passed away recently. He, um, he has some of her things, and I was hoping to sort of find him and see if he has something that's of particular sentimental value. I, um, I don't know how to look him up at all, because she never brought him to meet us."

This sounded like bigger bullshit than he'd fed the girl in the Life Center.

"So, um, I don't have a name or anything, I just know they were involved in the club here," he finished. Hopefully Hallie would mis-take the frustrated tears stinging his eyes for true desperation to find the "artifact" he was looking for.

"Oh, man. I'm sorry to hear that. I doubt I can help any, though. I wasn't at school here then."

"Don't you all keep records of who was in the club way back when or something?" he fished.

She laughed. "We're *supposed* to have officers. A historian is *supposed* to do that. But you know how college is. Midterms, frat parties. Sometimes those things slip through the cracks. Our records are close to nil."

Thadius's chest deflated. What now?

She must've seen it on his face. "You know, you could try checking with Dr. Coppage. He teaches the history of film classes. I'm pretty sure he taught them to the velociraptors and woolly mammoths, too. Most people in the MM Society take his class at one point or another, even if they aren't filmmaking majors. He probably has better records than we do."

"Good thought! Any idea where I find him?"

She pointed out the window. "Right over there in Fine Arts. I was in his office an hour ago to pick up a makeup test for one of my friends who's sick. Room 201."

Thadius extended his hand, which Hallie shook in her meaty fist.

"Thanks a million, Hallie."

"No prob. Hope you find whoever you're looking for."

28

"You want me to *what*?" Hank asked when Jenna arrived back at the precinct building where Isaac Keaton was being held.

"Release Keaton's name, picture, everything we have. I don't even want the ferry shooter so much as breathed about."

"Jenna, the public will blow a gasket if they think we're not looking for the other Gemini."

"I know. But so will the ferry shooter."

Hank rubbed his head. "This is Claudia's influence?"

"I know, I know. Believe me, I don't like it any more than you do, but you have to admit the profile backs it up. We should've known without her," Jenna said.

"Let's forget for a second that for *me* the lucidity of this conversation is in question. It could backfire. Heck. Could *work*, but in the way that we end up with a severed head on our doorstep."

"Severed head, Hank? Seriously? The guy barely had the stomach to fire more than a few times when he had the means to take out a few dozen people. He's not severing any heads."

"Unless he was told to," Hank replied.

The theory said that the UNSUB might deviate from any and all plans if his buttons were pushed. No matter how much over the years Jenna had sold law enforcement officials on the "behavioral science" of profiling, the truth was, it was never exact. It was like a lot of other sciences: a start based on educated guesses.

"We don't have other cards to play, Ellis, and I have no doubt Keaton *has* told him to do *something*. We have no clue what it is, and I for one don't want to cool our heels and wait to find out. Let's roll the dice."

Hank flipped over a picture he'd been looking at of the fourth Gemini victim. Beth Abney had been shot twice in the neck at Rawlings Insurance Company's annual spring picnic in Delaware right after her boss had been killed by a single shot to the head. Her kids were two and six. Both boys.

"If you want to release it, I say we release it. Let's just make sure we've got a lot of people to answer tip lines, because the crazies are going to swarm like termites in a log cabin."

"Fine," Jenna replied.

She sat across the table from Hank while he talked to Saleda on the phone and instructed her to call a press conference. This was either a really good idea or a really bad one. No in between.

When he hung up, he said nothing. He continued flipping through the photos.

"Thanks," Jenna whispered.

He shook his head. "Don't thank me yet. This could be an exceptionally bad call."

Jenna wanted to look back through those files Irv had sent of the Sumpter Building workers. Isaac Keaton had to have worked at the psych hospital. It was the only way he could've met Claudia. If Jenna had a name, she could find out who Isaac was connected to in Denver, find out who he was connected to *everywhere*. Put away the ferry shooter, and put away the person who'd helped Isaac Keaton terrorize her family.

"Can I ask you something, Hank?"

"You just did."

Always the insufferable know-it-all. "A third question?"

Hank looked up from Rowen Lasder, victim number five. He and his twenty-year-old son had been shot having a drink at an outdoor pub. "Hit me."

Jenna swallowed hard. "Do you ever regret anything?"

Clearly not what he'd expected. The focus of the case melted from his eyes, and that deep-rooted thoughtfulness set in, the one once reserved for discussions about things like that breast cancer scare a while back. Most of the time it was easy to remember why she didn't want to raise Ayana with him, but when that face showed up, it was hard to imagine why she hadn't.

"You mean us?" Hank asked quietly.

The lump in Jenna's throat kept her from answering. She nodded. He did, too. "Yeah. Sometimes I do."

They stared across the table at each other, both obviously not knowing what to say. So much had happened between them, so much of it not fixable. And yet Jenna couldn't deny this man was part of her life, inseparable from the good or the bad.

The door at the side flew open.

"Irv found the MM emblem," Saleda said. "FCU. Movie Making Society."

She and Hank jumped from their chairs in tandem, as if powered by one brain.

"Let's go," Hank said.

Jenna would've thought with a technical analyst at their disposal that it would've been easier to find Hallie Majors, president of the MM Society. College students weren't always where they were supposed to be. According to another resident assistant in her dorm, Hallie had left duty early to pick up something at the health center.

Finally, after chasing the phantom Hallie Majors around campus for far longer than they should've had to, they found her at one of the dining halls. She played with her mashed potatoes while reading a tattered copy of *The Hobbit*. She matched the description, and had a tote bag with the MM emblem sewn on.

"Hallie?" Jenna said, pulling up a chair beside her.

The girl folded down the corner of the page she'd been reading. "Man, I'm popular today."

Jenna's introduction died on her lips. "What makes you say that?"

The girl squinted at Jenna, suspicious. "Who are you?"

Hank sat across from them. "I'm Special Agent Hank Ellis. This is Dr. Jenna Ramey. We're investigating a string of crimes, and—"

"Man, the weed is *not* mine. My roommate is always doing God-knows-what, and I have to live with her 'cause I can't afford the fees for a private room—"

"We're not here about anything like that," Jenna interrupted.

"Have you seen this man?" Hank asked, and he slid a small photo of Thadius they'd retrieved from his house over to her.

She chomped on a carrot stick. "Yeah, actually. He was here earlier. Said he was looking for his daughter's boyfriend or something. Is he a psycho? He seemed nice! I felt sorry for him."

"No, he's not a psycho," Jenna replied. "What'd you tell him?"

Hallie looked at the carrot on her fork, then set it down on her plate corner. She yanked out the holder from one of her pigtails.

"I told him we didn't keep records of old members, really. Said he could ask the film professor, Dr. Coppage."

"Where do we find him?"

Hank banged on Dr. Rutland Coppage's office door for the third time. "FBI! Open up!"

A woman's gray head poked out from the next office.

"FBI! Good grief, are you really? What in tarnation is going on?" the lady asked.

"Ma'am, we need to speak to Dr. Coppage as soon as possible. Can you tell us where he might be? In class?"

The bewildered woman shook her head. "Dr. Coppage left for the day. I passed him in the hallway coming back from my lecture."

One of two things had happened: either Dr. Coppage had already encountered Thadius Grogan on campus, or Thadius had yet to talk to the professor. If he came to see him during normal office hours tomorrow, they could have plants ready to intercept. Still, to Jenna, that seemed too easy. Garnet pulsed in Jenna's brain. The color of danger.

"We need to talk to Dr. Coppage immediately," Jenna said. "Do you have any idea how we can reach him?"

29

"Dr. Coppage, thanks for seeing me on such short notice," Thadius said as he stepped into Rutland Coppage's two-story Tudor on the cul-de-sac of Emory Place. He'd phoned Coppage's office and asked him for a meeting. He hadn't come on strong, because he wasn't sure this guy had met the man responsible for Emily's death. But this way, if he had to employ less than sociable means to get answers from the man, he'd be able.

"Oh, it's no problem, Mr. Gilmer. I try to help with these things when I can. I'm so sorry to hear of your daughter's passing, by the way," the elderly gentleman said as he closed the door behind Thadius and led him into the sitting room.

You didn't even know my daughter. "Thank you."

Dr. Coppage sat in an overstuffed chair across from the chaise he'd pointed Thadius to. The man crossed his legs. "How can I help?"

Thadius held out the envelope that contained the surveillance pictures. Coppage took the package and dumped the contents into his left hand, then spread the pictures out like a deck of cards.

"Your daughter's boyfriend, you said?" he asked, tilting his wire glasses up, down, and closer to him as he studied the photos.

"Mm-hm," Thadius assented, his chest tightening painfully. The excitement of finally doing something yielded to resigned, adrenaline-filled anxiety.

Dr. Coppage wobbled his head on top of his wrinkly neck. "Yes, yes. I think I do remember him."

If Thadius thought the adrenaline was coursing before, now it was like he'd been shot up with heroin. Heart racing, he leaned forward but didn't speak. *Let him talk on his own.*

"Yes, yes. I remember him very well. Film student, very passionate. Bright kid. Oh, what was his name? Always asked questions about the movies I showed. Particularly odd interests, he had. I was always amused by his dark side!"

Dr. Coppage chuckled, nostalgic, but Thadius's throat constricted. *Dark side.*

"How do you mean?" Thadius managed.

The professor leaned back now, relaxed some in his memories. "Oh, he asked lots of questions about the making of certain films and the tactics employed. Inquired if I thought the best way to get a reaction from actors portraying scientists in the Arctic would be to actually bring them to freezing temperatures, things like that. I showed one film he was interested in—old silent film called *The Passion of Joan of Arc.* He had a strong opinion that the fear the actress showed didn't seem real enough. Was curious how to make it more organic."

Thadius could hear his own heart in his ears, but mostly, he could feel the heartbeat of the SIG tucked safely inside his jacket, reminding him it was there, ready. This man had known that his daughter's murderer had a penchant for violence. He had to have known.

"Do you remember his name, sir?"

"Oh, what was it?" Coppage repeated, tossing his head from side to side as if to jar it loose. "I'm sure I know it. Hold on, now."

A beeping ripped the air, almost knocking Thadius out of his chair. Dr. Coppage rummaged through his pants pocket.

"Darned phone. Forgot to turn it off," he said. He jabbed the button to silence it and stuffed it back into his trousers.

A million questions sat on Thadius's tongue, every one of them impatient. He had to let the man think, but he wanted to know so much more, so many details of this kid's personality that had apparently charmed Dr. Coppage so much.

"Any papers he wrote that might jog the memory?" Thadius ventured.

"Hm," Coppage wondered out loud. "He checked out one of my films, come to think of it. I probably have a record somewhere in my office. Could probably get back to you tomorrow."

By tomorrow, the cops might still be far away from the MM Society, but if Woody had talked, told them everything they'd discussed, that was unlikely. Chances were greater than not that he *had* talked. That was the danger in leaving him alive.

"Which film?" Thadius blurted out, instinct.

"Good question! *The Bad Seed*, I think. We talked about the film in class. Interesting, that one. The film was written with three different endings, and the script for the actual one wasn't released until shooting. The original ending had the child survive, but the Motion Picture Code at the time stipulated that the perpetrator of a crime couldn't 'get away with it,' if you will. My, how things have changed. Don't see why it mattered, of course. That child got away with enough as it was. Come to think, that was why he wanted to borrow the film, I believe. Research for the fire scene."

Now Thadius's pulse thundered against his neck as if a live animal were trying to escape his arteries. "Fire scene?"

"Yes, yes. The film contains a rather gruesome scene where the child sets a cellar afire with the handyman inside in order to hide her crimes. Rather disturbing, that. S'pose she learned it from her mother. Earlier in the film, the woman finds evidence the child is guilty of a crime, and instead of turning her in, she instructs the girl to burn the evidence in the incinerator. Sad, the woman. S'pose there isn't much a parent won't do for their child, after all."

Thadius's hand came to rest on his leg on his right side, the same side where the gun was tucked inside his jacket. Emily's killer had all but done this! Emily's house, blown to pieces to cover his tracks. The film that pressed the idea into the bastard's skull, given to him by this ridiculous little man before him who thought the kid nothing but a harmless enthusiast.

Dr. Coppage snapped his fingers. "Waters! That was his name! Waters!"

30

Sebastian Waters hadn't been able to stop thinking about Zane since he saw her in the meeting in the hospital. He'd since been released from observation and sent home, which happened to be an apartment he and Isaac had set up in anticipation of him needing a home to go to when he left the hospital.

Now he sat on the threadbare orange velour sofa they'd bought at a thrift store and drank lukewarm tap water. Zane was a weird bird. The way she acted the cheerleader for that "Healing Celebration" she was volunteering for, you'd think she was a college kid promoting a sorority clambake instead of the girl with the speech impediment caused by half her face being a chargrilled deluxe.

But here he was, dwelling on her like she was a Brazilian supermodel, so much so he'd forgotten the *real* reason he should be thinking about her. Until now.

Luckily, she'd been more than willing to pass on her number to him. "We have to stick together," she'd said.

He needed to get on with it. Sebastian punched the numbers on the prepaid cell he'd bought at the local discount store and waited to hear her voice. Her awful, grueling voice.

"'lo?" The word sounded like half a greeting, what with the sucking sound her vowels made.

Sebastian cringed. He couldn't do this. Wasn't made for this.

He had to! He'd come way too far. This setup was perfect.

"Zane?"

"Sebastian? I didn't think I'd hear from you this soon!"

She knew his voice?

He regripped the phone. "Um, yeah. I wanted to talk to you about that City Walk event you mentioned the other day. I was wondering if I could, like, come with you to it."

A slurping noise. Maybe a gasp? "Oh, Sebastian! That'd be so wonderful! You'll love it. Music, games. It's the best. I'd love to meet you there!"

Sebastian stared at the dumbfounded look on his own face in the wall mirror across from the sofa, the one piece of decor in the place. No one had ever been so thrilled to hear from him in his life probably. Not even his own mom.

"Uh, okay. Right. Where should I meet you, you think?" he stumbled.

"Want to ride together? I have a parking pass. I don't drive—you know, I had trouble after I lost my eye—but if you can! Oh, man. This'll be so fun. I was going to walk around by myself all day."

Had she really just told him that? Tons of times in his life, he'd wanted to say things like that, but he'd never *actually* say them out loud. Heat crept up his neck, almost embarrassed for her.

Almost.

"Right, sure. I can drive us. Can I, uh, pick you up somewhere?"

No answer.

"Zane?" Sebastian said, afraid the call had been lost.

The shallow breathing gave away she was still on the line. "Pick me up at the hospital, will you? I'll be there that day volunteering."

Of *course* she volunteered at the hospital. She had time to do that in between saving an exotic species of barn owl and pulling babies from fires. And yet something about her hesitation sounded nervous. Self-conscious, even.

Sebastian thought of his father, of the day he'd torn apart Sebastian's room. He'd found Sebastian's stash of porn under the mattress.

His father's face was so glaring, accusing. Of course, he might not have gone so pale if they'd just been *Playboys*, but these weren't exactly Hugh Hefner's girls—or even boys. More like the kind of thing you'd find on the Cartoon Network, if it was rated for nudity and animals. From then on, Sebastian had been convinced every person who saw his father look at him could see the disappointment, knew the reason for the shame in his eyes.

If Zane didn't want to tell him about her living situation, who was he to ask?

"Okay, the hospital it is. What time?" Sebastian said, infusing his voice with a deliberate shot of confidence.

"Nine a.m.," she replied. Then, after another sucking noise, "Hey, Sebastian, are you sure you're up for this?"

Immediately, every muscle in his body seemed to stiffen. "What do you mean?"

"Don't get me wrong. I think it's great for you to be out and in the sunshine. It's only . . . it's a lot of people, and it's a crowd setting. I'm afraid it won't . . ." Her voice trailed off.

"I'll be okay," he said.

"Okay," she said. "Didn't mean to offend—"

"You didn't. See you Saturday at nine."

Sebastian clicked the phone off before she had a chance to say good-bye *or* to change her mind. This wasn't normal. None of it was.

He flipped on the little twelve-inch black-and-white TV he'd hooked up. Anything to drown out the misgivings.

"We've just been informed that authorities have revealed the identity of the man apprehended at the Enchanted Kingdom following the massacre there several days ago."

A picture of Isaac popped up on the screen. His mug shot.

"Authorities say Isaac Keaton is responsible for most of the deaths involved in the tragedy, even going so far as to call him the mastermind of the theme park shootings. When questioned about the other shooter at the park, the FBI remains stoic but seemingly unworried. Special Agent Saleda Ovarez says that while federal investigators are still searching for the other perpetrator in the park and other Gemini killings, they are skeptical that the second shooter is much of a danger now that Keaton is behind bars."

That was it. No mention of him, other than to say he wasn't a problem. None.

What was *wrong* with him? This is what they wanted! What *he* wanted!

Even so, the anger bubbled underneath. *Not again.*

They'd all know soon. He'd go to the City Walk event with Zane and be one step closer. He'd pick her up Saturday.

Now he just had to find a car.

31

Jenna walked under the crime scene tape at Rutland Coppage's house. When he hadn't answered their call, her gut said bad news, but she hoped he was busy taking a frozen pizza out of the oven or playing tennis. No such luck.

The local cops had arrived in the suburbs before them to find Coppage shot twice in the head. Ballistics weren't back yet, but the wounds were consistent with the gun used on the pawn shop owner.

"Man. What'd he do that the firework guy didn't?" Saleda asked as they entered the blood-spattered living room.

Coppage's body lay facedown in a pool of his own gore, dead limbs glued to his sides where his hands had stuck underneath him when he'd fallen. Two shots from behind, but one would've done. And that wasn't all. The same red Jenna had seen that first day at Thadius's home reading his journal burned bright in her mind. Rage.

"Oh, he did something, all right," Jenna muttered.

Angles of the blood spray, angles of the holes in the back of the professor's head. He hadn't been surprised. He'd been *kneeling*.

Hank had spotted it, too. "Execution requires a strong reaction. It's almost cold. Weird for a crime of passion. Coppage has some connection to Emily Grogan's murder. Has to have. But what prompted the style?"

Jenna glanced around the room. A nanny-cam would be too convenient. "Crime and punishment maybe? Working his way up to shooting him, maybe even trying to talk himself out of it? I think the better question is, what does it mean for where he's going next?"

"I thought you said we shouldn't be focused on Grogan," Hank answered, following.

Jenna's eyes fell on the DVD collection on the black-lacquered shelf across the room. Classics, most of them. Laurence Olivier in *Sleuth*, several Hitchcock films. Sherlock Holmes. Jungle green flashed in. She'd read loads of classic suspense novels in college, and this was the color she often envisioned when a piece of a masterful plot of one jumped out at her. Had been ever since she read *The Most Dangerous Game*.

She'd been so sure Grogan was a distraction, but after visiting Claudia, she wasn't so positive. Sure, Keaton planted Grogan, but Keaton did everything deliberately. He planned it all. Up to now, she'd figured Grogan was a *deliberate* distraction.

"I *don't* think we should focus on Grogan. Not directly anyway. But Keaton has laid things so perfectly, mailing me packages from God-knows-where. I can't help but think it'd be the sort of thing he'd do."

"*What* would be the sort of thing he'd do?" Saleda asked.

"Grogan is a *piece*. Keaton set it up for Grogan to be a piece of something bigger. It's his style."

"Are you sure you're not confusing that with *Claudia's* style?"

The bite in Hank's voice stung Jenna like a slap to the face. He expected her to step in, support his investigation, but he'd never once supported her about her theories on Claudia.

She spun around to face him, face flushed. "No. I'm not."

Then she turned her back on him and walked toward the door. Time to stop acting like a five-year-old and be an investigator. Personal crap couldn't get in the way.

"Where are you *going*, Jenna? We have to walk the rest of the scene. You know that," Hank scolded.

"No, Hank. *You* have to walk the rest of the scene. I'm a consult, remember? You called in a favor. I know he said he'd only talk to me, but you shouldn't confuse that with me being *required* to do anything."

Her face burned, and she could feel Hank on her heels as she hopped into the unlocked SUV and turned the key in the ignition. She jammed it in reverse.

Through the window, she could hear him yell, "That's an FBI vehicle, Ms. Not on Duty! How are we supposed to get back?"

She twisted the wheel and put it in drive with one hand while she hit the window down button with the other.

"Call a cab."

Forty minutes later, Jenna pulled into a parking spot at Bentley Memorial Park. She leaned her head against the steering wheel for a long minute before getting out. What the hell was she doing here?

Hunch maybe? Stupidity? But something about Yancy felt untapped, for sure. He knew things about this case even if he didn't realize it. She could pursue this case in her off time as much as she wanted as long as she didn't interfere with the investigation, right?

Besides, he was interesting, and not because he was a shooting victim. In fact, everything about his personality had *nothing* to do with him as a victim.

Yancy Vogul sat on a stone bench inside the park, little Oboe parked at his feet.

"Sorry I couldn't meet you at the coffee shop you suggested, but you know, the old ball and chain," he said, cocking his head toward the dog.

Jenna smiled at the stocky pooch. Its eyes followed a line of ants about three feet away. "Believe me, I understand. I have one not always allowed into fine establishments, too."

"Schnauzer?"

"Two-year-old."

Yancy's mouth sagged comically. "Nice breed, if you can get 'em. I gotta tell you, Doc, I haven't had any miraculous feats of my Herculean memory since we talked last. So to what do I owe the pleasure?"

If only she knew. How to tell someone you thought they could unlock something you yourself had no keys to?

"I have a problem," she said.

"Heh. You and me both, but mine involves awkward moments of that debate I have between needing to go to the bathroom and whether or not I'm too lazy to put on my foot."

Jokes about the foot a lot. Draws attention to it to deflect any awkward, silent scrutiny. All in all, not bad.

"Are you always in this good of a mood, or do you save it for the weeks when you're shot at?"

He grinned. "Another freak genetic mutation. Really, what's your problem? Lay it on me. One-footed people are great listeners."

"Because they can't run away?"

"Damn! You're fast. I need a head start. Okay. I'm ready."

He was part of the investigation. Technically, she shouldn't tell him anything she hadn't discussed with Hank. Then again, as she'd just screamed at Hank out of a moving vehicle, she wasn't *technically* part of the official investigation squad, either.

"Can I trust you?" she asked before she could stop herself. As if you could come out and ask someone that and expect a straight answer.

"Won't tell a soul. Scout's honor. But careful of the dachshund. He's German," Yancy replied, popping the dog's collar to pull him back from making a move toward the ants.

Jenna didn't say anything. She'd called him out here on some whim to try to pry some unknown information out of him, and now she was about to spill case details to him for no apparent reason. What was it about him that made her want to?

Then the reason popped in. It pissed her off even more. Color.

Yancy leaned forward into her vision, caught her eye. "Hey. You okay? Look, no pressure, but no worries, either. I'm good at keeping my mouth shut, and I'm good at problems. You called me for a reason, didn't you?"

His voice was eager, but not in the looky-loo way she'd seen with so many "interested" people in cases over the years. He sounded more like a curious kid who'd missed his shot at the big time and finally had his chance.

Details, but not too many.

"All right. The guy? The Mr. America you picked out from the lineup? He found another guy. A killer."

"The ferry shooter?" Yancy asked.

Jenna didn't answer but kept talking. "He knew things about this guy to have pushed some really specific buttons. At first I thought it was something unimportant, but the more I think about it, the more I think it's the key to figuring things out."

"Makes sense," Yancy said, nodding along.

That's because you think it's the ferry shooter.

"So what buttons are we talking here? Blackmail? Mommy issues?"

"Suffice it to say he has a past with violent crimes," Jenna answered. Then, as an afterthought, "As a victim."

"Oh, I see. Fancy."

"Yep."

Yancy unscrewed the cap of his bottled water and took a swig, then poured some in front of Oboe, who lapped at the stream as it fell to the grass. "So the problem is, where'd he find the guy? I take it the guy's not famous like . . . well . . . *you*."

The hair on Jenna's neck prickled. "No. But I thought along those lines. Tried to get records of articles he might've shown up in, stuff like that. Checking local victim support groups, among other things."

"No dice?"

"Not so far. I'm stuck. Plain stuck, and the ferry shooter won't catch himself."

"Geez. I don't know, Doc. I might have to think about that one for a few. Articles would have been my best guess, too, though I don't know if *I'd* have thought of it if you hadn't told me. Wanna walk?"

Jenna followed Yancy's lead, and together they ambled across the stone bridge. Yancy's metal foot made a strange *clank* on the walkway. Timed with Oboe's toenails, they blended into a weird sort of a song.

"How'd you get wrapped up in all this anyway? I thought you weren't with the Bureau anymore," he said.

Better not to tell him about Isaac's request yet. Not because he couldn't handle it, really. More like she couldn't handle him knowing.

Jenna's phone buzzed in her pocket, but she ignored it. Five minutes of fresh air and some radio silence never killed anyone, especially since most of the phone calls she picked up these days involved already dead folks.

"Remember that two-year-old I mentioned? Her father *hasn't* left the Feds."

"Oh, I see, I see. Exes. Can't live with 'em, then you're away from 'em, and they still drag you into all kinds of hell. Yours brings you into a serial murder investigation, mine manages to get me shot . . ."

Jenna stopped walking. "You didn't say she was an ex. The girl you were at the theme park to see?"

Yancy stopped a yard in front of her and turned, calculating. "And you didn't introduce yourself as Dr. Jenna Ramey, S.A. Ellis's former spouse, either."

"Who said he was a former spouse?"

A smile fought past the poker face Yancy wore. "Touché."

Almost on cue, Jenna's phone buzzed again. This time she pulled it out. Hank. Again.

"Sorry. Have to take it, no matter how much I don't want to," she mumbled. After all, she did steal his vehicle. At some point, she'd have to return it. If he was calling to tell her to come pick him up, though, he could forget it. "I'm busy, Hank. Don't you have other lackeys you can call?"

"I need to talk to you. Where are you?"

Her stomach dropped. His voice wasn't authoritative or angry, not even as a commanding officer who'd just been left at a crime scene. No, this was a personal voice. Serious.

"What is it? Is it Ayana?" Jenna asked, her little girl's face forming in her mind, the package from Isaac still fresh. What had he done now?

"No. It's not that. It's—just tell me where you are. I'm coming to get you."

"I can drive, Hank," she said.

"No. Just tell me where you are," he repeated.

Had he ever not answered her like this before? He was usually so damned blunt it was ugly. Fear licked her insides. She rattled off the park address and agreed to wait for him. Then she hung up.

"What was that? Are you okay?" Yancy asked.

Jenna jumped at his hand on her shoulder.

"Sorry," he said, yanking it away. "What's up?"

She shook her head. "Don't know. Hank is coming to pick me up here. Wouldn't tell me why. He sounded . . . I don't know what."

Jenna sank to the lip of the wall they were next to, scenario after scenario chasing each other around her mind. The case, their daughter. He said it wasn't Ayana, but if not, what would make him sound so worried?

"Want me to wait with you?" Yancy asked, taking a seat beside her.

Oboe leapt after a butterfly flitting by. His front legs stubbed the ground on the way down, and he yelped.

"Yeah," she said. "That'd be nice."

Explaining Yancy's presence to Hank would be fun, but right now the last thing she wanted to do was sit here and wait for Hank without distraction from all the horrible ideas forming.

Yancy leaned down to examine Oboe's legs, which had nary a scrape. "You're all right, you big sissy. You sure do talk a big talk for such a whiny dude." Then, as if he could read her thoughts, Yancy winked. "I'll tell Hank we ran into each other here."

The BAU had so many years profiling liars, and this guy planned to bald-face it to the best of them. "That'd be a big coincidence."

"Maybe so, but the *truth* is, he'll never know. He might *suspect*, but believing and knowing aren't the same thing. And like I said, I'm good at keeping secrets."

Yancy swallowed hard as he watched S.A. Hank Ellis striding toward them, confusion on the agent's face melting into frustration at the sight of Yancy with his ex. Yancy's neck burned. He knew he shouldn't be here. Just because he'd trained as an investigator once upon a time didn't make him one. *What are you doing here, smart guy? Playing with the big boys?*

Hank reached them, seeming to battle with himself for what to say or do. In the end he must've decided whatever brought him was more pressing than Jenna sitting in the park with one of the Gemini shooters' victims.

"Mr. Vogul, good to see you again. Excuse us, will you?"

Jenna put her hand up to her ex. "He's fine, Hank. Just tell me what's going on."

Awkward. Ellis glanced back and forth from Yancy to Jenna, and Yancy averted his eyes to study Oboe's progress scratching his left ear.

"Jenna, we need to talk in private—"

"Please, Hank."

A loud sigh. "Fine. It's about Claudia. She's . . . Jenna, they're releasing her from the Sumpter Building."

At this, Yancy's head jerked up. "What?" he and Jenna echoed at the same time.

"How is that *possible?* She's charged with murder and attempted murder!"

Yancy knew that technically, Jenna's mother had only been officially charged with the attempted murder of Jenna's brother and father and the murder of one of the previous husbands. The books all talked about how the other murders were suspected, but no prosecutor would pursue them for lack of evidence. By the time anyone suspected Claudia of wrongdoing, the bodies couldn't be investigated for the signs of foul play needed to convict her.

"The charges were dropped, Jenna," Hank said.

All the blood drained from Jenna's face. "They can't have been! What judge in his right mind—"

Hank cut in. "She fired her old lawyer. New lawyer presented evidence to a judge today that her old lawyer and the DA have been living together in secrecy for several years."

"What?"

Jenna's voice sounded high, shrill. Panicked.

"New lawyer argued the prosecutor has been conspiring to violate Claudia's right to a speedy trial, and the judge agreed. Hesitantly, but he agreed."

Jenna's knees buckled, and Yancy saw it coming and caught her under the armpits just in time to keep her tailbone from striking the stone wall. Oboe clawed at the pavement against the tightening leash.

"Wait a minute, boy," Yancy said out of the corner of his mouth as he eased Jenna to a seat on the wall. "But isn't she insane? I mean, they can't just let her go free, right?"

Jenna shook her head. When she spoke again, her voice was

eerily quiet compared to the piercing notes of before. "Not insane. Not legally. She was found *not competent* to stand trial. It's not the same as being found guilty by reason of insanity."

"But she's schizophrenic, right?"

"Legally, she's not even arachnophobic," Ellis replied.

Jenna sat forward and let her head droop between her knees. She breathed deeply and blew the breaths out of her mouth.

Yancy watched her back curve up and flatten with the gasps, and he clenched his fists at his sides to resist the urge to touch her shoulder. God. So this was what helplessness felt like.

"When?" Jenna whispered.

Now Hank sat on the wall next to her. "Tomorrow morning."

Jenna lifted her head. She looked like she would vomit at any second, but she didn't. Instead, she reached down and scratched Oboe on the scruff of his neck.

"Tomorrow. Great."

"Jenna, they'll watch her. You better believe I'll have her on surveillance twenty-four/seven from the moment she's out. We'll work on this constantly if we have to. We'll find evidence. There are new techniques, new ways to solve cold cases. She'll be held accountable."

By the look on her face, Yancy could tell she didn't believe him. Somebody really needed to tell this guy that if he wanted to preach about life ending up fair, he was playing to the wrong crowd.

Who could possibly decide to release that woman? Everyone knew she was guilty as—"Hey, Jenna. Wait a minute."

Jenna stared at Yancy through glassy eyes, questioning.

"The Gemini mastermind found this guy with buttons to push. What about this violent crime you said was in his past? What about the jurors on the case?"

Jenna squinted like she was trying to read writing that was far away. Then she blinked rapidly. "There wasn't a trial. No jury to look at."

"Oh." *Too good to be true. Stupid. Trying to bring up the other case at a time like this.*

Yancy caught the look Hank shot at Jenna, but luckily she didn't see it. She was too busy staring at the ground.

"Has Claudia's release been on the news?" she asked.

"Not yet," Ellis answered.

She hung her head again. "I have to tell Dad. Charley."

"I'll come with you," Ellis said.

Yancy swallowed his urge to say he would come with her, as well. Talk about insane. Her mother wasn't the only one.

Jenna patted Oboe once more. "Thanks for the talk."

Yancy watched the two walk away, their heads together as they talked furiously in hushed tones. Just like when he was lying on the pavement at the theme park. Couldn't help anyone.

He'd think of a way. Had to. It had to be a lot easier to help other people than to help yourself, right?

Okay, smart guy. Time to do some research.

"Awesome. I'll see you later," Charley said.

He couldn't be serious.

"Did you hear me?" Jenna asked.

Her brother picked up his guitar case and hoisted the strap on his shoulder. "Yes. Claudia released, technicality, out tomorrow. Good deal. I'm sure she'll have found wedded bliss and be fixing her new hubs a special arsenic burrito in no time. Ten-four."

"And you're just going out? At a time like this?"

Sure, he'd been little when everything happened, but she knew he remembered. He'd had nightmares throughout his teen years. Probably still did.

"What am I supposed to do, Rain Man? Huddle in here and board up the windows? Wait for the Big Bad Wolf to come calling? I think not. I have better shit to do."

He turned the doorknob, but Jenna grabbed his shoulder. "Charley, we need to figure out—"

"Figure out nothing. We can't change it, Jenna. We try, and all we'll get is a foot in the ass and a pat on the back. Trust me. It's better we don't waste our time. Easier to let it wash by than fight it, lose, *then* have it wash by. See you in the morning."

Charley kissed her forehead and squeezed her middle, then he was gone. She stared after him for a long minute. Sometimes it seemed like maybe it was easier to be the stabbed, unconscious one. At least then you didn't have to see other people stabbed.

Jenna wandered into the kitchen. Her father was pacing nervously, and a pot of broth boiled over on the stove, the liquid sizzling on the burner. Jenna turned down the heat.

"I'm surprised the floor hasn't given way yet with the path you've worn in it over the years. One day the people under us will have surprise guests for dinner," she said.

Vern muttered something indiscernible. Then, "Hank gone?"

"You thought he'd stick around after you screamed in his face how he ought to have to take Claudia's place in the asylum? Yeah, I'd say he felt like he'd overstayed his welcome."

Vern wrung his hands. "Didn't mean to. Just antsy."

Jenna's eyes followed him as he moved. Her poor dad. He'd really loved Claudia. For that matter, she had, too. Maybe. Could you love someone if you never really knew them?

"It'll be okay, Dad. She won't hurt you," she whispered.

He turned to pace the way he'd come, but she stood in his way. He hugged her tight, tighter than he had in years. She squeezed him back.

"It's not me I'm worried for, Jenn. I worry for you."

She pulled back from him. His eyes were tired. Sad. "For me?"

Her dad extricated himself from her embrace and padded the floor again. "I know you hate it when people say things like this, because I know you can take care of yourself. Different than me."

"We're not that different, Dad. I don't pretend to know what it was like for you, but we all lived through it, didn't we?"

"No," he said, flat.

"Excuse me?"

Vern glanced at the baby monitor, which had crackled. Ayana murmured a few sounds, but then it went quiet again.

"Jenn, you lived with it longer than we did. You knew alone for so long."

The shame in his voice brought tears to her eyes. "Dad, you knew it, too. You just weren't a stupid kid who thought she could play detective. You loved her, so you gave her the benefit of the doubt."

His back to her again. He walked slowly back toward the hallway. "You care more about *truth*. And you weren't *that* young."

"You couldn't have stopped her, you know," Jenna said.

Vern halted in his tracks. "Why not? You did."

"Dad, I'm so sorry. I wasn't trying to say you were weak—"

Vern waved her off, but this time, he walked straight into the hall. "Never mind. I know you weren't trying to say anything like that. I guess I just think it enough on my own." He sighed heavily, and his shoulders drooped, the weight of the moment seeming to manifest on top of them. "I'm going to get some shut-eye, hm? Maybe you should do the same. Take the baby monitor with you, okay?"

"I will," Jenna muttered. Lecture from her ex on talking to a potential witness, brother gone, and now Dad upset, too. She was on a roll tonight.

Jenna lifted the pot her dad had started like he often did when he was disturbed. She poured out the forgotten broth. She set it on the counter, which was still coated lightly with the fingerprint dust the evidence clerks used to dust the package.

The station had gotten almost a hundred calls in the past few hours since the spot on Keaton aired, all from people claiming to be Isaac Keaton's math teacher, childhood best friend, astronaut buddy. None of them sounded even remotely like the ferry shooter was taking the bait. If only Jenna could figure out where Keaton had found Thadius Grogan, maybe she'd come across where he got the ferry shooter, too.

Too bad Yancy's thought about the jury had been off base. If Emily Grogan's killer had been put on trial, the trial and its circumstances would've been a nice place to start looking for connections to Thadius.

Then again, it wouldn't have mattered. If they'd caught Emily's murderer, he'd most likely have gotten off on a technicality like Claudia. Hell, the exact same thing would probably happen with Isaac Keaton. They'd caught him with the gun in his hand, but Jenna had handed the cops all the information they'd needed to convict Claudia, and *she'd* managed to get out. Isaac came from the same mold. He'd met her mother somewhere. All his schemes of letters and packages were mailed after he went to jail. It wouldn't surprise Jenna if Isaac had planted the damned evidence to get Claudia off.

Again, the purple of narcissism colored Jenna's thoughts. Isaac thought he was so smart, brilliant enough to place every piece of a puzzle. But that was a weakness. He didn't think he could slip.

Isaac would not be another Claudia.

She grabbed the baby monitor and tiptoed past Ayana's room. She tapped on Vern's open door ever so lightly. "Dad? You have to take this. I have to go back out."

Vern rubbed his eyes from where he was reclining on his bed, though she could tell he hadn't been asleep yet. "Tonight?"

"Yeah. Can't wait."

She set the monitor on his bedside table and, before he had a chance to ask questions, left the room. Isaac Keaton might know exactly what he was doing, but she did, too. Games and tricks and even Claudia out of Sumpter didn't change that. She could outsmart them.

One of them anyway.

34

"So we meet again, Dr. Ramey," Isaac said when he smelled the pretty young psychiatrist at his back. He'd looked forward to her coming back. To the next move.

She sighed heavily as she sat down in the chair outside the infirmary. He couldn't see her, but he could tell what she was doing on instinct by her breathing.

"You know, I could live my whole life without knowing you had picked up my scent," she replied.

Smart girl.

They'd put him in the infirmary, he knew, because it was the best place for criminals like him—the famous ones. Safe from the general prison population, better for watching for suicidal tendencies, as if he'd do such a thing. Still, it was a nice touch, having his own cell. Better for sure than the grime of some cell mate he might loathe.

The infirmary was also great for his purposes.

He turned around to see Jenna Ramey, hair slicked back in a wet ponytail, navy blue blazer over jeans. Classy.

Irresistible.

"Do tell me. Did Ayana enjoy my present?"

She tensed for the slightest, most delicious second. Then her chest relaxed, her nostrils flared.

"I thought we had a deal about that," she said.

Ah. They had, hadn't they? Though he'd never exactly applied that logic to *him*. Sure, he'd offered her an agreement. That didn't mean he ever planned to keep it. Oh, well.

"So we did. To what do I owe the pleasure?"

"I want to talk about your partner. The ferry shooter."

Isaac couldn't suppress the grin that spread over his face. "Fairy shooter! That's a good name! Though I suspect he'd not be thrilled with it on the whole."

"Why do you say that?" Jenna Ramey asked.

"No specific reason."

"Not because the two of you had some type of homoerotic relationship?"

"Are you insane?"

"No. Just observant. He's submissive, you're dominant. You're a male partnership. It's not that huge of a leap."

"And how do you know it's a male partnership, Dr. Ramey? The magic crayon box in your brain tell you that?"

She crossed her legs and leaned back. "No. You told me a second ago he was a he."

"I'll be damned."

"If he's a male submissive, I'd say that he's somewhat reclusive, avoidant. Doesn't make friends easily. Doesn't trust easily. That probably means you met him in an unthreatening environment before you flattered him into trusting you. That personality type lends itself to overreacting in the most harmless of situations, which probably means you had plenty to feel like you could control him by, be sure he wouldn't go off his rocker when the big stuff happened. Sexual relationships are powerful mental motivators, strong in emotional attachments. Maybe knowing you had that authority over his psyche helped you feel secure in sharing your jaunts with him. Did it?"

Isaac's heart thumped hard against his ribs, and he let his breathing accelerate. She wanted to play games, huh? He could play games.

Keep this clean. "You think you're so clever, don't you? Think you'll tease me with ideas, maybe boil something out of me if you get me angry enough. It's not going to work." Now his voice had reached fever pitch, the fast slur of someone angry enough to have a stroke. "Just because that little queer has a preoccupation with me doesn't mean I had to have one with him. Fucker *lives* in Dreamland!"

Jenna Ramey stood up, smoothed her gray slacks. "Thanks, Isaac. You've been a joy, as always."

Then she walked away.

Go, go, good Doctor. Enjoy the hunt.

Thadius wasn't about to try to buy a plane ticket under the circumstances, so he now drove a rented U-Haul through Asheville, North Carolina. It hadn't taken long to pull up Facebook and search the school networks for the years surrounding Emily's graduation year, scroll down to the letter W. Only one Waters was listed. Sebastian Waters.

Sure enough, the profile picture looked like the one in the printout he'd gotten from Howie Dumas from the pawn shop video. Among Sebastian Waters's other networks was Cramer-Corrington High School, class of 2003. Asheville it was.

As he eased into a parking spot at Cramer-Corrington High, he still couldn't believe he made it. The entire drive, he'd expected to see blue lights in his rearview mirror, to be pulled over. He'd taken precautions to make sure no one traced the U-Haul, but the police resources outmatched his.

Then again, they hadn't found Sebastian Waters, had they?

Thadius hopped out of the truck and knocked on the walkway door of the room in front of him to his right. Mrs. Eckley told him her room would be directly ahead of her black 4Runner's parking space.

The door opened to reveal a woman a bit younger than he'd expected. The teacher he'd talked to on the phone sounded at *least* seventy. This woman couldn't be a day over forty. Either that or she knew the city's finest plastic surgeon.

"Mr. Gilmer," she said, offering a hand. "So nice to see you. Come in, come in."

People. So full of crap. He should be used to this by now, but somehow it never ceased to amaze. Mrs. Eckley greeted "Mr. Gilmer," the father of her well-remembered former student, Emily Gilmer. Too bad Emily Gilmer wasn't a student *or* a real person.

"I was so sorry to hear of Emily's situation. She's such a sweet girl," the teacher lied.

"Thank you," Thadius said. He squeezed into one of the wooden desks.

Mrs. Eckley propped her hip against her own desk. "I'm surprised she got involved with someone like Sebastian personally."

"Why do you say that?" Thadius inquired. Never mind that he'd told her Emily Gilmer ran away to elope with Sebastian Waters. Never mind he hadn't mentioned he'd found out that Sebastian Waters had killed his daughter.

Mrs. Eckley shifted on her feet, suddenly uncomfortable. "I shouldn't have said that . . ."

"Please. That's why I came to you. You taught psychology to both of them. I don't know Sebastian that well. If I knew more about him, I might know where to look for them, or at the very least find some kind of peace that she's okay with him," Thadius said.

She crossed one ankle over the other. Still seeming to weigh her words, she said, "It's not that he was a bad kid. Not really. It's just . . . his emotions took him over. Anger. He was *very* smart. Don't get me wrong. He was a gifted kid. But he was negative and moody. Those moods manifested in outbursts when things were going badly for him, you know?"

Strange how she remembered so much about this "not bad kid" and couldn't even remember that she'd never taught an Emily Gilmer.

"He sticks in my brain for that reason, actually," Mrs. Eckley said like she was reading his thoughts. "Sebastian and I argued once over a test grade he received. I confronted him about his study habits, because his grades had dropped off. He'd gotten the first F I'd ever known him to have, and I served as the Beta Club sponsor at the time. Because he was a Beta Club member, his other teachers had to notify me about his grades slipping. The organization requires us to keep records of everyone in the honor society. So when I started to hear from his other teachers, too, I asked him about it. I have to say, I wasn't prepared for his reaction."

Thadius stared at her, unable to speak. *Violent? Cold? Unfeeling? What?*

"I'm sorry. I'm probably not helping your peace of mind," Mrs. Eckley said.

"No, no. I'm just trying to understand," Thadius said, waving his hand. "How did he react?"

"Well, he cried. Hard. More depressive than anything I'd seen up to that point from him. He wanted extra help. Asked me if I could find a tutor for his algebra class. Yet when I found someone to tutor him, he screamed at me. Told me I was nosy, that he didn't need anything from me or anyone, to back off. I wrote up the incident for the principal, because I thought we needed to inform his parents. Nothing came of it."

"Ever? No more incidents?" Thadius asked.

"Not until *the* incident," she replied. She squirmed again, stood straight up.

"What do you mean?"

Mrs. Eckley cocked her head. "Obviously you know about what happened before Emily's graduation."

Thadius quirked his head. *Think!*

"Apparently, I haven't been informed of everything."

"Oh, my. Sebastian didn't graduate. As a private prep school, we hold our students to high standards, as you well know. The police arrested Sebastian the Friday before graduation on Monday. He was expelled."

E ven though Jenna picked Yancy up in the wee hours of the morning, he looked like he hadn't been asleep. Either that or his good looks were immune to fatigue.

"So why are we doing this again?" Yancy asked as he climbed into Jenna's Blazer.

She'd thought and thought about her interview with Isaac, but she kept coming back to a bright burnt orange that popped in her mind when Isaac made a certain statement. It had long been the color that showed up when her instinct said something was a lie.

That color was the reason Jenna and Yancy were now on their way to meet up with the ex-girlfriend he'd been going to see at the theme park when he was shot. What she was looking for was anybody's guess. Either way, she wasn't leaving until she found it.

"I'm ninety-nine percent sure Keaton tried to send me on some kind of tangent. I need to make sure I'm right."

Yancy groaned. "If you're gonna make me call up my ex at four a.m. to ask if she can return us to the scene of my own shooting, the least you can do is to tell me why I'm doing it."

Probably anything to keep from stalking the governor in the middle of the night to convince him to stop Claudia's release. "I went back to interview Keaton tonight on a whim, and he said something. It wasn't even what he said so much as how he said it. Or what he *did* when he said it maybe. He was trying to play me."

"You mean like a tell? I thought body language stuff didn't apply to psychopaths. They can lie to you and look you in the eye, right?"

Unfortunately. "Yes, that's true, but it wasn't that. Not quite. Some of it I chalk up to the way sociopaths talk in general. You ask a question, they don't give a direct answer. They talk around things."

"What did he *say* exactly?" Yancy asked, impatient.

Might as well tell him. He was helping, after all.

"I thought I'd rattle his cage some, see if I could shake something loose. He called me on it, said it wouldn't work. But it did. Sort of. When I said that he and the ferry shooter probably had a homoerotic relationship, he got upset. Might've been for show. Either way, he told me the guy lived in dreamland. It didn't escape me, of course, that Dreamland is the part of the theme park where the castle is. The part Isaac shot from."

"Okay. So he gave you a lead."

"No. I don't think he did. I . . . I think he's too smart for that. I believe he *meant* for me to think it was a lead."

Yancy fiddled with the clip of his seat belt. "You said he did something to make you assume this?"

"Like I said, Isaac didn't answer me directly when I asked if the sexual relationship made him feel secure in sharing his kills with the ferry shooter. He didn't deny it, but he spun out that random comment," Jenna explained.

"And from that you got that he wants you to think you have a lead?"

Explaining this one was going to be precious. "Well, those things combined with the color."

Yancy smirked. "So I get to hear about the famous colors?"

"Not if you call them 'the famous colors,' " Jenna replied.

Yancy lifted his hands in a gesture of surrender. "Okay, okay. I'm sorry. What about the color?"

Jenna swallowed hard. The damn things could be so helpful, but they could also be such a pain in the ass. "When he said the words, something about the way he was talking made fuchsia pop into my mind. It's a color I tend to get when I'm interviewing a subject who's being disingenuous."

"So he was lying?"

If someone didn't have the synesthesia phenomenon, delineating the particulars was like describing sight to a person who had been blind since birth. They might be able to fathom it, but they didn't have any experiences to connect the thoughts.

"Not lying," Jenna said. "Lying is more of an orange color. Kind of brown. The fuchsia is more of . . . intentionally misleading."

Yancy stared at her from the passenger's seat. "That doesn't make any sense."

A dry chuckle escaped Jenna's throat. "That's the great thing about grapheme-color synesthesia. It doesn't have rules. That's why I have to put together the colors with other things I know. They help me narrow down the location on a map, but I have to find the exact coordinates myself."

"Sounds tedious," Yancy replied.

"You don't know the half of it."

"Okay, so not denying something, making a random comment, and fuchsia. Is that all?" he asked.

"No. A few more things. He emphasized the word 'lives.' Usually, a liar emphasizing a word indicates a true statement."

"Are you saying the ferry shooter lives in Dreamland? What does that mean? He doesn't pitch a tent every night and camp out."

"No, not literally, but I think Isaac wanted me to chase that thought. He wants me to think the ferry shooter escaped because the guy works at the theme park."

"But you think that's not true? I thought you said fuchsia didn't mean a lie," Yancy said.

"It doesn't. But Isaac himself is a liar. That's why the fuchsia tells me something. If it was straight up burnt orange like a lie, I wouldn't be overthinking his statement at all. But the fuchsia—he's not lying, but he's not telling the truth, either."

"Isaac is that self-aware? That he knows to emphasize words to make you think a lie is true?" Yancy asked.

"I doubt it. That's what's bugging me. My gut says he lapsed into that speech pattern because that part of the statement *is* true. I just don't think he'd give me that huge of a lead that easy."

"We're talking double meanings now?" Yancy asked.

Jenna nodded. "Yes, but I don't have a clue how to prove it or what the hell the other meaning could've been."

Theme parks might close at night, but they apparently weren't empty. The employee lot Yancy's ex-girlfriend directed them to was packed, and they had trouble finding a spot.

Finally they squeezed the Blazer into a space between two industrial vans and hopped out. Jenna followed Yancy toward a slim girl with coppery ribbons streaking throughout her lengthy banana-blond hair.

"I'm so glad you're okay!" the girl whined. She pulled him into a tight hug.

Something angry bubbled inside Jenna's chest. The girl hadn't been worried enough to visit Yancy in the hospital when he was *shot*. He'd told Jenna as much.

"Oh, yeah. No permanent damage done. I might need years of therapy to get over this, but lucky for me, I've already got some under my belt." Yancy returned the chick's hug as halfheartedly as a middle-schooler on a first date.

The ex-girlfriend pulled back from him and slapped his arm playfully. "Yancy! You do not!"

Gag.

"Who's this?" the girl asked, catching a glimpse of Jenna.

As if Yancy hadn't told her about Jenna when he called. *Wow.*

"This is Dr. Jenna Ramey. She's part of the FBI investigation," Yancy answered. "Jenna, this is Phoebe."

Jenna offered a hand. "Nice to meet you, Phoebe."

Phoebe returned the shake like a queen offering her hand to a gentleman to kiss. "Ditto. Yancy says you need some information about workers."

So he did tell you I was coming. "I'm trying to find out if a certain person worked here . . ."

Jenna's voice died away. Telling Yancy about the case was one thing, but this girl seemed a few Cheerios away from a full box. Trust-inspiring, she wasn't.

"This lot isn't easy to find if you don't know where to look. Are there other places like that for workers only?" Yancy cut in.

Phoebe twisted her hair off her neck and fanned herself with her hand. Then she released her locks to cascade down her neck again. "Sure. Lots of them. Which ones do you want to know about?"

"All of them," Yancy said.

"Sure. Come on. I'll give you the grand tour."

Phoebe swooped her arm to hook Yancy's elbow with hers and dragged him alongside her. Jenna trailed behind them.

Through the park gates, they first stopped at the employee locker room, which wasn't very interesting, especially if the ferry shooter *didn't* work there. Yancy asked Phoebe to move on, and next, they toured the cafeteria and the costume department. Also unremarkable.

However, when Phoebe led them down a flight of stairs into a fluorescent-lit area about fifteen feet wide, Jenna's ears perked up. Underground crew passages.

"So most of the cast members get around down here. It's less crowded, easier to move fast than trying to weave through tourists taking pictures of snotty-nosed kids. Cooler, too. Sometimes we have to walk the park if we're in costume and on duty, but if not, we can take these," Phoebe explained as they wandered the tunnel.

"Are there surveillance cameras down here?" Jenna asked.

"Good question," Phoebe said.

If the ferry shooter *did* know about the crew passages, they were a prime way to leave the fray and exit on, say, the other side of the park to throw suspicion. Jenna made a mental note to check on the surveillance cameras with Irv once she was back aboveground and in cell range.

"Does the Enchanted Kingdom keep *any* records from these tunnels? Like an ID card you have to swipe to use them, or can anyone get in?"

"Now that you mention it, anyone can technically get in, I guess. They can't *leave*, but they could get in," Phoebe answered.

"What do you mean? They have to swipe a card to come out in a different place in the park?" Yancy prodded.

Phoebe changed direction and motioned for them to follow. In a little while, they came to an alcove off the main tunnel labeled SOUTH EXIT.

"You can come out of any of the crew passages still *in* the park without a pass. However, if you leave *the park* in the passages, you have to scan your thumbprint. That way on-the-clock employees can't sneak out early without someone knowing. Otherwise they'd have no clue. There's way too many of us for them to keep track of at a given time. But the outside gates won't open without a thumbprint scan."

Excitement rose in Jenna's stomach. In other words, if the employee bull Isaac implied was true, the ferry shooter had to have scanned his thumbprint to exit. All of the employees who were still in the park after the shooting had checked out. It was the only way he could be an employee and have gotten away.

Jenna looked to Phoebe. "Where's your HR department?"

37

As they journeyed across the park, Jenna marveled at how a place that had been a crime scene only days ago could now look like no one had died there. Groups of maintenance workers filled the park, conducting routine test runs of all the rides and attractions. Cleanup crews swept and placed new trash bags in bins. The FBI had fought to keep the park closed a few days longer, but even a governmental investigation agency couldn't compete with one of the biggest corporations in the country or their even bigger law team.

Phoebe led them up a set of metal stairs to a brick building off the beaten path. She knocked on a door. "I doubt the HR manager's here this early."

Nevertheless, a voice came from the other side. "Enter."

Phoebe shrugged and pushed the door open. Jenna followed her inside the dingy room, Yancy on her heels. Hank was going to kill her for this.

Inside, a woman younger than Phoebe sat at a card table, laptop at her fingertips. For a place that spent millions on everything the public saw, the desks left something to be desired.

"Hi. I'm Dr. Jenna Ramey. I'm working with the FBI task force regarding the shootings."

"Oh, not again! Haven't I answered enough questions? I thought working here was supposed to be relaxing and fun. Now I'm questioned by the FBI every ten and a half seconds. I've given you guys every record I have! That's why I'm here at this butt-crack-of-dawn hour. Reprinting my paper records. I told you all I'd give you every computer file printout on earth, but could you wait? No! You had to have the ones in my *cabinet*. It's not enough that I'm trying to run a staff of hundreds here. Good grief!"

"I'm so sorry to bother you, Miss—"

"Wyche. Tori Wyche. But apparently *you* don't have the records, since you don't know who I am. You need copies, too? Want the fresh batch I just printed for my files?"

The FBI might need to work on its people skills. "No, Miss Wyche. I really *don't* mean to bother you. I'm *not* actually an FBI agent. I'm a consultant, a forensic psychiatrist. I need five minutes of your time."

The brunette pushed back from her table, and her rolling chair scooted a few feet with the force. She folded her arms, the chair teetering as she leaned back. "What's five more?"

"Thank you," Jenna said.

She glanced around for a chair to sit in, but there was none. Instead she dropped to her knees at the folding table and pulled out the paper she'd sketched on in the tunnel. The only time the ferry shooter had to escape was between when the shooting started and thirty minutes later when police locked down the entire park. During that half hour only a certain number of access points existed that the shooter could've reached from the ferry bridge. He couldn't get to the outer parks without taking the ferry itself or the monorail.

Jenna snapped her pen from where it was clipped to her pants and circled the spots in question, then passed the paper to Tori Wyche.

"I know you've already given the cops your records of everyone who entered that morning, but did anyone leave through these access points in the crew passageways between nine thirty-three and ten forty-five the morning of the shootings?"

"The *crew* passageways? But—"

"Can you access those records?" Jenna asked before Tori could protest. The girl already looked panicked at what Jenna was implying.

"I . . . sure," she said, her eyes wide.

Tori's feet pedaled the carpet until her chair was back to the folding table, and she pecked a few keys on her laptop. Several clicks later, the girl shook her head. "No. No one left through those passages until well after the park was out of lockdown."

When they'd said good-bye to Tori Wyche and Phoebe, the Blazer's clock registered 6:40 a.m. Jenna hadn't slept in over twenty-four hours, and all she really wanted to do was go home, take a long, hot shower, and sleep for about ten days. But no sleep for her yet. She still had a few chores to do, the least of which was dropping in to visit the DA.

As soon as they were in with the doors shut, Yancy blew out a heavy breath. "You were right. He's not an employee."

"Nope, but now I have to figure out what he *did* mean if the Dreamland reference wasn't theme park–related. His speech pattern said truth there. I just know it. Dreamland *has* to have a double meaning," Jenna said, distracted. As much as the burnt orange of Isaac's lying clashing with the fuchsia that screamed misleading bugged her, other things tugged at her attention. Her eyes flitted toward the clock, then from the clock to the road again. She jerked the steering wheel hard to the left to keep them from running off the right shoulder.

"You turn into a pumpkin at seven or something? Can't be vampire, because the sun already came up."

"Oh, I forgot I need to take you home!" Jenna blurted out.

"No worries. I've got nowhere to be for a while. Oboe sleeps like a log until at least nine on a normal day, and that's when I *don't* take him out at four a.m. I can tag along wherever," Yancy replied.

"No, no. I'll take you home. I just forgot." Still, Jenna couldn't help the way her eyes slipped toward the clock again. The hours ticked down to Claudia's release, and she hadn't done a thing. Distracting herself from doing something stupid in the middle of the night was one thing, but ignoring that the person who'd tried to kill her father and brother would be released was a different story in daylight.

"Oh, come on. Where do you have to be?"

What was it about this guy inspiring confidences?

"Claudia. I was planning to go by the DA's and see if I can do anything about her," Jenna whispered.

"Ah," he replied. "I *better* go with you then. I hear murdering the DA comes with heavy time."

A stiff smile stretched her lips. Coming from anyone else, she might've thought that joke in poor taste, given the circumstances, but Yancy had no filter.

"You gonna keep the engine running just in case?" she asked.

"Engine running, trunk popped. You'll have to get over the border somehow."

38

The sun peeked through the bathroom window, and the stem of Lyra's wineglass slipped from her fingers. The shatter sounded far away. Her eyes trailed downward over her naked breasts, her legs under the water where all of the bubbles had long melted into nothing.

Blood? No. Red wine mingled with the suds. How many glasses had she had? Lyra blinked and tried to focus, but all she saw were the tiny shards of glass that sparkled throughout like little stars in a watery sky. This feeling never would get easier, no matter how many times she had it. Never.

Oh, dear brother.

She glanced at the biggest piece of glass. It would be effortless to slide it into her flesh, rip open her arteries. Lie here forever, no one to stop it. Isaac didn't care. He'd done this. Left her. Knew she'd find out at some point he hadn't told her everything.

Lyra flipped the glass over with her right hand into her left, closed her palm over it. For her, it could all end right here.

No! That's why she couldn't. They'd never understand him without her.

Isaac didn't know better. It was the only explanation. He did everything he'd done because he believed he had to. Without her, he'd have no one to explain for him, help him. He'd be stuck.

When Lyra was five, Isaac had walked her through the church's tiny graveyard at the end of the road. Lyra had been scared, wanted to go back home, but Isaac took her by the hand. His hand had been so warm, bigger than hers. Safe.

"You see that, Lye?" he asked when they reached a smooth, black stone in the back corner of the resting place.

She looked down at where her brother held her fingers between them, then back up at the stone. She knew they were letters on the stone, but she didn't know them well enough yet to tell what they spelled out.

"That's where Mom is," Isaac said.

The stone didn't look like Mom. Just a rock. "How?"

"Under the rock. She's buried here. It's what they do with dead people. Bury them."

Now Lyra shifted in the tub, and the water sluiced up the sides and splashed onto the bare tile. She'd known what dead meant even then. Not breathing anymore. Not alive. She'd been told about it ever since she could remember, after all. Her mother died giving birth to her. How could someone forget *that*?

Isaac squeezed her hand. "Don't worry, Lye. No matter what anyone else thinks, I know it wasn't your fault. No one should make you feel different. I'll always make sure you feel safe."

Lyra stared down at the rock. Earlier in the day, Isaac had told her that Daddy was getting married again because he was lonely, that he wanted a girl in the house who didn't kill Mom.

Tears surged to her eyes. Daddy hated her for what she'd done. She hadn't meant to, but she had anyway.

Isaac moved in front of the stone and kneeled in front of Lyra, his eyes

burning into hers. "You have to promise me you know I think it wasn't your
fault, Lye. Promise promise?"

She sniffed, wiped her nose. "Promise promise."

The travel dates matched, of course. She'd read back in her
journal to find the times Isaac was on business trips, compared them
with the dates of the Gemini killings. It was all real.

Somehow, deep down, she'd always known it would be.

She kicked the gold faucet hard. For once, why couldn't he make
her life easier?

Her toe started to swell instantly, but the alcohol had numbed her
so much she barely felt it. Maybe she wished she did.

Everything was so blurry. So exhausting. Fixing things for him,
making sure he wasn't in trouble. Was she that ungrateful? Wasn't
that what he'd always done for her? Wasn't this how all the ways she
took care of him started?

*At age eight, Lyra trudged up the road alone, save the plastic grocery
sacks she carried. The creepy fence to the graveyard squeaked. If only Isaac
was with her . . .*

*She couldn't worry about that now. Too much work to be done, all for
her brother's sake. Lyra knelt beside the black gravestone and began to paw
at the ground with her hands. Don't think about what you might see.*

*Still, the entire time she scooped earth away from where Mom was bur-
ied, she shook. At any second, she was sure she'd see a skeleton like the ones
in the haunted house at Halloween.*

*At last she managed a big enough hole. She held her breath as she untied
the grocery bags. If only she could've dug a bigger hole, she'd have just put
them in, too, but she couldn't go any farther.*

*The white kitten lay limp in the bottom of the bags in the exact position
in which she'd found him. Lyra reached under the bag, lifted him, and
dumped him into the hole.*

"I'm sorry, Snoogles," Lyra whispered. Then she covered him with dirt.

Lyra plunged her hand into the water, pulled the drain plug, and watched the liquid swirl away. She didn't bother to move. There was nothing she could do. Not yet.

When she arrived home that day so many years ago, her father looked at the dirt under her nails in disapproval, asked what she'd been doing. She'd fibbed about making mud burritos. He told her to take a bath, which she did gratefully. Anything to wash the kitten from her hands.

Lyra had known when she'd found the kitten that Isaac had done it, though she never was sure how she knew. She'd never told him what she'd done, and he'd never asked. Dad had looked for Snoogles for a few days, but in the end everyone agreed he'd run away. She'd cried, and Dad had thought it was because she missed Snoogles.

Now she leaned her head back onto the edge of the bathtub and closed her eyes. Maybe she'd sleep here awhile. Only a nap, until she knew how to fix things this time.

39

Visiting the DA's home in Winport might be the craziest thing Jenna had ever allowed herself to do, and on a Saturday morning no less. She knew better than anyone that if you wanted sympathy from authority figures involved in criminal cases, the last place you should show up is their home. And yet here she was on the front stoop, banging on Tad Ulschafer's door.

Tad opened his porch door in gym shorts. His T-shirt with cutoff sleeves and lengthy hair parted down the middle made him look like a strange cross between an art gallery manager and a personal trainer rather than a district attorney.

"Jenna?" he said through the screen.

"Yeah, I'm sorry to bother you," she stammered.

Tad's eyes cut to the Blazer, where Yancy waited in the passenger's seat, then back to her. He shook his head.

The look on his face mingled with the violet pity Jenna's mind conjured made her stomach sink. He knew why she was here.

"I can't do anything, Jenna. We've been friends a long time. I know how awful this must be for you, but it is what it is. I filed everything I could, called every judge I knew. It's not possible."

Jenna could hear her voice shake as she laughed an odd, foreign laugh. "She killed four people!"

Tad opened the screen and stepped outside.

"The state only charged her with *one* murder, Jenna. You know that, and you know why," he said calmly.

"Well, charge her with the others!"

Jenna wasn't making a case, and she knew it. Still, falling off a cliff had this funny way of making you flail as you fell, even if it helped nothing.

"You know I would if I thought *anything* would stick, Jenna. We didn't charge her with the others because we couldn't. Not enough evidence. We couldn't exhume one of the bodies because the injunctions held it up, and another was cremated. You know good and well trace evidence of arsenic poisoning can't come from ashes!"

"What about Lowman?" Jenna asked.

Tad shook his long, greasy hair out of his face. "Neil Lowman was first. Claudia hadn't figured out her game then. We have *nothing* to tie her to Lowman's death other than our Spidey sense."

"That, and a bottle of nitroglycerin pills."

"Jenna, the man had a heart condition. The nitroglycerin makes our case *worse*."

Charley's face flashed in.

So white. She had to run for help, but leaving him meant she might never see him again . . .

Jenna glared back at Tad, pleading with him to see her terror, how much she needed him to *do* something.

"Charge her with something else, then. Anything," Jenna said.

"Go home, Jenna. Get some rest," he whispered.

The sympathy in his voice made her want to run into the street and pray a semi happened along this humble suburban road. How in the hell had she gotten here?

"Yeah. Home."

"You're quiet." Yancy's voice pinged Jenna from the fog that was her head. She hadn't even realized they were on his street.

She eased the Blazer into park. "Long night."

"Long forty-eight hours is more like it, right?"

"Something like that," she conceded. Seventy-two hours? She couldn't remember anymore.

Yancy hopped out, but he kept the door open. "Come in. I know they say it's five o'clock somewhere, but even nonalcoholics have a Bloody Mary at breakfast, yeah?"

She shook her head. So much to do, so many things to figure out. She needed to check on her family, somehow decipher Isaac Keaton's Dreamland bull, and find a magical link from Isaac Keaton to Thadius Grogan. No time for a cozy breakfast break.

Yancy climbed back in, turned the keys, and took them out of the ignition. "Come on. Even rock stars need breakfast. I make killer pancakes."

Jenna groaned and climbed out of the Blazer. "That's the second bad murderer joke you've cracked today, you know."

"What can I say? Mad social skills."

Oboe's nails scratched the door from the inside. So much for that whole sleeping until nine thing.

"Back, back, back, back," Yancy said, shoveling the dachshund away from the door with his metal foot as he entered.

Jenna followed him inside into the kitchen, where she leaned against the counter and watched him retrieve glasses, tomato juice, and Worcestershire sauce. He plucked ingredients from cabinets, finally pulling down the vodka from the cabinet above the refrigerator.

They didn't say much while he made the drinks. Despite all the information crammed in her mind, Jenna couldn't help but be impressed with his mixing knowledge.

"You used to be a bartender?" she asked.

He swirled her drink in her glass, checking its consistency, then held it out to her. "Nah. Dated one."

"Classy," she replied. "So what *do* you do exactly?"

"I'm a graphic designer. Companies pay me to build their websites."

"You get to work from home?" Jenna asked.

"Yeah, most of the time. Good work if you can get it."

Jenna sat on his couch and stirred the drink with her finger. She should be doing a lot more to fight Claudia's release than sitting here drinking an early-morning cocktail.

"In a perfect world, someone like your mother would be in the pen for the long haul, huh?" Yancy said as he took a seat next to her.

He was so uninhibited. Most people tiptoed around all Claudia-related subjects. He had no problem spitting out whatever he thought. Part of her wanted to lash out, and yet the other part was almost relaxed by it.

"In an *ideal* world she'd be in the electric chair," Jenna replied.

He nodded. "Well, that, too. Shame about the other bodies. Seems like it should be easier to have them tested."

"You'd think. But the one family put up a huge fight. Religious reasons. Never mind that their dad's killer is walking free, so long as they don't disrupt his ascension into heaven."

"God *is* really picky about technicalities, huh?" Yancy said.

"Then Neil Lowman can't be used, and Logan Brady is in an urn on the mantle. Bam. Done deal."

An unnaturally loud voice filled the room. "Hey, Yance, you gonna make it for the raid tonight?"

"Oh, crap," Yancy said, jumping up. He moved to his computer, where he held down his tab key. "Hey, Buddy. Can't chat right now. Trying to wine and dine a hot chick. Catch you later, 'kay?"

Yancy winked at Jenna.

"Hot chick? She have a big rack? You sonofa—"

Yancy double-clicked his mouse, and the computer fell silent. "Uh, sorry about that. I'm in the a.f.k. room now."

"A.f.k.?"

"Ah, yeah. Nerd alert. Away from keys. No one bothers me there unless it's a dire emergency."

Jenna choked on her sip of Bloody Mary. "Dire emergency? What kind of emergencies can there be in the computer gaming world? Don't tell me you're really into all that stuff."

Yancy sat back down, slurped some of his drink. "You'd be surprised how much losing a foot can affect your soccer game."

"Oh, geez. I didn't mean—"

"Just kidding, just kidding. I was a nerd before the elevator crushed my leg, don't worry. It's actually kinda nice being able to joke with someone about that. Most people go all sympathetic on me when I crack foot jokes. You take them in stride."

"No pun intended?" Jenna asked.

"Pun *entirely* intended. See what I mean?"

It was true. Even Hank, who knew everything Jenna had been through, was horrible at taking Jenna's sarcasm about her past lightly. Refreshing, talking without a barrier. "Yeah, I do see what you mean. You make one poison joke at a dinner party when you're Claudia Ramey's daughter, and suddenly everyone at the table looks like they're about to puke."

"Are you sure it wasn't the gazpacho?"

Jenna snorted. "You've read too much. Korbin Dale didn't really eat poisoned gazpacho. She put it in his morning coffee."

"Oh, bummer! That was a good one."

Jenna stared into the drink Yancy had made. She'd watched him put each ingredient into it, not realizing at the time she'd been monitoring it the way she had everything someone had cooked for her since she was thirteen. For the longest time she wouldn't eat anything unless she poured it straight from a can or sealed container herself.

"It was the same for my dad, we think."

"They took him to the hospital, right? Is that how you ended up telling the police what you knew?"

Her head spun now, and not from the drink. The knife flashed in, the bloody handprints.

Jenna followed the trail of handprints to the front door, but then they veered off to the left, up the stairs. She had to find Charley. Save him.

"Dad was in the hospital, yeah. But no, I wasn't ready to tell a soul what I knew. I didn't think anyone would believe me. That was when she found my journal."

Jenna tiptoed through the hallway, opened the bathroom door. Charley lay on the tile in front of the commode, half-collapsed against the wall. Red covered his front. Jenna could hear her mother's voice calling her. She had to decide right then.

Jenna slammed her glass toward the edge of the coffee table right before she dropped it, but Yancy caught it in one deft arm movement. He set it down, then pushed her hands away and helped her sit back.

"Whoa, there. Steady."

"I'm sorry. I try hard not to think about it too much for that reason," she said.

Yancy shook his head. "No, no. It's okay. Things like that sneak up on you. Believe me, I know."

His forehead creased with worry, and his lips parted as he stared at her. He seemed to be waiting to make sure of something, but she couldn't tell what. Then he leaned forward.

A second too late, her mind flashed the crimson that should've warned her this was coming. Her brain screamed no, but her head tilted back, eyes closed. God, she was so ready for this. It'd been too long. His breath came closer, the Bloody Mary still lingering there.

"Hey, Yance! I know you're busy wooing your early-morning boo-tay call, but if you want that BH-91, get your ass on. We're ready to go to sleep!"

Jenna's eyes flew open, and Yancy's weight that had been pressing in sprung away from her. For a long second, they stared at each other, frozen in the moment.

He leapt up and crossed toward the computer. "Jesus!"

The couch cushion Jenna was on sprung back to shape from where his hands had braced him on either side. She propped up on her elbows. "You've gotta be kidding me."

"No!" he said. "It's not what you think. I need to show you something . . ."

His fingers flew over the keyboard. Some kind of map popped up on the screen, though it wasn't of a country Jenna had ever seen before. The graphic in the corner said, LAND OF VALOR. Some kind of video game map.

"Yancy, I get this is a big deal to you, but seriously, I don't understand it. I don't know that I really *want* to understand it. I mean—"

"No, no, no! Stop and listen to me for a minute. BH-91. It's a . . ."

His voice trailed off, and he scrolled down the screen, then clicked the map to zoom in, mumbling. "Come on."

He clicked another button, and a new map came up. "BH is a bounty hunter quest. Ninety-one is the level you have to get to in order to play it."

Man, she had really misjudged this guy. "So?"

Yancy spun in his chair to face her, saw her confusion. "Um, okay. Imagine a big monster in a video game, and if you kill it, you can gather a bunch of cool loot. Every big boss guy is in his own land within this big land."

"I follow," Jenna answered, eyes following his hand as he gestured at the screen.

"BH-91 is one I've been trying to . . . well, you have to have a certain number of people to go do this, and . . ."

"And you don't want to let it pass just because I'm here. I get it," Jenna said, trying to hold in the eye roll until he turned his back.

"No! Stop putting words in my mouth!"

The anger in his voice took her by surprise. He'd been so laid back this whole time. *What the . . .*

"Okay, okay. I'm listening," Jenna said.

"BH-91 is here," Yancy said, clicking the zoom on his screen. "I hadn't thought of it until now! I had no reason to . . ."

"No reason to what?"

"I know where your dude found the ferry shooter! It's Dreamland! I know what it is. It's right here!"

Yancy jabbed his pointer finger at the screen. "It's BH-91!"

The City Walk bustled with people in bright colors, and the water shimmered in the early sun. Instruments everywhere, the smell of hamburgers lingering in the air. Boats puttered by on the lake, and yet Sebastian's eyes kept coming back to Zane.

She smiled as they walked, occasionally introducing him to people. Sometimes they'd stop and listen to a band she noticed or take a picture of a random sight she thought pretty. From where he stood beside her, the burned side of her face wasn't visible. Her profile looked perfect, whole.

"Oh, let's do that!" she said, pointing.

In front of them stretched a giant piece of butcher paper the length of the stone wall in front of the café. A rainbow of handprints covered it, and the sign above read, HANDLING IT RIGHT.

He had yet to broach the subject he was supposed to be here for, but maybe this would be the time. "Sure."

Zane practically skipped over to the wall and plunged her hand into a pan of purple paint. She pressed her hand to the paper, excited.

"Come on, Sebastian! You next!"

Sebastian wandered over, looked into the variety of paints available. All of them seemed too vivid for his handprint.

He felt Zane's eyes on him as she waited to see his choice, but somehow, right now, his shoes were filled with concrete. Nothing was the right decision. Isaac had prepped him and coached him, but he'd said nothing about handprints and paint colors. This was so wrong.

"Here. Let's pick together," Zane said.

She grabbed his hand and dragged him forward. Her hand felt something like the newt he'd had as a teenager: wet and dry, cool and hot all at the same time.

Zane knelt in front of one of the pans, and her downward pressure on his hand caused Sebastian to follow. She grinned, her lip curling and catching at the burnt spot. At this angle, his gaze fell from her lip to her neck, which was milky and smooth. He'd not seen it before.

Ponytail. Her hair didn't drape her face like the first time they'd met but, rather, was knotted in a ponytail.

She pulled his hand to one of the tins and pressed it into the paint. Her fingers looked so small on top of his.

"Now wall," she instructed.

Sebastian obediently rose and stepped to a blank spot on the canvas. He smashed his hand onto the paper and pulled it away fast. The paint left a messy glob there, and he couldn't see the individual ridges and patterns of his fingerprints the way he could in Zane's. But still, it was there.

They both accepted the paper towels offered to them by volunteers, but even after Sebastian wiped his fingers, the paint stuck as a reminder. Purple, like Zane's.

She bought a corn dog at a stand, and he ordered nachos. Then they ambled onto the bridge that stretched across the lake, and Zane plopped down on a bench.

"What a great day for it, huh?" Zane mused.

Now or never.

"Yeah. Glad we got it in while it's not too hot. Weather says this week will be a scorcher."

Zane chomped on her corn dog. Through a full mouth, she mumbled, "Tell me about it!"

She laughed and chewed, holding up one finger to signal she'd finish her thought once she'd swallowed. "I have another event this week outside, and I'm *dreading* it. It's supposed to get up to ninety."

Sebastian breathed out. The bridge reminded him of the ferry bridge, of looking down at all of those people. Moving targets. In games, they seemed to go down so easily, but in real life, the blood was different. Not only were these real people instead of elves and dwarves and sorcerers, but he didn't have his clan all there to back him. That, and screams had accompanied the falling bodies.

"Oh yeah?" he asked.

"Yup. I'm kind of organizing that one, so it'll be a little different from this," she said.

So many thoughts whirred through his head about instructions he'd been given, things he was supposed to accomplish, but right now, there was only Zane in front of him. Weirdly enough, her burnt face in this light almost looked comfortable to him.

"You need any more volunteers?"

41

I f Hank might kill Jenna for going to the theme park without him, he'd definitely be ready to shoot her on sight for bringing Yancy with her to the precinct. Either way, she didn't have time to get the information she needed from Yancy and *then* drive over and grill Isaac Keaton. A serial murderer remained at large, and time might mean lives. Technically, the ferry shooter had been "silent" as far as they knew, but he wouldn't stay that way forever. Keaton was too much of a planner for that. You had to look no farther than Thadius Grogan to know it. If Keaton planned for the ferry shooter to escape, they had to bank that there was a reason for it.

One thing at a time. Jenna had called Irv and had him check Land of Valor for an account under Isaac Keaton's name. Of course, nothing. Irv was pulling up lists of all the Isaacs and Keatons registered, but in a game with millions of users, those lists weren't as limiting as she wished.

Back to square one: Isaac himself.

On the way to interview him, Yancy gave her a crash course about Land of Valor. So far, she'd learned that MMORPG stood for

Massively Multiplayer Online Role-Playing Game, and that the world of MMORPGs proved far more complex than most people thought. The stereotype of role-players as loners was only about half-true in that even if they were somewhat antisocial in real life, they were anything but online.

"You have social circles, kind of. Clans. A bunch of people who know each other and work together online," Yancy explained.

"How many people in a clan?" Jenna asked, expecting him to answer ten or twenty.

"A hundred, maybe? Give or take."

"Whoa! Really?"

"Yep. Most of the adults communicate with each other using voice software like I have. They know each other's usernames, but most of the time they know real names, too. And each other's voices, and probably some about their real lives."

"Scary," Jenna ventured, though she filed away the coral her mind registered: the shade reserved for all things goofy and lacka-daisical. Most of these guys were probably harmless.

"Ah, yeah, well. Most guys don't think about other players being something to be freaked out about. If someone pisses you off or weirds you out, you can block 'em."

Spoken like a guy who doesn't deal with sociopaths for a living.

"Can anyone sign up? What stops you from creating an account as a different person?" Jenna asked.

Yancy laughed. "Apparently nothing, if this Isaac dude is any indication. For most people, it's a payment issue. You have to use a credit card or debit card. I guess you *could* get a prepaid gift card or something, but most people end up using a credit card at some point or other. Christmas presents don't last forever."

"Hm. Unless you're Isaac and you want to make sure your infor-mation isn't recorded."

"Exactly."

Jenna sighed. "Not that it would matter. We wouldn't find his name anyway since we don't know what his real name *is*. For all we know, he *did* pay with a credit card."

"How are you planning to get this out of him? From what you've told me, you can't simply tell him you figured out where he found the ferry shooter and expect him to dish the details."

"Leave that to me, okay?" she said, the purple that had occasionally flashed in during her conversations with Isaac doing so again. While it had given her the idea for what she was about to attempt, and exploiting this bastard's pretentious side was going to be fun, the facts had to come first. "Tell me more about the tribes or clans or whatever. You're familiar with each other's voices, names, anything else?"

Yancy took a minute to think. "I guess you'd know some about looks. Characters pass each other, work together, run into each other within the game."

"Looks?"

"Yeah, they're customizable. You can even buy certain wardrobes. Knew a guy once who had a character who wore assless chaps. Wasn't in *my* clan, though."

"So you know *other* clans, too?" Jenna asked, perking up.

"You know some people within other clans, sure. Depends on who you hang around with and who they know, too. Kind of like real life, I guess, only you can take breaks from it and don't have to put up with people you hate. Like I said, block button."

Other people in other clans could be acquainted. So technically, Yancy could've run into Isaac Keaton's character and never have had any idea it was him. Given the number of players worldwide, the odds were astronomical, but the sheer fact that the *possibility* existed seemed insane.

"Wait a minute. If you recognize people in other clans, are there players *everyone* knows? Like famous people?"

"Kim Kardashian, they ain't, but yeah. Everyone is ranked in the game, all the way down to the billionty-first character created. But most people know the names of or recognize the really high-ranked players. Top one hundred, maybe most of the top thousand, if they're into it enough. I know what you're thinking, but I doubt this Isaac guy is ranked. Seems like he's too busy with other craziness to invest as much time into it as you have to put in to be that level. Don't mean to toot my own horn, but *I'm* pretty good, and I'm nowhere *near* that high."

"But if Isaac was in that Dreamland place where you were, he'd have to be at least that good, right? You said it depended on your level," Jenna countered.

"Good point. Also means the ferry shooter would have to be at least that good, too. Since when do serial killers use Internet games to find shooting partners?"

The answer was easy enough as to why Isaac was using the method he was, though this particular method itself was new to Jenna. "It isn't uncommon for sociopaths to have places they frequent to find targets to use as followers. They love to be surrounded by people who virtually worship them, and they have ways of sidling up to certain individuals, making them feel valued, and essentially, hooking them in to do their bidding. It's what Isaac Keaton would've been doing with the ferry shooter. They do it wherever they find is their comfort zone to find these particular types they're looking for, usually where they can appear an expert of some sort. Some sociopaths hunt in religious circles, some in arts clubs. I guess Keaton just happens to use the Internet gaming world."

They'd reached the precinct, and Jenna parked the Blazer. "Whatever you do in here, just keep the things we've talked about on the down low until I'm done, got it?"

"You're the expert."

Inside, Jenna walked straight past the desk without explaining

42

Being found in the park with a man's ex was awkward enough. Now, as Yancy stood next to S.A. Hank Ellis in the police precinct—*Hank's* territory—that discomfort took on a whole new meaning. "Come here often?" didn't seem appropriate.

Instead, Yancy turned his focus on the two-way mirror that showed him everything inside the box. There sat Isaac, the all-American boy Yancy had run into that day. Guy looked smugger than a foreign ambassador pulled over for a speeding violation.

"Do you have a *clue* what this is about?" Ellis asked Yancy.

"Can I say no?" Yancy replied. Wasn't a good answer, but the truth was he didn't know. Had Ellis asked him what they'd been talking about for the past hour, Yancy could tell him honestly, but he knew Ellis's team had already told him about the Dreamland angle. As for Jenna's current move, Yancy was as in the dark as Ellis.

"Didn't figure out enough during our last rendezvous, Dr. Ramey?" Isaac asked.

"Oh, I learned a thing or two," Jenna replied. She leaned against the back wall, crossed her arms. "I'm guessing you told me more than you planned."

Next to Yancy, Ellis coughed.

"Oh, really?" Isaac leaned forward, propped his head on his fists. "Do tell."

Like the cat that swallowed the canary.

"Dreamland," Jenna said, adopting her own self-satisfied expression. "I'm not stupid, you know."

"Oh, I know that, Dr. Ramey. It's why I wanted to chat with you in the first place. You figured out my little joke then, hm?"

She was going to *tell* him?

"Wasn't that hard. So where in Dreamland does he work, Isaac?"

Isaac's head tilted to the side, but the expression on his face remained unchanged. "Do you really think it's that easy?"

Jenna stood up from where she'd been leaning against the wall. Then she winked. "You can't blame a girl for trying."

She sat down in the chair opposite Isaac, and Yancy could almost see the wheels of thought turning in her head. She smiled again, almost like she was *flirting* with the bastard.

"Your partner must've been a lower-level employee to have gotten a job there, huh? From what we've already determined about his profile, I already knew he was most likely a bottom feeder. You confirmed it for me, too."

Isaac mimicked a scale with his cuffed hands, weighing imaginary ingredients. The way they were bound, his hands couldn't move much, but the imagery came across. "He wasn't too bad."

"Smart," S.A. Ellis grunted like it pained him to say so. "She's playing to his narcissism."

"What do you mean?" Yancy asked.

Ellis glanced over at him, squinted. "You had law enforcement training, right? You tell me."

S.A. Ellis turned back to the mirror.

Ass.

Yancy shrugged off Ellis's comment, focused on Jenna and Isaac.

"You're saying the ferry shooter *didn't* get hired because of affirmative action laws?" Jenna asked.

"Oh, come now, Dr. Ramey. You know he's white. Let's not pretend you're getting something out of me there. Then again, perhaps there *is* affirmative action for very ugly people. Of that, I'm not sure."

Jenna looked him straight in the eye. "Bad joke."

"Like the bad joke you made about me being in a homoerotic relationship with him?" Isaac asked.

She shrugged. "It was my only card. I had to play it. You have to admit it worked to some extent. You told me something, didn't you? Still, that he's ugly is news to me. Even then I wasn't insinuating you were in a homoerotic relationship with a very ugly person."

Now Isaac looked proud of himself. "I jest. I wouldn't associate with him if he was *that* hideous. I have standards."

S.A. Ellis muttered under his breath again. "Son of a bitch. He thinks she couldn't possibly know what he's really talking about."

"Standards, huh?" Jenna said. "So he's management? Upper management? I would've figured *you* were the management type, Isaac. He has to be lower on the totem pole than you."

In a social setting, yes. In Land of Valor, no.

Isaac stared straight ahead, deep in his own head. It seemed he was weighing words. "You can't climb too high on the pole when your head's in the clouds, Jenna. I told you. Fairy."

Brilliant.

Jenna nodded vigorously. "Right, right. So you *knew* he wanted you then?"

Isaac laughed. "'Course I knew! Wanted me, wanted to *be* me. Take your pick."

Jenna closed one eye, looked at him through the other. "You have that problem a lot?"

"People get attached, Dr. Ramey. You give them what they need, they're *bound* to get attached. You of all people should know that. She did it a lot."

For the first time, Yancy saw Jenna flinch. She sat straighter.

"True. She was good at what she did," Jenna said.

"Not as good as you."

"Get out of there, Jenna. Don't let him start this shit," Ellis breathed.

"I think she's holding her own pretty well," Yancy muttered.

"You've known her about five minutes," Ellis said.

Not long enough to hold preconceived notions against her.

But it was like Jenna had heard Hank. She pushed back from the table and stood.

"Isaac, I'm not as good as you think," she said.

A minute later, Jenna was back on Yancy's side of the mirror. She collapsed against the door and stared at her feet, breathing hard. Then her eyes rose and met Yancy's. She grinned.

He smiled back. He'd read so much about Jenna Ramey, but the stories didn't compare to watching her work in real life.

"No," Yancy said. "You're way better."

43

"I felt like that was worth something to you," Jenna said. She looked only at Yancy. Tolerating Hank's disapproval wasn't conducive to focus right now, and his condemnation wouldn't help this case move forward any more than her anxiety over Claudia's release.

"Perfection. He said, 'head in the clouds.' Don't bet your two good legs on this or anything, but since I've only got one, I think I'm reasonably safe betting the bad one that the ferry shooter's playing a Celestial."

"Which is what?" Hank asked. Now no animosity in his voice. Only intrigue. Luck with an UNSUB would do it every time.

"Imagine if a thousand years ago an angel did the nasty with a human, and they spawned really attractive descendents with special powers," Yancy answered.

"Angel X-Men. Got it," Hank said.

Yancy's visual tick didn't escape Jenna, but he shook it off well. She stifled a small laugh as red colored her thoughts. The males were battling for dominance.

"Assuming Isaac met this guy *through* the game also assumes he had to have targeted him. Isaac would've had to have seen him somewhere. Either the ferry shooter has to have been Isaac's clan, or the ferry shooter was a top-ranked player," Jenna said.

"Isaac commented about his high standards, so I'm guessing the ferry shooter was ranked. If he's playing a Celestial, that narrows it down some."

"How much?" Hank asked.

Yancy shook his head. "Crap. I don't know exactly. It'll vary depending on servers the game goes through. Worldwide, there are a metric shitfuckton of servers, but the ferry shooter and Isaac would have had to have played on the same one, say, the East Coast one. I say that because unless the ferry shooter plays twenty-four hours a day and takes his food through a tube, he's not gonna be ranked in the top thousand in the world. So you're talking thousands instead of millions."

"Okay. Dialing Irv for the ranked Celestials," Jenna said, hitting the speed dial on her cell.

"He might not be ranked today, though," Yancy muttered.

Jenna hung up immediately. "What?"

Yancy shook his head. "He'd have had significantly less playing time after he got started playing pop goes the weasel with Isaac here. Anytime you're not on for days at a time, you're at risk of dropping. There's a reason the stereotype of gamers who live with their mothers exists."

Mother. Claudia was probably being released from the Sumpter Building as they spoke.

Jenna picked up her phone again. Irv answered on the second ring.

"Hey, buddy. Odd request," she said.

"You say that like your requests usually involve taxes or grocery lists," he answered.

"Odder than usual, I mean. I need you to check out the accounts of the top thousand ranked players in Land of Valor, but this time, narrow it down to accounts with Celestial characters whose rankings dropped around the date of the first Gemini killings."

Irv chortled. "Your very specific wish is my command, ma'am."

Jenna hung up just as Hank's phone rang. She hoped answers would come soon. If they had the ferry shooter, they'd have more information on Isaac Keaton, and then maybe the link from Isaac to Thadius. The more they had on Keaton, the more they could charge him with. Right now they might not have a death penalty case, regardless of what he'd confessed up to this point. With the ferry shooter in custody, they'd be able to prove Isaac masterminded the Gemini killings as well as somehow manipulated Thadius's spree.

"If the ferry shooter is a Celestial, does that mean Isaac played one, too?" Jenna asked.

Yancy made a face. "Doubt it. He'd probably want to play something more supposedly all-powerful, like a warlock. Not as much skill required. Completely over-rated. Assholes."

"So a Celestial isn't that powerful but has a lot of skill?" Jenna asked.

Yancy cocked his head back and forth, weighing. "Eh, I wouldn't say that exactly. They're just different types of people entirely, and usually different types play them. Celestials tend to be people who don't want to lead *or* follow. They want to stand on their own, separate."

Jenna nodded. Colors coalesced in her mind, confirming the royal blue hue her mind had settled on for the ferry shooter long ago. Submissive traits influenced it, but those alone would've been lighter. Beta males usually showed up as a gentler sky color. Omega males, however, were the types of men who preferred to strike out as lone wolves rather than be a part of the pack. Alphas tended to stay on the warm-colored end of the spectrum, betas cool but pastel. But nearly every omega male Jenna had met simply settled into a brighter, more jewel-toned version of the color her mind conjured up when she first talked to him. Based on her profile of the ferry shooter up to this point, everything Yancy was saying made perfect sense.

It also didn't bode well, because the ferry shooter wouldn't want to blend into the background if he was an omega. He'd want to strike out on his own path if he wished to be known. Maybe he was under Isaac's complete control, and yet maybe he wasn't. The scary aspect of the possibility canceled out any comfort Jenna found in it.

On the other side of the room, Hank spoke in hushed tones on his cell. "Keep me posted. Yeah. Bye."

When Hank turned around to face Jenna, he didn't wipe the panic off his face fast enough.

"What?" she asked.

"Irv's finding the Celestials?"

"Hank . . ."

He bit his lip, the dark skin whitening under the pressure of his bite.

"Who was that?" she demanded.

"Saleda," Hank replied.

Just Saleda. Another one of the team. And yet Hank's face.

"Oh, Jenna. I'm so sorry," he said.

Before she asked, before he said it, she knew. Even so, she needed to hear it to make it real. "Say it, Hank."

"I put Saleda on Claudia when she left Sumpter this morning," Hank said. He sounded like he was going to be sick. "She followed her to the lawyer's office. She didn't come out. By the time she went in, Claudia was gone."

Jenna's head spun, and the ground seemed to sink under her. "I have to go."

"Jenna, you can't do anything! The best thing you can—"

She spun around and pointed a finger in Hank's face. "The best thing I can do is get my little girl, father, and brother the hell away from our home. *That* is what I can do. *You* apparently don't know shit about protecting people from Claudia. I *do*."

44

Thadius knelt beside a bearded Jasper Jeremiah Higgins. The man's whole body trembled like a pine tree in the breeze, and sweat slicked the seat of the plush leather office chair underneath him.

"I'll ask you again, Jasper. Tell me *why* you represented Sebastian Waters."

Thadius had known going in this wouldn't end well for the man. Others, he gave a chance to explain themselves. This guy, though? The lawyer knowingly worked so Sebastian Waters could walk away from the courtroom with nothing but probation. Police arrested Sebastian Waters for possession of illegal firearms, which he'd planned to use to gun down his peers at his high school the day of graduation. If helping a would-be school shooter get off free didn't contribute to Sebastian making his way toward Emily, Thadius didn't know what did.

Which was why he hadn't messed around with pretending he was someone else when he paid Jasper Jeremiah Higgins a visit that morning. Secretary wasn't there on a Saturday, and Jasper shouldn't have been either. Not technically. But when Thadius called as a potential client needing immediate assistance, Jasper lived up to the advertisement on his business card that said available anytime.

They'd come in, Jasper offered him a cup of coffee. Thadius offered him a seat and a belt to tie him to his chair.

Unfortunately, the more brazen technique had resulted in one squirmy, tongue-tied lawyer. Not surprising. These weasels were all the same.

Thadius expected the guy to say he *had* to defend Waters. He'd preach how everyone deserved a fair trial and representation. Probably give some BS about how Sebastian was only a kid at the time, deserved another chance. But hearing the truth was important to Thadius even now. Maybe even more than before.

"He was young. I . . . I know it sounds bad, but his parents called me. They were upset. Needed someone to help them."

Don't talk to me about his parents' desperation.

"Waters planned to use those guns on other *kids*," Thadius growled.

"I know! But *he* was a kid. Just a pissy kid. Surely he didn't have the guts for something like that! Probably didn't hang around with the popular kids, I don't know! He made a mistake, and if he went to jail, his life would be over forever. He seemed nice enough. Remorseful."

Thadius leaned in toward Jasper's ear. "He wasn't."

Jasper jumped at the gun at his head, then shook harder. "I'm sorry if he hurt you somehow! I didn't know! It was a long time ago! I can't take it back!"

Emily's face filled Thadius's mind. Her first day visiting home since she'd gone to college, she'd stood in the driveway plucking honeysuckles from the bush, twisting off their ends. "Never gets old," she'd said.

"You're right. You can't take it back," Thadius said. He stood, aimed the gun.

The lawyer's feet backpedaled, and the chair wheeled backward. "He got what was coming to him, didn't he?"

Thadius's trigger finger relaxed reflexively. "What did you say?"

For the first time, Jasper's shakes eased. "Yeah! He got shot!"

"What? How? Where?" Was Jasper making this up?

Jasper nodded toward his desk at the newspaper. "The Gemini killings at the theme park! Waters was one of the victims."

Thadius's heart thumped fast, and he reached for the newspaper. Sure enough, the front page bore a list of the victims of the recent shootings at the Enchanted Kingdom. Sebastian Waters, wounded. Plain in black and white.

"Wounded?" Thadius whispered, again facing Jasper. "I wouldn't exactly call that revenge."

He closed his eyes and pulled the trigger.

Jenna threw Ayana's things into a bag. If she forgot something, they could buy more. Stuff wasn't important.

Hank was already on his way to a new crime scene that most likely contained Thadius Grogan's latest victim. Jenna opted not to go with him this time. More important things to do.

Her dad stood in the corner, watching, his own little duffle at his feet. Yancy waited in the living room reading *One Fish Two Fish Red Fish Blue Fish* to Ayana.

"Do you think the pink hoodie or the green? The pink is warmer, but this time of year it probably doesn't matter—"

"Jenn, do you really think all this is necessary?" Vern asked quietly.

She stopped folding the green jacket. "You think we should test it out first?"

A door shut in the living room. "Who the hell are you?"

"Uh-oh," Jenna muttered, pushing past her dad into the living room. "Charley, this is Yancy. A friend."

Charley's hackles visibly relaxed. "Hey."

He glanced past Jenna to the packed diaper bag on the love seat, the bedroom pillows set there. "Weekend trip no one told me about?"

This was a battle she wouldn't win, but she had to try. It was for his own good.

"Claudia's out, Charley. They lost track of her."

"Lost track of her? What is she, a tomcat? Don't answer that."

"Charley, you have to come with us. We're moving you guys to a safe house."

"No way, Rain Man. I'm good here."

"I don't ask you for much, Charley," Jenna pleaded. Why couldn't he do this one thing for her? After all, he was the one who wouldn't leave Florida and his band and his friends when Jenna first begged him and her dad to move to Virginia to help with Ayana after she and Hank broke up. Vern had been ready and willing to leave this godforsaken town behind, but Charley had insisted on not letting Claudia run him away from the one place he'd ever known. So she'd come back here, to be with her dad and brother, the brother she'd saved from the woman now running free. After everything, he couldn't do this one thing.

He took her by the shoulders. "I didn't say you did. But I can't do it, Jenn. Can't. Won't. Take your pick. I can't miss a dozen gigs—one of them huge—and hide like a scared rabbit. Besides, Claudia's not stupid. She knows she can't get away with that I'm-insane-but-not-insane bullshit again. She's not coming after us."

All of Jenna's blood rose to her face. "She doesn't work that way, Charley! She doesn't always think with her brain!"

Her brother let go of her, walked past. "Well, neither do you."

It felt like he'd pulled a rip cord in her heart. "What is *that* supposed to mean?"

Charley yanked off his bandanna, worked the knot slowly with his fingers. He frowned. "You're thinking with your heart and your *past* right now, Jenna. Do you really think uprooting Ayana is best for everyone?"

Jenna stared at him, stung. "If I remember correctly, thinking with my gut saved your guitar-playing ass once before!"

"No."

"Excuse me?"

"I said *no*. Your gut got Claudia charged, but she still stabbed my guitar-playing ass, if you'll back that memory up a few megabytes."

Tears battled toward the corners of Jenna's eyes. She couldn't argue. He was too right. Technically, she hadn't saved any of them.

Charley noticed her watering eyes. "I'm sorry. I didn't mean that. I'm only trying to say we can't live our lives running, Jenn. I don't think she is, but if Claudia's planning to catch up, she'll do it. No hiding place will be good enough."

"Charley, please . . ."

"No, Jenn. No. Take Dad and Ay if you have to, but I'm staying put. If Claudia comes back here, I'll knife *her* this time."

For the first time since this whole mess started, Thadius Grogan finally made some sense. Logic and reasoning only went so far. Jenna could deduce everything about Thadius's state of mind through profiling, but until now, it had all been theory to her. Keep records and notes and the system will help you, she'd thought. Put her away the right way, just like the rest of the criminals she worked for years to put behind bars.

Yet against all odds, despite Jenna's trust in the system, Claudia was free. Thadius's kid's killer was never caught, and here Jenna was, hunting Thadius like she wouldn't do the exact same thing if someone hurt Ayana.

But Jenna would want someone to stop her.

This whole time, she'd been so intent on learning Thadius in order to learn Isaac, which would in turn help her catch the ferry shooter. What if she was going about this all wrong? What if by learning Thadius, she could find him and put an end to his misery? Then along the way she could *ask* him who Isaac was.

Now her brother wouldn't come with her to the safe house, which was one *more* thing to worry about. Sure, he'd learned a lot over the years. But so had Claudia.

"Please think about it, Charley," Jenna said. "Ready, Dad?"

"As ready as I'm gonna be," he said, shooting Charley a glance.

Jenna lifted Ayana, nuzzled her nose to hers. Charley or no Charley, this little girl wasn't ending up in any crime files. "Ready, Freddy?"

But Ayana had eyes only for Charley. She curled her finger once to beckon him toward her, as though to tell him they were ready to go. Jenna's heart cracked right down the middle.

"Not this time, kiddo. See you later, alligator?" Charley said, cheerful.

Ayana grinned behind her pacifier. "After while, cr'c'dile!"

After they got Vern and Ayana settled at the safe house, Jenna and Yancy set off for the next stop: the university where all of Thadius's troubles began. Irv might be a magician, but even he couldn't seem to get past the bureaucracy that was the university system of Florida. Either that or their record-keeping skills sucked harder than a brand-new Hoover.

"The college used to keep up with everything by social security number, but some bright individual eventually figured out that wasn't the best method on earth," Irv explained on speakerphone.

"Maybe not the most *secure*," Jenna replied.

"Ergo, they dumped *all* records leading up to the switch. Numerous lawsuits. Hence a giant ever-loving gap in the student history."

"Perfect," Yancy grumbled.

"You're telling me. The registrar wouldn't even be able to give the Pope information if he called for it. This was before everything went digital. If my computer doesn't have it, no one's does," Irv said.

"While I have you, anything on the Land of Valor Celestials?" Jenna asked.

"Eighty-three Celestials in the East Coast top thousand. Fifteen of those accounts dropped in rank near the first Gemini killings. I'll have those names to you ASAP. I'm digging up some details on them first. Those bastards try to keep those files private, but we're bitch-slapping them with a subpoena as we speak."

"Great. Thanks."

Jenna hung up. If just one solid lead would come through on any of these, maybe she could get somewhere with either Thadius *or* the ferry shooter.

"If neither the registrar's office nor the MM Society has records, the next place to look might be individual professors' offices. What do you think? I know Coppage's files have been taken as evidence, but surely there are others."

"Gotta be a faster way," Yancy said. "Remind me about the MM Society."

"Movie Making Society. The guy in the firework store said the kid had a button on his backpack. Grogan made him sketch it. Hank and I talked to the kid who runs it now."

Yancy hit the dashboard. "That's your answer! Way faster than digging through tons of old professors' records hoping to find some student with some *random* connection to Emily Grogan. We don't have a clue which classes she took. It'd take forever."

"I told you already. We checked with the MM Society. They don't have records."

"Don't need theirs. We can find out easy who was in the MM Society. Colleges keep plenty of records that have nothing to do with registrars. Yearbooks."

In the bowels of the University Library, Jenna and Yancy sat at a huge oak table with an aging volume of *The Crusader*. The yearbook was only six years old, but judging by the dust, Jenna wasn't the only person who'd forgotten these things existed. God willing, no one would ever think to look up her class albums. She liked to think her previous hair styles had never been the product of characters on popular television shows. Why did everyone on earth think that just because the "it" girl of the moment had the right face shape to pull off a trendy bob, it meant they must, too?

They flipped through the pictures of students and finally reached the shots of organizations and clubs.

"Jewish Life Center, Intramural Referees . . . Movie Making Society. Just sitting here waiting for us," Yancy said.

Jenna's heart leapt, and she jabbed at a kid in the left-hand corner of the photograph. "That looks like the guy in the pawn shop photo!"

Yancy skimmed the caption, which named the members from left to right. "Sebastian Waters."

The skinny youth in the picture looked harmless, like any other kid Jenna had ever seen at any college in Anywhere, USA. She texted the name to Irv with, "Pronto."

"That name sounds so familiar to me," Yancy mumbled.

Now that he mentioned it, Sebastian Waters's name tickled the back of Jenna's mind, too. She examined the picture harder, but the only match she could come up with was the profile in the pawn shop photo.

The light on Jenna's phone blinked, and she opened the text from Irv. In all caps, it said: CALL ME.

She punched the callback, and Irv answered on the first ring.

"Not sure if this is like Christmas morning or Halloween night," he said.

"Hit me with it, Irv."

"For starters, Sebastian Waters is a former client of a Mr. Jasper Jeremiah Higgins, also known as the lawyer Thadius Grogan popped between the eyes last night."

"Oh, my. That's solid."

"Hold your horses, sweet pea. The other half is cuter than pictures of a senator with his mistress the day before an election. Sebastian Waters was one of the shooting victims at the theme park."

"What?" Jenna gasped.

"What is it?" Yancy asked.

She mimicked writing something to ask for a pen. Then, to Irv, "Like, a dead one?"

"No, ma'am. Alive and schtickin'."

Jenna's brain fuses blew before any of the connections could lock in. She managed, "His history?"

"So glad you asked me that, Dr. Ramey. It would seem that as a juvenile, Waters was arrested for possession with intent to harm other students at his high school. Court psychiatrist cited maladaptive behaviors, anger management issues, and severe anxiety. Problems with daydreaming. Fast-talking lawyer got him off on probation. Argued he had some problems, made a mistake, but that he wouldn't have gone through with an actual shooting. He was *such* a fine kid, excellent moral compass and all. Came from a good family, raised right. Nothing a little counseling couldn't iron out. Waters completed court-ordered anger management classes and went on to the university. Led a quiet life riddled with depression. Treated by one of the on-campus health center psychiatrists."

Yancy handed Jenna a scrap of paper from his wallet and a pen, and she scribbled *Waters = theme park victim* on the slip. She ignored his gasp to keep on track. "Perfect recipe for a bigger, badder killer with less remorse to swoop in and lead him on his righteous path to destruction."

"This is why you get paid the big bucks."

Still, the colors gnawed at Jenna. The ferry shooter's blue clashed violently with the colors she associated with Emily Grogan's murder. The girl had been strangled with her own intestine. The red of ultraviolent crimes didn't make much sense. Could the ferry shooter have changed that much over time?

She pushed the thoughts of the colors away. "I'm guessing you've already cross-referenced Waters with the Land of Valor names?"

At last they would find out who Isaac Keaton really was. The question still remained as to how in God's name he'd found Grogan and how he knew what the guy would do. He'd set Grogan off on track to find Emily's killer, who he presumably knew ahead of time was Sebastian. Smooth way to get rid of *that* loose end, but what about Grogan? He was a loose end, too. Keaton wouldn't leave one and not the other.

"No dice on the Land of Valor game, but like I said, I still have some work to do to get info on all these names. I'll keep you posted."

"Does Hank know?" Jenna asked.

"He and Saleda are already en route to Waters's home address."

He won't be there. "Okay, great. Let me know on the names."

She hung up with Irv, and the string of curse words Yancy had been holding back flew out.

"Bastard! Isaac *shot* the guy to help him get away! That is *insane!*"

"Unfortunately, it's as sane as it comes," Jenna replied. She shut the yearbook and shoved it back into the pile in front of her. "Come on, we have to move fast."

"Where are we moving?"

"Hank's on his way to Waters's house, but Isaac will have planned all this. Waters is long gone. But if Grogan knows what we do—and he *does* since he just offed Waters's lawyer—he'll do what he's done every other time and head for where he knows Waters was last."

"The hospital," Yancy supplied.

"Yep," Jenna said, jogging toward the elevator. "Waters isn't still there, but Thadius Grogan is about to be."

47

Though Jenna had called the police to get them to head toward the hospital, too, when Jenna and Yancy arrived, no sirens and no cars.

No backup.

They hurried toward the entrance.

"I'm still amazed Isaac knew Waters killed Grogan's daughter. Even for Keaton, that's pretty specific targeting," Yancy said.

Jenna and Yancy slipped through the automatic doors. "You said yourself people talk way too much on these games. Isaac probably has a knack for eliciting confidences."

They took the stairs, Yancy in the lead. Jenna followed, knowing he would remember which floor the shooting victims had all stayed on. Yancy jumped the stairs two at a time. For a guy missing a foot, he was more athletic than she'd have given him credit for.

When they reached the right floor, Jenna and Yancy burst through the doors. The nurses' station seemed empty, everything quiet.

Yancy headed to the other side of the station, opened the EMPLOY-EES ONLY door.

"Yancy!" Jenna whispered.

"Don't worry. I know where the buzzer is."

The buzzer was the last thing on Jenna's mind. Regardless of what she'd posed as or been brought in as, technically, she was as much an agent as Ayana was. If something went wrong, her ass wasn't even padded, much less covered.

Then the door unclicked, and she grabbed the handle anyway. So much for that half of her conscience.

They peeked inside every room on the way down the hall, including the one Yancy had occupied a few days ago. Some contained patients hooked up to beeping monitors, some bore only empty beds.

And a strange absence of medical professionals.

Just as danger garnet flashed in Jenna's mind, a young, thin nurse backed out of a room on the right. At the sight of Yancy and Jenna, her face crinkled with confusion.

"Can I help you?"

Very different from the nurse the day they'd been in to interview Yancy, who would've taken one look at them in an employee only area and shot them on sight. In fact, seeing Nurse Twyla might be refreshing, given the situation.

"Is Twyla on duty?" Jenna asked.

The younger nurse's mouth quirked as though the request was the strangest thing she'd ever heard. Having met Twyla, it probably wasn't far from the truth.

"Wow, she's popular today. She's here. Her brother's in with her now. Is there some kind of emergency?"

Brother?

"Where?" Yancy asked.

The girl nodded toward the end of the hall. "Last room. Is everything okay?"

"Call 911. Page hospital security. *Now!*" Jenna said as she passed the young nurse on the way to the last room.

The girl nodded hard, backed away a few feet, then turned and ran.

Jenna's heart thundered. What the hell was she doing? She had no gun, no badge, no cuffs. No way to restrain a two-hundred-pound father hell-bent on revenge.

Which was why she gasped at the sight of Yancy removing a Ruger .380 from his prosthetic leg.

"What? I have a license to conceal and carry," he said, defensive.

"In your *leg?*"

"If you gotta have a custom-made fake leg, you might as well use it. Now, go!"

She stood to the side of the last door on the left, and Yancy took up position on the other side. No sounds from inside.

"Three, two, one," Yancy said.

He pushed the door inward, gun first. Jenna entered behind him, careful to shield herself.

Thadius Grogan stood near the window holding Twyla in front of him, a human shield. He held a SIG against her temple.

"Thadius, drop the gun! No one has to get hurt!" Yancy said, clear and loud. He leveled his gun with Thadius's head.

Twyla trembled in front of Thadius, squeezing her eyes shut, saying something under her breath. *The Lord's Prayer.*

"Somebody's already been hurt!" the gray-haired man said through gritted teeth.

Most cops would think it wise to say something about how all this bloodshed wouldn't bring Emily back, but Jenna knew Thadius wasn't looking to change the past. Not by a long shot.

"Twyla didn't save Sebastian, Thadius. You know that. She wasn't even in the emergency room when he was brought in. She wasn't on the team that evacuated him from the park, either. She isn't responsible," Jenna said calmly.

Thadius's hand holding the SIG wobbled. "She helped him."

"Twyla did her job, Thadius. She didn't know who he was or the things he'd done to hurt other people. How could she have?"

Twyla didn't look at Jenna at all. Her eyes stayed upward, and her mouth kept praying. The nurse's stubby fingers grabbed at Thadius's hand around her rib cage and arms, almost as though she was using it for safety.

Keep saying Twyla's name.

"Twyla didn't know Sebastian hurt your daughter, Thadius. But we know. We know what he did to Emily and to other people. We'll find him, and we'll punish him. Put down the gun. Let us help you."

Thadius edged backward. "That's what they said last time."

Then, before Jenna could scream, Thadius's gun jolted away from Twyla's temple and toward Yancy. He fired.

Jenna hit the ground behind the hospital bed. The gun fired again, glass shattered.

Jenna peered around the corner of the bed. Thadius had disappeared. Twyla lay on the floor where he'd dropped her, shrieking and covering her head but unharmed.

Yancy. Jenna twisted her head to look for him, dread creeping up from her toes.

But Yancy was back on his feet, charging full-speed at the window.

48

Yancy leapt through the shot-up window after Thadius Grogan. Fucker might have fired the shot at him as a distraction so he could get away, but Yancy had had enough gunshots fired at him to last a lifetime and then some.

The outcropping wasn't that wide, but Thadius was already out of sight. He couldn't have jumped to another building. Even if the bastard was more agile than he looked, the closest rooftop was too far for an Olympic high jumper.

That's when Yancy heard more gunshots.

His metal foot scuffed the granite of the outcrop as he ran toward the lip of the roof. He could hear Thadius screaming.

"Crank now!"

Yancy leaned over the side to see Thadius holding one of the window washers, gun to his head. Thadius had shot out one of the ropes stabilizing the swing scaffold, which explained the swaying platform.

The operator below ran toward the rope crank, yelling for Thadius to calm down.

"I'll calm down when you crank! Do it now!"

The operator worked the pulley. Thadius pressed the SIG harder into the washer's skull. "Hand over hand! Take us down!"

The side of the platform where Thadius stood with his hostage eased lower, but the other side remained stationary. Thadius took aim at the rope on the stationary side and fired. The bullet missed.

If Thadius hit the rope, he would go down. Fast. Problem was, so would the other guy.

Yancy leapt onto the scaffold and grabbed the rope. His eyes locked with Thadius's, then he yanked at the rope, hand over hand, trying not to fumble his own gun. The scaffold descended, sloped. Yancy pulled faster to keep up with the other side.

"When we get to the bottom, you make one move, and this guy's blood is on you," Thadius said. "Leave your hands on the rope or he dies."

Yancy hardly listened, just kept moving. *Please let the cops be here by the time we hit ground. For once in my life, let me be lucky.*

They closed in toward the ground, the platform swaying precariously with their uneven, uncoordinated efforts. Yancy's heart thundered, the Ruger heavy in his hand.

"Nobody moves!" Thadius warned.

The platform crashed into the cement on Yancy's side first, jarring him off his feet. His bad grip on the gun slackened, and it dropped.

Thadius's side hit bottom, and the man pulled the window washer with him, still holding him tight to his chest. "Don't follow me!"

Dazed, Yancy glanced around for the Ruger, saw it a few feet away. He rolled to his stomach, his head throbbing.

Yancy pushed to his knees, crawled toward the gun. He didn't know where Thadius was or if he was watching. He could only hope Grogan wouldn't shoot him since he'd done nothing wrong. After all, Thadius had had the chance to shoot him in the hospital room and didn't.

Yancy's fingers found the gun. He grabbed it tight and twisted to face the direction Thadius had been. Nothing.

Yancy collapsed onto the cement on his rear end, then he used his arms to boost himself to his feet. *Follow him!*

"Where?" he yelled to the crank worker.

The guy pointed to an alley to the side, and Yancy staggered that way. Thadius had a hostage and the advantage, but where could he go?

When Yancy turned the corner, though, that answer became abundantly clear.

The window washer leaned into the brick wall, face first, counting. Yancy looked past him to where the alleyway spilled into the opposite parking lot. A taxi line.

Thadius was gone.

49

Thirty minutes later, while nurses stitched up the gash on Yancy's head, Jenna considered bashing her own against the wall. If it would get her out of Hank railing at her for moving in on a suspect without police, she might.

"You could've been killed, you could've gotten other people killed! What were you *thinking*?"

She glared at him. "I was thinking there was a spree killer two rooms away from me and that letting him *go* would be worse than confronting him. He didn't kill the nurse, did he? In fact, the entire hospital made it through his visit alive."

"It could've easily gone the other way, Jenna."

"I guess it's a good thing for me it didn't, then."

All the ways the confrontation could've gone awry had already run through Jenna's head, and even considering all of those, she still came to the conclusion she'd done the right thing. Thadius would've killed Twyla, whether Hank believed it or not. Finding out about Sebastian's arrest history and that someone had the chance to put him away and didn't had sent him on a worse spiral, and Twyla would've likely borne the brunt of that if Jenna hadn't been there to talk Thadius down. Now Twyla was alive, and that made her a prime witness. They could talk to her, find out what Thadius wanted to know from her. That is, if Hank stopped wasting time arguing about what might have happened.

After Yancy had run after Thadius, Jenna had attempted to go after *him*. She'd been stopped by Twyla, who'd grabbed her leg and begged her not to leave. The pleading had been insistent, but the grip was what actually kept Jenna there. Looking back, it was a wonder Twyla hadn't been able to take Thadius down, gun and all.

It had taken Twyla ten minutes to stop screaming at a full-on bloodcurdling level, then an additional two injections of Valium to stop crying and yelling at random intervals. Now the woman rested in the bed of the room where she'd been held hostage.

"How long until we can talk to her?" Jenna asked.

"You're not talking to anyone! Do you realize how much hell I'm going to take for this?"

Jenna shrugged. "Probably a lot more if you don't catch Thadius Grogan *or* Sebastian Waters."

"I know how to profile, Jenna."

"I'm sorry. I could've sworn it was me that showed up at the hospital when Grogan was still here. Or did I hallucinate that?"

Hank folded his arms. "Fine. But I'm present for the interview, and I know your next move before you *make* it. Clear?"

"Crystal."

"Fine. I'll go check when we can interview her," he said.

When Hank walked away, Yancy stood from the bench in the waiting area where he'd been seated. "How'd that go?"

"You shouldn't be walking around. Concussions don't like movement."

He waved her off. "Nothing compared to the blood loss you sustain when you lose a leg. Besides, they haven't said it was a concussion yet."

"Yet," Jenna repeated.

"Come on. What'd he say?" Yancy pressed.

Jenna sighed. This day might be longer than the previous, and that was saying something. "He wasn't thrilled about the Ruger."

"Ah. It's always the guns that get you. Next time, I'll bring my trusty baseball bat. Would he rather you have hijacked some tranquilizers to fight Thadius? Or ask him politely to surrender?"

Despite everything, Jenna laughed. It was so true. Hank had called them both into this mess. Maybe she'd dragged them further than Hank intended, but if he expected to tell her half the story and let the other half remain a mystery, he had another think coming.

Hank ambled back over. "We can go in, but we can't stay long. She's 'resting comfortably,' whatever that means. Come on."

Jenna stood, and Yancy followed. Hank put a palm to his chest. "Not you."

At this point, best not to fight Hank. She shook her head at Yancy, who bit his lip and backed away.

Jenna walked beside Hank toward the room where everything went down.

"You know, you could cut Yancy some slack. He did keep a guy from splatting on the concrete out there," Jenna said.

"Lawsuits," Hank muttered.

Lawsuits. Ego. Same thing, right?

Nurse Twyla lay on the hospital bed. An industrial blanket covered her up to her waist, her pink scrub top gently rising and falling with her breathing. She stared at the ceiling, wide-eyed.

"Twyla? My name is Jenna Ramey. I need to ask you a few questions, okay?"

The nurse didn't say anything, only nodded.

"The man who was here earlier. Can you remember what he talked to you about when he first came in?"

She nodded again. When she spoke, she sounded about a decade older than when they'd visited Yancy in the ICU a few nights ago.

"He put the gun to my head. Said they'd told him I was on duty when the park victims were brought in. I don't know who 'they' meant."

"Did he ask you any questions about any of the theme park victims?"

"One," she whispered.

"Who was it, Twyla?" Jenna coaxed.

"The Waters kid. S-Sebastian."

Easy, girl. Twyla was tearing up, but pushing through this was paramount. "He wanted to talk about Sebastian Waters. What did he say about him?"

She clutched the blanket tighter, inched it up toward her thick neck. "Was angry. Said Sebastian killed his daughter." Twyla gripped the rail of the bed with her right hand, then twisted her head toward Jenna. "Did he?"

The answer wouldn't help Twyla sleep at night, for sure. Better to keep her centered on the matter at hand. "Did this man ask you any questions about Sebastian Waters?"

The woman's eyes returned to the ceiling and slid in and out of focus. "He told me to tell him who Sebastian left the hospital with. Who picked him up."

"Do you remember the answer to that?"

She shook her head vigorously.

"Did he ask anything else?"

"Who he talked to while he was here. Who visited."

Jenna had let her doctor side take over in the past few years because it was far more patient than the cop side. But right now, the two were definitely dueling.

"Can you remember what you told him?" Jenna asked.

"N-No one visited him. Nobody except police. He only talked to the support group while he was here."

The lavender Jenna saw anytime she had a sense of déjà vu flashed in. She swapped a quick glance with Hank. Support groups. Again.

"Thank you, Twyla," she said. "Feel better soon."

They exited the room, and Hank was already talking. "We need a list of everyone involved with the support group Waters attended while he was here. Any chance it could be the same one Thadius Grogan worked with?"

"Slim. If it was, Thadius would've gone another route to find him, no?"

"You've got a point."

"We need names and meeting places. I have no idea where Thadius will go to track down a member of the hospital support group, but all the people involved need to be notified that they could be in danger. Not to mention, we need to know who talked most to Waters while he was at the meeting. I'll get info from the hospital, you put Irv on notice."

"On it," Hank said.

Jenna sprinted down the hall. Minutes were precious. Assuming Isaac Keaton shot Sebastian Waters so the latter could escape the park shooting, Sebastian didn't go to that meeting because he was a victim in need of camaraderie.

They didn't just need to know who Sebastian Waters had talked to. They also needed to know *why*.

"I had a great time today," Zane said as Sebastian eased his neighbor's borrowed Chevy into the parking lot of the abandoned Piggly Wiggly off the interstate. Funny how even the people who'd known you for only a few weeks could be swayed by the words "neighbor" and "shooting victim."

He'd brought Zane here to meet her friend who was supposed to pick her up. She'd mumbled something about a friend needing company for the night, but Sebastian knew. He didn't press.

"Me, too," he admitted. So hard not to look at her, but he didn't dare. Her face was weird from this angle. Better not to see that side of her.

"She'll be here any minute, I'm sure," Zane said.

Maybe Zane had homed in on his awkward inner conflict, or maybe she was reassuring herself. Sebastian couldn't tell anymore.

The minutes ticked by. No sign of Zane's friend.

"Maybe you should call her," Sebastian suggested.

Still, in his gut, he knew this feeling. Had it too many times. No one was coming. Zane's "friend" wasn't a friend at all.

"Oh, I'm sure she'll be along. I don't mind waiting if you don't," she said, her voice wavering, unsteady.

"No. I don't mind at all."

The truth seeped out so easily, effortless. A lot different from most things he'd talked about today. In fact, Sebastian couldn't remember the last time sitting with someone was so simple. Usually, he felt so inconspicuous, like the world had no idea he was there, and he had a love-hate relationship with it. If they didn't notice him, he analyzed why. If they did, it made him endlessly anxious. But Zane was aware of his presence constantly. What's more, he liked that she was.

A few minutes turned into thirty, but they sat and talked. About anything, nothing. Sebastian wasn't about to bring up the "friend" again. He wouldn't remind her of the thing he'd tried so hard to escape.

"And that's how we ended up keeping the ferret as a pet," she said.

Sebastian had only half listened to the story. "Cool."

She giggled, and the sucking noise her mouth sometimes made tagged the end. When the laugh died out, Zane sighed hard. "Yeah, I don't think she's gonna make it."

What was next, then? Either way, he didn't want to ask. He didn't really care.

This was the point people usually told him that their "friend" had probably gotten tied up, or that some stupid mistake was to blame, like they thought they were meeting at a different abandoned Piggly Wiggly parking lot. That sucked worse than the actual ditching. He wouldn't do that to her.

Instead, Sebastian finally looked at Zane and was surprised to find her looking at him as though she had been the whole time. His ears burned. The rippled skin on her cheek was turned away just enough so he wasn't staring at it head-on.

"I'm glad she didn't show," Sebastian said.

Before he knew what was happening, Zane had lurched across the front seat. Her lips pressed hard against his, her curved upper lip oddly smooth under his. She kissed him, and her hands gripped his nonexistent biceps.

He didn't kiss back, but he didn't stop her, either. He felt sensation pulse through him, nice. Calming, even.

Zane's eyes were shut tight, but Sebastian never closed his. He glanced down, lifted his hands to her hips and placed one on either side. She was small, soft. Warm.

Finally, Sebastian convinced his mouth to close in time with hers. Awkward. More like eating pudding than what he'd heard about making out with a girl.

If Zane noticed that he didn't seem to know what he was doing, she didn't let on. Maybe this was her way of thanking him for his earlier discretion?

She pressed herself closer into him, halfway over the cup holders between them. Her knee bumped the drive shaft, and his hand acted of its own accord to pull her leg over the barrier and out of the way.

The stirring in his jeans interrupted his concentration on the feeling of her lips. *No, no, no. Not this. Not now.*

But in the next moment, Zane's hand closed over his, small and tepid. The memory of the handprint on City Walk washed over him, and the taste of her salty tongue overpowered his doubts. He let his own tongue roam over the scarred surface of her lip, his worries about how he was doing flitting away in the stale air of the Chevy. She breathed out as he tasted her, and she emitted a tiny gasp, which caused her mouth to squelch.

She didn't flinch, and shocked as Sebastian was, neither did he. Noticed, sure. But it didn't stop him from wanting to do it again. Hell, maybe he wanted it all the more.

That was what was perfect about her, after all. She was infinitely fucked up. Just like him.

The hospital pointed Jenna and Hank—and to Hank's chagrin, Yancy—toward the workplace of the hospital support group's leader while Richards and Saleda visited the guy's home. Les Quaney turned out to be a chef at a local Thai restaurant called Chatchada, which was located in a hole in the wall on Second.

"Les Quaney around?" Hank asked the man behind the bar of the restaurant.

"Whatcha want with him?" the hefty bartender asked.

Hank whipped out his badge. "FBI. We need to talk to him as soon as possible."

The guy wiped his dark hands on a cloth from the shelf under the bar, then stuck one out to Hank. "Les."

Doesn't seem surprised to see us. In Jenna's experience with federal investigation, most people were knocked back by a real live visit from an FBI agent. However, these folks with histories involving violent crimes tended to be the opposite. They weren't necessarily thrilled or welcoming, but they had a quiet acceptance about them. A life of constant drama would do that to a person.

"We're here to ask you some questions about Sebastian Waters. You may have met him at one of your recent meetings. He was a victim in the Gemini theme park shootings."

Les Quaney scrubbed the counter with the same cloth with which he'd wiped his hands. *Nervous tick.*

"Not sure I know the name. Park shootings, you said? Any clue which meeting? Sorry. I try not to pry into people's business. Don't keep up with who's there, either. Anonymous is anonymous, you know. 'Sides, I have enough to think about on my own."

"We understand," Hank replied.

"It would've been a meeting at the hospital, probably only one. Sometime last week," Jenna explained.

Les looked up toward his left. Memory accessing. A lot of people thought looking a certain direction or other was the "tell" of a liar, but Jenna had hung around with enough sociopaths to know the rules about this weren't hard and fast. Still, in normal people, looking up usually meant they were looking to their brain—or rather, their reservoir for memories.

"Oh, yeah. Guy they brought from upstairs. He didn't say much, really. Listened. I didn't talk to him, either. Seemed in his own world. Mostly, everyone let him be. I think the only person who chatted with him was Zane. Of course, she chats with everyone. I'd be impressed if he made it away *without* talking to her."

"Zane?" Jenna repeated.

"Yeah, Zane Krupke. Really active in the local vic support scene. Cheerful to the point of aggravation. I warn you, you talk to her, you might wanna take an Imodium first. The verbal diarrhea gets to you."

"Any idea where we can locate her?" Hank asked.

Les folded his lips, scrunched his nose. "Not a clue, actually. I don't know where she works or where she lives. I know she helps organize a bunch of events, but that's about it. If you'd dropped by a little earlier, you probably could've caught her at the City Walk thing today. Would've ended a few hours ago, though."

"All right. Zane Krupke, right?"

"Yep," Quaney said.

"Got it. Thanks," Hank replied.

Jenna and Yancy followed Hank out of the building. Jenna already had her phone to her ear. "Need everything you have on Zane Krupke, please, sir."

Irv cackled. "Zane? That her real name?"

"Far as I know."

"Coming up. By the way, I found your boy in Land of Valor. Sebastian Waters was using his mom's credit card, turns out. Since I've been known to play MMORPGs on occasion, I'll refrain from the sarcastic comments."

"Really, Irv? *You?*"

"I know. See any pigs in the sky above the Thai?"

Jenna looked up on reflex. "Pork free. So now that you've found his character, can we find more on Keaton?"

"Maybe. I'mma do some fancy footwork and talk to some of these jokers in this clan and see."

"Sounds good. Keaton would've isolated Sebastian as much as he could from others, not wanted him to play with anyone else."

"Kinky," Irv said.

"Something like that."

"Zane Krupke, 56 Thurmond Place, apartment 4. The projects. Sounds like a fun evening you have in store there."

"Wish us luck," Jenna said.

"Happy Tasers," Irv replied. The phone clicked.

"Got an address. Get Richards and Saleda off Les Quaney's home and onto notifying other people on the support group list to be on the lookout for Waters. Let's go see Zane."

52

Jenna climbed out of the SUV at Zane Krupke's apartment complex. *Note to self: Never come on a case like this again unless they issue a handheld.*

"This looks like a nice place to *become* a victim of a violent crime," Yancy muttered.

The joke might've been funnier if it was farther from the truth. The derelict buildings boasted more graffiti than clean wall, and bars graced some of the apartment windows.

Jenna, Yancy, and Hank climbed a flight of rickety stairs, complete with no lighting, up to where number 4 nestled in the left corner. The landing smelled of cigarettes and urine, and a broken Bud bottle lay in place of a welcome mat.

"Here goes nothing," Hank said. Then he knocked.

A door opened the length the security chain would allow, and a man's eye stared back at them through the crevice.

Hank held his identification close to the crack with his left hand, his right on his holstered weapon. "Sir, we're with the FBI. We're here to speak to Zane Krupke."

The door slammed. *Great.*

Hank beat hard on the door with the side of his fist again. "Sir? Sir, open up."

Crashing and banging came from behind the door, whispered voices. Always a good sign.

"None of the drills can prepare one for the *actual* hiding of the stash," Yancy quipped.

Hank rolled his eyes. "You'd know, wouldn't you?"

A minute later, the chain unbolted, and the door opened.

"Sorry. Had to get a shirt on," the man said.

Now that was a euphemism Jenna had never heard. The salt-and-pepper-haired man had been wearing a shirt—and pants, for that matter—when he'd cracked the door earlier. Times like these made Jenna wish they had time to search the place, just for fun.

She stepped into the apartment behind Hank. Two guys lounged on a beige sofa to the right. One leaned back, dozing, clearly too stoned to be worried about the Feds showing up. The other perched on the edge of the couch pretending to be intent on the game show on the forty-two-inch LCD.

"You said you want Zane?" the man asked.

His right eye was fixed permanently in toward his nose, but his left stared straight at Jenna, not Hank, who'd originally spoken to him. God, she needed a shower.

"Yes," Jenna answered. Wasn't going to be hard to find Zane, apparently. Guy seemed about as ready to sell her out as he was to "put on his shirt."

He jerked his head toward a small hallway to the back of the apartment. "First door on the right."

Jenna said nothing else, but wandered that way. She felt Yancy on her heels. Hank stayed behind to cover them from the rear.

"Gee, the butler service must be nice. He announces visitors like she's a queen," Yancy whispered.

"You find something funny about poverty?" Hank asked.

"Cut it out, you two," Jenna said.

Yancy had a point. The guy pointed them right to Zane's room without so much as a warning to her. Made Jenna wonder who Zane was and why she was living with this guy.

The door to the bedroom was closed. Protocol for entering a bedroom: not in the manual.

Jenna tapped the door. "Zane? Zane Krupke?"

Shuffling sounds. The click of a lock twisting.

The door opened to reveal a pencil of a girl so pale she glowed in the light of the orb under the ceiling fan. After Jenna's eyes adjusted to the light change, the girl's pallid color wasn't even her most striking feature. Half of her face appeared melted, like a candle left burning too long.

"Who're you?" the girl asked.

No accusation. Curiosity.

"I'm Dr. Jenna Ramey. This is Yancy Vogul, and Special Agent Hank Ellis. We're working on an FBI case, Zane."

Zane blinked, and her eyes widened. "About the school?"

How had Jenna not figured out by now that when approaching these violent crime victims, when you said you were with the FBI, you should specify you weren't visiting about their own case? This was the second time this week she'd made the mistake not only of not clarifying up front, but also of not researching the particulars of the case of the person she was visiting.

"Um, not exactly," Jenna said. "May we come in?"

What a weird thing to ask about someone's bedroom.

Zane shook her head but said, "Sure."

The girl moved fast as they entered the room, scooping up books and clothes off her bed. Her frenzy was different from the one they'd just heard prior to entering the living room. This was more housecleaning, welcoming guests.

"Your roommates?" Jenna asked, quirking her head toward the den.

Zane shoved colored pencils at the wrong angles into a box, and the cardboard bulged. She closed a doodle-filled notebook, plopped it onto the desk.

"Oh, no. That's my dad," Zane whispered, her cheeks tinging pink.

Zane hadn't mentioned the other men in the living room, but either way, the news took Jenna aback. The short, graying man in the other room looked nothing like Zane and seemed old enough to be the girl's grandfather.

Hank and Yancy crowded into the room behind her, and Jenna took a seat on the bed where Zane had cleared a space. Courtesy was important. "That your mom?"

The picture on the desk next to a cup of pastel-colored flair pens, a Koosh ball, and a stack of loose-leaf paper was the only one in the room. The jet-black hair of the woman in the photo matched the color of Zane's. Framed in ornate gold, the photo looked out of place with the hodgepodge of yard-sale items in the room.

"Yeah. Mom doesn't live with us anymore."

So Mom wasn't dead.

"Mom left a long time ago. I don't remember a lot about her. She wasn't around for all this," Zane continued, and she gestured to her face. She shrugged.

Long time ago. Healing.

"I see," Jenna replied. This visit wasn't even about Zane, but somehow, the girl's smile made Jenna crave knowing more of her story. She saw light pink, the pure version of the color usually associated with babies. The color reminded Jenna of childlike innocence. Zane could be trusted.

Hank jumped in. "Zane, we're here to ask you some questions about someone you may have had contact with recently. I don't mean to alarm you, but this person may be involved with some pretty serious crimes."

"What? What crimes?"

"The Gemini killings. Have you come into contact with a man named Sebastian Waters in the past few days?" Hank asked.

Zane's cheeks flushed, and her face splotched maroon. Could she *know* about Sebastian's connection?

"Yes. I . . . he and I met at group. He was one of the people shot."

"That's right, Zane, but we believe Sebastian Waters may be responsible for some of the shootings," Hank explained.

Zane shook her head feverishly, and her color slipped from maroon to ashen. "No. That's impossible. Sebastian is a really sweet guy. He's not . . ."

Jenna's hand drifted to Zane's. Damn it. The girl had befriended him, hadn't she?

"Zane, he's one of the Gemini shooters. I know this is hard to hear, but we have to find him," Jenna answered.

Zane continued to sway her head side to side, though the movement slowed. Terror washed the side of her face that wasn't already frozen.

"But he can't be . . ."

"Zane, do you have any idea where we can find him?" Jenna asked. She squeezed Zane's hand. This was beyond awful.

"I . . . no. He . . . he's coming to volunteer with us at the event tomorrow. It's the only place I can think . . . I don't know other than that."

"What event?" Hank pressed.

The girl stared at the floor. Her forehead crinkled as she spoke, and the words sounded like she was talking to herself, not to them.

"He asked if I needed volunteers for the rally. He . . . he *knew* about the rally already. I didn't notice it before, but looking back, he had to have. He asked me about it like he didn't know, but he *knew!* He had to have!"

"Knew about *what* rally, Zane?" Jenna coaxed.

Zane blinked up at her. "It's an anti–death penalty rally. They're executing Fordham Beach day after tomorrow. We're doing a rally-slash-vigil thing."

"Who's 'we'?" Hank asked.

But Jenna didn't care who "we" involved or how strange some might think it was that this victim of a violent crime was attending a death vigil for a convicted rapist and murderer. The same jungle green she'd seen at Coppage's house, the green her mind connected to brilliantly laid plots, shone in her mind. Suddenly, every little thing Isaac Keaton had said to this point, all his intimate knowledge of her family, his thorough planning, the fact that he'd orchestrated a way for Sebastian Waters to walk away from the theme park, all made sense.

Isaac hadn't shot Sebastian to tie up a loose end. He'd shot him so Sebastian could execute another plan.

Sebastian lugged the black-painted rubber hose into the closed block where the vigil for Fordham Beach, convicted of raping and murdering a thirty-one-year-old mother of two, would be held in only hours. It was just like Isaac had pointed out to him for so long—people were sick. These pathetic losers would light candles and pray for this man who'd done so many things wrong, and yet most didn't even know Sebastian's name. Stupid conscience had kept him from setting off those chemical bombs at the school years ago, from blowing so many people away with the guns he'd brought. Maybe if he had, they'd have taken notice of him *then*. None of this had to happen.

And yet he might've created a Zane.

The thought whipped chills into his nerve endings, prodded him to the core. Sebastian didn't need Zane to be there tomorrow. She wasn't part of this.

The crew putting up the stage at the north end of the block near the prison was already working in the wee hours, and to them, Sebastian looked like any other cargo-pants-clad workman, paid to get in, get done, and leave. This would be fast and painless. Just like the end.

Then the world would know and remember him. After it was over, he'd never have to wonder about his fate like Isaac. Then again, Isaac *wanted* a chance to have this vigil, people fighting for him to win. Sebastian never had.

Before Sebastian set out, he followed Isaac's instructions with precision. Black hose, packed with filter treatment from the pool supply store, fuses every ten feet. The end capped tight, duct tape to place it. He'd been nervous, buying the stuff, but Isaac told him to go to three different stores, gave him details on what to say at each. Sebastian had wanted to use matchsticks, since he could've bought an unlimited supply without raising a brow, but crushing match-sticks was too volatile, Isaac said. He was right, too. Sebastian knew a guy who'd lost a hand that way.

Then the only task left was to go to the toy section of a few chain stores, buy a handful of the normally harmless toys Isaac had men-tioned. The metal shavings that made the things work would be a nice fuel to combine with the other chemicals. Stuffed the hose with thumbtacks, BBs. Shrapnel as a secondary weapon might be as good as the actual bomb.

"The ultimate irony," Isaac said. *"They'll be fighting for this guy's freedom, and you'll send them on their way. Instant fame."*

No one so much as looked at Sebastian while he laid the hose.

As he applied strips of duct tape over the hose to hold it in place, he couldn't help but think that in the coming days, people would wonder why he'd done this. They'd try to guess, try to make them-selves feel like if they'd known, they could've understood. Helped. Stopped it. Or worse, they'd paint the act like it was senseless and nothing they *could* understand. So much easier to make him a mon-ster than find out who he really was, probably.

When Sebastian and Isaac first started talking on Land of Valor,

Sebastian hadn't been amazed someone knew him. On the video game, he was a god. Isaac had given him a way to be great in real life. Isaac knew what Sebastian needed, and he'd shown him how to achieve it.

Isaac showed him it was better to be a monster with a name than a good guy without one.

Zane knows your name.

"Can I give you a hand?"

Sebastian jumped at the voice. He looked up to see an older guy with a handlebar mustache kneeling on the other side of the hose. Guy ripped a few strips of duct tape off the roll, tacked the ends on his pant leg. Then he started taping with Sebastian.

The sweat dripped down Sebastian's forehead and onto his neck. He had to get rid of the guy before they came to the capped end.

"Nothing like prepping electrical at this hour, huh? Guess it's a job."

"Yeah," Sebastian grunted.

"You get to go home after this, or are you on crew tomorrow?" the man asked.

Friendly conversation never had been Sebastian's forte.

"Home." Shit. He should've said crew. Mistake.

"Ah. Good for you. I'm stuck here 'til seven. The wife won't even be awake when I get back," he said. He chuckled. "Guess you young guys don't have that problem, eh?"

Zane's mottled face entered Sebastian's mind, the feel of her clammy hands on his chest. Her smooth, scarred lips had been detestable, and yet he'd wanted more of them. Crazy.

What would a normal guy say to that? Sebastian forced out a laugh. "You know how it is."

It was the sort of thing he heard men say all the time, but he never knew what it was supposed to mean. How could someone possibly know how something was for somebody else unless they'd lived their life?

They taped the cord in silence, and Sebastian floundered for a diversion. Having the man see the end of the hose would ruin everything.

As it turned out, the geezer gave him an out, almost like he knew and took sympathy on Sebastian. "You need any hookups or anything at the end?"

Question of the century. "Oh, nah. This one's for a private group's equipment. Just supposed to have it laid out and ready for them to plug in when they get here."

The lie came so easily, it was almost like he'd known he'd need it.

"Ah, okey dokey, then. Might want to toss a tarp over the end just in case. No rain in the forecast, but if the weather turns bad, tarp'll give the crew a chance to cover up the rest. If the outside of the line gets wet, that's not such a big deal, but if that adapter head gets drenched, you've got problems."

"Good call," Sebastian replied. He hadn't thought of rain.

Probably a lot he hadn't thought of.

The guy got up, moved on to the next random project. Too bad the geezer wouldn't be here tomorrow. The guilt that he'd helped with setting up this disaster would probably make him wish he were.

If Sebastian somehow made it so Zane wasn't here, she would probably wish she'd stopped him, too. Maybe her being here *was* kinder to her, after all.

He could call her, pretend he was someone else. Lure her away. No. That was no good. This event meant too much to her. She wouldn't leave.

The thought pissed him off, made his face burn. Someone had taken her face from her, someone like the guy she was fighting to keep alive tomorrow. She was sick, too.

Sebastian tossed the tarp over the capped end of the hose, taped it down on all sides. The last thing he needed was someone trying to inspect that end. When he was done, he walked the same way he'd come in, no one bothering to stop him to talk. They wouldn't, after all. He was a nobody here, too.

No deciding about Zane tonight. He'd sleep on it. Maybe when he called her to meet up tomorrow, the answer would hit him just like the lie to the old man.

If no ideas miraculously developed, at the very least he wouldn't have to be around to see what happened to her.

54

Jenna and Hank stood in the Krupkes' hallway to talk. Turned out, Hank appeared somewhat grateful for Yancy's presence, since Yancy could sit there with the heap of sobbing Zane while they strategized.

The stoners in the other room seemed oblivious to their chatter other than the dad, who occasionally stalked back and forth to glimpse what they were doing. He always had some "reason," like watering his aloe plant, but Jenna could tell.

"We station men to monitor the crowd for him, *all* plainclothes. Snipers posted, as many vantage points as we can," Jenna said. Hank knew all this, but talking it out helped her feel in control of her thoughts.

"What about windows? He could take kill shots," Hank pointed out.

"Not likely. Sebastian wasn't the marksman of the group. We know that from the ferry shooting. Isaac will have him take out a chunk of the rally in a way that feels less personal to Sebastian. Sebastian will have doubts, and Isaac foresaw that. He's foreseen a lot."

"You're thinking bomb?"

"Bomb, maybe preset sniper rifle, but then again, I doubt the rifle. If it was an option, they'd have used it at the ferry shooting. Isaac might've gotten a kick out of being able to get Sebastian out of the park without detection, but he'd have known Sebastian wouldn't have the stomach to kill as many when separated from him."

"True. So we need to check every car, bus, van in the area. All the equipment trucks coming in," Hank replied.

"The ones already *there*. We need backgrounds on personnel if we can, a sharp eye on any left bags, boxes, et cetera."

"Jenna, this is risky. We should call the event off."

Jenna raised her eyebrows. "You seriously want to *try* to cancel an anti–death penalty rally? You think that's even *possible*? On a good day, you're talking about riots and some really pissed off bureaucrats. FBI messes in a hot button issue like death penalty? We'd cause a shitstorm. Not to mention, this may be our one chance to catch the ferry shooter. We don't know his plans. He gets away from this scene, our trail turns cold, and he plants the next bomb. We don't know how many Keaton put him up to."

Hank blew out a breath. "I hate it when you're right."

"Don't I know it."

"We could screen everyone who goes in," Hank ventured.

"He'll spook faster than Punxsutawney Phil on a bright June day."

"This is a nightmare."

"No. It's a nightmare if the bomb goes off. This is a *challenge*. Figure out Keaton's brain, and we win," Jenna said.

If they knew more about Keaton, maybe they'd know about the modus operandi he'd choose for Sebastian. This was Keaton's show, not Sebastian's. Sebastian hadn't chosen one thing about how this would go down other than committing to it.

"We *could* go back to Keaton," Hank suggested.

Isaac's face flashed in Jenna's mind, his smug expression. Riddles. "No. He wouldn't tell us anything at this point. Not even to toy with us. He knows Sebastian's volatile, I'm sure of it." Not to mention Thadius Grogan. At least they'd found Zane before he had.

"In that case, Zane's our best option," Hank said, nodding toward the girl's room.

"Let's hope."

Jenna sat next to Zane Krupke on her bed. The girl had stopped crying, but she was now rocking herself back and forth, hugging a purple sham pillow to her chest.

"How could he do this to me?" she whimpered.

"These things aren't easy to understand, Zane. Trust me," Jenna said.

"I would've never known. All the things I've been through in my life, and I'd never have picked him out," she muttered.

Jenna looked away from Zane, whose hair was wet from her own tears. This never got easier no matter who it was, but especially when it was someone who'd already been through the ringer.

"This is a hard thing to ask of you, Zane, but we need your help. We need you to help us find him tomorrow."

"Tomorrow?" she echoed. "What's tomorrow?"

"The rally, Zane. We're trying to find Sebastian before the rally, but in case we don't, you're our best chance to get in touch with him before something bad happens."

She scooted back on the bed, fumbled her way to her knees. "Tomorrow? You can't let him come tomorrow! It's not . . . I can't . . . he . . ."

"I know, Zane. We know. But if we call off the rally, he could hurt other people somewhere else another time. We have to stop him while we know where he is."

"My friends—"

"We're going to do everything we can to make this safe," Hank said.

Oh, go on. Reassure her when we have no reason to think this will be safe. Promise her the same way you promised me you'd keep an eye on Claudia.

"Zane, we can't tell you this plan is perfect. But we don't have another one. We could prepare for years, and we might not know what's coming. The truth is, this is the one chance we have to catch him. We need you, Zane," Jenna said.

Zane sank back to her rear end, her breaths rattling in and out of the mouth destroyed by another freak just like Sebastian. The girl shook her head from side to side, and her black locks drifted over her shoulders.

"If I have to," she whispered.

Reluctant but accepting. Man, did Jenna know the feeling.

"You said this is an event you've worked on a lot, right?" Jenna asked.

The girl nodded. "Yeah. I organized at least half the volunteers."

"Do you have lists of their names?" Sebastian's name wouldn't be on one yet, so it couldn't be a *complete* list. But it was a start.

"Yes, I do. I'll give you all my notes about the rally. Hang on."

Zane got up and moved to the desk. Her forehead wrinkled as she shuffled a few papers, picked up a book or two. "It's gone."

Trepidation crept up Jenna's back. "What's gone?"

Zane shifted a few more books, this time more frantic. "My binder. The rally binder. It's not here."

Oh, no.

"Is anything else missing?" Yancy asked, standing as though he knew the room well enough to help look.

Zane glanced around, leafed through a stack of books she'd dropped into her closet. "I don't think so."

"Did you talk to *anyone* else about Sebastian Waters, Zane? Anyone at all?"

The sinking in Jenna's stomach was deepening even before the answer, because somehow she knew what had happened. The room glowed red in her eyes, a red very clearly associated with this case. No way this could turn out well.

"No. I just got home a little while ago. I haven't seen anyone since Sebastian actually," Zane said. She blushed.

"Anything odd about home when you got here? Even the tiniest detail? Think hard," Hank said.

Zane closed her eyes like she was taking mental inventory. She shook her head twice, then stopped. Her eyes fluttered open.

"My door wasn't closed."

"Is it usually?" Jenna asked.

Now Zane nodded her head hard. "Always. I don't like the . . . well, I don't like Dad to see what I do in here."

Or you don't like the smell of pot.

Either way, they had bigger problems than Daddy's marijuana problem right now. The dread encircling Jenna's stomach tightened, squeezed. They needed to talk to Daddy now, stoned or not stoned. The red glowed brighter. It was the color that one man involved with this case had appeared as all along.

It would seem Thadius Grogan might've found Zane first after all.

yra sat on the cold earth in the dark, waiting. She'd come as soon as she'd sobered up—enough to call a cab anyway. No way she'd be brave enough to try this without a drop of alcohol in her system.

This was the only plan she could think of, though. The one thing that might be worth a try, the sole idea with the potential to help Isaac out of this impossible scenario he'd dug his way into.

She checked the glowing face of her phone for the hundredth or so time. Ten minutes had passed since she last looked. *Be patient.*

Freaky, hanging out in this place by herself. Hard to be still, keep the jitters in check. But Lyra couldn't risk moving, giving herself away until *she* came. The woman might leave without showing herself, or worse: sneak up on her.

Lyra couldn't be sure what told her to be here. Somehow she knew the woman would show up, and it had everything to do with the fact that *Isaac* would if he were in the same situation. She'd learned a lot about his patterns over the years.

Lyra wandered down to the lake one day after her Girl Scouts meeting. Their dad said her brother had gone outside carrying sheets and blankets to build a fort. Super cool. Lyra knew she could help him.

When she reached the bank, she didn't see Isaac anywhere. He wasn't on the dock soaking his feet in the water, nowhere around the boathouse. Maybe he was in the boathouse . . .

The door pushed open without a sound. Isaac faced the wall, tearing a sheet into strips. He ripped and ripped, harder and angrier, until only shreds remained. He hovered over them, still facing away from her. For a moment, she thought he was staring down at the strips, examining them, until she heard the trickle. He was peeing on them!

Isaac turned, and Lyra crouched. For a split second, her breath caught. Had he seen her?

His gaze lingered on the door, but then he kept moving. He climbed into Dad's boat, lifted the bench seat. Under each section, he placed a strip of soiled sheet before returning the seat to its regular position.

Before she could think, he was out of the boat and heading her way. Hide!

Lyra tried to sneak behind the door, but a hand grabbed the back of her neck, yanked her to her feet. "You wanna be nosy, Lye-RUH? Huh?"

Isaac shoved her nose into the side of the boathouse, and a splinter pierced the soft skin on its tip. She didn't yell. She shouldn't.

He leaned close to her. "Don't follow me, Lye-RUH. Not ever. I take care of you. You don't try to keep secrets from me, understand? Don't try to know things about me I don't tell you, either."

She'd tried to nod, but her face was too smashed into the wood. "Promise, promise."

The pressure slackened. Her nose stung, but her heart hurt worse. Tears burned her eyes as she faced him, ashamed but even more bruised by his words.

"Oh, Lye. I'm sorry," he said. He hugged her tight. "If you did that to

other people, they might hurt you. I had to teach you that lesson. Under-
stand?"

"Uh-huh," she said, burrowing her face into his shirt. His underarms
smelled so strongly of sweat she could barely smell the urine in the boat
anymore.

"Why'd you do that to the boat?" she asked, her face still buried in his arm.

"Funny prank," he said. "Don't tell, okay?"

She promised again.

It wouldn't be the last time Lyra saw him do that, though it was
definitely the last time she let him catch her watching. Sometimes he
put the sheets in the boat, other times the car. Always places sure to
cause a musky problem no one could find, least of all Dad. Isaac always had an excuse for what happened to the old sheets. They'd
blown into the lake, he'd forgotten one in the woods. Once, he told
Dad they used one to make a kite that got away.

After a while, Lyra added two and two and realized this ritual
occurred on days after her father chewed Isaac out for wetting his
bed. She'd never tell Dad, though. She didn't blame Isaac. He and
Dad had huge screaming matches about how Isaac was too old to
wet his bed, and Lyra felt bad for her brother. Isaac couldn't help it.
Everyone always said when you had to go, you had to go. She'd
never been told this applied only to a certain age, and she was always sure Isaac hadn't, either.

As an adult, Lyra recognized the difference, but it didn't change
her level of sympathy.

Even after Dad was gone, sometimes Isaac still went to the boathouse and piled sheets in a musty corner there. Lyra never understood it, but it helped him some way. Somehow it cauterized his
shame.

It was like all of the habits Isaac had, the ways he would visit
places that meant something to him. Something dark she didn't al-

ways understand. But even if she didn't understand what they meant or why he visited them, his habit of revisiting his own little chaotic memories was the reason she always knew how to find him, even if the first time, only intuition led her to him.

It was the same reason that now Claudia Ramey would show up here.

A n hour or two passed before Lyra sensed someone in the graveyard with her. She steeled herself to be strong for her brother. She was his only hope.

The footsteps came closer and closer still until they were almost upon her. *Please, let this be the right thing to do. It's all I have.*

"Who are you?" Claudia's cold voice asked when she saw Lyra sitting beside the gravestone.

"I'm L-L-L-Lyra Mintelle," she stuttered.

"Oh, I see," Claudia said, amused. "You come here often?"

The woman was playing with her, Lyra knew. Claudia had to be well aware Lyra was there waiting for her.

Lyra's body shuddered as though she were in the middle of the Alaskan tundra.

"I need your help," Lyra said.

Claudia Ramey practically cackled. "Help *you?* Why would I want to help *you?*"

"Because I know things that would be mutually beneficial."

Claudia cocked her head, examined Lyra like she was a strange artifact in a museum. "What could you possibly know that could be of any service to *me?*"

"I know things about your daughter. Jenna." Lyra trembled, afraid to say the next part. Once she did, there would be no taking it back. "And I know how you could get to her, hurt her most if you wanted to."

"Is that so, young lady?" Claudia asked. The woman sounded skeptical, but Lyra could tell she'd touched a nerve by the way Claudia's eyes widened, the wildness reflected in the moonlight.

Lyra nodded.

"Well, well, well. If that's the case, you might be my new best friend."

Zane's father washed his hands three times while Jenna and Hank questioned him. Keeping yourself busy always made it easier not to panic while talking to cops, right?

"Mr. Krupke," Hank said, "think one more time. Was anything different about your house when you came home this afternoon?"

Krupke dried his very clean hands on the dirty dishrag next to the sink. "I told you. I've *been* home. I cooked dinner, had the boys over. Haven't left."

They had to be going about this wrong. It would help if the man didn't think they wanted to trap him in some kind of drug bust. They hadn't explained what was missing from Zane's room yet, but only because, as Zane pointed out, her father didn't know much about the contents of her room anyway.

"Did anyone besides the boys come over today? Any pizzas delivered, maintenance men come by?" Jenna asked. Thadius had to have had a chance to gain entry to the house, but how? All the access points were intact, no locks tampered with. Mr. Krupke hadn't gone out, so Thadius must've come in and taken the book while he was here. Too stoned to notice maybe?

"Nothing like that, I told you! Just been us," he said. Then, to Zane, "The one guy from your group came by, but he left shortly after—"

"Wait, what guy?" Zane asked.

"You know. The guy you sent over for the record thingie."

"*What?*"

"Mr. Krupke, what record *thingie* are you referring to?" Jenna asked, heart thumping.

The man dried his hands on the towel again, which was more soaked than his palms at this point. "Guy from the victim what-a-jig. Zane sent him over for that picture keeper thing she has for the get-together-whatnot."

"Did he go in and *get* it?" Jenna pushed.

"I'm not *that* much of an ass! 'Course I didn't let him go in my daughter's bedroom. Went in and got it myself."

"Dad!" Zane gasped, head in hands.

Jenna couldn't help but feel bad for her. Retrieving the notebook for a stranger seemed so stupid. But really it wasn't. The pretext was simple. Perfect. Thadius Grogan, master of disguise.

"What did the man look like?" Jenna asked, even though she already knew.

As expected, Krupke gave a pretty decent picture of Grogan: on the large side, older. He didn't have a mustache or beard anymore apparently, but they'd known for a while he'd probably have shaved.

"Wait, wait. Back up. You said he asked you for records. He knew Zane wasn't home?" Hank asked.

Krupke opened the fridge, stared into it blankly. "Nah. He wanted to see Zane, come to think. Told him she wasn't here. He asked when she'd be back. Told him I didn't know, that Eva was bringing her home. Then he asked when he could come by tomorrow, that he needed to get together with her on some stuff for an event."

"What'd you tell him? How'd the records come up?"

Krupke shut the refrigerator door, seemed to think better of it, and opened it again. "I said she wouldn't be here tomorrow, either, because she had that thing-a-ma-jig. He said oh yeah, he remembered that. He needed to meet up before it, because she had some records about it he was organizing. Asked me if I could find the information for him. 'Course, I didn't know when Zane'd be back, and the guy was kinda frazzled. I didn't wanna make him freak out. I went in there and looked around, found the thing he seemed to be talking about. Brought it to him. He left."

"Dad, how *could* you?"

"How could I *what*? He was helpin' out, I thought."

Jenna turned to Zane. "Who's Eva?"

Zane blinked, stuck between being pissed at her dad and answering the question. "A friend. She was supposed to pick me up tonight, but then she didn't show up."

"Last name?"

"Delaney."

"Call Saleda and have her find Eva Delaney, pronto," Jenna said. God willing, Thadius Grogan had no reason to have a beef with this girl, but Jenna wasn't willing to bank on it.

Hank nodded and pulled out his phone.

"How *did* you get home tonight, Zane? Sebastian didn't bring you, right?" Jenna asked.

She shook her head. "No. I called a taxi."

Zane's eyes darted toward her father, but he was still busy expecting the contents of the refrigerator to magically change or multiply.

"All right. We need to station an agent here at the apartment with you tonight, Zane. For your own protection," Jenna said.

At this, Mr. Krupke slammed the refrigerator door. "No way."

Hank covered his ear not pressed to the phone listening to Saleda. He stepped away from them.

"Sir, I know it's inconvenient, but the man here earlier is extremely dangerous," Jenna explained. "Zane's safety has to be our first priority."

The dad shook his head back and forth. "They have protocol for that, yeah? Protective custody and all?"

"It's important we don't *move* her, either," Hank cut in as he hung up with Saleda.

"I don't have to consent to this!"

Hank leaned on the counter toward the man. "And *I* don't have to ignore what I've seen at this apartment so far, but I'm willing to, if you cooperate."

"Seen? Seen nothing! I haven't done anything wron—"

"Are you kidding us with this?" Hank replied. He cocked his head toward the men on the couch. "Those two would probably *bleed* weed if we stuck them right now."

"I'll stay."

Jenna turned, wide eyes on Yancy. As if Hank didn't think he was interfering enough already. This would be a doozy.

"What? I'm not a cop, so the Pot Brigade here has nothing to fear. I can keep lookout without being conspicuous," Yancy said.

"Yancy, you chased Thadius Grogan down a painter's scaffold, for God's sake! He'd recognize you in a second!"

"Might be all the better, actually," Hank said.

"You're not serious." This was unbelievable. Now Hank was trying to get Yancy killed outright?

"I mean it. Grogan knows Yancy will confront him, plus Yancy *could* theoretically know Zane through victim support. May be better for everyone if we walk out and leave no reason for anyone to think Zane's being tailed, just in case *Sebastian's* watching. Yancy's less of a threat," Hank said, and he glanced at Yancy's leg. "No offense."

Yancy's eyes narrowed. "Of course not."

"It's settled, then. Yancy'll stay, hang with Zane tomorrow. No-body will be the wiser," Hank said.

"You don't think there's a chance of Sebastian remembering this is one of the people he might've *shot*?" Zane piped up.

Jenna locked eyes with Yancy. He sent a lot across that fierce look, but the main thing was *do this*.

"No. I don't think he knows who any of those people were," Jenna answered. "His aim isn't that good."

H ank's phone rang almost the moment they got back in the SUV. He put Saleda on speaker.

"Eva Delaney?" Hank asked.

"Grogan spoke to her all right," Saleda replied. "Sending an agent to her house now. Grogan called her, pretended to be another volunteer for tomorrow. Told Eva he was supposed to pick Zane up at the Roger's Road Emporium so they could hash out details. Eva argued, said *she* was picking Zane up at the abandoned grocery on Wilshire, that Zane had been out with some guy. Grogan acted confused, didn't realize Zane was on a date. Eva told him she hadn't met the guy, but Zane recruited him for tomorrow, so they'd have one more. Then Thadius told her not to worry, he would give Zane a ride. Said he was in the Wilshire neighborhood and could swing by and pick her up."

"Get a car to the old Wilshire grocery store ASAP," Hank said.

"Already on it," Saleda replied.

Hank hung up. "Be nice if tomorrow could be anticlimactic."

"You think Grogan caught up with Sebastian already?" Jenna asked.

"Don't know. You doubt it?"

"Zane made it home safe and sound. I wouldn't think Sebastian would hang around after Zane got in the taxi."

"True. Unless Grogan was lying in wait and followed Sebastian after Zane left? Thadius isn't into killing innocents, after all."

Jenna shrugged. "No way to know until tomorrow."

They pulled into Jenna's apartment complex.

"You want me to come up?" Hank asked.

Jenna already had one foot out the door. "No, thanks. Charley's probably home by now."

"I'm surprised you're staying."

"Me, too."

She hurried across the lot to her door, climbed the stairs. She shoved her key in the lock, turned it, and rushed inside. She closed the door behind her, bolted it. If Charley came home, he could call her to let him in.

Shadows slithered across the walls, moonbeams eerie through the blinds. So weird, coming home to a dark apartment. She hadn't done this in years. Someone was always up: Dad making a pot of coffee and walking with Ayana, Charley writing music in the living room under the lamp.

Ayana was probably fast asleep by now, warm and cozy in her porta-crib, gently sucking her pink pacifier. God, Jenna ached so much to be near her.

In the bathroom, Jenna twisted the shower knobs and pulled the curtain closed to keep the spray confined to the tub. She closed the door and flipped the bolt. She might be the only person in this building with bolts on every door *inside* her apartment.

Her phone dinged with a text message. Yancy.

Checking in to make sure you made it home okay.

Jenna smiled and typed back. You were worried about me?

After a few seconds, the text chimed again. Nah. Just didn't want to be left to face the crazies tomorrow with only Hank at my back. He'd push me toward the bullets.

Jenna typed back. Have no fear. I'll back you up. Gotta run-shower.

She laid her phone back on the counter, turned to step into the tub. The text alert went off again. *Damn you, Yancy.*

Jenna picked up her phone. It said: So, what color is your towel? *wink wink*

She bit her lip. Of all the things people ask about colors, I think that's the first time anyone's asked me about a towel, Yancy Vogul.

Jenna stood holding her phone now, stark naked, waiting for his reply. *Ding.*

I think light blue would be a nice towel on you. Unless you have some freaky color association with towels I don't know about.

Despite herself, Jenna giggled. She wrote back: Nope. No towel associations. Light blue works fine for me. Good night, Yancy . . .

Ding. Good night, little blue. ;-)

Jenna grinned. She put down her phone and climbed into the shower. The spray beat down on the knots in her neck, warm and delicious. Tomorrow would be hell. Thadius Grogan knew Sebastian would be at the rally, so he'd go after him. Sebastian's target was the rally itself. Both Thadius *and* Sebastian were Jenna's targets. A giant battle royale set so the victor would be whoever lucked out. At this point, Jenna had no idea who to expect that to be. Crazy thing was, Isaac Keaton probably wasn't even sure, either.

She squirted shampoo into her hand, lathered it in the tangles of her hair. Sure, Isaac had some contempt for a weakling like Sebastian, but in a way, it would be part of the fun of it for Isaac. In a way, by pitting Sebastian up against a worthy opponent like Thadius, he was testing his own skill in training and preparing Sebastian. He'd set up this little cat and mouse game, and he'd probably get some sick pleasure knowing that at any moment it could go either way.

And whatever else Isaac was, he was confident. He had to have been reasonably sure the two of them would make it to the rally, if only because he had controlled the level of information Thadius Grogan had access to, through Howie Dumas, just enough that he knew it would take them a while to come head to head. Could Thadius get to Sebastian before that? Sure. But a gamemaster like Isaac Keaton who thought himself flawless in his planning wouldn't assume so. And for Isaac, really, anything that happened from here on out was a win in his book. No matter who did what at this point or what chaos went down, he had caused it. He had lorded power over these people, pulled the puppets' strings so that ultimately he had been the only one truly in control of their destinies. Whatever happened to any of them would all be at his mercy, exactly how he would like it.

Suds dripped from her hair and fell to the tub floor. This would be a crapshoot, all right. They had Zane, but whether or not she could lead them to Sebastian depended on Sebastian's own plans. If Jenna, Hank, Yancy, and the team had any karma going for them, they'd find Sebastian and he'd show them his plan in time for them to stop it.

Even though they didn't know what Sebastian was up to, Thadius was the *real* wild card. Grogan would want Sebastian no matter the cost. The profile said Grogan was in pain, probably so much pain that he didn't care about *anything* but making Sebastian pay. In fact, Thadius might very well *expect* to go down in the process.

For so long, Jenna thought she had it bad, what with how her life had gone. But really, she still had her dad, Charley, and a beautiful little girl. Thadius didn't have anything—anyone—to live for. Wife gone, daughter killed. *That* was pain.

Jenna was going through a rough time with Claudia out and her family stashed away, but hard times passed. Keeping Ayana safe mattered most, and as long as they didn't know where Claudia was, Ayana's well-being took precedence.

What if they never found Claudia? What would she do? Hide Ayana forever? Stay away forever?

Jenna had to stay away, though. Claudia had plenty of reasons to come after Jenna. Her mother might go after Ayana to hurt *Jenna*, but at the end of the day, it was Jenna whom Claudia wanted.

Right?

The question was moot. Jenna knew it the same way she knew a lot of things. The same way she knew her mother.

It wouldn't be long before Claudia and Jenna would come head to head. The calm before the storm. Sooner or later, Claudia would surface, and when she did, Jenna had to make sure the woman could never hurt her family again.

57

The next morning, Jenna stood with Hank in a storefront on the block shut down for the vigil for killer Fordham Beach. The place was something like a Thanksgiving Day parade minus the giant Bart Simpson and Garfield balloons. People ate hot dogs and carried signs that said things like, THE DEATH PENALTY ADDS MORE MURDER and HATE DOESN'T HEAL. Kids too young to know what they were wearing were dressed in T-shirts with Beach's face and the words, HE HAS A KID LIKE ME.

Behind barricades set up on the other side of the block a different group of people hunkered, and they held signs, too. One lady behind the barricade wore a neon shirt that proclaimed JUSTICE FOR KAREN. Jenna assumed Karen was the name of Beach's victim.

Then again, maybe Karen had nothing to do with Beach, and Beach just represented everything the protesting woman hated. Who knew.

"No chance we're spotting Sebastian at random here," Jenna mumbled. Not like she'd expected to be able to, but the thought of not having to put Zane in the position appealed to her.

"Nope. We'll have Zane call. Yancy has a headset. We're good to go," Hank replied.

They'd met Zane in the wee hours of the morning to brief her, get her ready. Zane would start the day stationed at the volunteer booth, Yancy alongside her. Yancy wouldn't be able to tag along with her everywhere, but he'd blend in well enough to try to keep them posted.

Thadius Grogan's whereabouts were an entirely different matter. The BAU team had given his photo to all the agents working the rally, but other than that, they had no way to find him. They'd sent agents to search the area near the grocery store where Zane was supposed to have been picked up just in case, but no sign of Grogan. Whether he'd ever ridden that way to try to head off Sebastian or if he'd thought today's rally was the better option was anyone's guess. But since Thadius's kills were about as subtle as the smell of pot in Zane's father's apartment, the fact that they hadn't found a dead Sebastian anywhere near the grocery store told them the two men had yet to run into each other. This meant today, the best plan of attack was to keep a sharp eye out and hope when they found Sebastian, they'd find Thadius, too. Hopefully before *Thadius* found *Sebastian*.

Jenna and Hank's vantage point—an abandoned storefront at the corner of the first block after the main entrance to the vigil—gave them a limited view of three blocks in either direction of the street closed off for the event. It might not have been so limited if not for the thick crowd. All in all, a remarkable turnout for a murderer's vigil in rural, middle-of-bumfuck-nowhere, Florida.

From where Jenna and Hank were, they could see the table Zane ran where volunteers passed out bottled water, bananas, and fliers. Zane herself disappeared from view depending on foot traffic, but that was why Yancy was at the table. A sniper waited in the loft above them, and he could cover most of the area within the blocks of the rally. A second sniper on the west corner covered his only blind spot.

"What time is it?" Jenna asked for the fifth time.

"Five more minutes," Hank replied.

She glanced in the binoculars again, spotted Yancy. He looked natural, maybe more natural than she'd have been able to come across. Calm or not, watching him made Jenna's heart flutter. She didn't like that he had less protection than her Kevlar gave *her*. Hank had forced Yancy to check his Ruger at the surveillance van, dead set against a gun in that crowd, even given the circumstances. Jenna and Yancy had both protested, but the fact was, they were still *invited in* by the FBI. The Feds' word was law.

No suspicious vehicles so far, no abandoned suitcases. Everything progressed as if this was just any other rally.

In about four more minutes, though, if Sebastian hadn't contacted Zane, she would call him. Big risk, since Zane didn't need to come across as too anxious. But there was a point at which they'd have to know where Sebastian was.

Two blocks away, a band jammed on the Frito-Lay-sponsored stage. If nothing else, the drums matched Jenna's mood, pounding and building.

Jenna's phone buzzed. Irv. Normally, she wouldn't answer in this situation, but the color of traffic cones flashed in, the same color she'd seen every time a "Breaking News" bulletin came on TV since she was young. Irv knew she was at the rally. Something must be up for him to call now.

"What's going on?"

"I've been going through some chat transcripts on Land of Valor, and I'm pretty sure I found our friend Isaac."

"Oh yeah?" If there was anything to trump her surveillance of the events outside, it was this.

"Yup. A goddamned warlock. Like you predicted, other guys pointed out his monopoly of Sebastian. Sometimes seemed like he was wooing him."

"Name?"

"Ain't that the question of the year? Account's listed under Rover McPhee, if that tells you anything. Prepaid cards only."

Great. Isaac Keaton was a golden retriever. "I'm guessing you aren't calling to tell me the finer points of their online battle strategies?"

"Eh, not exactly, though I think you'll find my news equally interesting. I'm pretty sure Emily Grogan's murder is mentioned."

Jenna almost dropped the phone. "By Sebastian?"

Bragging could've opened the door for Isaac to approach Sebastian to join him on the hunt, but it didn't sit right. Sebastian was lower-key than that. Grandiosity didn't match his style. Maybe Jenna had pegged him wrong all along.

"Bonk. By Isaac."

"What?" How could Isaac have known Sebastian killed Emily unless he knew Sebastian in real life?

" 'Enable Flaming Wrath. Dude, I heard some girl was killed in your neck of the woods.' End Isaac quote. 'Yeah. Popping a health pot.' End Sebastian quote. 'You didn't kill her, did you? Wouldn't put it past you. Watch those adds on the left hill.' End Isaac quote. 'Got 'em. What do you mean?' End Sebastian quote. Isaac says, 'She was hot, man!' Sebastian says, 'Was she?' 'You know she was!' End Isaac quote. 'Do you know how big this school is, man?' End Sebastian quote. 'I heard it was like, the bloodiest murder the cops there had ever seen.' End Isaac quote. Sebastian says, 'Gross.' "

"Is that it?" Jenna asked, the peridot color she'd come to associate with fishing for information dancing in front of her eyes. She tried to pull it closer, to let another color surround it, as often this particular color came in first, then another color would follow. A color that felt most like the intent behind the fishing.

"Not quite," Irv said, breaking her concentration. "Isaac quote, 'Gross. This coming from a guy who packs heat for fun and laughs and walks away. Admit it: you wouldn't mind seeing her sizzle.' At that point, Sebastian kind of ignores him. Continue the warlock rambling in between battle junk about the girl, trying to get Sebastian to bite, but he doesn't. Ever. Also doesn't react to the conversation like it's uncomfortable or anything different from any other ol' talk."

"Didn't Sebastian ever try to *end* the conversation? You're kidding me."

The clash between Sebastian Waters's blue and the red Jenna associated with the violence of Emily Grogan's murder popped to mind. It had never made sense why the colors didn't match. Someone with such a cool blue hue in all other aspects of his profile committing something as violent as strangling someone with her own intestines was about as likely as Jenna joining a mother-daughter beauty pageant with Claudia.

"Nope. He's too casual, Jenna. Either Sebastian is one extremely cool cucumber—and I mean under the on-high icemaker—or . . ."

"He didn't do it," Jenna finished.

"Precisimo, ultima," Irv said. "Sound like I took a foreign language class, huh?"

"Huh. Thanks, Irv."

She hung up and relayed the information to Hank. "Isaac waved the murder in front of him, but Sebastian gave up nothing. Which, it's not like Sebastian's profile for him to come into Land of Valor openly bragging about killing someone, but it's also unlikely that he'd say *nothing* to Isaac when it was brought up. Here's a guy he doesn't know in real life, and someone like Sebastian is on edge as it is, not chill under pressure the way Isaac would be. He'd be dying to get it out or shut it up. One of the two."

"*And* if Sebastian knew her, the talk would at least elicit some embarrassment, nervousness."

"Exactly! He also says the way she was killed was gross. I ignored it before for so many obvious reasons, but Emily Grogan's murder was *so* personal. The killer had to be up close, not to mention have a stomach of steel in order to strangle her with her own *intestines*. Sebastian couldn't even aim his gun at specific people at the theme park. Couldn't stand the kills."

"Yeah. It's a lot easier to fire from a bridge than gut a girl a foot in front of you," Hank replied.

Jenna shook her head in disbelief. From Sebastian's standpoint, the Gemini shootings had always been about *him*, not the people he killed. Emily Grogan's murder was far too individualized. That violent red she'd always seen had to do with hyper-violence, but also crimes of passion. Sebastian wasn't capable of something so close to home. The cool blue of his planning to bring weapons to school but not going through with harming anyone showed that.

Thadius Grogan was after the wrong man, and Isaac had sent him there.

"Wait a minute," Jenna said, her heart speeding up. "Isaac mentioned something about Sebastian packing heat for fun and walking away. Land of Valor has a lot of weapons, sure, but I don't think Celestials 'pack heat' exactly."

Hank stared at her, blinking. "Are you speaking English?"

She was already dialing Irv again.

"Yes, my queen?" he answered.

"Land of Valor. Celestials. Would they carry guns?"

"Do Care Bears wear bandoliers to strap ammo to their chests?"

Jenna coughed. "Um . . . no."

Irv chuckled. "You're right. They don't. Neither do Celestials, though I wouldn't say no to a nice cloud car if the game invented one. Why do you ask?"

"Isaac talking to Sebastian about packing heat for fun. I was just thinking . . . he probably wasn't talking about the game, was he?"

"Heh," Irv laughed. "We're gonna make a nerd out of you yet, good Doctor. Good catch. No, most of the time a Celestial would carry a sword. Maybe one with some godly component. A fire sword, maybe. A hammer could happen, but yeah, no guns."

"Right. Thanks," Jenna said, and she hung up.

She relayed the info to Hank. Before he could fully expound on his confusion, she tried to quickly explain where her head was. "So if Isaac talked to Sebastian about packing heat for fun in some context that *wasn't* to do with the game, and he mentioned Sebastian walking away, it sounds like Isaac might've known about Sebastian's past at his high school."

"So what? He found Sebastian within the game, targeted him, and started researching him? Found all his deep dark secrets, then used them to somehow assume Sebastian killed this random girl Isaac heard had been murdered? Now *your* head's the one in the clouds," Hank said.

Jenna shook her head hard. "No. I think I was wrong," Jenna said as the peridot from her first hearing of Isaac and Sebastian's conversation gave way to indigo flashing in, rather than the goldfish color of natural curiosity. Indigo usually showed up when the person fishing for information had a deliberate intent, an answer they wanted to hear. Other colors burned bright, but Jenna tried to ignore them long enough to get her thought out. "Isaac wasn't just idly pumping Sebastian for information to see if he knew anything about Emily Grogan. He—"

She couldn't think. The colors came rapidly now, one after the other. First indigo, then the sable color of knowledge, then fuchsia, disingenuous . . .

Slow down, let me process.

Jenna closed her eyes and took a deep breath. When she opened them again, Hank was still staring at her, but he showed no signs of impatience. Though he'd never understood her process, he knew when to shut up and let her work through whatever was flitting through her mind.

"I don't think he ever thought Sebastian had anything to do with Emily's death or that he was even trying to find out what Sebastian knew about Emily's murder. I think . . . well, I think the way he was talking to Sebastian was more deliberate than that. Call it instinct, but to me, the words he used, how much he knew about Sebastian already . . . he wasn't being sincere. It was almost like bragging. He was almost mocking Sebastian for not knowing the things he knew, only Sebastian never would get the joke. He *was* the joke."

Hank shook his head. "What are you talking about, Jenna?"

"We might never know how he managed to do it so perfectly, but I think I was wrong when I said Isaac happened upon Sebastian in the gaming world. Maybe the gaming world is Isaac's comfort zone, and maybe he even uses it as a hunting ground for targets. But in this case, I think he set out to target Sebastian specifically *because* he knew all about him and his past for whatever reason. It made Sebastian the perfect fall guy for Emily's murder, but Sebastian didn't ever actually *take* that fall."

"And you're thinking that for years, Isaac has watched his fall guy not get burned. How would he have not gotten caught?"

"Could've been any number of reasons. We see crimes every day that go unsolved, cold cases where an obvious answer comes out decades later when a certain piece of the puzzle jams into place. Maybe something just slipped through the cracks. Who knows?" Jenna answered.

"I guess I can see it. So Isaac watched Sebastian not take the fall he set up for him. And yet he knows enough about Sebastian to know how volatile he is, how ripe for direction in all things horrific . . ." Hank said, playing along.

"Yep. Not only watched his scapegoat walk away free and clear, never needing to use him, but also cultivating a target. A perfectly willing follower with all the makings of a partner in crime. He knew Sebastian had all the wiring. He just had to figure out which buttons to push," Jenna finished.

Hank nodded, but he frowned. "Okay, so he somehow manages to take Sebastian to the next level, and the Gemini killers are born. Why bring Thadius Grogan back into it? Just a fun game to see if his loose ends will tie each other up?"

Jenna was quiet. That, she didn't know. Not yet. Obviously, Isaac had staged Sebastian's shooting and everything else with a mind of getting Sebastian out of the theme park unnoticed and getting him to this very day and place. As for what was in store next or why all the events were lining up quite the way they were, Jenna could only badly speculate. There was still a missing piece.

Next to Jenna, Hank gripped his binoculars. "Zane just answered her phone."

Jenna's attention jolted back to the rally, pulse racing.

"We need more water at the stage," Yancy's voice crackled through the radio.

The code they'd decided on.

Hank picked up the other radio, this one connected to Saleda. "She's on. Stay with her."

Saleda lingered outside in a sundress on the arm of another agent holding a sign that said, DEATH IS NOT THE ANSWER.

Jenna lifted her binoculars and tried to home in on Zane, but she kept losing the girl behind taller people. As far as Jenna could tell, Zane remained at the table.

Three guys in face paint walked in front of her. When they moved, Zane was gone.

"She's moving!" Yancy crackled in, all pretext lost. He sounded panicked.

"Do *not* follow," Hank replied. He flipped a switch to disconnect Yancy's radio.

"What are you doing?" Jenna gasped.

"He's freaking. Not following protocol won't help us *or* Zane. We need to be able to listen for the real info." Hank radioed Saleda. "Have her?"

The radio came back. "Yes. Walking toward the west side. Coming your way. Zane's still on the phone."

The hair on Jenna's neck stood up. She drifted to the side of the storefront window, waiting for Zane to pass. It'd be at least a few more seconds, even if Zane was walking fast. She'd been a good football field away at the table.

"Still coming at you. I'm pressing, but trying to hang back a safe distance," Saleda replied.

Then Jenna saw Zane several yards down, talking furiously. Zane didn't glance at the storefront where they were, because they hadn't told her where they'd be.

The girl passed beside them so close Jenna could've reached out and touched her if not for the window. Zane turned sharply into the alleyway next to the storefront.

"Down the west alley," Saleda called.

Hank darted toward the back of the abandoned building. Connected to another structure in back, the attached building was adjacent to the parking garage behind the alley. The alley wasn't barricaded—the barricade was on the other side of the parking garage, putting it on the next block. Surveillance Van B was parked in the garage, but the garage wasn't one of the interception areas they'd anticipated. Zane had instructions not to leave the main crowd. Where was she going?

"Dropping her at the alley. Crossing through the coffee shop," Saleda said.

No way Saleda could follow Zane into the alley without someone knowing she had a tail. Saleda would go in through another access point and come out the other side. Still, Jenna's breath caught as she followed Hank. Letting Zane out of sight couldn't be a good thing.

Hank peeked out the exit of the store, moved into the space between the garage rails and the building. "Nothing."

They'd lost her.

58

Yancy had agreed to hang out with Zane. So far, he'd done everything he'd been told, but now he was left to juggle Gatorade and fruit, no idea what to do. Jenna was with the other agents, and yet he had no clue where they were.

He should stay. He should stay. He *should* stay!

Yancy's feet moved anyway.

The alleyway was up to his right, and that was where Zane had disappeared. She'd either gone down the alley or come back into the main crowd.

He walked straight up the center of the road and reached the gap where the alley jutted off right. People everywhere, but the alley was empty. Only puddles and power cords. Good combo.

Yancy's hooked prosthetic caught something under him, and he tripped. After a few quick steps, he regained his balance and looked down to see what his foot had snagged. His eye line followed the cords from the alley to where he was standing. They were all tagged with tiny labels: LAKE HARP BAND AMP 2. RAAZZER 3. MC TABLE MIC B.

His chest squeezed painfully when he saw the next cord. Duct-taped down like the rest, tacked in place, it didn't trail to the side with the others. Instead, it ended abruptly in the middle of the street.

CHARLEY PADGETT MIC.

Jenna's brother's face burst forth in Yancy's mind. "Oh, no . . ."

Isaac, Sebastian, this whole place. Isaac's plan wasn't just about the irony of dead people at an anti–death penalty rally or a high death count and infamy for Sebastian. It was about *Jenna.*

"I have a situation here!" he said, jamming the radio button.

He tried again, but he couldn't hear himself in the other end of his radio. They'd turned him off. Why would they turn him off? *Shit!*

Yancy glanced around, hoping to see an agent near him. Fucking plainclothes. He'd have to do it himself.

He squatted next to the end of the cord and pried the duct tape from the ground. The tape came up, and the end of the cord turned out not to be the end of a cord at all.

It appeared to be a hose—with a cap screwed onto the end.

The cops had been looking for abandoned cars and bags, searching *people* for this very thing. Yet here it was, all because he'd *tripped* on it. *All in a day.*

Internship in law enforcement didn't exactly train you for everything, including how to disarm a fucking *bomb.* Christ.

Still, Yancy had opened a champagne bottle or two in his life. Pressure was bad.

What's the worst that can happen? I have a hand to match my foot?

Slowly, carefully, he unscrewed the cap on the end. It slid away from the hose's end as easily as the top on a ginger ale. He stared inside the hose for a few seconds, stunned. It was packed with black stuff, tacks.

Yancy was sweating through his shirt now, too hot for comfort.

Someone needed to know about this. Anyone. Jenna. But Jenna

and Hank were God-knew-where, and Yancy was crouched in front of a bomb.

Jesus. Jenna!

Then his head swam, thoughts cramming in faster than he could react. If the bomb was here, and it wasn't the kind you saw in movies with a timer counting down to zero hour, that meant someone had to light the thing. He imagined Wile E. Coyote creeping up to a stick of dynamite with a match.

Yancy's eyes flew in the direction the cords snaked away from the alley. The stage.

Sebastian might've changed his mind. Maybe he *was* meeting Zane.

But maybe he wasn't.

Yancy bolted toward the stage. He shoved people out of his way, ripping through the crowd in a dead run. It didn't matter where Jenna was. She was off chasing Zane on the other side of the alley. She was nowhere near this thing.

Charley Padgett *was*.

59

The parking garage was completely quiet as Jenna followed Hank, the Glock issued to her for today trained in the direction they were moving. Zane was nowhere in sight.

"Something's wrong," Jenna whispered to Hank. "This isn't right. No one's out here. Sebastian's not."

"Are you saying Zane led us into a trap?" he asked.

"No. I'm saying maybe Zane isn't going to lead us to Sebastian, because *he* isn't leading her to *him*." This felt off. All the people and the main event were behind them. Isaac would've designed this plan to cause the maximum damage and chaos. There was no one in the garage. Nothing would happen here.

Jenna closed her eyes. The rally area glowed orange. Hot. The color of traffic cones and breaking news. The parking garage radiated blue or gray, the color she saw every time she thought about the incident with Charley and Claudia, of Charley's pale face. Defensiveness. Protectiveness.

"Oh, God," Jenna said. "He's saving her. We're going toward blue."

"What are you talking about? Blue could mean we're going *toward* Sebastian, right? You told me his color was blue," Hank said.

Jenna shook her head. "Not how it works. It's not Sebastian's blue. No time to explain! We need to get back to the rally. He sent Zane out here because the main event *is* far away. She's here so she won't get hurt. Sebastian's in *there*, and that's where he's going to execute Isaac's plan."

She pointed back toward the rally, but she was already taking off toward it. Whatever was about to happen, Zane wasn't part of it.

S ebastian lingered at the south corner near the barricade, watching the crowd. Not quite time. Yet something had sparked in the middle of the crowd, and it wasn't the hose.

People were getting restless somewhere in the back, but he couldn't see why. They parted like a sea. Could they have found it? No. He was too close. It was almost over! This was *his* moment.

Then a man burst from the crowd, running toward the stage. All eyes were on the sprinting figure. Confusion, chaos.

Time to go.

T hadius Grogan sat inside the cop car at the east side barricade near the stage. The officer who normally drove the car was safely tied and gagged in his home, knocked out with a couple Xanax that Thadius's doctor had prescribed for him once upon a time. Having the cop out of the way for the afternoon was the kind of anti-anxiety Thadius enjoyed most.

Inside the car, a picture of Thadius issued for the manhunt stared back at him. All the cops had one. But they assumed if you had Officer Brenniman's badge, uniform, cell phone, and car, you must be

Officer Brenniman. This was exactly why cops didn't get things done.

Thadius scanned the crowd again, but so far, nothing. Not a big deal. He would see him. Obsession was a powerful, magnetic thing. Only so much you could plan something like this. Fate had allowed Thadius to come this far. He'd spot Sebastian Waters, even in a crowd this big.

The crowd stirred, though. A man split off the side and ran past Thadius's vehicle. The guy's face was wrought with panic.

Thadius's head snapped away from the running man, the cops moving toward him. The crowd skittered like bugs from a rotten log. They gushed out from the center, steady lines of traffic forming in all directions that led away from the stage.

Which made the single person slinking from the barricade corner directly *into* the fray light up like a neon sign.

Him.

The kid was younger than Thadius had expected. Chubby-cheeked, almost like he hadn't lost all his baby fat. Dusty bangs in his eyes.

Thadius looked to Sebastian's hands. He imagined those fingers on Emily's neck, his body twice the size of hers forcing her to the ground.

Somehow it seemed fitting that in this moment, Thadius would have witnesses by the hundreds. Just like the execution planned for this evening inside that prison; a brutal crime deserved a brutal answer. It didn't matter who you killed—as long as you were right.

Thadius opened the cruiser's door.

Charley Padgett stood by the stage with his guitar, and Yancy practically bowled him over.

Jenna's brother tripped backward with the blow, dazed. Charley reared back to hit him, then noticed who Yancy was. "Dude, what *is* this?"

"Charley . . ." Yancy gasped. "Jenna. Bomb. You. We have to move!"

"Hold it right there!" a cop yelled from behind him.

Yancy wheeled around to see three guns trained on him. "You've got this all wrong!"

Then all hell broke loose.

Jenna's feet pelted the asphalt as fast as she could make them move. Had to get back! Almost to the alley opening. Ten more feet.

BOOM.

60

Jenna burst out of the alleyway in time to see what looked like a giant fiery snake whip through the air. People ran, screamed. Something near the front of the block was on fire. The stage? *Yancy!*

"Here, here, here!" Jenna yelled as people passed her, running down the block.

She wound her arms as if she were a little league coach sending kids to home plate. The alley was the fastest way out, and the safest. Now on the ground, the flaming cord tore a path through the middle of the crowd. Running from it was a gamble. Breaking off was the best chance.

As the crowd rushed by her into the quickly cramming alley, Jenna looked hard at every male who went by. Sebastian had lit his bomb. Surely *that* wasn't how he'd expected his precious bomb to blow. If he was still alive, he might be here somewhere. She was giving him a route to safety, damn it!

No helping it. Had to get as many people out of that vacuum as she could.

The bomb squad had been standing by, but even they didn't seem to know what to do about the bizarre beast thrashing its way down the street. A fire truck toward the barricade at the second block eased its way through throngs of opposing traffic. The basket went up over the crowd, and the fireman directed his CO_2 extinguisher toward the flame. The fire had to look electrical to them, but Jenna was sure it wasn't. Highly combustible, yes. Electrical, no. That tiny extinguisher would do nothing against this large a fire.

Lights flashed at the prison, and a foghorn blared to signal a lockdown.

If God existed, Yancy would be somewhere in the crowd moving into the alley past her. She looked toward the ground, hoping to spot a metal foot.

What she saw made her heart sink.

Charley.

Jenna ran toward the lashing, semi-failed bomb and the massive pillar of flames that was the stage.

Thadius approached the man who'd killed Emily, who'd taken his life away from him. The blast had knocked Sebastian Waters off his feet, and he sat in a heap between the fiery stage and the hose bomb. All around Thadius, people cried, helped each other. Some were bleeding, others lay on the ground, unmoving.

His daughter's killer's face was slashed up the side, and his shirt torn down the sleeve, revealing the bloody mess that was his arm. The man looked around him at the horror he'd created. Guy was clearly in shock.

He didn't see Thadius coming.

Thadius lifted Sebastian by his collar to his feet, backed him up. "Do you know who I am?"

Sebastian's eyes widened, took in Thadius's face. He didn't answer. His mouth hung open, slack like a stroke patient's.

Jenna reached the front of the crowd just in time to see hands release a body into the inferno that was the stage. For a moment, the person in the fire almost seemed unreal, like a ghost. Then he felt the flames and began to flail.

Another shadow stood still in front of the fire, not running or yelling or panicking in the horror. No. The stocky figure watched, entranced.

Thadius Grogan.

"Stop right there!"

The words were out before Jenna considered she had little way to enforce them. A gun would have to be good enough. Handcuffs were for amateurs, right?

Her feet surged toward Grogan, who had turned to see where the yelling had come from. In his second of hesitation, she gained on him. Now the only thing that stood between them was the giant power supply box.

Jenna took aim at Thadius through the flames. "Don't move!"

It would be *really* helpful if she could tell him he was under arrest.

Thadius Grogan backed toward the barricade on the left side as Sebastian Waters's screams died with him.

"You don't have to do this, Thadius! I know why you did it. I can't say I blame you. But you can choose how it ends. Come in with me. Quietly. It'll go better that way."

The lies were quick and smooth, but even as Jenna said them, she knew they were a mistake. Her brain wasn't working right. Charley, somewhere in the fray. Yancy.

Focus.

Thadius laughed. "Nothing is going to go well for me! You don't have a clue!"

Claudia flashed into Jenna's mind. "Yes, I do. You have to believe me."

"Ha! You don't *know.* You couldn't possibly *know* what it is to know *that* man killed your daughter!" He gestured toward the fire.

Charley.

"But he didn't!" Jenna screamed.

Thadius stopped moving. "What did you say?"

Mistake number two.

"I . . . he didn't do it, Thadius. Sebastian Waters didn't kill your daughter," she said. Too late now. Better try to salvage this as best she could.

"Of course he did. I hired the private investigator. I know *everything!*"

"No. He didn't. Everything you know is a lie, Thadius. The PI was a fraud, a sociopath that lies with every breath. You were taken in, Thadius. I'm sorry," Jenna added. *I'm so sorry.*

Thadius gripped the sides of his head like his brains were leaking out, wrestled with his own face. "I don't know what you're talking about. You couldn't . . . he couldn't . . . no way it wasn't right—"

"Sebastian Waters didn't know Emily. They never met. But that's not why you should believe me. He couldn't have killed her because of who he *was*, Thadius, any more than you could kill Woody Fine at his fireworks store. It's not in you to kill innocent people, and for Sebastian, it wasn't possible to kill someone up close and personal. It takes guts to do that, and you know it."

"But the gun . . ."

"All a setup, Thadius. I'm trying to tell you. This sociopath knew you'd go after Sebastian. He *wanted* you to go after him. He knew about Sebastian's past, what you'd find when you went looking for him. He knew it'd be all too easy for you to hear about Sebastian's history, see the evidence connecting him to various places linked to your daughter's death, and render judgment. Because Sebastian *was* a likely suspect, and he *had* been everywhere the killer showed him to be. The only problem was, the *real* killer knew about Sebastian and where he'd been, too. Think! Everything the PI fed you was meant to lead you to this moment. Come in quietly, and we'll try to make this less painful. I promise I will try to make it move *fast*."

It was all Thadius really wanted, she knew. For it to be over. That was who *he* was.

Thadius glanced toward the fire. His chest began to heave. Hands pressed to his knees, he threw his head down and screamed.

Jenna inched closer. Thadius had a good hundred pounds on her, but if he turned himself in . . .

"How could they do this to me?" he yelled.

"Who? Who is 'they,' Thadius?" *Keep saying his name.*

He looked back up at her, the anguish translating through the steam. "I have to . . . Oh, God. I can't. I need to . . ."

Thadius took off running.

62

"Go, go, go!" Hank yelled from behind Jenna, and three agents bolted after Thadius.

They didn't have a chance. Thadius climbed in the police cruiser at the barricade and was already moving before he slammed the door. The car's lights whirled to life and he careened through the lingering crowd still trying to gimp away from the fire.

One agent fired at the car.

"No!" Jenna screamed. Even though the shot had no chance of hitting Thadius, the reflex took over. She had to catch up with him. If Isaac Keaton orchestrated this entire thing not only to have Thadius tie up his loose end, but because Charley was there, Jenna had to find out what Thadius knew. Keaton had made it personal for *both* of them. But why?

Charley.

The others could take over. Jenna could worry over Thadius later. She shuffled through the area around the stage and checked the couple of still bodies on the ground. No Charley.

"Charley! Charley Padgett!"

The cry didn't sound like it came from her own throat. High. Desperate.

Please, not again.

A whistle. "Here. Over here!"

Jenna followed the whistles toward the other side of the stage, calling out from time to time. "Where?"

"Here! Beside the gray van!"

Jenna scanned the immediate area, spotted the van. She trotted toward it. Yancy.

Beside him, Charley lay, a huge spike jutting through his right arm.

"Medic!" Jenna shouted in futility. Everyone within the block was already working this way. She jammed buttons on her cell phone. "Get someone behind the stage *now!*"

Charley used his good arm to push himself to a sitting position. "Nothing a little duct tape won't fix, Rain Man. I'm okay."

Easy for him to say. Charley didn't know he was the target of this whole thing yet. Or did he?

Jenna glanced to Yancy. He'd gotten to her brother. Must've realized it.

His hazel eyes met hers, and he nodded. A veteran of stuff like this, he'd already tied off the blood supply to the shrapnel, had Charley hold the arm over his head.

"You okay?" Jenna asked Yancy. He didn't seem to have a scratch, but then again, she hadn't really looked yet.

"Best I've come out during one of these," he joked. "Where is he?"

Yancy meant Sebastian, of course, but the first to come to Jenna's mind was Thadius Grogan. "Dead. Thadius Grogan killed him."

Yancy drew his head back, disbelieving. "And where is Thadius?"

"He . . ." Jenna's voice trailed. So much to catch him up on. "I don't know. He's . . . Sebastian didn't kill Thadius's daughter. I found out just before we lost Zane. I . . . I made a mistake and told him. He's . . ."

Probably going after the private investigator who gave him the wrong information. That'd steer him right.

"Thadius never met the PI," Jenna mumbled to herself.

"So who did?" Yancy asked.

"No idea," she answered, distracted by the paramedic arriving to attend to Charley. Jenna and Yancy waited while the medic started an IV, loaded Charley into the ambulance.

"We'll follow you," she promised Charley.

The paramedics shut the doors, and Jenna's little brother was whisked away from her. Yancy's hand found hers, squeezed hard.

"Not too different from a long time ago?" Yancy asked.

Jenna pictured Charley's younger face, much less conscious then than he was just now. She should've been an accountant.

"A little more fire," she answered.

"Heh." Then, "Zane?"

"I don't know that, either. The team is on it. You coming with? I need to find a car." For once, the wrap-up had to be somebody else's problem.

Yancy glanced around as if he expected to see Zane in the immediate vicinity. When he didn't, he shrugged. "You should steal an FBI SUV. That's gone well in the past."

"Oh, shut up."

Hank stepped over the smoldering cords near them. "They got the hose put out. The stage is next. We couldn't get through the crowd to follow Grogan. Too much debris between him and the next cruiser."

"Unfortunate," Jenna replied.

"What next?" Hank asked.

"I'm making sure Charley's all right."

"Then?"

Then I figure out why Isaac Keaton is gunning for my family. I track down how Isaac Keaton found Thadius Grogan in the first place. I determine how all of this shit is connected.

"I find out who the hell Isaac Keaton is."

Thadius knocked on the door of the suburban home. He would have answers, and he'd have them *now*. Christ alive. What had he done?

"Thadius! What the—"

Thadius pushed his way into the man, gun first. "Back up. Where is she?"

"Whoa, whoa, man! Put it away! You don't need that here. We don't judge. We—"

"One more time. Where. Is. She."

The guy put his hands up like it was a bank robbery. "Who?"

"Your *wife*."

The man's eyes betrayed him. He glanced toward the living room.

Thadius cocked the gun that way. "Walk."

When they entered the room, the woman shrieked. She jumped up, scrambled toward the phone, but Thadius cocked the pistol and leveled it with her husband's head.

"I'll put a bullet in his head. I swear I will."

She stopped, whimpered. Then she backed up and collapsed back into her chair.

"You set me up. I know it. You gave me her name *because* she had the PI contact. I know you knew. You never *used* the PI. Couldn't have. He wasn't real."

The husband trembled. "What are you talking about?"

Thadius looked at the woman, however. "She knows. I want to know *why*."

"Thadius, I didn't mean for any of this to—"

Now Thadius reared back and smacked the husband aside, aimed between the woman's eyes. "I don't want to hear it! Tell me *why*. Your recommendation is the *only* reason I sought her out. Who *is* she?"

"I'm sorry! I didn't mean—"

"I'm *only* going to ask you one more time. Who *is* she?"

The woman stared at her feet, then looked at her husband. Her feet again. "I met her at another support group meeting I went to. *She* found *me!* She knew about Leah! Said if I helped her, she'd . . . she promised she'd give me *my* answers!"

"What is going *on?*" the husband asked, exasperated.

"So you sold me out," Thadius replied. Everything he'd wanted, she'd done for the same reason. Only she was willing to throw him under the bus to get it.

"I didn't mean it, Thadius! I swear, I—"

"Save it."

Thadius stepped toward the woman and leveled the gun at her forehead.

"Please, Thadius! Please don't do this!" her husband cried.

"No," she whispered.

"Didn't think of how it would be, did you? How it would be if I ever found out? Maybe you think I'm some pathetic loser who stayed still for so long after what happened to Emily that I wouldn't react no matter what happened, huh?"

"No," she repeated.

Emily and Narelle. Narelle and Emily. So long since he'd seen them. God, he'd thought he'd give anything for them back. Even so, he wouldn't have given *them*.

"How could you do it?"

Don't answer me.

The woman squeaked as the SIG pressed harder against her face. "What would you have done? Seriously, Thadius! You're telling me you wouldn't have done the exact same thing?"

"No," Thadius said. "I wouldn't have."

64

saac dreaded the next part, but he couldn't put it off much longer. Even though he couldn't see the news and didn't have any way of knowing, the clock told him that by now, everything was complete chaos in one way or another.

He stared at the ceiling from the infirmary cot, imagining the dirty cement was a giant television screen, playing out the events of his own masterpiece before his eyes. Too bad he had no popcorn, because he had a damned good imagination.

On the big screen in his mind, he pictured it different ways: Grogan pummeling Sebastian's head into a brick building. The cops nabbing Sebastian as he attempted to set off the makeshift bomb. Sebastian cleverly tricking Grogan into standing too close while he lit the fuse.

And despite his initial contempt for the sniveling little wretch that was Sebastian, he chuckled as he realized that, deep down, he was rooting for him. No matter which way it went down, of course, it was all gravy. But for whatever Isaac had initially meant Sebastian to be, the kid had shown scrap. He'd grown.

"Give 'em a little sunlight, water 'em, cultivate 'em. If it's a daisy seed, it'll still end up being a daisy, but if the seed is a rose with thorns, the rose and the thorns will show up," he muttered.

Maybe that was it. Maybe there was something about the underdog in this scenario. After all, when Sebastian had first shown up on Isaac's radar, he'd been of no use to him other than someone to conveniently take a fall. He hadn't wanted Sebastian in his life at all, for anything.

Now the cement ceiling became the backdrop for another image as though it were being projected there in widescreen. The photograph of Emily Grogan that Jenna Ramey had tried to tease him with, get a reaction.

Oh, Dr. Ramey. How can you understand so much and so little at the same time?

For all her profiling and gut feelings and textbook knowledge, the shrink had seemed sure she would recognize the signs of a murderer looking at his victim. She'd been watching him for dilated pupils, sweating. Maybe even a pant or two. That would be what she was used to seeing in a guilty party.

But I'm not like your other monsters, Doc. That's why everything is working out exactly as I'd hoped.

After all, Jenna Ramey hadn't considered that if a person strangled someone he wanted but could never have with her own intestine without his pulse ever creeping past sixty, that person might have a wee bit more control over himself than some of the other miserable vermin she'd studied.

Isaac closed his eyes, inhaled. He could still smell the soft lotion Emily wore, the salty hint of perspiration that wafted off the back of her neck into his nostrils the day the campus bus had screeched to a sudden halt, throwing the standing Emily backward into him.

He'd hopped the bus in the afternoon rush, a time the drivers were just so grateful to squeeze all of their charges on that they didn't bother to swipe passes. What had started as his own laziness to get to where he'd parked his car without having to traipse across the college campus from downtown had turned into a pretty girl in his lap. She'd thanked him for catching her, and he'd accepted her thanks by "allowing" her to take him to lunch.

Early on, it had worked just like any other target he saw and desired. He flattered her, paid her more attention than anyone should ever be paid. In essence, became the exact person she needed him to be to be her perfect companion. But then, his lies about which classes he had when and why he didn't seem to attend any of the university events started to add up, and unlike so many, she didn't turn a blind eye. She started asking questions, and his persona unraveled. It would've been fine if it hadn't been for him following her so much. Because when she finally figured out he wasn't even a university student, suddenly their chance meetings on campus no longer made sense. What were run-ins with a familiar person had become scary encounters with someone whose presence didn't belong. She'd tried to exit the situation gracefully, but Isaac never *had* been very good at being told he couldn't have what he wanted, when he wanted it.

That's why he'd gone to Pembry Pawn that day. He'd browsed the store, trying to win over his anger by telling himself he still had her. It wasn't too late to put her blinders back on. He just needed a distraction. Emily was a sucker for vintage clothing and jewelry, and this place reeked of heirs who couldn't wait to hock Grandma's pearls the day after she died.

Then the little movie nerd had walked in, gone to the counter, and talked to the man about a gun he needed as a prop for some student film he was helping with. Kid also asked about fireworks. The shop owner sold him the gun, gave him directions to another store, and the nerdy kid had left.

Isaac had put down the strand of beads he'd been looking at and headed for the door. He'd watched the pimply-faced kid with the backpack climb into an old, light blue car and crank it.

At the time, he hadn't known why he memorized that light blue car's license plates, only that something in his psyche told him it was the thing to do. Another brilliant little stroke of his own brain's genius, he now knew.

That gun had stayed in his mind, as had the fireworks, for the next twenty-four hours. He'd molded them like clay he was trying to shape over and over again until finally he'd begun to wonder their worth. They'd given him such spectacular ideas. He'd become obsessed with not just them, but with the nerd driving the light blue car.

Some searching the Internet had led him to not only Sebastian Waters's name, but his past. A past filled with dark things, scary ones. A past that would look very, very bad if ever it came to light, say, close to a murder.

But that had never happened. Why, he wasn't sure. Sebastian had been lucky, he supposed, though the dipshit would never know it. But a stroke of luck like that wouldn't mean anything to Sebastian when he found out he'd had a moment of bad luck like the one when Isaac had run across a familiar handle in Land of Valor, one he'd run across during his little jaunt into Sebastian's past. Sebastian's name online had also been associated with the Undertaker Gaming guild of elite gamers, and he remembered thinking at the time how intrigued he was by the fact that Sebastian's favorite pastime was the very one where he himself hung out much of the time. He'd thought then how maybe it was fate that Sebastian hadn't been caught, how maybe he should've looked more into all they had in common . . .

Now he glanced at the clock. No time to get lost reveling in times gone by. Those events had been important, but there was still so much left. He pushed to his rear end so he sat on the edge of the cot, legs hanging over the side.

Showtime.

Isaac Keaton charged the infirmary wall head first. His temple exploded with pain, the room twirled. Lovely.

Again.

He screamed the high-pitched squeal of a five-year-old and launched himself again, this time arms stretched forward as though he were pushing someone invisible.

"Noooooo!"

His right hand jammed into the cement hard, and his vision blurred. This would get ugly *really* fast.

"Not my stuff! You won't take it!"

All just words. No clue what he was saying. Didn't matter.

Ruckus outside. "Get someone down here! He's going batshit in there!"

"You won't, you won't!" Isaac shrieked. Wow. Until now, he had no clue his voice could sound like this.

Isaac rushed the wall again and kicked it. Over and over, he slammed his feet into the wall as though it were assaulting him. One toe went down for sure. Maybe more. Losing feeling and in the zone. A good thing.

Guards hollered outside the infirmary, none with a damned clue what to do. They stood yelling, watching, calling people. None brave enough to stop him. Imagine that. Stupid pigs.

He bitch-slapped the wall.

This time, his hand had to be broken. Flames shot through it, and it swelled almost immediately. He backhanded the wall again, and blood spattered from his knuckles.

"Get away, get away, get away!"

"He's gonna kill himself in there! We have to move!"

The door locks clicked as they unlatched. Isaac didn't look, didn't flinch. He beat the wall harder, damaging the hand more and more. Hell, it was already gone. Might as well do the thing right.

Then every muscle in Isaac's body flexed at once. Daggers of ice shot through him, and his control went rigid. Pulsed. The walls fell away.

When his muscles came back, he was on the floor. Officers on either side grabbed his arms, pinned him.

Struggle.

"You can't have it! I won't do it, assholes! You can't have *her*!"

He forced his arms to flail as much as he could, but his body stung. Stupid sons of bitches had *Tasered* him!

"Over here!" one guard said.

The infirmary nurse hovered above him, and a band squeezed his arm. A prick, then a needle stung his arm, chilled him. Sedatives.

His vision swam, and his muscles relaxed against his will. This could be bad.

Isaac fought the drug as much as he could. He'd always known it was coming. This was the dangerous part.

"Omelet's in the kitchen. Ready for Bunny. Okay?" he said, his rehearsed script.

It was the good thing about following a template that worked, though. He'd been able to prepare for what was coming, and as long as he stayed the course, he could trust the result. If he hadn't practiced so many times, this would've been trouble. His words slurred more than he'd expected, and fogginess overtook him.

"What happened?" the nurse asked.

Isaac tried to speak, but it was like someone had stuffed a sock in his mouth. He licked his lips, then took a swipe at the nurse with his limp fist.

She pressed it down gently, a mother cat correcting a weak kitten.

"That hand needs to be x-rayed. Ambulance. If we need special detail for a transport, get it."

"On it," the guard replied.

Before his eyes closed, Isaac saw them moving into action for what had to be done.

Mission accomplished.

65

Jenna sat in the hospital lobby while the doctors attended to Charley. He would be fine, she'd heard. The ER team would anesthetize him while they removed the shrapnel from his arm, but as soon as he had some stitches, a tetanus shot, and heaping doses of antibiotics and pain medication, he'd recover nicely. Too bad they couldn't say the same about everyone at the rally.

"Five people died in the explosion, about a dozen others injured from shrapnel and the fire. Five is better than five hundred, I guess," Hank had said on the phone.

She'd inquired about Zane, who'd been found standing in a parking lot about three blocks away from the garage. She called the BAU team when she hung up with Sebastian and realized he wasn't coming. Turns out Sebastian had a conscience, just as Jenna had suspected all along. Guy probably thought he was doing Zane a favor.

Jenna made a mental note to contact Zane, refer her to someone good. She was too close to help her.

Yancy wandered back into the lobby with a Dr Pepper for Jenna, a Coke for himself. "Any word?"

She nodded. "He's out of surgery and in recovery. We'll be able to see him in a bit."

Yancy plopped down beside her and propped his real foot on the chair across from him. "This mean you're out of the thing now?"

"If only."

So far, no sign of Thadius Grogan, but Jenna hoped that would change soon. Thadius was part of this case, and this case involved her family. Not exactly something she could ignore.

"I need to know why me," Jenna said.

"Yeah. I get that. Isaac asked for you from the start, right?"

"Yep."

"And that wasn't weird?"

Jenna sipped the soft drink and thought. The easy answer was no, but if you hadn't lived her life up to now, it might be a hard concept to understand.

"Not really. Yes but no. Other perps have asked for me before. It's the famous thing. They're sick puppies, and they get off on notoriety. What's more notable than bringing in a high-profile forensic psychiatrist to question you? Usually it's their pathetic attempt to gain some more publicity. Not to mention they like to try to get me to tell them what color they are."

Yancy downed half his Coke in a few gulps. "And you don't tell them?"

"Nope."

"Any reason?"

She cracked up. Chaos and sleep deprivation would do that to you. In between laughs she managed, "Because why should I?"

Yancy smiled. "Solid logic."

He sat back, arms folded. From the way his mouth curved, the way he breathed, Jenna could tell he wanted to say something more.

"You want to know yours, don't you?" she asked.

"What?" Yancy asked, surprised.

"Your color. You want to ask me."

His grin reappeared. "Maybe. But I won't."

Jenna's phone buzzed, and she groaned. "Not now."

"You know, you really ought to turn that thing off for a couple days a year. A couple *hours* a year," Yancy said.

Jenna shoved him and stood up. The receptionist's glare was evil enough to scare her outside.

"Yes?" she answered.

"Dr. Ramey?" The voice on the other end of the phone was hesitant. Frightened?

"This is she."

"Thank God. Dr. Ramey, this is Shawn Snow."

Shawn Snow's face flew into Jenna's mind along with his colors. The day she'd visited Shawn and Amy Snow at their home to question them about their relationship to Thadius Grogan seemed so long ago. It had only been a few days. She'd given Shawn her card but hadn't expected to hear from him again. The couple had seemed less than eager to talk.

"Go ahead," Jenna said.

"I . . . You have to come. Thadius Grogan. He was just here."

Jenna and Yancy arrived at the Snows' home on the heels of the 911 first responders. The paramedics were inside treating Amy Snow, but for what, she had no idea.

Shawn met them at the door, eyes red-rimmed. "Dr. Ramey."

She offered her hand, and he shook it, though she preferred to skip the niceties.

"Shawn. I'm glad you called. How's Amy?"

The question was met with a face completely foreign to the Shawn Snow she'd met days ago. He'd been so concerned about his wife's mental state when the woman realized they weren't there because they'd found *her* daughter's killer. Now, if Jenna wasn't mistaken, Shawn showed disdain at the mention of Amy's name.

"They're treating her for a panic attack," he answered.

Cold. Unfeeling. Gray. Not the same protective gray she saw at times or the coal guarded color she'd seen at the Snows' before. No. This was the same stark cement color she'd seen when Isaac had told the person on the other end of his jail phone call he loved them. A gray as flat as the emotions behind it.

The shock over his reaction trumped the shock that the medics weren't treating Amy for a gunshot wound. In fact, knowing Thadius's state of mind when he left the rally, he could only go two ways: spiral down or be done with his shooting spree. Killing the wrong man had sent Thadius in a direction, but until now, Jenna hadn't been sure which.

"Did Thadius Grogan give you any clue where he might be going next?" she asked.

"Oh, yeah."

"Excuse me?"

Shawn Snow stepped out of his door much like he had the last time. He kicked the pine straw of his immaculate flower bed, and it littered the sidewalk.

"Apparently, Amy set Grogan up."

"How do you mean?" Jenna choked. Harnessing the pulse pounding in her chest wasn't easy.

Shawn bent over and began to pluck leaves from the bush beside the porch. "She met some chick at a meeting. Not a double-F double-V C meeting, but some other place she went. I don't know why she went without me, but I'm guessing . . ."

He ripped a leaf in half and let it litter the ground, too.

"Yes, Mr. Snow?" Yancy prompted.

Jenna examined the way Shawn didn't look at Yancy or question who he was. Maybe he assumed Yancy was an agent, and telling him otherwise wouldn't help. Shawn seemed pissed, but mostly his disappointment shone through.

"I guess she was still trying to find a way to hunt down who killed Leah. The support groups have . . . they're very good for support, but you can either go for a meeting, or you can go for other things."

"Like what?" Yancy asked.

"Services," Shawn Snow answered.

Like private investigators. "What did Amy find, Mr. Snow? Or who?"

"You have to believe me, I didn't know anything about this," Shawn said, tearing more leaves and chucking them to the ground.

"Mr. Snow, we're not here to judge you. It's important we know where Thadius Grogan is heading next."

Besides, it wasn't for Jenna to decide whether or not Shawn Snow was guilty by association, though he sounded sincere. The strain in his voice screamed innocence, and if Jenna needed to recount this conversation, her professional opinion would be he had nothing to do with it.

"The girl Amy met approached her at the second meeting at the new place. Told Amy she could give her information on Leah's murder but wanted a favor in return. Amy figures maybe the girl was following her, but until today, she hadn't thought about it. The offer was *apparently* too attractive," he spat, bitter.

The orange-brown color Jenna had seen around Amy the first time she met her flashed in again. It had been close to denial, but she'd known that day denial didn't feel quite right. Now it all made sense. The orange showed up because Amy Snow's upbeat persona *wasn't* denial. It was orange, just like other lies.

"The favor?" Jenna pushed. *Get back on track.*

"Get her a job with Thadius Grogan."

That made sense. They hadn't been able to find a connection

between Thadius and Isaac Keaton within the support group network because the connection didn't *exist*.

Which begged the question: Who would Isaac trust enough to involve in his plan? A girlfriend, most likely. Wife? No. Isaac wouldn't be married.

"Who was she, Mr. Snow?"

He laughed, dry and sardonic. "I know her. I should. She and Amy talked. Amy hired her. Hell, I even knew she'd met Thadius, but it didn't occur to me to think she might've cleaned his house. She came in a few times a week to do our laundry."

The elusive housekeeper.

"Name? Do you have her address?"

"No address," Shawn answered. "But her name is Lyra. Lyra Mintelle."

The name collided into Jenna with the force of an industrial wrecking ball, and for a moment she couldn't breathe. Papers flashed in, photographs.

Names.

Yancy pulled her to the side. "Excuse us," he said to Shawn. Then, when they were out of earshot, "What? What is it?"

"Dover Mintelle was . . . Claudia's second victim. Lyra is his daughter from another marriage. And she had a brother."

"Wait. Really? You're saying Claudia is Isaac's evil stepmother?" Yancy asked.

Jenna was frozen, and all she could think to do was shove her cell phone toward Yancy. He took it and started texting. God willing, he was sending information to Hank or Irv. Both.

This was why Isaac Keaton had asked for her from the beginning. It was why he was gunning for her family at the rally, why he had always been so interested in how she figured out Claudia all those years ago. He wanted to play a little game, all right, and in his life, Claudia had been as close to a perfect player as they came. In fact, in his mind, there would've only been one person more perfect. One opponent he'd know hadn't been beaten, even by the devil Claudia herself.

Isaac had wanted to see if he could do what Jenna's mother couldn't. He wanted to beat *her*.

"Come on," Yancy said, pulling her in the direction of the car they'd borrowed from an officer at the rally.

God, the fog. They didn't even know where to go yet! "Shawn Snow . . ."

"The local cops will take care of the Snows," Yancy said.

But then Hank came into her vision. He couldn't be real, right? Why not, though? Thadius's name had to have been mentioned on police radar.

"Jenna, I need to talk to you!"

Yancy stepped in front of her. "Not now, Hank. She needs time. We just found out . . . I sent you a text. Thadius Grogan is connected to Lyra Mintelle, the daughter of one of Claudia's victims."

"*What?*"

Jenna swallowed and stepped out from behind Yancy. "Dover's kid. She had a brother. I'm guessing that's how Isaac found Thadius. Lyra was the housekeeper."

"Jesus," Hank said. The news seemed to throw his mind off topic, and he stared at her.

"Hank?"

He shook his head hard as if to clear it. "Jenna, they've filed paperwork to move Isaac Keaton to the Sumpter Building. He's showing *signs of schizophrenia*."

Jenna's breath caught again, and this time, it chased the cloudiness from her head. Everything was a little *too* lucid. Claudia's brilliant plan to stay out of prison, and all along, Isaac planned to duplicate it.

He'd met Claudia. Isaac had never worked at the Sumpter Building, but he knew Claudia's birthmark. The guy knew everything about Jenna's family, and he'd targeted Jenna from the start.

He had to be the other kid. Lyra's brother.

"I have to get to the prison. I need Claudia's case file," she mumbled to herself. The answers to Isaac were in there, but there was no time to go get it. She couldn't let him be transported. Once he was in Sumpter, they might never get him back out again.

"What? What can you do?" Hank asked.

The burnt orange of lies shone in Jenna's mind, as did what she saw Claudia as. She could smoke Isaac out if only she could make it.

"I can fix this, Hank. I know I can. But I need the case file on Claudia. It's at the apartment."

"Keys," he said.

She fished in her pocket, tossed him her apartment key. "Meet you at the precinct."

Jenna and Yancy hopped in the car and sped away. *Please let us get there in time.*

"He's in the infirmary," Saleda said as she and Jenna walked down the hall.

She had met Jenna and Yancy at the door to take them in, but Yancy got checked at the gate. Hank not being with them was a problem today. Apparently when a high-priority criminal starts banging his head into a wall, security becomes very particular about who they let into the prison.

"It's cool," Yancy'd said. "I'll wait in the car."

She hadn't had time to argue.

"Drugged up?" Jenna asked.

"They gave him a fast-acting, so he should be more than lucid by now, at least for the record. Besides, if he's really schizophrenic, the lucidity issue wouldn't matter."

"So true." They'd reached the infirmary, where Isaac was now sitting peacefully on his cot, his arm splinted by the infirmary nurse. The jail had called for a portable x-ray, but it hadn't arrived. "Wish me luck."

"Luck," Saleda said, and she left to go monitor the interview on camera.

The guard unlocked the doors, and Jenna slipped inside.

Isaac didn't look up at her.

"I hear you had a rough day," she said.

"To say the least."

He'd gotten the first part right anyway. Malingering schizophrenics nearly always blew it on that one. They'd exhibit *continuous* symptoms when in reality the real schizophrenic would show only intermittent signs.

"What happened?"

Isaac smiled up at her. "Dr. Ramey, you know what happened."

The statement sounded honest enough for video evidence, but Jenna knew exactly how Isaac intended *her* to hear it. He'd wanted her to hear in his voice how he was planning to win his ticket right out of jail and a murder trial by faking insanity, just like Claudia had. "Why don't you tell me in your own words?"

"Saw some stuff."

No details, good hesitancy. He's studied up on this.

"What kind of stuff?"

He grunted. "Sister."

"You heard her voice?" Jenna asked.

Isaac shook his head. "No."

Consistent. "Saw her?"

Again, Isaac said, "No."

"Can you tell me what you *did* see?" Jenna asked. So far, he was a good mimic. Then again, she already knew that much from their first meeting.

"What did I see? A man trying to take her. Trying to take important things of our family's. Hard to explain."

With that, his first sign of psychopathy pushed through, at least in Jenna's eyes. Repetition of the question. It wasn't enough, of course, but the sentence bolstered her. She could trip him. Now, to find the way to prove it.

She glanced over the report of the guards present during Isaac's little staged tantrum. He ran into a wall, kicked a wall, screamed at a wall. Then a tiny notation at the bottom about something he'd said.

Jenna held back a sharp intake of breath. "*Biscuit time . . .* and the omelet?" she asked.

"The omelet?" he repeated.

"Yes. You said something about an omelet. Was someone making you an omelet?"

Not that the answer mattered. If Isaac truly had the episode, he wouldn't remember it. Either way, the statement wasn't cohesive with the hallucination he was presenting her with. Too random. Too ready.

And it sounded just like something Claudia had said a lot. She always asked about biscuit time.

Isaac Keaton's acting skills were admirable, but he hadn't studied the right material. He'd studied *Claudia*.

"I'm not sure," he said.

"Back to the hallucination where someone said they were taking things. Did they intend to hurt you?"

"The man I saw was going to take my sister. Hurt her. I just knew. You should understand that, Dr. Ramey. He was going to hurt my *sister*."

As Isaac said the word, he looked up at her, blue eyes cold. Charley's pallid child face popped in, and Jenna's pulse quickened. *Don't do it. He's fucking with you.*

Isaac had learned everything from Claudia. *Everything.*

"What did he look like?" Jenna asked, a specific detail in mind.

"Tall, lanky. Slit-like eyes."

"Did he have hair?"

"Yeah. It was short, like a crew-cut."

"What color?"

"Black," he answered.

Bingo.

"What color was his shirt?"

"Black."

"Did you see any colors on him?" she asked, forcing her breathing rate not to change.

Isaac looked straight in her eyes. "No. He was black and white. All black and white."

Jenna smiled, then bit her lip, trying to stop. She couldn't. The grin broke, and the laugh jerked its way out of her.

"What's so funny?" Isaac asked, his eyes examining. He thought she'd cracked, she was sure.

She stood up. "You should've done more research, Isaac. Claudia isn't *really* schizophrenic. You know that. Not only is she not schizophrenic, but you didn't even *know* her after she started portraying her schizo *character.*"

He stared at her, but he didn't speak. For the first time, he looked less than sure of himself. Fearful.

"I don't know what you're talking about," he finally said.

Jenna plopped the guard report on the wooden chair the nurse had brought in for her interview. "The omelet was a bad choice. Gave you away."

"I don't—"

"Papers always talk about my mother and her hallucinations, and the *interesting* 'fact' of how I saw her as black, the black widow. You mentioned it to me when we talked that first day. I told you back then I didn't see her as black, but even then, you didn't realize you'd made a wrong move. You'd read all those reports about my mother's 'black and white hallucinations' and the coincidence that I saw her as that color. But the reports were inaccurate, Isaac."

Isaac's mouth twitched slightly. She should leave now while he wondered, just like when she'd told him she didn't see Claudia as black. But she couldn't. For once, passing on the knowledge was too delicious to pass up.

"Claudia never claimed to have visual hallucinations, Isaac. She feigned auditory ones. And even if she *had* claimed visual hallucinations, real schizophrenics don't hallucinate in black and white. They see colors."

saac leapt from the bed, closed in on Jenna. "You stupid, horrible, smelly cunt!"

Jenna backed away, but she didn't have much room to get away. She was locked in.

"Guard!" she yelled.

"Miserable piece of shit! Claudia should've killed you when you were a pissant cunt kid!" All pretext was gone from Isaac's voice now. He knew he'd been beat.

"Easy, Isaac. They'll be keeping you in lockdown now, don't want to give them any reason to lengthen your sentence any more than it's already going to be. Though trust me, I wouldn't be sad," Jenna replied.

Isaac cornered Jenna in the infirmary cell. "For your sake, Jenna, you'd better *hope* I never get out of here. You *and* your little girl! I'll get you both."

"Sure you will. Just like Charley, huh? He's fine, by the way. You sure went to a lot of trouble to orchestrate the climax of your little plan to revolve around him for it to not pan out. Hope you just saw his name on a flier somewhere and that sparked your idea for the rally. I'm sure if this idea wasn't a whim, you'd have scouted a location he was playing, made sure nothing was left to chance. You know. Put your best foot forward? It's okay, though. I'm sure you'll plan better for that first prison shower."

Then Isaac charged her, his plaster cast poised to crush her. Jenna ducked, beat the walls, screaming for the guards.

"You miserable bitch!" Isaac yelled, finally upon her. He knocked her across the face with the cast, his good hand reached for her throat.

Jenna scrambled underneath him, kicked as hard as she could into his groin. He grunted when she made contact just as she heard the doors unlatching.

Guards rushed in, one took down Isaac Keaton with a Taser. Another helped Jenna to her feet. "You okay, Dr. Ramey?" he asked.

Jenna stared down at Isaac Keaton, who was now frothing at the mouth. Depended what "okay" meant. Before this encounter, Isaac Keaton probably had nothing but curiosity about Jenna, however dangerous that curiosity might've proven. He might've hurt her in the midst of trying to prove he was even better at the game than Claudia herself, but any pain he'd planned for her and her family before was entirely incidental. All for the cause.

Now he didn't just want to test her skills as a worthy opponent. If he ever had the chance at her again, this time he'd be out for blood.

She looked away from the pitiful creature on the floor and brushed off her slacks. "Nothing a nice long bubble bath won't fix."

As she turned to leave the cell, Isaac's voice grated after her.

"Dr. Ramey, you'd better pray they keep me here forever or kill me, because if they don't, I swear to God, I will finish what your mother started. I swear, I will take you *out*."

rv sent Lyra Mintelle's address to Yancy with the text: You with Jenna and Hank? Can't get either. Please pass along.

In the car, waiting. Waiting in the car. No Jenna, no Hank. Thadius Grogan might be at Lyra Mintelle's right now. If Thadius got to her first, she might not live to tell what Isaac put her up to. If she lived and they could get it out of her, Lyra could be the key to keeping Isaac behind bars and from following in Claudia Ramey's footsteps.

The choice seemed obvious.

Yancy caught a wheel pulling out of the prison parking lot. He'd text Jenna so she'd get it when she was out. His plan for when he got there, however, was pretty much nonexistent. At best, maybe he could make sure Lyra didn't let Thadius in if he showed up. Maybe Yancy could stop Thadius if he was already there.

This might be the stupidest thing you've ever done, buddy.

The address turned out to be all the way in the boonies. Maybe Thadius hadn't found it, because Yancy wasn't sure he'd taken all the right turns, even with the help of the car's built-in GPS. Finally, he reached the driveway.

No car in the drive. The garage door was closed, so someone could be in there.

Yancy didn't knock, but instead tiptoed around back as best he could with one metal foot. The porch was screened in. Should be easy enough to get in there.

Turned out, way easier than he'd thought. The screened porch was unlatched, and Yancy let himself inside. The home was quiet except for some distant music. Classical?

Upstairs.

Yancy pulled his gun, which he'd demanded back from Hank post-rally. He let the barrel lead around the corner at the top of the staircase. *Checking all the downstairs rooms first would've been good, smart guy. Some cop you'd have turned out to be.*

Too late for intelligence. Balls to the wall recklessness for the win.

Yancy proceeded into the bedroom, gun first, following the music. He was closing in on it. Had to be. It swelled, an orchestra reaching a crescendo.

A twenty-something-year-old redhead lay on the bed, limp. *Oh, man.*

Yancy ran to her, felt for a pulse. Nothing. She was still warm.

He yanked his phone from his pocket. The battery blinked red. He pressed speaker, dialed 911. Then he started CPR.

Was that a breath?

He leaned closer to her lips. Yes. She was breathing. He'd brought her back from . . . something. She had no apparent wounds.

"Nine-one-one, what is your emergency?"

Please, battery. Live through this call.

"Yes, I'm at 6514 Chestnut out in . . . heck, I don't know where I am. There's a woman here who's unconscious."

"What appears to be the trouble?"

"I have no idea! Just *get* here!"

"Who are you?" Lyra Mintelle asked, voice faint.

Her eyes fluttered open and closed, and Yancy glimpsed the green flecks in her irises.

"I'm . . . help. Help is coming. Did Thadius Grogan do this to you?"

She coughed and tilted her head back, trying to breathe better. "Thadius?"

"Yes! Where is he?"

She tried to shake her head, but it made her cough more. She grappled at Yancy's shirt collar like a life line.

"I don't know where . . . Thadius hates me now. I don't blame him . . . I hate . . . me, too."

If this was Yancy's only chance to find out about Isaac Keaton, he needed her to talk, but he'd be damned if he knew what to ask her. On the way here, he'd imagined fighting Thadius Grogan on a rooftop, not trying to question a half-conscious Lyra Mintelle on her bed.

"Why?" was all that came out of Yancy's mouth.

Lyra coughed again. "I . . . horrible things . . . I knew . . . tried to help anyway. Now I've only . . . hurt . . . lots of hurt."

"Where's Thadius, Lyra?"

"Gone," she answered.

"He was here?"

A terrible rattling breath came out of Lyra. "Yes."

"Did he do this? What did he do?" Yancy asked, panic gripping him. That sound couldn't mean anything good.

"He told me . . . I had . . . to live . . . with . . . myself."

Then Lyra's breath rattled one more time and stopped. Yancy tried starting CPR again, but this time, nothing.

Shit.

That's when he saw the envelope on the nightstand. It bore the handwritten words "For Isaac" in the middle.

Contaminate a scene when cops were on the way, or wait patiently for someone to come so he could explain the situation. What a choice.

Yancy grabbed the envelope and ripped it open.

His eyes skimmed the paper. A suicide letter to her brother.

In it, she didn't call him Isaac.

Joey,

By the time you read this, I'll be gone. I did everything I could to protect you. I really did. It's only . . . I understand why you needed to do the things you've done, but your way and my way were never the same. I'm sorry I couldn't keep going. I did the best I could. You needed to meet her, find out why she was how she was. I think I get why. She did things we couldn't do, especially as far as Dad was concerned. We couldn't save him, and I know how much you tortured yourself over it.

"Yeah right," Yancy mumbled. Isaac, if anything, had only wanted to meet Jenna to find out one thing and one thing only—how to win. If Yancy had learned anything in profiling, it was that Isaac didn't want to meet Jenna because of some emotional need. Sociopaths never did. They needed power, and in Isaac's eyes, Jenna was the most powerful person he knew of. Beat her, and he was invincible. Beat her to become God.

Yancy read on.

Knowing what I do, I don't know if you'll ever come home, and facing a world without you in it is something I'm not sure I'm capable of. Knowing the things I've done, I'm not sure I could live even if you were by my side to help me. I know I'm weak, and you hate weakness, which makes me despise myself even more. I've let you

down, and for that, I'm sorry. Please just know that I've tried to do
what you needed all along. I sent the letters and the package, but I
also took steps to make sure even if you don't ever come home, the
end will do you justice.

Yancy kept going, read the final paragraph of the letter. His heart
dropped into his stomach. "Oh, no. Christ no!"

He grabbed his phone again, but when he pressed a button, the
red light at the top blinked once. The screen went black.

"Oh, God! No . . ."

He left Lyra and the letter and ran for the car.

69

Jenna finally finished the appropriate paperwork at the prison. The state psychiatrist would take over now, and the FBI would bring in another forensic psych to evaluate Isaac Keaton. Even though he'd get another crack at the next psych, she'd made sure he wouldn't be able to pull Claudia's little trick all over again, and that was all that mattered.

Still, Hank hadn't shown up with the folder. Thank God she'd been able to wear Isaac down without it.

Saleda eased open the door of the office Jenna was borrowing to fill out the necessary reports. She tossed Jenna's cell phone to her, which she'd had to check with the guards earlier. "Long day. Anything from Hank?"

Jenna pulled up her texts. Nothing. Something, however, from Yancy.

"Oh, Jesus! Yancy . . . Thadius Grogan . . . Lyra—"

Saleda held up a hand. "Not to worry. The locals arrested Grogan at his house ten minutes ago. Found him in his daughter's room, sleeping off a handful of Xanax. Lyra Mintelle wasn't so lucky."

"What do you mean?" *Yancy, what did you do?*

"Dead. Nine-one-one had a call a while ago from her home. Injected herself with potassium chloride. Being a nurse opens doors when you have mental issues, I guess."

"She called 911?"

"No, some guy. No sign of him, but she left a suicide letter. Most of it was a bunch of gibberish, but given everything we know, doesn't look like there's any reason to think someone else did it. Plus, the only set of fingerprints aren't anywhere near the room where she shot herself up. Only in one place. Looks like the mysterious male tried to save her."

Yancy.

Jenna stacked the papers, then clipped them together. She rose, handed Saleda the forms. "You mind taking care of these for me? I'd love to get home and shower before I head back to the hospital. I'm covered in days of this monster's shit."

"No problem," Saleda said. "Let me know when you run into the fearless leader, hm?"

"You'll probably see him before me," she answered. "Think we can finagle a cop to escort me home?"

"Heh. I hear Moose has taken a liking to you. Doubt you'll have trouble persuading him," Saleda said, winking.

Great.

The ride home would've been relaxing, what with the case finally not hanging over her, only Moose insisted on telling her his life story about wanting to become a cop. The story might've been interesting, too, had he not taken every opportunity to interject his lack of a significant other.

Relief washed over Jenna as they pulled up to her apartment.

"Thanks," she said as she climbed out.

"Need me to walk you in?" he asked, his voice shadowed with mild disappointment.

"No, thank you. I'll be okay." *Once you're no longer hitting on me.*

"Okay, Doc. Take it easy."

With that, Moose drove off. Jenna entered the building and trudged up the stairs to her floor. Of all days she ought to have taken the elevator, this was it. Somehow she never thought about it until she was halfway up.

Upon exiting the stairwell, Jenna could see from down the hall that something about her door looked different. An envelope sticking out?

As she approached, though, it was obvious the obtrusive object wasn't an envelope. It was Hank's key, and it was left *in* the keyhole.

Hank would never . . .

The key was something Claudia would do. On purpose.

Jenna reached into her purse, extracted the Glock. Sweat crept down her neckline, slid toward her stomach.

The door pushed open, and from behind it she scanned the right side of the room. Clear. Pointing the gun muzzle downward, she swept into the room toward the left, ready to shoot at legs if someone was there. Nothing.

She pulled the door closed as she moved in. Some things you don't forget, and one is not leaving your rear end wide open.

The kitchen would be scary. No cover, no partner for backup. She should call the cops and wait, but no time. If Claudia was here and had intercepted Hank, minutes mattered. Jenna ripped out her cell, dialed 911, then slipped it back in her pocket. The noise of a phone call would just act as an alert to her presence.

She pushed into the swinging door that led to the kitchen, and through deep, sharp breaths, she covered the 360-degree radius. No one.

Hallway.

Heat ascended Jenna's collarbone, cheeks. Her arms tingled on high alert.

The key in the door.

Her feet shuffled faster over the carpet down the hall, and she cleared one room at a time. Ayana's, hers, Charley's. Empty.

At the end of the hall she came to her father's room. The door hung open, and Jenna cut in with the Glock, pulse mounting.

"Motherfu—"

Jenna ran to Hank's side, where he lay in a pool of blood right outside the door of the tiny bathroom. One glance told her no one was in the shower, on the toilet. Nowhere else in the room to hide.

She knelt next to him, checked for a pulse. Nothing. She'd already known there wouldn't be.

He was shot three times in the chest at close range. His eyes stared straight in front of him, surprised.

The father of her child, the man she'd loved—tried to love—for so many years, gone. Angry tears sprung to Jenna's eyes as she thought of Ayana. Her little girl's laugh sounded like Hank's; her nose was shaped just like his.

Jenna tipped her head so the tears would fall on the carpet instead of her cheeks. She couldn't stand the thought of wiping them away right now.

That was when she noticed Hank's holster unclipped. No gun.

Something back toward the living room rustled. Jenna's head shot up. The living room door.

Her hand stiffened, her grip on her Glock tightened. She crouched, then stood and crept swiftly down the hallway. Charley's room was the perfect cover between her and the kitchen, so she eased behind the door and waited, barely breathing. She could hear steps on the tile, then the muffled sound of feet hitting the carpet.

The intruder passed Charley's room. Now was the time.

Jenna burst out of her brother's bedroom, gun trained on the perp.

"What the fuck?"

Yancy turned around, his own gun aimed at her. He lowered it. "Jenna! Christ! I almost shot you!"

"Ditto. What are you doing? Where have you been?"

"No time to explain. Claudia knows this address, she's probably on her way . . . it's not safe!"

"I know," Jenna answered. She stood rooted to the spot, shaking. "Yancy . . ."

He moved toward her, face written with concern. She fell into him, clutched him with every ounce of strength she had left.

"Jenna. Hey. Hey. It's going to be okay. What happened?"

She pulled back from him, stared in his eyes. Then she took his hand and led him to the back bedroom.

Upon seeing Hank, Yancy swallowed hard. "Called the cops?"

"Oh, shit." Jenna grabbed the phone out of her pocket, picked up the 911 dispatcher. She relayed who she was, what had happened. They said they'd send help, and she hung up.

"Why wouldn't Claudia stay and wait for you? Charley?" Yancy asked.

She left the key. She wanted me to know she'd been here.

"Oh, no," Jenna said. She rushed back to Hank's body, panic crashing over her.

Hank's gun was missing. What else? Jenna frisked him furiously, already afraid of what she'd find.

"No cell phone!" she said, jumping up.

The safe house. Dad. Ayana.

"I'll drive," Yancy said, fast on her heels.

They stumbled down the steps of the building. Jenna's mind raced to keep up with her feet. Claudia couldn't know where the safe house was located. Even if she had Hank's phone, he didn't keep the address of the place in there.

This was Claudia. She'd figured it out.

"It's why I came," Yancy explained as he huffed and clanked down the stairs. "The suicide letter. Lyra said she gave Joey's . . . Isaac's . . . oh, whatever the hell his name is . . . she gave his mom their sister's address. Lyra knew what would hurt you the most, even if she wasn't planning to stick around to see Isaac out of jail!"

They hit the bottom floor and reached the car. Yancy cranked it as Jenna climbed in, and they peeled out.

"Where am I going?" Yancy asked.

"West Norfolk Street past East and Seventh. I'll get you there after that," Jenna answered, dialing Saleda for backup. She'd tell Jenna not to go, to wait for help. She'd say it was a horrible idea, playing into her mother's hands.

Saleda was also the person who'd lost Claudia the first time.

"Floor it!"

70

ank's FBI SUV sat in the driveway of the tiny cottage that was the safe house. Claudia was here.

No one else was.

Jenna had Yancy park in front of the house two mailboxes down. Surprise was a good thing, though surprising Claudia probably wasn't in the cards. After all, they weren't so much crashing a party as showing up as invited guests.

Either way, Jenna had backup this time, which was always better than being alone.

The softest entry point would be the cellar door. Jenna might not have been here before, but when they'd moved Ayana and her dad there, she memorized the layout of the place, top to bottom and side to side. What had been paranoia at the time was now turning out to be a useful bit of obsessive-compulsion.

Jenna's key would open it, and they could sneak in without anyone realizing they were there. The difficulty was in climbing those steps without alerting anyone to their presence. Coming in from below might be stealthiest, but it didn't offer the best vantage point. Still, better than knocking on the front door.

Jenna and Yancy climbed over the back fence of the house next door and crept toward the crawl space, then to the cellar door. Jenna slid her key in, turned.

When she opened it, the bloody, bruised body of the FBI agent assigned to the safe house met her. Dead.

This would be Claudia's idea of a welcome mat.

So Claudia knew Jenna would enter this way. To continue or not. Yancy lifted his arms as though to ask.

Claudia thought Jenna would come in here. Therefore, Claudia wouldn't watch other areas of the house. Even so, Claudia wasn't the potted plant, conk you on the head type of bitch, either.

"She won't be near the door. Won't be watching it. She'll make us go in deeper either way. We're keeping this way."

The layout of the safe house was fairly simple: Through the cellar door, up into the kitchen, which led to a dining area. Off the dining area was the living room, then bedrooms from there. Tiny, compact. Its dense structure was one reason they'd chosen it.

Jenna hoisted herself up the cellar ladder without lowering her gun. No way she'd put the Glock down now. Yancy climbed behind her. Jenna stopped when they reached the door. He stepped up level with her.

"Left," Jenna said. The dining room would be at her left.

She turned the knob, peeked through. Nothing. She let the door fall open.

Jenna and Yancy entered back to back like they'd been partners forever, and Jenna swept the dining side, corners. No one. Jenna crouched forward into the dining room, Yancy covering her rear.

"Jenna, tsk, tsk. You know better than this nonsense, right? We've played hide and seek before."

Claudia's voice made Jenna's skin prickle from head to toe.

Yancy shifted, prepared to aim low, as though he could tell from Claudia's voice her position in the room, but Jenna put a hand to his chest.

"You'll not want to come in guns blazing, dearie. Not when Grandma has your wee-bitty-baby girl on her lap."

Ayana. Jenna lowered her Glock. *Only one way to play this.*

Jenna walked out, gun at the floor, and faced her mother.

"Aren't you going to ask your friend to join us?" Claudia asked.

Her mother sat on the floor with Ayana in her lap. Ay sucked calmly on her pacifier and flipped pages in *If You Give a Mouse a Cookie*. Hank's gun lay beside Claudia's knee within easy grasp of her right hand. "And please, do put the gun down. It's always awkward to talk holding them, and we both know who has the upper hand right now."

Jenna squatted to place her gun on the floor.

"Where's Dad?"

Claudia turned a page of Ayana's book with her left hand, pointed at a picture. "Ooh, look a there! He's drawing a picture!" Then she turned coldly to Jenna. "It depends. Where's your friend?"

"Yancy," Jenna croaked.

Yancy stepped around the corner. No gun.

Claudia's eyes hit Yancy's leg first, then roamed up to his face. "Oho! You've really matched yourself well this time, huh, Jenna? It's okay. Didn't like the other one anyway, even if he did give us this *precious* angel." Claudia kissed the top of Ayana's blond head, eyes never leaving Jenna's face.

"Dad," Jenna said, fighting for even tone.

"Oh, right. Your father. He's, um, resting *comfortably* in the bedroom," Claudia replied. Her head gave a little toss to indicate the room to her right.

Jenna felt her composure slip, and she frowned. *Please, no.*

"Oh, not to worry. He's not dead. Yet."

"Claudia—"

"Jenna, haven't you ever heard that little ditty about honoring thy father *and* thy mother? Really. I'm hurt."

"What have you done to Dad?"

Stop talking to her this way. You know you won't get a thing out of her if you rise to the taunts. She enjoys it too much.

Claudia didn't answer. Instead she pointed out another picture to Ayana, who laughed and clapped her hands.

"See, Jenna? Most children like me. You were an extreme exception."

Bile rose in Jenna's throat, and her hands tried hard not to form tight fists. *Ask a better question.*

"How long does Dad have?"

Claudia tilted her head. "Long enough, if someone gets him to the hospital. Fast."

"Will you let me check on him?" Jenna asked. *Stupid question.*

Claudia laughed. "No. But . . ." Her eyes trailed back to Yancy, down to his leg, and back to Jenna again. "I'd rather the business we have to, um, take care of . . . be attended to with . . . just family."

She winked.

"Are you saying Yancy can take Dad?" Jenna asked.

Jenna glanced to Yancy, then back to Claudia, unwilling to go too long without keeping an eye on her.

"Ooh! Quick on the uptake. That's what I love *and* hate about you, Jenna. Smart girl."

Jenna chanced another look at Yancy, whose gaze was locked on Claudia. God, she wished they had a plan.

"Tick tock, Jenna."

"Yancy, go."

"Jenna—"

"Go now!" she demanded. The thought of losing her only ally was rough, but losing Dad was way worse. Jenna probably wasn't thinking clearly, but it was the best chance they had. Plus, once out, Yancy could tell Saleda and Richards the layout of the living room, where Claudia was sitting, holding Ayana. Might be enough to give the SWAT team a tactical advantage.

Yancy skulked toward the bedroom, then disappeared. A long minute later, he reentered the room supporting an unconscious Vern over his shoulders, fireman style.

"Wolverine here has more oomph than I gave him credit for!" Claudia said, amused.

Yancy shot Claudia a look but continued to drag Vern toward the front door. Jenna's father looked ghastly, his face the color of the whitewash of the walls.

Yancy wobbled under Vern's weight. As he struggled to regain his footing, he turned his full back to Claudia. Yancy made a show of steadying himself, but Jenna found his face. His eyes were locked on her even though he continued to teeter for effect. His gaze cut sharp to the bedroom, back, then again. Then Yancy glared at Vern's pant leg. There, tucked in Vern's pocket, was a hand towel. The canary color Jenna saw so many times when she knew someone or something was part of something even when she didn't know the meaning flashed in. Relevance.

Then Yancy was gone.

"Ah. That's better. Now that it's the two of us, we can catch up a bit."

Play to her. "I have to admit I'm impressed you found the place."

"Wasn't that hard, Jenna. Hank E. Poo left me more than enough tools."

Jenna's mind cast a net for an idea. *Come on, come on!*

Then the words caught up to her, and purple ego flashed in. Of course Claudia would be ready to talk about her crimes. To this point, she hadn't gotten to brag to anyone. She'd been too busy keeping her nonexistent mental disorder secret. She was probably dying to tell someone how she'd managed it. If Claudia and Isaac had one thing in common, it was their penchant for narcissism. All good sociopaths had it. All Claudia needed was a little nudge.

Jenna nodded to Ayana. "I know she's small, but she has ears. If you ever do anything for me, let it be this."

Claudia regarded Jenna with shrewd eyes. Then, for whatever reason, she nodded. "True. I somehow doubt hearing—or seeing—this will do me any favors should she end up growing up like her mother . . ."

The woman rose, leaving Ayana to sit with her book. The little girl glanced up, confused, then looked to Jenna.

"It's okay, baby." Then, to Claudia, "Can't we at least put her in her crib where she's safe?"

"Be thankful for small miracles, Jenna," Claudia said. She gestured toward the bedroom with the gun.

Jenna walked that direction, nerves jittery. She'd only have one chance.

When they were in the next room, Jenna sat on the edge of the bed. "So come on, Claudia. You're dying to. Tell me how it went down with Hank."

Claudia cackled. "Wouldn't you rather hear about something else, Jenna? You've always been so morbid."

"You're planning to kill me anyway, right? You wouldn't leave me alive. You know I'm the only one capable of putting you away again. So I figure I give myself a fighting chance if we keep talking."

"And the other agents rush in and save the day, huh? That's a nice fantasy."

"Oh, give it a try. You like games. If you didn't, you wouldn't be here, wouldn't have chanced leaving the key. I could've easily sent someone else."

"If you think you know me, Jenna, would it blow your mind to hear that everything I've done, I've done because I knew you would show up here and not someone else?"

"In other words, I'm the only one you'll *get* to brag to for a while. Let it out."

Claudia smirked, shrugged. "Hank E. Poo came by the apartment before you. I intended to see you first. Turned out just as well. Wouldn't have had a chance to say hullo to Hank if it hadn't gone that way. Fate and all that."

Jenna fought tears at the image of Hank lying dead in her apartment. Vern, who'd looked so pale moments before as Yancy carried him out.

"I take it Hank didn't see you right away?"

"Aw! The sniffles are adorable, Jenna. You'd almost think you cared about Hank E. Poo. Ha. Yes. I waited for him. Had a chance to look over my file, too, by the way. Impressive."

The file had been in the bathroom. Jenna had it in there last, looking over it in a hot bubble bath. Hank must've gone in to retrieve it.

"So you hid, waited. I get that part. How'd you manage his gun?"

Claudia let out a vicious giggle. "Men. So predictable. He actually went in the bathroom *without* it. I guess even time-sensitive issues are nothing compared to the call of nature and taking a nice, luxurious crap."

Jenna winced. *What a horrible way to—*

"Unsnapped himself, left his holster on the bed with his keys, wallet, and phone. You'd practically think you two were still married and he was nothing but an amateur security guard, the way it went down. No dignity about it, really. He closed the bathroom door all but a crack. I snapped off a text or six to the agent in charge at the safe house to gather some information to find the place. They really should prep those guys better, you know. I was ready for Hank when he came out."

"How did you get past the door if it was cracked? That's good even for you, considering the apartment layout," Jenna pushed.

"Not really, Jenna. All you have to do is crawl across the bed and not go around it. We evil geniuses come up with out-of-the-box things like that," she said dryly.

"Wouldn't work."

"Oh, really?" Claudia asked.

"Couldn't. That bathroom has too much of a wide-angle view."

Claudia squinted at Jenna for a second, then moved toward the bathroom side of this bedroom. Jenna was counting on Claudia's penchant for dramatics taking her over. It had always been part of her charm.

"This bathroom is set about the same way, dearie."

"True, and there's no way to escape the view from there, either."

Claudia rolled her eyes. "I'm not stupid enough to turn my back on you while I go in this bathroom to try it out, Jenna. Sorry."

"Fine. But you're still wrong."

"Ugh," Claudia groaned. She motioned toward the bathroom with the gun. "In."

Jenna went inside, and as expected, Claudia pulled the door until only a small crack remained.

"See?" Claudia said. "We didn't have to make it this difficult, but since you asked."

Jenna reached for the bulge in the towel crumpled on the floor, discarded from someone's previous shower. She'd eyed it the moment she'd walked in the bedroom. She and Yancy had texted about the light blue towel, the towel he'd tucked in Vern's pants pocket.

Her hand found something hard, grabbed it. She could hear sirens in the distance wailing, coming to help her.

The door creaked back open, and Jenna planted Yancy's infamous hidden leg gun right in Claudia's chest.

"Was it like this?" Jenna asked.

And she fired once, twice, a third time.

Claudia staggered backward, thrown off balance. Then Claudia looked down at her chest, clutched it, staggered toward the living room.

Ayana!

Jenna jumped to get between Claudia and the living room, gun trained on Claudia, but in the split second she'd taken to move around the door, Claudia aimed at Jenna. Her shot was wide, but it hit Jenna directly in the left shin, which collapsed underneath her as she came down on it. Jenna fell back onto her right, and her head clocked the dresser. She slid down it, her vision spinning. The fall shook her, and her grip on the gun slackened.

Claudia kicked the gun away from Jenna's hand and stood over her.

"Yahtzee," Claudia said, calmer than ever. She lifted her shirt to reveal a Kevlar vest. "You didn't check Hank E. Poo close enough, I guess. In case it's relevant for you to know, he removes his outerwear as well as his holster for more comfortable potty breaks. I find these vests are much more effective hidden."

Jenna's leg burned, and pain shot up her thigh and radiated into her stomach, her head on fire. She felt Claudia close.

Her mother's breath was hot on her ear. The sirens so close but so far away.

"I have to be going now, sweet daughter. But I'll make you a deal. I'll leave you alone if you leave me," Claudia whispered.

Claudia stood above Jenna. *Get to the gun.*

She tried to roll over and couldn't. Her stomach threatened to hurl its contents.

"I don't believe you," Jenna mustered.

Claudia's hand at her pocket, taking Jenna's phone, keys. Her mother was nothing but a silhouette in the door in Jenna's blurry eyes.

"I don't either. That's the fun of it," Claudia replied.

Then everything went black.

When Jenna woke up, she was in the same hospital where she'd met Yancy, where she'd left Charley only hours ago. She blinked a few times into the fluorescents above her, groaned. Her head felt like it would implode.

She tried to sit up but was met with pressure from a hand on either shoulder. "Settle down, hoss."

Yancy stood above her, worry in his eyes.

"Ayana?" she forced out of the dry thickness that was her throat.

"She's fine. Perfectly fine. Not a scratch on her. She's with Charley right now. He's not on full babysitting duty again just yet, but he's up and about. The nurses can't keep him in that bed longer than five minutes at a time. Only way they could get him to be still was to put Ayana in the bed with him and force him to read to her."

"Dad?"

"No, he's not reading to her," Yancy said.

"Don't mess with me, Yancy."

"Sorry, sorry. Bad time for humor. No, Vern's . . . not perfect. Claudia overdosed him, they think, using psychiatric medications she found at Lyra Mintelle's. Though how she got them in him, we might not know until he wakes up."

"He's still—"

"Calm, calm. Yes, he's still unconscious, but it's not as bad as it sounds. They pumped his stomach, and he's stable. They have him in ICU on constant watch just in case, but they think he's gonna be fine."

Ayana, Charley, Dad. All safe.

"Claudia?" she forced out.

Yancy didn't answer. It was what she was afraid of.

"Tell me," Jenna said.

"Claudia was, ah, gone by the time the cops got there," Yancy admitted. "They're searching for her, road blocks set up, everything. I think they're, um, hoping you'll be able to tell them more."

Same old, same old. They'd never find her. Claudia'd find them all. One day.

"You, by the way, are going to make it, too. You have a pretty good concussion and a nice bullet to the leg, but, you know, nothing to amputate over."

Yancy's smile swam in her vision, and she couldn't help but sleepily smile back. "Thank you, Yancy."

"For what?" he asked, but his grin said he knew.

"Leaving me a gun, saving my dad, being here. Being you. Take your pick."

He laughed, and he smoothed Jenna's bangs back from her forehead. "You know, I do charge a pretty steep fee."

She rolled her eyes. "Let me guess. You want to know your color."

Yancy shrugged. "I'd settle for Claudia's."

Jenna pushed her head back against the pillows, hoping the pressure would ease the headache. Worse. She shifted again.

She'd never told anyone, including her family, what Claudia's color was. Not the police, not Hank. No one.

But if anyone deserved to know, it was this man standing at her bedside.

Jenna locked eyes with Yancy. "She doesn't have one."

The words surprised Jenna as she said them, and just like that, the secret was out. It didn't seem to linger in the air, though, like she'd always imagined it would. Instead, it was like the words moved straight from her to Yancy, no room in between them for the knowledge to be intercepted.

His eyes got bigger until they were full-on saucers, then his face relaxed. "Huh?"

Jenna closed her eyes. They were so heavy, and sleep threatened to pull her in. She fought to reopen them and drank in Yancy's rugged features. She'd always known time was valuable, but Hank was gone in an instant, and now it seemed more pressing than ever. If something ever happened to her, she wanted someone to know how she'd figured Claudia out all those years ago.

Finally, after so long, someone she trusted.

"Claudia is the only person I've ever known that, well . . . been around that much . . . who didn't have her own color. She simply blended . . . a chameleon . . . into whatever she needed to be. When it came to her, I might as well have been colorblind. It's why I knew she wasn't the same as everyone else."

Yancy stared back at Jenna, unblinking.

"You should sleep, Jenna. You've had a rough day," he said gently. Then his grin reappeared, stretched across the length of his face. "And for the record, I didn't expect you to tell me Claudia's color. In fact, I doubted you would. I'd already decided on a second request for my fee when you'd denied that one."

Jenna let her eyes drift closed. "You're welcome then. But . . . what was the second?"

Yancy's voice was softer, closer. "I'd have settled for a kiss."